Hiroshima

Bomb

Money

Hiroshima

Bomb

Money

a novel based
on family stories Terry Watada

NeWest Press

Library and Archives Canada Cataloguing in Publication
Title: Hiroshima bomb money : a novel based on true stories / by Terry Watada.
Names: Watada, Terry, 1951- author.
Identifiers: Canadiana (print) 2023057498X | Canadiana (ebook) 2023057503x |
    ISBN 9781774391006 (softcover) | ISBN 9781774391013 (EPUB)
Subjects: LCGFT: Historical fiction. | LCGFT: Novels.
Classification: LCC PS8595.A79 H57 2024 | DDC C813/.54—dc23

NeWest Press wishes to acknowledge that the land on which we operate is Treaty 6 territory and Métis Nation of Alberta Region 4, a traditional meeting ground and home for many Indigenous Peoples, including Cree, Saulteaux, Niitsitapi (Blackfoot), Métis, Dene, and Nakota Sioux, since time immemorial.

Editor for the Press: Sheila Pratt
Cover and interior design: Michel Vrana
Author Photo Credit: Tane Akamatsu
The Bomb Money Photograph: Tane Akamatsu

NeWest Press acknowledges the support of the Canada Council for the Arts, the Government of Alberta through the Ministry of Arts, Culture and Status of Women, and the Edmonton Arts Council for support of our publishing program. We acknowledge the financial support of the Government of Canada through the Canada Book Fund for our publishing activities.

NeWest Press
#201, 8540-109 Street
Edmonton, Alberta T6G 1E6
www.newestpress.com

No bison were harmed in the making of this book.
Printed and bound in Canada

*Dedicated to Setsuko Thurlow, who fought for world peace,
Takeo Yamashiro, who created peace with his music,
and Chiemi Tanigawa, who survived war, for a short time.
May she rest in peace.*

In Memory of Mr. Akamatsu

Form is emptiness, emptiness is form.
from *The Heart Sutra*

I.   OBON SEASON :: AUGUST 6, 1945

THE WOMAN HAD NO NAME. She had no recollection how she came to stand outside in the hot, searing wind. Her head throbbed, straining to remember, but black oily areas of her brain had formed, blotting out memory. Humidity leapt up from the ground and knifed at her throat. She hoarsely coughed it clear. She spit but no phlegm came out. With her eyes feeling like they were welded shut, she was blind and couldn't move. With great difficulty, she managed to crack them open a slit. She realized she was standing in front of an anonymous building, its walls fractured, crumbled in part, and charred by fire.

She lifted her arms and saw that her skin was black and scaled; it crackled with every further attempt to twist them for inspection. She was in pain but in so much pain that she suspected she could no longer feel how bad it was. She felt herself crying but there were no tears. With difficulty, she touched her hair, crinkling it; the smell rising around her told her it was burnt to a crisp. Her legs ached with every attempt to move. When she was finally able to shuffle forward, her joints cracked loudly. The skin split open here and there. But no blood, just a raw red interior, like a lava flow beneath the surface. The ragged, singed material of what was left of her clothes was plastered against her body; it was part of her now, a new layer of skin. Her eyes slowly opened fully. She noticed how blistered her skin had become. Yellow and clear pus seeped out and covered her arms. It acted as momentary relief. She then became aware of her surroundings.

The sky was thickly overcast burying her in an anonymous grave. The sun was gone, gone nova; that, she recalled. The end of the world: the landscape barren, grey, scraped down to its stone and clay foundation. Lumps of debris everywhere. The surrounding buildings were flattened into piles and piles of rubble. Nothing was familiar, all the landmarks gone. She turned to see the half-standing building behind her. Words sputtered in her mind.

I know this place. What is it? It's a...it's a...I know it...It's a hospital...Shima...Hospital

Faces whirled around her, but they remained nameless. Except: *a captain...there was a captain...* A glimmer of recognition that soon faded.

✿ ✿ ✿

Water gushed somewhere, but she couldn't tell where. She was alone, no one was anywhere, yet she heard a choir of cries, moans and then screams of agony or fearful distress. Somewhere a woman wailed incessantly, her voice torn to shreds. But nowhere to be seen.

A roar suddenly vibrated the air. She lifted her gaze and even managed to turn around. It took some doing but she finally realized the sound came from a gigantic approaching fire and the voices came from underneath the debris. The gun-metal clouds changed into a blazing red. People were trapped and could not extricate themselves.

"Tasukete!" they cried weakly or loudly. "Tasukete." *Save me.* The dissonant choir continued unrelentingly. Cries of desperation, cries of fear, cries of capitulation. The pathetic cries for Mama... Okaachan...

But she couldn't help; she couldn't save them. Too weak and damaged to even lift a finger. She could barely walk.

The fire approached like an invading army carried by strengthening breezes. It was a *Fire-Wind.* And as the unstoppable flames conquered areas of the wreckage, the screams intensified until abruptly silent. The horror was palpable. She thought she saw a hand or leg jutting out of the rubble, trembling as the entire pile caught on fire. The *Fire-Wind* crackled with sadistic glee.

Something crept along the ground. A current of air, carrying a toxic swirl of smoke within. It wrapped around the legs and crawled up the body. The smell made her gag, her body convulsed, and she nearly toppled from the new pain. She realized it was the smell of bodies roasting within the rubble maybe only a few feet away.

She steadied herself and willed herself to shuffle forward, easier now that she was getting used to moving again. She put the victims out of her mind. Despite being in a daze, dizzy with every movement, words entered and randomly floated across her consciousness. Screams of agony, screams of sorrow, squeals of joy and delight...

Kuniya...Takeshi...

Who were they? She couldn't remember, except she knew they were young boys, babies really. That glimmer of recognition sparked again and suddenly ignited into full-blown images.

Kuniya...Takeshi...my babies. My babies.

Were they beneath the collapsed hospital or some other building? Were they twisting and writhing to get away from the devil flames? Were they held tightly for sacrifice? *No, they are alive—well and safe. I'm sure of it.* She felt the weight of their little bodies against her chest—the comfort and warmth of it. She suddenly wept. Streams finally poured down her cheeks. The ground at her feet turned red.

She moved forward instinctively. Her legs were held down by what seemed like sacks of wet, burnt rice, *kome*. The throbbing ache was now indescribable, but she endured...she endured. She had to find them, find the familiar, find hope. She must find them. But how? The trolley tracks were torn up, misshapen and broken apart. She knew she had to drag herself to the edge of town. To safety.

Mizu, mizu. Please give me some water. Chikuso, bring me water! Damn it!

She ignored the pleas, weak voices growing weaker, as she approached the Aioi-*bashi*, the closest bridge to her, its distinctive t-shape intact save the buckled asphalt and the cracks in the foundation. The Yokogawa Bridge came to mind, but it was too far away. Her limbs barely obeyed her commands as she stood before the mangled structure. On the ground to the sides of the road across were piles of twisted, black corpses. They looked like the ants that Hideki tortured and burned into contorted masses with a magnifying glass back when he was a boy. *Hideki? Another name. Her brother. But what of her sister? Her name gone...erased. Where is she? On a ship sailing somewhere, so long ago. But to where? Far away from Japan. Is she safe? How could she be safe in this world?* Her sister's face a smooth blank surface, like a demon, a *noppera*. The memory of her blacked out.

She gingerly stepped past the piles, keeping her gaze straight to the other side, though she caught glimpses of some bodies impaled by glass shards or pieces of jagged wood, some decapitated, some with rubbery and stretched limbs, some with melted faces, their features distorted into monsters. Some still alive, most dead, she guessed and hoped. Each body spoke of the abject terror and utter agony of the day. Death patiently awaited them.

She came to a standstill. Another intense pure white light ignited before her eyes. She was blind again; her mind burned with memory:

Akamatsu...my name is Akamatsu...Chiemi. I am Akamatsu Chiemi.

A cool breeze came down from the distant mountains, and her sight came back. She turned to see the horizon. Though not understanding anything more, she intuitively knew the way.

Follow the river...follow the Motoyasu River...to the Ota...to home.

2.   OBON: BUDDHIST FESTIVAL OF THE DEAD :: AUGUST 1938

SUMMER IN HIROSHIMA IS HOT. No one can overstate how hot it is. The oppressive daytime heat slowly falls on everyone until condensation forms on the skin. Every movement, however slight, causes a sweat that does not evaporate. Soon the whole-body shimmers in a liquid film like a saturated washcloth; the *yukata* adheres to the body and forms a new layer of skin.

The night is sticky, making sleep uncomfortable at best. During the day, it is easy to see the ripples of heat enveloping everyone as if consuming the body, but at night, the heat becomes insidious. Nothing can be seen, only felt, like being struck blind in hell.

But Chiemi sat in a room filled with the sacred aroma of incense, the only one in the house of weather-worn wood siding, long halls and multiple chambers of polished floorboards that was cool; a room covered with comfortable *tatami* and enclosed by opaque *shoji*, paper doors. That was what Akamatsu Chiemi enjoyed most about this corner of the compound: the pools of fresh air settling above parts of the *tatami* (straw mats) especially in August. Her father called it "the room of whispering *oni*" when she and her siblings were children. The family referred to it as the *Oni Room*. The *Devil's Room*. He said it, she reasoned, to keep them out of it, especially her younger naughty sister, Chisato.

Chiemi, the eldest sister called *Oneesan*, was a tall woman, a family trait, "big boned" with an attractive face with high cheek bones, smooth pale skin, extraordinarily dark eyes, and short but thick hair. No one however could ever convince her that she was a beauty. Though the *kanji* for "Chiemi" meant "blessed with wisdom and beauty", she often scoffed at anyone who said she was appropriately named and would soon be married as a prize catch. To her mind, her age, not her looks, stood between her duties as a daughter and her independence. Marriage was the farthest thing from her mind. She was content to live and wait, caught by her obligations as the oldest child.

The only other area that was as cool was the large kitchen, but the floor and walls were concrete and brick, the sink with a water pump was metal and wood. Not comfortable enough for sitting and meditating alone, though there was a set of wooden steps leading down to the kitchen from the main part of the house. She could truly be comfortable listening to her own thoughts, clearly, while sitting *seiza*, (in meditation) in a relatively isolated room, whispering devils or not. The cicada's whining, heard just beyond the open ricepaper door to the garden, called to her. Being the oldest of three children, she was forever taking care of her younger siblings, dealing with their quarrels, dealing with their problems. She didn't think it fair, but she obeyed her mother implicitly.

Outside was no better. Even though the Akamatsu Compound stood on the border of the city and country, really part of the countryside, the noise of traffic intruded. When *Otousan, Father*, built the place, it was hoped the mountains and hills with their thick forests that separated them from the city would offer peace and a measure of temperate air. But the dirt road gently curved up from between the barrier-mountains, bringing the traffic right by the front of the house. The rumble, clouds of exhaust and dust of automobiles, trucks, and horse-drawn wagons disturbed whatever peace could be found in their lush courtyard garden with the babbling stream and *samurai* statue brought all the way from far-off Tokyo by her father years ago.

Then again, the scowling face of the *samurai* with raised *katana* (*sword*) had given Chiemi a frightened pause ever since she was a child. There was something in the fierce misaligned eyes that always gave her chills. It was like an avenging god threatening to strike anyone who dared intrude. Maybe he was the whispering *oni*, the whispering devil.

In the blazing summer heat of the street, the possible intruders went about their business, men in stylish Western suits or women in bright, garish *yukata*, all rushing towards town to do what and where was unknown. It didn't seem Japanese to Chiemi somehow.

But by the road, one of the many tributaries and estuaries of the Ota River, the mother river that divided into six at the delta, flowed downhill to the city. Chiemi and her sister during their childhood often hunted for fireflies among the reeds and slow-moving shallow water with its smooth rocky bed. Chiemi liked the comfortable feel of the slimy stones on the soles of her feet. The stream offered a respite from modern Japan.

❊ ❊ ❊

August was also the time of *Obon* when the dead came back to visit for a time. And so Chiemi sat in the *Oni Room*, before the open *butsudan*, the altar's interior dark with black-and-white photos of sad ancestors peering out as if waiting for some sign of remembrance, while offering incense in their memory. The bell still vibrated with the presence of the Buddha. Chiemi leaned back on her haunches and brought her hands together in *gasshou*, (in supplication). She felt her fingers press to her palms, as she chanted her gratitude.

As she did so, she took in the perfume of plumeria wafting in from the outside. It was sweet, fragrant of course, and beautiful in its blossoming. Her eyes closed as her thoughts settled.

Around the compound, several vegetable, tree, and flower gardens proliferated. It was Chiemi and Chisato's job to take care of the plants. Chiemi was particularly proud of the beauty of the *sakura* trees in the spring. Hideki was not expected to help since he was a boy, *chonan* or oldest brother in fact, a much-revered position in the family.

Chiemi touched each of four green incense sticks with the flame of a match. An ancestor instantly came to life, the flame eventually calming to a steady glow. The smoke climbed and swirled in the cool, haunted air, mixing with the scent of flowers. Quickly it filled the room and her lungs. She breathed in and then exhaled without choking; clouds of ghosts swirled about her. She continued the recitation as the curls of smoke engulfed her, blessing her. Chiemi couldn't help but fall into a dreamy reverie.

She is running through the streets without panting for breath, without strain in her legs, without perspiration. She suddenly becomes aware she is not alone. To her left and then right she sees the kindly faces of her grandmother, her grandfather, her uncles and aunts, and some lost cousins. How is this possible? Her mind tells her that her grandparents had died as did the aunts, uncles, and cousins (some in war, others accidentally, or naturally of old age). Yet there they are as alive as she; confusion swirls within and around her. She somehow manages to look behind her and sees a crowd of followers, all familiar, but she didn't know them. A cheer rises as she continues to run.

She notices a sound, a noise about her. It is like a gurgling; no, more like water sloshing. It comes from her ample breasts, flopping up and down under her shirt. They didn't hurt; she laughed. Her leg muscles grow sharply defined as she moves; her arms flex large. And she has long hair! Long black hair whips about her shoulders, exuding the perfume of youth. She hadn't worn it like that since she was a child.

She then begins to glow from within. Her body vibrates. A bright corona forms around her. It gives her comfort, but then her clothes start to rip away. First her white school shirt, her blue scarf and then her pleated skirt. She can't explain it, but she had on the uniform of a student. It is as if she had grown younger in the process. When her outer clothes fall away in shreds, her underwear begins to fray and tear. She can do nothing to stop the unclothing.

But she does nothing to cover herself. Her relatives and crowd cheer as she becomes naked, but still running.

A grin scratches across her face as she fights the shame of being in her "all-together" in public. No one seems to mind.

"Why are you smiling?"

The intrusion shocked Chiemi awake. She raised her hand to her neck under her chin and grasped it lightly to catch her breath. "You startled me! Don't sneak up on a person like that."

"Sorry." It was Chisato-*chan*, her baby sister, looking a bit guilty with eyes askance. She was about half-a-foot shorter than Chiemi but much more mischievous. She had a pretty round face with a telling grin, long hair, and a touch of compassion about the eyes. Being sixteen years old, she was starting to display signs of womanhood, but, in Chiemi's estimation, none of the maturity. She was still a baby to her older sister.

"What is it?" Chiemi snapped.

"Why were you smiling? Did the Buddha say something funny?"

"Baka!" *Idiot!*

"Well?"

Still the rudeness of youth, Chiemi thought. "None of your business why I was smiling. You didn't scare your sister to find out what was so funny."

"Okaa says we should get ready for the Bon dance," she said matter-o-factly.

"Good, you can help me."

"Do I have to?"

"Chi-chan!"

"Oh, all right."

The two began rummaging through a convenient closet, Chiemi pulling out several *yukata* for selection. Chisato perfunctorily took them and put them aside.

"Neesan?" she started with a pout. *Eldest Sister.*

"Yes...yes," she answered somewhat distracted.

"I have something to tell you. A secret that only Otousan and me know."

"Yes, yes, yes."

"Can I tell you?"

"Don't be so irritating. There's no time now. Help me find an obi that goes with...yes, tell me later."

✿ ✿ ✿

As Chiemi waded into the festive tides of community and celebration, she felt the joy of the familiar. On August 1st, *Otousan* had suspended the paper lanterns along the width of the front of the house. Both sisters, all gleeful and exuberant, climbed to light them. Hideki, their brother, teased and shook the ladders to scare them. They complained and laughed wildly but no one fell. With the lanterns lit, the ancestors were assured to find their way back home. Both girls always liked the way they swayed in the wind as if beckoning the spirits. To be sure, one incense stick for each relative continuously burned in their memory. The Buddha was always present.

Otousan went to see the Mayor to let him know the land next to his estate was available for the *Bon* Dance later in the month. It was a formality since Gunhei always made the area available. The *Akamatsu Obon* wasn't the only one in the city, but it was large, not the largest but substantial.

The community dance was as expected: the crowds encircled the centre of the clearing, in all manner of dress, but mostly in *happi* or *yukata*, the women with fans, clappers, and other *Bon* dance paraphernalia. The young girls with typically long hair and fresh complexions, the young boys with ruddy complexions and closely shaved heads, almost blue in the reflected light, milled about the central *yagura* tower as the drummer readied himself at its base and the musicians tuned their instruments perched atop.

Smoke drifted across the field. It carried the aroma of cooked meat: chicken, octopus, and pork from supplies held back from the military by local fishermen and farmers, no doubt. Incense floated from the in-town temple's large portable incense burner. The Buddhist priest chanted the *sutra* in a constant stream.

Folks greeted each other like they hadn't seen one another in a decade, when they probably saw them at the morning market trying to find fresh fish or vegetables or a bag of rice to buy. Still available but getting harder to find. Under a new law, the government conscripted factory workers to fight in China. Subsequently, the powers-that-be forced men and women out of their farms and small businesses to take the place of the factory workers. The fields abandoned, the businesses empty. At least with *Obon*, those factory workers and others could be together again. As if nothing else was going on in the world.

But then an impressive man in full Western suit with a vest and cravat (rather than a tie) stood before the crowd. He raised his arms and an audible hush fell. He began to speak in a loud, clear voice. Most within earshot turned away but stood in place. He cited the *"Five Races under One Union"* motto: the Japanese, the Han Chinese, the Mongols, the Koreans, and the Manchus were all one people. He insisted, "We must all hold to the belief that the *'Go zoku kyouwa'* will preserve the house of Asia. And the roof of the Asian union is Japan. And the Emperor is Japan.

"With the united help of Japan, China, and Manchukuo, the world can be at peace!" He ended with the motto written on posters all over town. *Go zoku kyouwa. Five races, one union.*

"Obey the demands of the National Mobilization Law," he added as an afterthought. "It is all for the good of Japan."

Ignoring his ridiculous manner of dress, the patriots in the crowd cheered, "Banzai!" Chiemi remained mute. She thought of the Emperor. Would He command her or her family to die in His name, His glory?

Life is dukkha. A childhood lesson from the *Dharma,* the *Teachings of the Buddha,* repeated constantly throughout the month of remembrance. *Life is suffering.*

The speaker's words did serve to remind everyone of the troubled times. Everyone knew of course but no one talked about what was happening all around them.

An ominous pall had fallen over the city. Hiroshima, with its mix of simple wooden houses with shale roofs and two-storey buildings with timber frames and stucco walls, was at war. As part of the movement of patriotism, the government started confiscating property, razing the structures, and constructing large industrial plants to supply the military campaigns in China. These were indeed troubled times.

✿ ✿ ✿

As if on cue, the *taiko* sounded with a loud thud, the *shamisen* plucked and rang out, and the choral voices intoned the words of folk long past. Like a huge gear rustled out of its inertia, the *odori* dance began to turn in a large circle. Arms swayed and went through the choreography and the legs moved as the feet went through the various positions.

Chiemi scanned the dancers until she found Chisato, her petite sister with her innocent face tilted just so. Chisato seemed like a natural going through the movements with great ease. Chiemi had stopped participating just last year. Women and men of all ages indulged in the celebration, but, for herself, she felt it was time to think about the future and not engage in something she had learned as a young girl. She was too old for such nonsense, though she stood swaying to the music and swinging her arms in the remembered choreography.

Hideki, their brother, watched from afar, not participating because he had serious concerns to consider.

3.

DESPITE OBON WITH ALL ITS colour, noise, and activity, Chiemi was really mesmerized by the black surrounding forests and the distant mountains. She felt she could walk among the trees while bowing below the welcoming branches and melting into the serene darkness. The fresh smell of cedar alone was intoxicating. But she admired the presence of the mountains most of all. Something that would last for all eternity.

The evening went well. The elderly Takanaka paid her respects to her parents as the family sat together on portable chairs watching the dance.

"It's so hot!" Takanaka-*san* complained as she wiped her neck with a hand towel while fanning her face with an open paper fan.

Akamatsu *Okaasan* nodded agreement and observed, "There's a cooling wind coming in. You'll be able to sleep tonight."

"Ach!" she complained. "I don't sleep with shoji open. Too dangerous. Who knows what would come in and kill me?"

Takanaka-*san* was paranoid and believed that one day she would die in her sleep, probably by some tragic agent. Chiemi and Chisato always laughed about her in their bedroom. *Okaasan* would scold them if she caught them, but always with a half-smile as she reproached them.

✿ ✿ ✿

"Can I tell you my secret now?" The voice was timid, soft, and somewhat reticent.

The *Bon* dance was over, and men started to tear down the kiosks and the tower. Some cleaned up the grounds. Merchants counted their profits. The musicians gathered their instruments and music before heading to a local café to celebrate their performance with *sake* and song. The women, old ladies, and young wives, put away the precious leftover food into convenient boxes for people to take home for later consumption.

Otousan left the proceedings soon after the mayor thanked him once again for the use of the land. *Okaasan* supervised the food packaging. Hideki left with friends to carry on somewhere away from prying eyes. The two girls strolled to the house, taking their time since their reverie had diminished to a post-celebratory dullness.

"Well, can I?" Chisato asked insistently.

Chiemi had forgotten about the secret. It was her baby sister after all. What could be so important: did she break Mother's porcelain dish sent to her by Hideki's chum in Kuomintang? She stole something from Takanaka-*san*'s store? She was in love with some boy? Now that would be a secret, but why tell Father?

"I'm getting married," she said with a dry mouth.

"Yes, one day you will."

"No, I mean now...well, not now exactly but soon."

"Don't be ridiculous," Chiemi harrumphed. "You're too young."

"I'm sixteen."

"Too young."

"Okaa was seventeen when she married!"

"Yes, well, a year makes a big difference."

"Don't tease. I am serious. I asked Otousan and he said exactly what you said, but he listened to reason. He saw I was serious."

Chisato didn't wait for a reaction as she pouted and continued to explain. "I went to Otousan and asked him to arrange a marriage. He argued but gave in as I knew he would."

Chiemi recovered enough to gain control of her doubt and dismay. "Why do you want to do such a thing, and at your age?"

"I'm not a baby!"

"I know but—"

"I want to see the world. The Emperor said we should. He did."

"So, you're royalty now. The world is in a terrible state."

"All the more reason to go to *Kanada*."

"*Kanada*? You don't even know where that is."

"Near *Amerika*, I think. It doesn't matter. Kiyoshi will take me there and protect me."

"Kiyoshi? Who's Kiyoshi?"

"The man I'm marrying. Father's arranging it with his friend from Kure." In the heated pause, Chisato continued. "He lives in *Kanada*. Has a good life there."

"You're marrying a gaijin? Are you—?"

"Am I what?" Chisato said with some anger.

"A gaijin! Chi-chan, it's bad enough you're marrying so young, do you have to marry a foreigner?" she said with disdain. "Marry someone here. What about Shiomi-san? He's a good catch with a good rice farm."

"Shiomi-san? He's bucktoothed and a simpleton."

"That's not true!"

"Oneesan, you have to understand, this is a modern, exciting world. Everything is changing. And I want to be a part of that change," she insisted. "Talk to Father. He understands."

Chiemi shook at the implications. Her sister was the youngest in the family. She should, at least, wait for her older siblings to marry. It just wasn't done. But she knew her young sister was headstrong and, once her mind was made, she would not listen to reason. All Chiemi could do was accept the facts. Marriage crept into her thoughts as well.

"Well, at least, you are appropriately named," Chiemi sighed as she watched her sister walk into the darkness of the house. "You will live in a thousand homes."

Chiemi began to feel abandoned. She knew her responsibility; she must take care of her parents. *Impermanence.*

✿ ✿ ✿

Chiemi suddenly remembered that her dream had turned into a nightmare when her flesh became enflamed resulting in a painfully black crust rapidly spreading over her skin. She stood horribly naked before crumbling into the darkness that was the entire world.

She shivered in the wake of the apparent premonition. *Life is suffering.*

CHISATO

The Charter Oath of the Meiji Restoration
1868

4.   SPRING–SUMMER 1938

AKAMATSU CHISATO HAD NOT TAKEN the decision to marry lightly. She had no idea what her husband would look like, a man more like a *noppera* since he had no face, no specific body type, and no name. Surely not a demon, however. An anonymous man of her dreams and not a nightmare, never a nightmare. So Chisato went to talk to her father.

Akamatsu Gunhei was tall, like most of the Akamatsu clan, with intense eyes, which clamped into slits whenever angered; he possessed a reputation for having a strong work-ethic. But he always brought home gifts for his children from his many business trips, mainly to Tokyo. For his wife, he bowed to her wishes most times. He bestowed upon his family understanding, despite giving the impression that he was not one to tolerate nonsense.

These days his face was lined and creased with worry. About half his workers had been forced to supply labour for the various war industries in town or were conscripted into the military. His rice crops and lumber supply suffered as a result. The government had promised compensation for losses, but he had no faith they would honour that promise.

He was hard to get to know, for he was a quiet man. He never let his emotions show in an obvious way, whether celebration or tragedy, unless provoked to the utmost. Hardly ever. The most he would ever do was smile or frown.

So, it was that Chisato, his youngest daughter, came to talk with him.

She could approach him, that she knew. He would listen to reason; he was not the dictatorial *shogun* of the house. She knew she was her father's daughter.

Though he dozed in a seated position, he looked like he knew she was standing at the doorway to the *Oni Room*, the ideal space just for him; she felt her underarms grow wet with perspiration, embarrassing her. Odd as cool air reached out to her and swirled around her, almost pulling her inside.

No family members were allowed in the sparsely furnished room whenever he was there. There was a comfortable, square *ofuton* cushion on the floor and a low-lying stand upon which to rest an arm, with a newspaper or documents handy to peruse. He often took a nap in there. A nearby *shoji* could be slid open for a view of the private garden at the side of the house. Somewhere within the outside vegetation, water gurgled from a bamboo tube and dripped into a small pond. All was very peaceful; the walled green space nearly cancelled out all the near and distant city noise.

She gingerly placed one foot across the threshold. She almost betrayed her presence when she shivered in the change of temperature and let out a small cloud of breath. It was cold, unusually cold, especially for summer. The presence of whispering devils. An *oni's* breath streamed in from the outside garden and around her father, like a wind current close to the ground. No one could explain it; they just accepted it.

Chisato stepped farther into the room, quickly moving to stand behind her dozing father.

As if on cue, Gunhei woke with a start, but did not face her. "Chi-chan, what are you doing here?"

Chisato too was startled, but she carried on. "Chichi-ue...," she addressed her father in a formal tone of voice as she crouched to her knees and bowed, almost touching her forehead to the floor.

"So prim and proper. This must be important," he said.

Ignoring the tease, she continued, "I...I'm sorry to disturb you."

"It's perfectly fine," he said with a note of forgiveness in his voice. "What would you like?"

She quivered again trying to ignore the cold and moved to face him. "I came to ask you... That is... I'd like..."

"Yes?"

"I'd...I'd..."

"Out with it girl!" he commanded.

"I'd like to get married," she blurted out.

Gunhei frowned and said nothing except to growl a bit. He finally turned to look at his daughter, but not in anger. "So, you want to get married? To anyone in particular?"

"I'm serious, Father!"

"All right, all right," he said waving away the complaint. "Why do you want to get married?"

"Because it's time," she insisted in a pout.

"You're only sixteen."

"Okaa was seventeen when she married you."

"A year can make a world of difference."

"I want to marry and move to *Amerika*."

That surprised him more so. His youngest was always stubborn, wanting her way, but this was too much. "Overseas? Are you out of your...No, I...Forgive me. Have you thought about this?"

"Yes, Father, I want adventure in my life. And I can't find it here in Hiroshima!"

"How do you know?"

"The Emperor said, 'Go overseas; get an education,'" she said puffing up her chest to mimic royalty. "All His predecessors said so too. I'm just obeying Their order."

Gunhei rose to his feet and snapped, "How dare you use the Emperor and His ancestors to justify your own female daydreams!"

"But Papa!"

"No, you are wrong here. Such insolence."

Chisato's eyes rimmed with tears as she stammered, "But Papa...please...listen...it's not like that...I didn't mean that—"

"How disrespectful. The Emperor would be outraged if He heard you!"

She bent her head down and began to sob quietly.

Gunhei softened his anger. As gently as he could, he asked his young daughter, "Do you know what you're asking? I worry that you don't know what you're in for."

She started to speak as an explanation, "What's my future to be? Marry some anonymous businessman or farmer, give birth to as many children as possible and take care of them until grown, and then what? Take care of his aging parents until they die? Take care of him until he dies? All the while taking care of the garden plants, the cooking, the cleaning of the house. Then and only then can I do what I want to do? Too late. Much too late."

Gunhei paused a good long while, taking in all the emotion, she guessed. "You were always a willful girl," he finally said and sighed before he next spoke. "Yoshi, if you are serious...are you?"

She nodded enthusiastically.

"I have a friend in Kure City, who has a son looking for a wife," he continued. "He lives in *Kanada*. You know where that is?"

"Hai. Of course, I do," she answered.

"There'll be time enough to look it up," he said as he grimaced. "My friend is Kimura Hideo. His son is Kiyoshi. Is that all right?"

"Kiyoshi? That's a wonderful name."

"Yes, yes, yes."

With that, he dismissed her. As Chisato stood and left the room, she turned her head and saw that her father sat worrying about his youngest. She heard him say, "I don't know...I don't know..." She saw him shaking his head and rubbing his chin.

Chisato skipped through the house and out the front door into the moist and sweltering heat. Though instantly sweating profusely, she smiled and hummed to the birds and the blue sky above. It was a marvelous day with her father's permission underlining the sunshine. She stopped in the moist heat and considered a moment. She yelled to the heavens, "Chiemi! I'm getting married!"

THE JOURNEY TO KURE WAS arduous since the town was on the Inland Sea coast, a bit of a distance from Hiroshima City. But no one complained, though Chisato's mother, Haruye, expressed discomfort sitting on the hard train benches. She nagged at her husband who had not bought a better class of ticket. He just ignored her.

The Kimura house was smallish with a vegetable garden in front. The one-storey structure with a roof of curved red clay shingles was on a dirt-road street surrounded by forest. The blue of the ocean could be seen between branches. A nice, steady breeze came in to cool the halls and bedrooms of the place. The wind was laden with moisture, but it took the heat out of the air, a welcome change from Hiroshima, simmering in its humid weather. The floor was made of an unfinished wood. "Kimura-san was too busy to bother," Chisato's mother whispered to her daughters.

There were various rooms, fitted with gleaming *tatami* (that Kimura had time to arrange), for sleeping, dining, reading, and communing. One featured a family altar. The kitchen seemed as large as the Hiroshima compound, all giving Chisato a sense of familiarity.

❊ ❊ ❊

Akamatsu Chisato was to become Chisato Kimura, married to a Canadian *gaijin*, in the Canadian naming style. Her father had arranged the union through a matchmaker, Inouye Nobuko, the most respected matchmaker in Kure City. She was thorough in her rooting out of sickness and insanity in the intended's family, even if he was a *gaijin* (foreigner). The union was soon approved.

The trip was all worth it when the Akamatsu family watched their youngest record her name in the Kimura register housed in the local temple, even if the groom was six-thousand miles away. Chisato watched as her mother cried. *Did Obaachan do this?* she wondered. *Grandmother.*

"Are you sure you want to do this?" asked her mother in an aside.

"Yes Mother," she reassured with some impatience. She turned away and gave a little groan.

Hideki did not attend. His head was buried in the *Shuho* (*To Preserve*), a magazine he was constantly reading again and again. Even old issues. The pages were filled with news and stories of the conflict in China.

It worried Chisato; they would be the subject of gossip about the absent sibling, but she was relieved, given the heated argument they had.

> "*What do you mean?*" she asked her brother angrily.
>
> "*I mean I've got more important things to do.*"
>
> "*More important than going to a family wedding? Your sister's wedding?*"
>
> "*Yes, the Emperor commands my attention,*" he said with pride.
>
> "*Aho. You a personal friend of the Emperor?*" she said as she remembered the same accusation of her. *Stupid.*
>
> His eyes bulged and grew large. He fell mute in his obvious outrage, but just for a moment. "*Don't be blasphemous! We all must be dedicated to vanquishing Japan's enemies. I must train…you've got to understand—*"
>
> "*I don't care about some stupid war!*" she said passionately.
>
> "*Don't raise your voice to me! I am an honourable soldier of His Majesty's Imperial Army.*" He finally had had all he was going to take.
>
> "*Oh, come down from that high horse of yours,*" Chisato said. "*You're in training…a recruit!*"
>
> "*Damare! You have no right to treat your oniisan like this.*" Shut up!

"I'm just thinking of the family, of our parents," she said, changing her tone. "Don't you understand that a wedding without the chonan looks bad. You bring shame to us."

"Perhaps, but it would be a greater shame if I died like a coward in battle."

Chisato threw up her hands, before turning on her heels and leaving.

The summer wedding reception was resplendent with flowers, colourful paper lanterns, and elaborate *kimono*. Her father paid the travel expenses for Fujita *Sensei* to preside. *Sensei* drew on his Shinto background to conduct the ceremony.

The celebratory dinner was opulent, surprising given the deliberate austerity the Kimura family embraced. But Kimura Hideo was an important man. The guests included many naval dignitaries as well as the local mayor and provincial governor. Chisato's father was impressed.

The food was lavish, including such delicacies as king crab and herring eggs (brought at great expense from Canada— Hideo's tribute to his son's adopted country, no doubt). Chisato smiled to herself seeing Kimura *Okaasan*, her mother-in-law, sitting glumly as the *sake* started to flow.

❊ ❊ ❊

So Chisato Kimura bid a tearful farewell to her parents and Chiemi *Oneesan*. She knew she would miss them, especially her sister, but it was necessary for her own sake. Her new life would begin in Kure and continue in Canada.

"Maybe we can go shopping together during the *Ebisu-ko* festival this year," Chiemi suggested.

That gave Chisato some comfort.

At night, when loneliness descended and the still muggy quiet of the house oppressed, her mind raced with all kinds of thoughts. She trembled with the fear that she had made a mistake, that she should be back home in Hiroshima. The vastness of the Pacific Ocean began playing on her mind. She couldn't fathom just how far away from Japan her new life would take her. Tears wet her *ofuton*.

❈ ❈ ❈

Kimura Hideo, Chisato's father-in-law, worked in the shipyard, but he never talked about it. In fact, he hardly ever came home. She did learn that his son, Kiyoshi, lived in Vancouver, British Columbia, and was employed as a clerk of some kind. Chisato said she liked the fact that he was an office worker, toiling in a "clean job".

Chisato's mother-in-law, Kimura Fumiko, was an overly serious woman with stern features, a scowling mouth, close-set eyes, and a set jaw. Not that Fumiko needed to say anything, her look could cow anyone, Chisato especially. Thus, with Hideo away most of the time, the daughter-in-law lived in a two-person house of silence. Little advice was given by or even conversation took place with her mother-in-law.

The only thing that Chisato could live for was her future, but the Canadian government would not allow her to immigrate for up to two years. Some speculated it was an effort by the Canadians to slow the propagation of the species.

A saving grace was the fact that Fumiko was about the same height as Chisato. Gave her a measure of equality.

To keep her spirits up, Chisato fantasized about her husband. At least, her mother-in-law had given her a photograph of Kiyoshi, a blurry one of a young man standing on a dock, Kobe perhaps, about to board a ship bound for Canada. A *noppera* no more.

It didn't matter, Chisato exaggerated his features. Kiyoshi was a tall, well-put-together man. His handsome face, from what she could glean from the photograph, was heaven-sent. She gazed at it every night when she was alone in her bed.

She remembered her friends talking about the act of love. The glory of a naked man's body. The touch, the kisses (sweeter than nectar, they claimed), and the final "connection" (a word an older girl used). She wondered what it all would feel like: was it the thrill of exploding stars with their beauteous light above, or as unknowable as the depths of the ocean? It was all a dream to Chisato.

But it wasn't until her mother had talked to her about her forthcoming wedding night that things became real.

> *"Chisato-chan, you must not be afraid."*
>
> *"I'm not," she said confidently. She had talked seriously and foolishly to her school girlfriends many times over the years. She knew a man's body from seeing her brother's and father's naked bodies and guessed at through hearsay amongst her friends what would happen when she was "with" one. Her friends were quite explicit.*
>
> *"That may be so, but it will be a new experience."*
>
> *"Oh Okaa," she said dismissively.*
>
> *Her eyes arched in surprise, but she carried on, "Do exactly what he says, and you'll be all right."*

As Chisato thought of Kiyoshi lying in the dark, she breathed faster, moved from side-to-side, hips rising and falling, until she quietly moaned in conclusion, falling asleep relaxed and satisfied.

6. EARLY SPRING–LATE SUMMER 1939

LIFE IN KURE WAS CONVENTIONAL if boring for Chisato. The town itself consisted of several low-lying wooden or stucco houses, the merchant area featured concrete buildings, like Hiroshima only built lower to the ground and considerably smaller in area. The summer humidity was the same, except it turned cold and clammy at night. At the centre of the town's reason-to-be was the shipyard, controlled by the Imperial Japanese Navy. And its main function was the construction of the Yamato-class of battleships.

Kimura Hideo, a stern man of serious comport and disposition, held a distinguished position in the design and construction process. Must be true, Chisato concluded, since he was seldom home and, when he was, he was constantly on the telephone conducting secretive business.

She liked him, though they seldom spoke. He often smiled at her; his eyes were full of compassion.

Chisato may have been a stubborn girl, knowing her mind better than anyone, but her mother-in-law was intimidating. From the get-go, Fumiko treated her new daughter-in-law as an undisciplined underling, as a spoiled child. Why was a mystery, she knew nothing about her.

Chisato was charged with doing the menial chores. She hand-washed all the clothes; swept and washed the floors; kept the outhouse as clean as possible; tidied the rooms; tended the garden, digging, weeding, planting. No cooking—that Fumiko did. Chisato's job was to slaughter, gut, and clean the chickens, pigs, and fish. The kitchen steam enveloped her as she watched.

As a result, her hands were sore and red at the close of a day of hard labour, her clothes heavy with dried sweat, her skin sore with an ugly rash. She always felt queasy. She may have had a strong will, but often, she broke down late at night in her room, the smallest in the house naturally. She kept quiet as best as she could, but she often called out for her mother, conjuring up her girlhood fears in her sleep. And when she awoke the next morning, doubt constantly nagged at her, though she kept it well hidden from her mother-in-law.

Her stubborn nature did aid her in enduring the work, but she never understood why her mother-in-law never let up, never modulated her tone of voice. Fumiko simply barked commands or mocked her.

"Haikara-san!" she would call in her sing-song voice. "It's time to clean out the outhouse! Hop to it."

She had never heard the term *haikara* before and therefore did not know what it meant, but there was a meanness to Fumiko's use of it. It played on her mind so much she wrote her sister.

A letter from Chiemi was quite illuminating.

Chisato-chan,
    I asked about haikara. Our old teacher from school days had no idea. Neither did Otousan nor anyone else for that matter. That is, until I talked to Fujita Sensei. He said he had read about the word in a book called the Origins of Meiji Phenomena. The term is meant to criticize people who have returned from overseas. It comes from the English words "High Collar". In other words, you are smug about having been overseas and you think you're better than everyone else.

But Chisato hadn't been overseas. She was going but that was in the future. And how could she act high and mighty about that?

Anger flushed her face. She decided she would come back from Canada and truly be *haikara*. Perhaps she would wear the finest *kimono* made of pure Indian silk. She would ride in a golden carriage. She wouldn't stay at the Kimura house; rather, a grand hotel in the centre of town. She smiled at the thought of laughing with her sister about the silly and petty Mother-in-law.

She would soon begin to fulfill that promise. The Canadian government unexpectedly ahead of schedule approved of Chisato Kimura's immigration to its country.

A vivid September sky creamed by swirls of thin cloud formed a canopy over Chisato as she waited on the pier with family members. The light-blue heavens gradually descended to the deep-blue sea to create a uniform landscape. The mugginess of the weather lifted to many sighs of relief. She gazed deeply into the colour and imagined being with her husband.

Her father, Gunhei, stood in a pinstriped three-piece suit and dark fedora, while her mother was resplendent in her floral *kimono*. *Okaasan* looked a little emotional despite her stoic outlook. She frequently dabbed away tears with a handkerchief. Gunhei for his part maintained his composure, yet Chisato thought she detected worry in his face. *Oneesan* Chiemi in her own formal *kimono* smiled at her sister. Chisato had expressed doubt many times to her through correspondence leading up to her departure date. *Was the Emperor right?* But in the end, Chisato gazed at the ship and savoured life away from Japan.

Things in the country were moving to back the people into a corner. The *National Service Draft Ordinance* or *Kokumin Choyo Rei* of March 1938 had sealed Hideki's fate and so he was not there to see her off. He was away at the military training camp. Chisato appreciated his absence since every time he was home, he spoke loudly in slogans.

> *We are the vessels of the Emperor to act as a shield for all the Pacific Asian countries! We must be ready for the coming war with Europe and America.*

She lamented every time she heard him. At some point, she had had it up to her neck. *What does a foreign war have to do with me?*

Kimura Hideo, in a rare appearance, and Fumiko were dressed in appropriate attire, the father in a black *kimono*, and Kimura *Okaasan* in a subdued grey *kimono*. Hideo wore, like Gunhei, a hat, but unlike her father, it was a skimmer. The attire, a mix of east and west, amused Chisato, but she said nothing having seen the style emerge recently. The couple were not as visibly emotional as the Akamatsu family. Chisato figured the time had come to let go; she was confident her life lessons had been learned from childhood to marriage. Kimura *Okaasan* must have been content that Chisato was ready to be with her son. She said nothing to her; instead, she just harrumphed every time Chisato looked her way.

In any case, Chisato was happy this was the last time she would have to deal with her mother-in-law.

The summer was hot as usual, but the Kobe dock, set some distance from the shipbuilding and cargo cranes, had a sustained cool breeze. The train ride from Kure was long and bumpy, but everyone enjoyed it. Chisato loved the company of her family, who boarded the train in Hiroshima. Her father allowed her to buy a boxed lunch through the window from a platform vendor. A lovely lunch of fried fish, pickled white radish, and rice with a bright red *umeboshi*, a single pickled plum, atop. Perfect for Chisato, though she thought she heard her mother-in-law say something under her breath, not quite within range but the word *haikara-san* came to mind. Certainly, the curl of contempt of Fumiko's lips was a clue.

She loved her father's gesture, but the look on his face bothered her. *Why can't he just let go? Be happy for me.* Chiemi said it was nothing.

The houses grew sparse as they rode through the countryside. Rice patties with skeletal bamboo drying racks carpeted the land. When the houses and then buildings began to reappear, she knew they were approaching the seaport city of Kobe. She smiled as her anticipation and anxiety grew.

The huge hulk of the single-stacked ocean liner, the *Heian Maru*, listed beside the pier as if anxious to depart. The breeze stiffened as Chisato bowed to her fathers, her mothers, and older sister. She straightened up and watched the porters take her luggage, two trunks and a suitcase, up the wide gangplank. A blast of a steam horn and the ship beckoned Chisato to come aboard. As she stepped up, she looked back one last time to see her family and Japan.

Almost at the last minute, Chiemi rushed forward to give something to Chisato. It was a plain coloured cloth bag. Chisato looked at her sister with a puzzled look as she saw it was heavy with its contents. When she took it and held it close, she understood. It was a satchel of soil from the Akamatsu compound. She squeezed it close to her breast and it felt warm.

Chiemi looked tenderly at her and whispered: "Remember the poem; remember your home; remember us."

The soil of home is here overseas,
The soil of my fathers, brothers, sisters, and ancestors,
The soil of my birth.
The soil of memories,
As I walk through it barefoot:
My mother's touch,
My father's voice.
I am always home.

A childhood poem recited in school. Chisato smiled and never loved her sister more than in that moment. Her life had become a series of farewells and it was hard to tolerate; she turned to hide the tears and walked up the gangplank.

✿ ✿ ✿

From that day forward, she enjoyed the sunset from the aft deck of the ship. With every nightfall, she realized she was that much farther away from her home and homeland. Hiroshima quickly disappeared like the exploding and slowly burning sun on the western horizon. She felt sad and wondered once again if the Emperors Meiji and Taisho had been wrong about leaving

Japan. But even the current Emperor had toured Europe for six months. She ruminated for only a few moments; the thought passed quickly.

7.   SUMMER 1939

AT THE END OF THE second week onboard, Chisato stared at the endless ocean behind the *Heian Maru* and shuddered. *How far?* She contemplated the unknowable depths of the ocean, the limitlessness of the sky, and the isolating distances in front and behind her. The plumeria in the garden came to mind—the aroma drifting across her thoughts. The cool dark forest surrounding the Akamatsu Compound appeared before her. And she felt the cupola of heat that encased her home and family. She opened her eyes wide and bent her head down watching the waters rush by the boat.

The waves swirled around the ship and in her imagination; she descended into the downward current and fell into an endless emptiness. She tried to put it out of her mind, but when her thoughts were replaced by the events of her recent past, her legs weakened and buckled. When she felt that her legs would give out, she had to grab hold of a railing to steady herself.

The rising and combined scent of fish, seaweed, and brine tickled a memory. The days her parents took her and her siblings to the seaside for a day in the sun and fresh air were the happiest of her childhood. During *Obon*, the family traveled to the island of Miyajima to express their gratitude to the Buddha. The temple, the *torii* (its ornate gate), and the various ceremonies were so beautiful. She cherished the time with her sister. She would do the same for her children; Vancouver is a seaport after all. *Do they celebrate Obon?* she wondered. *There are Japanese there*, she reasoned. The ocean brought all that back to her. She put her faith in the waves above the *Kuroshio*, (the Black Current) and the Buddha that guided her to the new land.

Her ship's cabin was small, perhaps cramped. She had no idea what conditions were like in steerage, though occasionally she spied some wretch who had crawled up from below. He was usually unwashed, scrawny with desperate thin yellow eyes, squinting in the fresh outside air. He raised his hands to block the brilliant sunlight. He would then be quickly chased back to the lower hold by a crisply uniformed crew member. At those times, she grimaced and turned away in disgust. She did not relish mixing with the riff-raff.

Other than the occasional steerage incident, the voyage was uneventful. It rained off and on, but the seas remained calm. She quietly thanked the Buddha. At this point, the clouds conspired to smother the skies overhead.

"Oh, it rains all the time in Canada," Terumi Takimoto informed.

How would she know? Chisato thought but didn't say.

She had made friends with a couple of women who were about her age: Terumi Takimoto from Tsuruga in Fukui Province and Sachiko Jikemura from Hiroshima. Both picture brides keenly anticipated docking in Canada. Sachiko loved to show off the photograph of her newly minted husband. Toshio Jikemura was a handsome man, Chisato had to say. With a smart three-piece suit and abundant hair, he looked like a film star, the kind in melodramatic movies seen in the *Shingeki-kaikan* theatre in Hiroshima. The straight-lined jaw with sharply defined lips, slicked-back hair, and intense eyes made him distinctively attractive.

"You are lucky," was all Chisato could say while Terumi nodded. She hid her own photograph. She denied she even had one.

Terumi, the know-it-all, had no such pretensions. She just wanted her new life to begin with a man who wasn't particularly attractive; in fact, he was ugly, by his photograph, with a pudgy body and acne-scarred and red-tanned face. But he worked steadily in the logging industry. She figured he would spend most of his time in the mountains and backwoods, while she kept house in the city or town (wherever they settled). Seemed like a good life, all things considered.

She herself was stocky with thick ankles and bloated arms and, though she said she was from Tsuruga, a substantial city on the Sea of Japan side of the country, she was obviously from the countryside. From a rice farm, no doubt.

Chisato spent most other times in her cabin, reading books or composing letters home. She saw her friends for meals or on deck when she wanted some air. They were forever gossiping, she assumed.

After Kobe, the ship had made a stop at Yokohama before heading out to sea towards Vancouver and Seattle. She looked up the two destination-cities at the library on board, a small cabin with only one row of books on a shelf. A convenient desk and chair allowed her to sit and read at her leisure the atlas and a text she pulled down. Both cities were found in the pages. The black-and-white pictures represented Seattle as being relatively flat with a huge mountain that dominated the distance. She couldn't pronounce the name *Mount Rainier* but the image of it reminded her of Mount Fuji, *Fujisan*. She smiled.

Surrounded by mountains and water, Vancouver seemed prettier, it was most like Hiroshima. Much more interesting land-scape with many hills throughout the city. She liked the Japanese section of town. At least, she wouldn't have to worry about the language.

The white men in both towns appeared unfriendly and rough. She did not look forward to dealing with them, but she steeled herself against the necessary evil. Her husband would be her protector.

❊ ❊ ❊

Despite knowing any letter she wrote would not be delivered until after she landed, Chisato wrote frequently to her sister to pass the time. She talked about her new "friends", the features of the boat, and her anticipation of her new life in Vancouver. She often expressed curiosity for her family.

> *How is Hideki-gun getting on with his soldiering? I hope he found his calling. And has Father let me go? Mother? I hope I*

didn't cause her too much heartache. I know you understand why I had to leave.

The days and nights of the third week passed slowly but the trip became short when Vancouver came into sight. On that morning, Chisato fussed about her cabin, putting things in order and arranging her luggage for pickup. She especially paid attention to her manner of dress for that day. *A Western dress for her new Western life*, she thought. A light blue dress with tiny flowers adorning it. That was the ticket. Her hands fumbled with the buttons as she slipped into it.

As the *Heian Maru* maneuvered under the Lions Gate Bridge and into Vancouver Harbour, Chisato stood on the forward deck with her two friends, eyes watering in the forceful and toxic, acidic wind.

"What is that smell?" complained Sachiko as she plugged her nose and wiped her eyes. "It stings!"

"That's the lumber-processing plant," Chisato informed. Her father's lumberyard smelled like that all the time.

"How do you know that?" Sachiko asked.

"Everybody knows that," Terumi claimed.

Chisato grimaced and followed the purser's orders to get ready to disembark.

8.

AS A SEAPORT, VANCOUVER HARBOUR bustled with ships and boats of all sizes and types. All the activity distracted Chisato from the strange, foreign country; she stood in anticipation of meeting her husband, even if a stranger, and beginning a new life.

The water was green and flecked with whitecaps as the ship created waves. It took a while but eventually the ship docked safely. The gangway lowered, and the three women began to organize their belongings to disembark. Each was dressed in a Western-style black coat with matching hat. Others wore the traditional *haori*, a short jacket, over a *kosode*, a flowing *kimono*.

As soon as Chisato stepped on the wooden pier, she experienced a shift in her perception. Japan, her homeland, was behind her; Canada was her new home. As she felt Pier 21 move slightly, a physical change came over her. The cloudless sky seemed bluer; the green of trees and plants more intense; the noise of the shipyard subsided to a whisper.

A tall white man in uniform directed them to a nearby building where they lined up to answer questions by other uniformed men.

After dealing with some immigration matters, Chisato was delighted to receive a small pile of letters from Japan. Her sister had written her!

She savoured every word as she started to read the first one where she stood.

Chisato-chan,

Welcome to Canada. I hope all is well and that the trip was not rough. Hiroshima is as you left it: peaceful but bustling with War talk. An odd contrast.

There's a lot of talk about the war with China. Two strangers in the street actually came to blows over Japan's involvement. Neither was hurt badly.

No one we know has enlisted or has been drafted (a new government edict), except, of course, our brother.

Hideki Oniisan is still in training though I suspect he will be in the army soon. I don't mind telling you, he and Otousan had a tremendous argument about his joining the military. Though they didn't think I heard, I did. I was hiding nearby...

Okaasan still worries about you. At least, she has stopped crying. Father pretends like he doesn't care, but I know he does.

I won't write more since the censors have started to ink out words and sentences. Inaba-san, the grocer, complained and was taken away. To where I don't know. Have not seen him since. I've probably written too much.

Write when you can.

Cheimi Oneesan

No "inked out" words. Chisato guessed a letter between sisters was not much of a concern. For now.

❉ ❉ ❉

Soon she had to stop. She, her companions, and all the others were directed back to the dock where a Japanese man met them. He hustled the crowd onto a bus, a green and yellow one with comfortable enough seats. They left without their luggage, the man assuring them their belongings would follow.

The bus moved easily through the city streets. As she clutched her letters, Chisato viewed the change of scenery; the urban setting reminded her of her hometown, yet it was different. The buildings were imposing (probably because she didn't know what they were), and the businesses sat in shadows. Everything in fact seemed rundown. The signs were all in the alien English language.

What she hadn't expected was the Immigration Building, a black, concrete mass in the middle of what appeared to be a railroad maze, tracks crisscrossing and leading everywhere before passing in front of the building's entrance. The building itself was five-storeys-high with bars on all the shuttered windows. As she approached it on the transport bus, she felt the building glaring at and awaiting all the new immigrants.

She wasn't intimidated by large buildings; after all, Hiroshima was full of them. The Hiroshima Prefectural Industrial Promotion Hall for one with its impressive dome. Inside, it housed a wide and high rotunda with well-lit hallway tributaries with shiny linoleum and waxed floors leading to various government offices. An abundance of light came in through the multitude of windows. Her father had taken her inside once when she was a little girl, but she had walked by it several times as she grew.

The Immigration Building, by contrast, contained shadowy hallways that twisted and turned away from the entranceway to unknown and thickly dark areas. Stairs were everywhere ascending and descending to pools of ominous shadows.

Several hulking guards moved Chisato and her fellow immigrants to a downstairs staircase. At the bottom, the building opened to a large area with minimal and subdued lighting and a segregated room. Inside it, obese white women in nurse uniforms stood, waiting for them. Another Japanese man, short with round glasses and greasy hair plastered against a balding scalp, stepped forward. He introduced himself as simply Kawasaki the Translator and commanded everyone to strip down to their underwear. Everyone hesitated, so outrageous was the order. He repeated his command but in a much louder and angrier voice. Some complied.

The guards then began grabbing at the garments of those nearby. They ignored the screams and words of complaint as they resorted to ripping the Western and Japanese jackets, robes, and dresses, and *kimono* off them. Material tore in the rising melee. Soon everyone obeyed the command.

Chisato felt her own light blue dress tearing away. Her letters were ripped away in the process and discarded somewhere. Standing in her undergarments, she gripped the rags in her hands as tight as she could. She glared defiantly. A sadness came over her as if she lost her sister, again.

The nurses then walked around, pulling down or opening the undergarments, and examining by manipulation everyone's intimate parts. Chisato soon went through the humiliation. Her face turned red, especially when one nurse smelled her fingers afterwards. Her stomach and throat filled with bile and disgust.

Once everyone had been inspected, Chisato led a chorus of protest, nearly screaming her objections. But then the men dragged out hoses and aimed them at the women; several gasped. A gushing sound emitted, and a white powder sprayed, covering the women, caking their faces, hair, and bodies. They tried to stop it by uselessly extending their arms with open palms in front of them. Some squealed in surprise, shame, and pain. Some fell to their knees and then the floor. Chisato closed her eyes as she turned her head away, holding up her tattered dress as protection against the onslaught. In the aftermath, the sounds of crying and rough coughing rose to the ceiling of the room.

Kawasaki's voice rose above the din, explaining that they had been deloused.

After a much-needed shower and dressing in their soiled clothes, torn in some cases (their possessions had yet to be delivered), the women sat and waited for what humiliation was to come next. Chisato's face turned red with the thought of meeting her husband looking like a poor wretch. She wept over the state of her pretty dress with the blue flowers all over it. The women soon endured seemingly endless interviews, interrogations more like it. Kawasaki and a small army of anonymous interpreters facilitated.

That night, she lay on a cot exhausted in a large upstairs common room known as the Dormitory. No one had eaten and not one of the guards or nurses cared, ignoring the complaints and protests. Chisato was too tired to grieve. She felt herself being dragged into a dreamless sleep.

9.

LIFE INSIDE THE IMMIGRATION BUILDING soon was a battle against fatigue and then boredom. Two days later, the luggage finally arrived, intact, but there was little comfort in the contents. At least, there were clean garments to wear. She carefully folded her soiled and torn clothes and put them away, almost as mementoes of her beginning in Canada. To her delight, there were books to read and old letters to pore over again and again. And the precious bag of Hiroshima soil given to her by her sister.

I am always home…

Chisato sat in the presence of Sachiko and Terumi.

"When are they going to release us?" Sachiko cried.

Terumi just sat with a scowl and said nothing.

"Don't worry, Sachiko-chan, they can't keep us forever," Chisato assured. "Think of the future!"

Chisato held onto the promise of life ahead, a life of happiness, prosperity, and adventure with a handsome husband. She encouraged her friends to feel the same way, though Sachiko sat with a wide-eyed stare into darkness.

At some point, Kawasaki told them in a moment of remarkable candour the officials and guards considered everyone in detention to be Chinese. Chisato knew about the Chinese Exclusion Act, but that did not affect the Japanese. And the Gentleman's Agreement between Japan and the West was no more. She sat on her cot confused. What happened next shocked her and Sachiko.

About three weeks into the detention, two stout white men and Kawasaki-*san* came into the Dormitory and called for Terumi Takimoto to come with them out of the room and down the stairwell.

Chisato and Sachiko had no idea what was transpiring. No explanation was given; Kawasaki said nothing.

"Another delousing?" Sachiko said in fear.

They waited about an hour before Terumi returned; she was in tears. So much so, it upset Sachiko. *It was another delousing.* Chisato immediately rushed to comfort Terumi. They had never seen her so emotional; quite unusual for their stalwart friend. She was inconsolable as she sat in a metal chair before them.

"What happened?"

Terumi kept blubbering and couldn't get any words out of her mouth. She hiccupped and gulped for air. Finally, she was able to gain a measure of composure. Her no-nonsense self soon returned.

"Deported. I am to be deported," she sighed and confessed.

"Why?"

"I don't know." She breathed in heavily. "Kawasaki just said I was unsuitable to enter Canada as an immigrant."

"That's stupid!" proclaimed Sachiko.

"There has to be a better reason than that," Chisato echoed.

"Don't you understand?" Terumi said. "They can do anything they want. I suppose I am to be an example to others. Or they think I'm Chinese." The words burned with bitterness as she said them.

Chisato offered, "Maybe it's because we're not Chinese."

"What do you mean?" Sachiko asked.

"Canadians don't like what our soldiers are doing in China." She had remembered what Hideki's magazine, the *Shuho*, had said back in 1937. Japan's reputation in the world had suffered because of its incursion. Not that the citizenship should care. *A useless war*, Chisato had thought at the time.

Terumi dismissed such speculation and revealed, "My husband can reapply after I return to my home village." She grew quiet.

Chisato shivered dread for she knew her family would feel the shame of their daughter's rejection by Canada. She wasn't even sure they would accept her since, once married, she was no longer a family member. She could live with the Takimoto family, if they accepted her.

What was going to happen to Terumi? What would happen to her if she herself were deported? She was sure her father would take her back into the family. Her mother-in-law would simply reject her, probably with a smile. *So, Haikara-san is not good enough for a white man's country.*

The next day, Takimoto Terumi and several others were escorted out of the facility with their suitcases in tow. Someone said they were headed for CPR Pier 21, the one where they had disembarked about a month prior, to meet the ship, the *Hie Maru*, sister ship of the *Heian Maru*.

"All of them are deported?" Sachiko asked.

"I suppose so." Chisato did not feel out of danger. She closed her eyes and waited for the sword to fall upon her. Fortunately, it never happened.

❀ ❀ ❀

When Chisato finally got out, well into autumn, she breathed in the free air of Canada. Outside the large doors of the Immigration Building, a crowd of Japanese men had gathered, every one of them waiting for their new brides.

It took some time, but eventually a man dressed in a three-piece black suit and a fedora stood in front of her. His shoes were tan and polished. It was her husband, Kiyoshi Kimura. He was not what she expected—his photograph paled in comparison. He was tall (certainly taller than Chisato) with a developed upper body and a kind face with bushy eyebrows, dancing eyes, and sharply defined cheek muscles. He appeared friendly with a smile that was as wide and bright as the horizon at daybreak.

He laughed a hearty laugh at her reaction to him and motioned to move away from the crowd. Just at that moment an argument exploded nearby.

Chisato looked around to see Sachiko flailing and whining in front of someone. Her voice rose to shouting and even screaming at him. It was an anonymous man much shorter than she. His face was grotesque, scarred and pockmarked as far as she could see.

"Would you have come if you knew I looked like this?" he shouted as he waved a hand over his deformed cheek and his balding head with a high forehead.

"You lied! You lied!" she shrieked loudly.

"Damare!" he shouted and tried to slap her. He missed in a comic fashion.

She guffawed at the effort.

He jumped from his standing position and let his hand fly. He caught her square on the cheek. She reeled as she covered her face with her hand. As she bent over from the shock and pain, he turned her around and pushed her to some unknown fate.

"You couldn't see," he growled as they walked, "that the photograph was of Sessue Hayakawa? A movie star?"

As Chisato was led away by her husband, she thought of a lesson taught to her by a Buddhist priest during her childhood. The main phrase *Sensei* Kiyahara uttered stood out in her mind: *the curse of impermanence.*

Without are dogs, and sorcerers, and whoremongers,
and murderers, and idolaters,
and whosoever loveth and maketh a lie.
Revelation 22:15

10.   FALL 1939

"HE LIED. HE LIED TO Sachiko," Chisato said to her husband
as they sat in a restaurant called Ernie's Café, partaking of what
Kiyoshi called a "coffee". The liquid was dark, bitter to the taste,
but she had not said a word of complaint. It resembled a cup of
mud. Cream and two sugars made it tolerable. She concentrated
on the sweet blueberry tart that accompanied the hot beverage.
That she liked.

Ernie's Café was unlike anything Chisato had ever seen. It
was small, but full of activity. *Must be a popular place,* she thought
given the number of customers there were. The long wooden
countertop especially impressed her. It was deeply polished with
several metal stools with red Naugahyde covers (as she was told)
in front of it. Many tables fanned out from it with an appropriate number of wooden chairs. A glass case rose behind, filled
with all kinds of pies and cakes. The variety and number of
strange unfamiliar desserts was a marvel to see. The menu itself
was delightful, though she didn't know what a "hamburger" was.
She would have to try it sometime.

Ernie Ohashi himself was a large, broad man with thick
arms; he wore a stained full-length apron over white shirt and
black pants. He had a perpetually kind expression on his face,
so it seemed, even if the unshaven look was off-putting to her.
There were no *neesan* or waitresses like in Hiroshima. Ernie
understood Japanese so Chisato could ask questions and order
whatever she liked. In general, she left it for her husband who
did the ordering. She would have to come again.

Kiyoshi Kimura was soft-spoken, but his intelligence shone

through as he spoke. Chisato found him very attractive, and for long stretches, she stared at him as if to memorize his face. She was careful not to let him notice.

In time, Chisato could see that people respected him. They listened closely, they often closed their eyes and lowered their heads to do so. People bowed to him in public, lower than he to them. A sense of pride swelled in her. *This is my husband!*

"Kimura-san, where do you work? Which store? Is it close to here?"

"Store?"

"Yes, where you're a clerk."

"I'm not a clerk," he said with a laugh.

"Manager?" she asked with hope in her voice.

"I don't work in a store. Where did you get that idea?"

A little concerned, she said, "My father told me."

"Well, he's wrong. I own a lumber company on Vancouver Island."

"A lumber company?" *Just like Father*, she thought.

"Yes, it's doing rather well. You won't have to worry about money," he assured her.

She wasn't worried about money, but it was nice he clarified things. Her mind moved to the recent past. "Sachiko, my friend from the boat, was lied to by this…this awful little man."

"Yes, that's common these days."

"Kimura-san, can you do something?"

"Call me Kiyo. Everyone uses first names in Canada," he said, seemingly delighted with the formality. "I'm afraid there's nothing I can do about your friend. It's a tragedy. Perhaps she will seek you out and ask for help."

She kept conjuring up the image of Sachiko being slapped by such a vile evil man.

"Do you know why my other friend, Terumi Takimoto, was deported?" she asked changing the subject. "She was right there with us when they took her away."

"My, you are full of questions, aren't you? I'm afraid I have no idea," he said. "Was she sick?"

"You mean, like a cold? She wasn't sniffling or sneezing or coughing."

"I mean, did she have consumption?"

"Consumption?"

"Yes, tuberculosis," he explained moving his chair slightly away. "A lung disease."

"No, I don't think so. As I said, she looked perfectly healthy to me."

"Perhaps in the past..."

She shook her head and the two fell silent.

Kiyoshi then said something she had not foreseen. "Now, I have a question for you. Are you a Buddhist?"

"Um," she said, caught off-guard. "Yes, I am. Aren't you?" she asked with some trepidation. She was more like a *Holiday Buddhist*.

"Well no. I am of the One-True-Faith."

"The what?" Chisato asked frowning.

"I am a Christian," he said with finality. He smiled broadly at her with the revelation.

"Why would you want to be a Christian?" she asked. In truth, she had never met a Christian.

"Oh, I don't know. It just makes sense to me."

"How...when?" Her series of questions must be off-putting to him, it would to her, she thought, but he gave no impression of such. He just sat smiling.

"One day, the Reverend James invited me to tea with a bunch of others. I accepted, and we all came together at his house. His wife served black tea and pastries. Very nice, actually. At the end, he invited us to a service at his church. I couldn't say no. *Giri*, you know—"

An obligation.

"And that did it?"

"I learned a lot that first Sunday. Christianity is a beautiful religion. Do you know anything about it?"

She lowered her head, embarrassed. "No, I don't." She lied; she did know that most Japanese and Foreign Christians lived in

Nagasaki but didn't know any of them. She also knew about the crucifixion. Nothing about the basic tenets.

"No need to feel ashamed. Come to the next service, and I'll explain things for you. What do you say?"

"Hai…" she said. What choice did she have?

"Good. Maybe your friend can come too. Uh…Sachiko, is it?"

Chisato nodded.

"Yes, Sachiko will find solace in the teaching of Christ and find peace within the church membership."

Chisato was skeptical but said nothing.

❈ ❈ ❈

After what Kiyoshi called a "welcome-to-Canada snack", he led Chisato to his house a few blocks away. It was early evening and the shadows had begun to grow.

She was impressed as she stood in front of a three-storey wooden house with an attic on Main Street, near Cordova, two streets she was determined to pronounce and to remember. There were unkempt bushes and overgrown small trees in the front yard but no flowers. *Typical of a man,* she thought. The smells of home came to mind.

The stand-alone, well-kept house fit the area, and probably the city too. It consisted of painted-dark-brown wood and a sharply peaked roof, very unusual to Chisato. A small grass area sat in front, defined by a low-lying white-picket fence, with a larger area in the rear. She saw the potential for a flower patch or two, while the backyard would be perfect for a vegetable garden. A wide and tall staircase led to the veranda and the front door. She noticed it was unique to the area. No other house seemed as grand. She kept looking around to make sure.

Inside was dark, the air thick with dust and humidity, the window shades drawn. As the two took off their outside shoes and placed them on the floor at the front, she coughed. The narrow halls closed in on her, lightly choking her, as she moved. The dry, stale interior attempted to suffocate. But then she made out a glimmer of light ahead, not bright but dull and flickering. Her husband led her to the source.

In what Kiyoshi called the dining room, Chisato first found her luggage. She sighed relief. Her husband had arranged to have them delivered. She then saw something astonishing. A multitude of candles burned before a large statue of a figure impaled to a cross. It was taller than she and certainly wider with its stretched-out arms. She knew instantly it was the figure of Christ during His passion. That much she could recall about Christianity.

"What is this?" she asked, more than a bit confused.

"The crucifixion of our Lord," he stated.

"Yes—"

"Grand, isn't it? I bought it as a donation to the church when the building was being reconstructed last year."

She stared at it. The painted blood from the hands, feet, and the gaping wound in his side was particularly disquieting. The extremities nailed to the cross were enough to upset her stomach. But the face, so much agony, so much pleading for mercy in its expression. The sorrow, the sorrow. A tingle of fear shot up her spine.

The statue reminded her of the stone *samurai* in the Hiroshima garden. That frightened her as a child with its fierce expression and raised *katana*; here, the crucifixion made her stomach queasy, but not enough to cause upset. What was its purpose? The *samurai* guarded against intruders to the *Oni Room*. To remind them of the Akamatsu past. What was the crucifixion for?

Kiyoshi went on to explain that he set up the candle display before he left for the docks. It was meant as a grand welcome for her. She kept staring at him and the icon.

Eventually, she decided to name the crucifixion statue, *The Jesus*.

Why worship someone tortured to death?

Kiyoshi turned on the one room-light, an ornate Victorian lamp that hung from the ceiling, and then other lights around the house. The first thing that struck Chisato was the fact that there were crucifixes, small and large, everywhere. Some were wooden, others a shiny silver.

"Wait till you meet the Reverend James," he said with an eager smile. "You'll like him. He's such a wonderful man, very forgiving, understanding."

A curious thing to say, she thought, but let it go.

"Let me show you the rest of the place."

There were many rooms, like the Akamatsu Compound in Hiroshima, but they looked different with smooth walls of dull white plaster and heavy furnishings her husband called Victorian. Paintings of Christ adorned the walls. And there were chairs and a heavy table in the dining room in front of but far enough away from *The Jesus* so as not to disturb the display, a fully equipped kitchen, though the appliances didn't look much used. The running water, without pumps, (even in the interior washrooms—no Japanese bath but something called a bathtub) was a handy convenience. Upstairs, she loved the large bedrooms with high beds and thick mattresses. She would have to get used to such Western luxury. The house seemed gloomy, because of the lack of bright lights. She would get used to that too, she imagined. At least, every room had a large window or two. She would make sure to open the shades every day.

Chisato was too tired and fatigued to explore the newness of everything in the house fully. The strange décor too weighed heavily upon her. But the so-called "wedding night" was ahead of them. She knew this and remembered what her mother had advised.

Do what your husband tells you to do.

Exhaustion pressed upon Chisato, and it must've shown, for Kiyoshi with his broad smile understood.

"You go to bed, Chisato-chan. We'll see how you feel tomorrow."

She appreciated his thoughtfulness and thanked him. She soon found that a nightgown had been placed on her bed as if waiting for her. Probably by Kiyoshi.

After she slipped under the covers and laid her head upon the comfortable pillow, she became instantly groggy. She thought she heard the front door open and close but was too sleepy to investigate.

She soon slept deeply and soundly in a new dreamscape.

With morning, she awoke to the sunlight and noise coming from downstairs somewhere. She sat up in bed and found her luggage had been placed in the room from the living room. *What a thoughtful husband*, she thought.

Chiemi felt tired still, but the house appeared brighter, its gloom dissipated with the window blinds drawn open, as she moved towards the source of the activity. The morning had conquered the empire of the haunted night. She was no longer queasy when she viewed *The Jesus*. It looked inert in daylight. The floorboards creaked no matter how lightly she stepped. Cooking smells greeted her as she landed at the foot of the stairs.

Kiyoshi was in the kitchen preparing something wonderful: a Canadian breakfast.

"Oh, good morning!" he said with his constant smile beaming as could be anticipated. "I made breakfast—bacon and eggs. Canadians wake up to this along with toast and coffee just about every morning."

A man cooking was a surprise. Her father never set a foot in the kitchen never mind handling the food except to eat it. She said nothing. *These Kanada ways!* she thought. The cuisine was also a new experience for Chisato. She liked everything; eggs she had in Hiroshima, usually scrambled, but bacon was new, crispy, and tasty. It was hard, with a pleasurable crunch. The taste was salty and meaty. She had had pork before but mostly stewed with vegetables, never fried. Having bread was also very unusual.

Where was the *miso* soup and rice? That she missed. The coffee was tolerable with cream and sugar.

After "breakfast", a new term to her, she stood before her luggage and began unpacking. She parted the wings of the trunk and opened a top drawer. She first discovered that her ruined dress was nowhere to be found. *Had Kiyoshi thrown it away?* She would have to ask. She then found the Hiroshima sack of soil. She held it to her chest. It was soft and strangely still warm.

Silly, worthless thing, she thought and began to hiccup with emotion. She placed it back in the trunk drawer, hidden and safe.

✿ ✿ ✿

Soon thereafter, Kiyoshi showed her around the neighbourhood. He explained the area was known as Powell Street and not Japantown. He pointed out the local food store, Matsumiya Grocery, that sold everything she might need for the kitchen. There was also the nearby Yamamoto Fruit Store and the farther afoot Union Fish Market and Matsuba's Butcher Shop. He showed her Sameshima Cleaners, Taishodo Drugstore, the New Pier Café, and all manner of restaurants and clothing stores. Soga's Department Store was large and well-stocked. She was told Chinatown was nearby, so she could buy Chinese barbecue meats and greens, if she so desired. That was something new again. She once visited the Chinatown in Yokohama, but that was when she was a little girl on a trip with her father. Only a vague memory for her.

Chisato's brain was overwhelmed. Her head spun with all the names she would have to memorize. Ernie's, she knew and would probably never forget, and she could find the grocery store easily enough, but the others, she would have to learn where they were in time.

The couple eventually stood before a large, mostly white building at a corner. Kiyoshi pointed out that this was his church at Jackson and Powell Streets. The United Church Japanese Mission, its spire above soared well into the sky. The wooden front doors were large and somewhat imposing. She was shocked that Kiyoshi had the temerity to walk right up the short flight of stairs to open them.

He turned and invited her inside.

❉ ❉ ❉

It was stuffy in the vestibule. The smell of what Kiyoshi called "Christian incense" lightly gagged her throat. The interior quiet clouded her ears. Farther in, the space opened to a cavernous hall with rows of chairs in an arched half-circle facing the front where what Kiyoshi pointed out was the altar. It featured yet another cross (gold this time) which sat in the centre of a table covered with a white cloth. Above was a stained-glass window depicting a Biblical scene or unknown saints, so Chisato surmised. More than a few stained-glass windows around the room.

It was noticeably quiet, something Chisato appreciated, until...

"*Kiyo!*" called out a cheery voice.

A slight, tall white man approached them in a rush. His face was smiling like Kiyoshi's as he reached out his hand. Must be the Reverend James, she reasoned. He was thin but solid. He towered over the couple, even taller than her husband. He was dressed in a dark suit with a distinctive collar, the collar of the clergy.

He seemed friendly enough, but Chisato couldn't understand a word as he took Kiyoshi's hand to shake it. *Hmm, no bowing here*, she thought.

"Nice to see you," the reverend said with Kiyoshi translating. "And you must be the new bride!"

Chisato didn't know what to do as the man grabbed her hand and pulled her in to him. Her face flushed red. It was rather shocking behaviour.

"*You must forgive her,*" Kiyoshi replied. "*She's not used to Canadian ways.*"

"Well, we'll have to work on that!"

"*Yes, we'll be here this Sunday. I just wanted to show her the church.*"

"Of course, of course. Come downstairs, some of the ladies are preparing tea."

And so, they went to the spacious kitchen below where several Japanese women were serving tea and cake to other women who had gathered for some volunteer work. Chisato was relieved to see other Japanese so she wouldn't have to bother with the translation.

"Ladies! Ladies!" the reverend called to gain attention. "Please, welcome…uh, what's your name, dear?"

Chisato looked at her husband who answered for her.

"Good. Welcome Chai-sato, Kiyo's new bride! Let's show her some of that good Christian hospitality."

An audible sound of pleased surprise arose from the crowd. Whispers murmured among the ladies before they applauded her.

Chisato bowed but she looked to her husband with eyes wide open. He said it was a Canadian greeting.

"Chai-sato, make yourself at home and see you Sunday," the reverend said with finality.

He walked away trusting the women would take care of her. Kiyoshi followed having further business with the minister. He was the President of the church after all.

Chisato was somewhat upset at the mispronunciation of her name and the informality of addressing her by her first name. But as her husband had said Canadians all were on a first-name basis. She suddenly grew small in the room. What was she to do now?

"Kimura-san," addressed a pleasant voice speaking Japanese. "Would you like some white cake?"

She felt a little ill-at-ease though the woman, Michiko Fujino, brimmed with kindness. Her face was round, and she had more weight than was necessary. But she was outgoing with that ever-present and ubiquitous smile. As it happened, she lived with her husband and two kids about a block or two away from her place. *This could come in handy*, Chisato thought.

At least some of the others in the room were smiling at her. Fujino-*san*'s ability to speak both Japanese and English was a plus. Chisato relaxed and made the effort to use the first name of everyone she was to address.

"Michiko-san, what is everyone doing here?" Chisato asked with a friendly grin. She couldn't help herself.

"We're putting together the newsletter. We come together once a month to do it," she explained. "Would you like to help?"

Out of politeness, Chisato said yes. She spent the rest of the day sorting pages and stapling them together. The publication was in Japanese and featured stories and information about the Japanese community in Vancouver. This she would read every month.

✿ ✿ ✿

At home in the front room with its comfortable Chesterfield couches, the newlyweds discussed the day. Kiyoshi walked around the living and front rooms lighting the candles while *The Jesus* played witness to the conversation. The icon glowed in the soft, indirect light.

The two enjoyed a long talk about the church and its activities. Kiyoshi eventually said there's time enough to learn about Christianity. Chisato also mentioned all the shops she had seen.

"I like Soga's," she declared. "There were so many nice things in the windows."

"You should shop there…shop there any time," her husband replied. "Just mention my name when you buy something. It'll all be on my tab, my running bill."

She was impressed and eagerly looked forward to shopping there, though she had no idea what a "tab" or "running bill" was. Something else to learn. She wondered if there was an *Ebisu-ko* festival when bargains could be had, just like back in Hiroshima.

The humiliating experiences of the Immigration Building came to mind. Tears seeped from her eyes. She quickly dried them. She vowed never to complain to her husband. The thoughts soon faded and disappeared.

✿ ✿ ✿

The cold autumn air chilled Chisato's skin. The warmth of the evening bath had evaporated as she faced her husband in the bedroom. The "wedding night" had been delayed enough. She could feel desire swell within her. It was time. She would do as her husband desired.

Kiyoshi sighed and inhaled deeply as he took off his robe after his own evening bath. He stood naked before her.

She dutifully allowed her robe to drop to the floor. Keenly aware of her nakedness, she demurely covered as best as she could her more intimate parts. Her legs were short, her stomach was not flat enough, her breasts were too small. Her face flushed red with the shame. But her heart started to race. Her breathing accelerated as he brushed her hands away and touched her left shoulder.

He led her to the bed and pulled the top sheet back. She quickly fell under the covers, and he just as quickly joined her. It was cold for only moments. The contact of skin on skin was electrifying. His kisses were as sweet and soft as she had imagined a first kiss would be. Chisato started to groan as he manipulated her. She never thought it would feel this good. As time slowed, she pushed and pulled for more until her eyes rolled back in ecstasy. It was from that moment that she knew she was in love and wanted to have his babies.

II.   FALL 1939

THE MORNING AFTER, CHISATO AWOKE disoriented. She found herself in a Western-styled bed in a strange city, in a new country. But she knew she was happy. Her muscles were perhaps a little sore, but that would not deter her from the day's activities.

She dressed. Her torn and soiled clothes had indeed disappeared. Kiyoshi must've discarded them, she decided. She then found a note and some money from her husband.

Must go to work. I hope you can manage on your own. I shall be home by dinner.

Kiyoshi

She imagined his smiling face, causing her to smile as well. The idea of leaving the comfort of her home was daunting, but if she stayed in the Powell Street area, she would not have trouble with the language.

She did have a goal for the day.

Cheimi Oneesan,

I am writing you to let you know my address in Kanada.

I am very happy to be here. My husband Kiyoshi Kimura is a wonderful man, successful, handsome, and well-respected. I'm very lucky.

She went on to talk about the neighbourhood, the house, the church, and some of the personalities she had met. She did not mention the Immigration Building experience. She didn't want her sister to worry. Nor did she talk about the lost letters.

She concluded with:

I hope all is well in Hiroshima, with the family. Write me soon and let me know about everyone.

All is good here.
Chisato-chan

She found an envelope and folded the letter into it. She then knew she had to address it in English, or at least with English lettering. She decided someone at the church could do it for her—*Fujiino-san, I mean Michiko* perhaps.

✿ ✿ ✿

Once outside, she began to walk along Main Street looking for Powell Street. The landmarks were familiar but not as a guide. When she encountered the busy East Hastings Street, she turned around and wondered if this was the right way. But then she smelled a familiar and wonderful aroma—bacon and eggs. She was hungry and so stopped in front of a restaurant a few feet away. It was not Ernie's; the interior was dark with the noise of food preparation and customers speaking English. She stepped inside, feeling her stomach growl.

She sat on a stool at the counter, a long one reminiscent of Ernie's, just not polished. She could not peer into its depths. A rough and burly white man in a long apron and cook's hat, like Ernie himself, stood in front of her. Unshaven and rumpled, he growled something she couldn't understand.

"*What'll it be?*"

Her face went blank; she looked back to the entrance.

"*C'mon lady, I ain't got all day!*"

She was about to run out when a friendly voice called out in Japanese, "He wants to know...what you'd like to eat."

Chisato turned to see, to her relief, a Japanese man in plaid shirt, jacket, and work pants.

"Oh, ba-kon to tamago," she answered.

"*Bacon and eggs, Mac*," he said to the cook.

"Coming right up. Coffee?"

That Chisato understood. "Hai."

"*Yeah, with cream and sugar.*"

She smiled and nodded.

· In normal circumstances, she would never talk to a stranger, a man especially, but the gentleman beside her seemed kind and he did do her a favour. She was in Canada now, where customs were different, she ultimately reasoned.

"Thank you for your help," she said.

"My...very good appreciation," he replied. His Japanese was not particularly good, but she understood. *My pleasure*, he meant to say.

"What is your name?"

"Osamu Otagaki, but you call me *Sam*," he said in a practiced way. Otagaki-*san* was a man of average height, balding head, and narrow shoulders. He did appear to be a friendly sort.

"What do you do for work?"

"I don't understand."

This was odd to Chisato since Sam seemed to be the same age as she and was Japanese.

"I am Nisei and I know no good Japanese," he explained clumsily.

They spent the next hour talking in an awkward, haphazard way, but they managed to communicate while Chisato ate. One thing she learned *Nisei* referred to the children of the immigrant Japanese. Made sense since she knew she was an *Issei*.

Otagaki worked odd jobs around the area. At present, he was a helper on a construction site—the *Showa Club*, a gentlemen's club on Powell Street. His boss was hired to renovate the place for Morii Etsuji.

She nodded not knowing the place or the name.

During the conversation, Sam revealed something that reminded her of her family.

"I join army soon."

Chisato just nodded. She thought of Hideki. Canada was at war with Germany, but she remembered her brother constantly spouting off a warning that Japan would soon go to war with Europe and America. Does that mean he'll be fighting Canada as well? She nodded and said nothing. This new war had nothing to do with her.

Having finished her meal, she had to ask one last question. "Do you know a beauty salon nearby?"

He didn't understand at first, but when she pantomimed her wish, he understood and pointed to a place down the street.

She thanked him for all his help and took out her money. He generously offered to pay. She couldn't understand his largess and offered to pay a few more times. She finally allowed the gesture. Lines creased her brow; she now owed him.

❊ ❊ ❊

The Gaiety Beauty Salon was a small storefront of East Hastings near the Patricia Hotel. It was owned and run by Mitzi Abe, an older *Nisei*, who took over from her mother, her *okaasan*, after she retired. The Abe *Okaasan* came in occasionally to pass the time visiting friends who patronized the business.

Mitzi was a short, squat woman with a sense of style about her. Her round, kind face welcomed all to the Gaiety. Chisato was no exception.

"Hello," Mitzi greeted in Japanese and then showed her to a chair to wait. She sat among a few women who nodded their welcome.

Chisato felt instantly at ease. She guessed that she must have looked like one of them. While she waited, she noticed a newspaper, the *Tairiku Nippo*. It was all in Japanese which she appreciated. Once she knew it was a daily, she decided she would ask her husband to buy a subscription.

"Better than that other paper," the woman next to her opined.

"Oh?"

"A new Nisei paper called *The New Canadian*. Just a bunch of loud, complaining young people trying to make trouble with the Canadians."

Before Chisato could ask how, Mitzi came and led her to a chair and asked what she wanted to do with her hair. Chisato answered that she wanted to look modern and Canadian to fit her new situation. Mitzi nodded and began the task of giving her a permanent in the latest "city style".

During the long, complicated process, Chisato overheard the gossip among various customers.

"Did you see that Otagaki down the street?"

"Yes, that ne'er-do-well," said another.

"You mean bokenasu!" *Ass!*

Everyone laughed or gasped.

"Can't speak proper Japanese if his life depended on it."

Sam Otagaki as it turned out had a bad reputation. He never had a steady job; he drank to excess at times; he would betray anyone for a price. He was cheap, always bumming free drinks and meals whenever he could.

This naturally confused Chisato who was just treated to breakfast by the man. Maybe they were talking about someone else. However, further talk confirmed the identity.

"Stay away from him," Mitzi warned.

Chisato nodded.

One last word of caution came from the corner of the room. "Stay away, he's working for Morii these days."

That name again. Who was this Morii? She would have to ask her husband.

❖ ❖ ❖

"How do you know that name?" Kiyoshi asked with some concern.

"At the beauty salon."

Kiyoshi, who had returned home at about five o'clock, noticed the new hairdo consisting of curls and an acrid processed scent.

He commented that it suited her. Before sitting down to a simple dinner of rice and cooked meat with vegetables, he began what was becoming a nightly ritual: the lighting of the candles, something Chisato decided to tolerate.

She was not a seasoned cook, but she could fix something with the meat and vegetables found in the icebox. Her mother taught her well.

His approval of the new hairstyle and dinner turned to dismay when Chisato asked about Morii. He stiffened when she mentioned the name. The expression on his face turned hard. His smile had disappeared.

"You don't need to know about that man," he said with finality.

"But Kiyoshi-san—"

"I said, you don't need to know."

And that was that. But Chisato's curiosity was piqued.

Death is meaningless.

12.   OCTOBER 1939

CHISATO THOUGHT HER LIFE IDEAL: married to a wonderful, handsome man, rich for all intents and purposes (she didn't
know, really; she presumed); lived in a big, comfortable house,
even if dominated by *The Jesus* and filled with Christian iconog-
raphy; loved the neighbourhood and all the people who resided
there; she was willing to give Christianity a chance, though she
quickly became irritated with what she privately called the *God
Talk*. At night, she avoided looking at *The Jesus*. The flickering
candlelight helped, giving everything a convivial feeling. In the
long run, she refused to let it upset her contentment. Soon reality intruded.

The Canadian newspapers started reporting the "real" numbers of dead in Nanking. At the church, Michiko Fujino as she
addressed Chisato's letter told her 300,000 to 400,000 Chinese
were slaughtered in the taking of the eastern city. Japanese soldiers were merciless in the battle.

"But Michiko-san, it's war after all," Chisato pointed out.

"Most were citizens, non-combatants! It's just evil to murder
like that. It's against Jesus. It's horrible, horrible, just horrible,"
she said, her eyes blurred with moisture. She lowered her head
in sorrow. "The Japanese are such horrible people."

Chisato frowned. *But she's Japanese,* she thought. *So am I
and everyone in the church. Except the Sensei, of course.*

In the end, she didn't believe the news. *Chinese propaganda.*
She had read in the *Tairiku Nippo* that the actual number was
4,000, and all were soldiers. In the end, 4,000, 400,000, what
did it matter? The numbers didn't mean anything. It was like
looking up at the stars and seeing infinite points of light. She
could never conceive of all the war-dead on a battlefield in
China; it was like knowing the totality of the heavens.

She soon put it out of her mind: an event that took place nearly two years ago in an obscure city and in a land over 6,000 miles away. But then she thought of Hideki. Oh, but he wasn't in the army in January 1938. Was he in training? Is he still? She gulped at the reported number of war dead in the paper and then imagined Hideki bayoneting a live soldier. A tingling like a pinprick struck her body.

Maybe Chiemi will tell her. She was determined to place the letter in the mail the first chance she got. Michiko did find her a stamp.

On the "home front", things began to change. Kiyoshi and she did not talk much at dinner. He mostly sat glumly and ate silently, his characteristic smile gone. After dinner, Kiyoshi would leave without a word and not come home until after she was asleep. But she heard when he opened the front door. She always looked at the bedside clock.

Eventually, he was not home for dinner at five o'clock, even if she had dinner ready and on the table. She dutifully waited for him, but often she ate alone, fearing the food would get cold; when he started returning at nine o'clock and later, he simply bypassed the dining room, ignored her silent self, for a bed in a separate room. Things came to a head when he finally stumbled into the house at about midnight.

His clothes were dishevelled, his tie eschew, his shirt dirty, and his suit jacket missing. His hair in a mess. She ran to him to help him to a chair.

She was about to ask if he were in a fight or was robbed. But then she noticed the rising stench of alcohol coming from him. He was drunk.

"Where have you been?" Chisato asked with an edge to her voice.

"Out," was all he said.

"Out where? And why are you drunk?"

"Damare, woman!" he shouted. *Shut up!*

She retreated, so unused to his anger.

He cast his gaze about groggily. "Why aren't the candles lit?"

"The what?"

"The candles, they should be lit," he proclaimed. He stood unsteadily before speaking again. "Jesus Christ our Lord needs venerating! Woman, every night you will light the candles and every day you shall clean the icon of Jesus Christ! That is my commandment, and you shall obey."

"All right, but where were you and why are you drunk?"

He said nothing and slowly dragged himself upstairs to bed, presumably.

She sat in the dining room puzzled, which soon grew to concern in the days ahead. When she washed his clothes, the alcohol odour pervaded, but there was also another smell underneath the fog of drink. It was faint but there. It reminded her of the plumeria back in Hiroshima. But it wasn't, it smelled like... like perfume.

✿ ✿ ✿

Canada was at war now. Chisato realized she must be mindful of and grateful for the Canadian soldiers' efforts. The Reverend James reminded the congregation of that fact during Chisato's first Christian service. Going to church on a weekly basis thereafter was a first for her.

This once-a-week ritual was odd. She went to temple any old time and mostly on important occasions. Then again, it was nice to see everyone on a regular basis; it also gave her a respite from Kiyoshi's strange absences and nearly nightly drunken tirades. He was civil in public.

The actual service gave her a sense of peace, except when the minister thundered from the pulpit. Besides the loud voice, there was Michiko's whispering a translation into her ear at the same time.

"Canada is at war! We have every confidence in our men who are about to go overseas. Pray for them and Jesus will protect them for their cause is a just cause. Let us sing!"

The piano rang out as the congregation stood and in full voice sang:

Onward Christian soldiers
Marching as to war
With the cross of Jesus
Going on before.
Onward then, ye people,
Join our happy throng,
Blend with ours your voices
In our triumph song.
Christ the royal master
Leads against the foe
Forward into battle.
See His banners go,
Crowns and Thrones may perish,
Kingdoms rise and wane,
But the cross of Jesus
Constant will remain.

Chisato saw that everyone knew the words for some reason, singing as they did from memory. She was perplexed as she
searched for a Japanese lyric sheet or book. No one, not even her
husband, lifted a finger to help. The sober Kiyoshi himself sang
with full-throated vigour. She remained mute, but she liked the
melody, despite not knowing what was being said.

And then *Sensei* asked everyone to pray for the soldiers.
What? *Blind devotion to a deity, just like in Japan,* she observed.
The act of prayer looked like everyone was saying *gassho* but
praying was much longer. The pressing of palms together was
no act of gratitude or contrition as in Buddhism. She was later
told it was "talking directly to God". In most cases, worshippers
ask for something, like guidance, like material gain, like health,
like anything. What confused Chisato further was the fact that
you could pray to Saints or Mother Mary. Were they gods too?
She thought there was only one god. No one had an answer.

The best part of the day was the luncheon prepared by the
women's club in the basement. The female volunteers, Michiko

included, were known as the Ladies Auxiliary. *Fujinkai* was a familiar term for Chisato. She considered joining, maybe later, much later.

As she waited for her husband to conduct church business, Chisato socialized while partaking of the simple lunch of and unfamiliar but delicious Japanese *chow mein*, rice, and pickled vegetables. The tea was lovely as she struck up conversations with other *fujinkai* women, introduced to her by Michiko.

Christianity was a mystery to her. If there was but one god, who were Jesus, the Father, and the Holy Ghost? Three gods? Never mind the saints. Mother Mary. Again, she thought there was only one. "But the three are one," Kiyoshi claimed. He also kept talking about the "good news". *That Jesus died?* she found. *Why is that good news?* Kiyoshi said she would find out at Easter. He ignored the questions about Mary and the saints.

Why were there two testaments in the Bible? Not that she could understand them anyway, though she was promised a Japanese version to come. Kiyoshi, with the patience of Job, tried to explain things to her, but it was all very confusing. *Who was Joubu?*

She did like the ceremonies, the peace of the processional hymn at the beginning of each service, and the companionship within the church. She was also obligated to go since her husband was such a prominent member.

But she could not reconcile the belief that "He died for our sins". *What sins? And what is Original Sin?*

The following weekend, a loud commotion again brought Chisato downstairs early in the morning. She spied various people in the kitchen banging pots and pans into position as one tall authoritative man with an intense stare barked orders which caused everyone else to hop to. He was flamboyant in dress and style. He even wore a funny looking hat.

"Good morning, Chisato-chan," Kiyoshi said as he appeared beside her. He was himself again; he had stopped disappearing into the night for the last little while. And he had returned to their bed.

"What's going on?" she asked with surprise.

"We're having a welcome party tonight!" he informed. "See that man?"

Fascinated with all the activity, she answered, "Can't miss him."

"That is Ryohachi Ryoji, the best caterer in town." Kiyoshi expanded his chest with pride. "He has access to the best seafood at Union Fish!"

"What's that on his head?" She brought her hand up to her mouth to suppress a laugh.

"A chef's hat. He's a master."

"Why all this fuss and expense?"

"I want to introduce you to the community," he said with that smile.

"But you already have."

"Not really. I've invited many others, so they can meet you. I would offend them if I didn't."

"Who are all these people?"

"As I said, I hired the Master Chef and his staff to prepare a grand meal!"

She stood mystified but enjoyed all the chaos.

That evening, the noise level increased ten-fold. Maybe fifty people came through the front door. They crowded around makeshift tables in the front rooms. Ryoji-*san* thought of everything. Besides the plates of Japanese delicacies, there was a multitude of *sake* bottles.

Lit candles (but not as many) greeted the guests. *The Jesus* as a result stood in the shadows, so much so no one paid it any mind. She was sure they knew about it anyway.

She watched her husband and the bottles of alcohol. To her surprise, he only partook of a few drinks to be polite, and only whenever others insisted. He was on his best behaviour.

Kiyoshi and Chisato eventually sat at the head of the main table, both dressed in white. He had insisted. She was confused since white was the colour of death—in Japan. Who knows what it meant in Canada. The array of food before her was impressive as many of the guests complimented. Chisato turned her head to hide her red face. Instead, Kiyoshi did most of the talking to introduce his wife to the many who were in attendance.

"Matsuyama-san owns the largest grocery store in Powell Street. You know Michiko. Her husband, Tamotsu Fujino, has a very successful fishing business. Must pull in a few tons of seafood per year. Eh, Fujino-san? And of course, there's Kenji Yamamoto, who owns several rooming houses and the fruit market up the street."

Each nodded in acknowledgement of the praise. And so, the evening went into the wee hours of the morning with the volume of the crowd growing ever louder as the bottles of *sake* emptied and disappeared. Ryohachi's wait-staff were very efficient around the table. Though she was impressed that her husband knew all these prominent people, Chisato grew weary as her head became dizzy with the random conversations the longer the evening stretched. She dragged herself to bed and eventually slept without dreaming that night.

❊ ❊ ❊

And then there was Christmas, the *Hanamatsuri* of Christianity. Seemingly overnight, the house was transformed with glistening decorations. Kiyoshi bought and put up a tree in the living room. He came into the house awkwardly carrying it while laughing with joy. When Chisato asked him why a tree, he said he didn't know. "It's what Canadians do."

The fresh, pungent aroma was enticing and the ornaments pretty, as they glittered with the Christmas lights, something else she discovered for the first time. She particularly liked the bubble lights, individual bulbs that came alive with bubbles within their glass housing. The scene made her feel cheery, a sharp contrast to the cold wet weather outside.

Chisato's family did something similar at *Oshogatsu* (New Year's Day) just not as elaborate.

She then learned she had to shop for presents for friends (there were no family members) and their children. Soga's provided an array of goods. Chisato liked the variety of Christmas paper, the bows, and cards. Wrapping the gifts in such brightly coloured paper was such a pleasure, as she marveled at the finished collection of presents under the tree. Friends and acquaintances came by to replace the gifts to them with gifts for the blessed couple. Singing carols at church was also a grand activity, the music was beautiful. All the new customs, in fact, were part of the Canadian experience that she soon embraced. It truly was a festive season.

The *fujinkai* (women's club) provided cooking instructions for a turkey dinner. Chisato did not need to worry, however. She and her husband were to attend an opulent Christmas dinner at the church. All she had to do was try her hand at breakfast. She and Kiyoshi awoke early and ate before opening the presents: mostly household items like towels, teacups, and a knife with a penny glued to it.

"To ward off the danger in giving a weapon," Kiyoshi explained.

It was all mystifying, but she enjoyed the new customs of the holiday. Then breakfast: Kiyoshi laughed after she burned the toast and overcooked the bacon. She had no idea you could do such a thing. At least, the eggs turned out fine with Kiyoshi's help.

The Japanese-Christian community came together on Christmas Day to exchange presents, to pray in celebration of the Lord's birth, and to share communally in the turkey dinner, Christmas cookies and rum punch. Everyone, it seemed, was there.

Chisato was overjoyed to taste the tender turkey meat, coated with something called "gravy", a mysterious thick brown liquid, as well as the stuffing, mixed vegetables, and the cranberry sauce. She looked on with wonder. The women also provided rice and *shoyu* (soy sauce). They could not forget some Japanese elements.

New Year's, just a week away, was something she understood. Canadians, she was told, spent New Year's Eve drinking, so she was happy to learn the Japanese observed the old *Oshogatsu* traditions. *Only white men drink,* she thought naively.

Though she couldn't go to the temple to offer her gratitude to the Buddha or worship before the Shinto gods in a shrine, she could prepare the New Year delicacies or *osechi ryori*. She thought of her mother. Maybe Chisato should have paid more attention.

The ingredients were readily available to her relief in the Powell Street area, from stores like Union Fish, Seiya's, and Matsumiya's Grocery. She found buckwheat noodles for the *toshikoshi soba*, long buckwheat noodles, the perfect symbol for crossing-over from one year into the next, on New Year's Eve. To her delight, the church put on a *mochi tsuki* to provide everyone with the magical rice cake. They called it a *Mochi Bee*. It was great fun watching women like Michiko and men like her husband pound and knead the *mochi* rice once the rhythm was set. Some of the smooth, round cakes were displayed in front of the altar to commemorate the dead. Kiyoshi tolerated the Japanese altar Chisato had bought at Soga's, but after use, she stored it out of sight in the bedroom closet.

Kiyoshi had said he would be going to several drinking parties leading up to New Year's Day since he wanted to forget the business troubles of the past year and look forward to the coming year. The parties were held in local watering holes like the *Showa Club* (an establishment owned and operated by Morii Etsuji), she learned, and attended by co-workers and business associates. Only men were allowed. She dreaded the late-night argument that would surely take place when he arrived home.

He also told her she would have to stay home on New Year's Day and play host to all the men who would drop by to pay their respects. They would converse as she served *sake* and beer and food. He in turn would visit various houses to do the same. She accepted it all; it was just as in Japan. Her father and Hideki ventured forth and stayed out all day and evening. She thought of her mother and Chiemi on *Oshogatsu*. She had enjoyed the female camaraderie. None in Canada, however.

As expected, Kiyoshi came home late that night and drunk but, miraculously, there was no argument. The candles were lit, *The Jesus* was clean, and the delicacies had been prepared to the best of her ability. Chisato wasn't sure he had even noticed since he waltzed up the stairs to bed as soon as he came home, tossing off his shoes, overcoat, and jacket. As she gathered the discarded items, she was glad of the fact that there was no perfume odour on his clothes. That too had been a mystery.

❋ ❋ ❋

On New Year's Day, she proudly gazed at her table heavy with Japanese delicacies. Her mother and Chiemi would be proud, she thought. Maybe she had been paying attention.

Kiyoshi, sober, stoic, and silent, a bit red-eyed, left the house early as Chisato lit the candles and performed last-minute preparations for the feast. He wore a simple white shirt and dark pants with matching suit jacket; he barely combed his hair and seemed to be in a hurry. The only thing he said was that he would be bringing back the first guest. In less than an hour, he made good on his promise.

"*Chai-sato-san!*" greeted a friendly and familiar voice at the front door. The Reverend James followed Kiyoshi inside. Chisato initially held in her stomach as she welcomed the man by helping him take off his coat and bringing him house slippers once he took off his outside shoes. She then led him to the dining table.

"*Kiyo has always invited me on New Year's Day. This is the first time the food has been home cooked. He usually has it catered,*" he said as he grabbed her hand and pulled her into him.

"*Ah, the advantage of having a wife.*"

Once Kiyoshi translated, Chisato smiled, taking the lefthanded compliment. She would never get used to these "Canadian ways". She remained mum.

The reverend was dressed in a three-piece dark suit with an appropriate tie. He did not wear his collar. His face was animated whenever he talked, his red hair tamed with hair product, so it did not move. He smelled of a man's cologne, perhaps a bit too much.

"*So, Chai-sato, how are you getting along?*" he asked as he presented her with a bouquet of flowers. Where he had got them was a mystery, but she was grateful he had observed the custom and for the touch of beauty added to the house.

"*I fine...am good,*" she said in halting English as she accepted the bouquet and sought a place to put them. The kitchen sink would suffice for the moment.

They both laughed as Kiyoshi sat back in his chair smiling proudly.

"*I see the Lord's in a grand place of honour,*" the reverend observed, pointing at *The Jesus.*

"Hai," Kiyoshi agreed. "*Not too much, is it?*"

"*No, no, not at all. Wonderful piece of art. Really gives the place a sense of sanctity.*"

Chisato just nodded after the translation.

Rev. James then went on about the church, which Kiyoshi translated but left Chisato a bit cold. She wasn't interested in the business of the church. She still had many questions about Christianity, but now was not the time to bring them forward. And besides, the constant *God Talk* was getting tiresome.

She stood and went back and forth from the kitchen to serve dishes: whole shrimp, *chow mein, sashimi* (tuna and octopus), and rice. The minister helped himself but talked more than ate. He avoided the *sashimi. Raw fish,* he shivered. Kiyoshi listened and drank some beer, even though it seemed a bit early. Occasionally, he offered an opinion, and the reverend countered. Chisato said nothing, listening politely but not taking in anything.

About an hour later, Kiyoshi announced that now it was time to go. The minister had other stops to make and Kiyoshi as president and interpreter needed to accompany him.

Chisato bid them farewell and cleared the table to set it for the next peripatetic guest. She then found out the importance of the October party.

❊ ❊ ❊

A parade of men came to the door from noon onwards. Michiko's husband, Tamotsu Fujino; Matsuyama-*san*; Yamamoto-*san*, the rooming-house owner; Mitsuo Abe of the Gaiety Beauty Salon (his wife was the owner actually); and more than a few others.

They came in groups of two or three. More than half shook her hand. All wanted to talk to the pretty young bride. By 4:00, Chisato was exhausted, her hand and wrist sore.

There was a nice lull at that point. She sat at the dining room table and exhaled as deeply as she could. She moved a clean plate over a food stain to hide it. She had no idea if any others were coming, but maybe. Couldn't imagine anyone else; she felt she had accounted for everyone she had met. But then there was a knock at the door. She sighed and got up slowly.

As she opened the door, she was surprised to see a familiar face, a little gaunt, drooping eyes, and balding head. Sam Otagaki stood in an old, slightly rumpled, three-piece suit. He smirked when he saw her.

"Kimura-san, akemashite omedetou gozaimasu," he said as he bowed. *Happy New Year Kimura-san.*

Well, at least, he didn't want to shake hands, she thought. "How did you know where to find me?" *And how did you know my name?* She remembered she hadn't mentioned it in the café.

"I hear around town," he said in his awkward Japanese.

"Come in, come in, don't stand out in the cold!"

Sam explained clumsily that he thought he would see how she was doing. He complimented her on the *osechi* she had put on the table, and the *sake* was sweet and easy on the throat. He particularly liked the different types of *sushi*.

Chisato watched him with a gracious smile.

He looked at *The Jesus*, momentarily, but didn't bat an eye. He continued to help himself to the food. Chisato served him a beer.

Sometime during the proceedings, Sam grew serious and turned to a different subject, probably the real purpose of his visit.

"Can come to *Ernie's* next Thursday at 11:30?" he asked as Chisato struggled to understand.

"I suppose so. Why?"

"Someone meet you...want to meet."

"Someone? Who?"

"Can no tell. It a secret. Come can?"

At that precise moment, the front door swung open, and Kiyoshi stood in the entrance. His smile quickly fell to a frown when he came into the dining room. His red eyes turned fiery and glowed with rage. "What's this man doing here?" His teeth flashed.

"Kiyoshi-san, this is—"

"I know who he is," he said flatly, his voice raised.

Sam came to feet immediately. "Kimura-san, I sorry to be here. I go now."

Kiyoshi grabbed him by the back of his collar as Sam made his way past. Sam began to shriek.

Chisato had never seen anything like this before and uttered a protest, and she even tried to stop her husband. It was so out of character. Sure, he raised his voice to her, but her husband had never been physically violent.

"Woman! Out of the way," he commanded as he pushed her aside with one hand. "This has got to be done. You have no idea who this is."

She recovered and watched in shock as Kiyoshi roughly rushed Sam to the door and out. Sam comically stood on his tiptoes and twisted since Kiyoshi had jerked his jacket up with his hand.

When peace descended again, Chisato sat at the dining table and glared at her husband.

"Why did you do that to Sammu?"

"'Sammu' is it? When did you become so friendly with him?"

"He just showed up and introduced himself. I thought he was one of your business people." She lied but the truth would've been too long a story, and she suspected her husband would not have approved.

"Well, he's not."

"Who is he, then?"

"Never mind. You don't need to know."

And that was that. They both fell into the cave of a silent evening.

13.   JANUARY 1940

CHISATO WAS INTRIGUED AND CAUTIOUSLY anticipated Thursday. *Who wants to meet me? And why all the secrecy?* She also wondered about Sam Otagaki. *What had he done to make my husband so angry with him? Who was he? I will have to find out.*

Ernie's Café was as busy as ever, even for a Thursday morning. And Ernie was as brusque as expected, talking rudely to his many customers. The New Year had not lightened his outlook, she surmised.

"You don't like the service, get the hell out and go somewhere else!" he yelled more than once. Either in English or Japanese.

She smirked, bemused if a little offended by his gruff personality. In her peripheral vision, she saw a man leave his chair and approach her.

"Kimura-san! So nice see you. Happy to be here." Speak of the devil, she recognized the familiar bumpy Japanese. It belonged to Sam Otagaki. Involuntarily, she rotated her head to see if her husband was nearby.

Sam soon situated himself in front of her. His grin was as wide as the horizon. He then shifted to the side while pointing back to his table. Sitting there was a guest, a woman.

"You know, I know," Sam pronounced.

At first, Chisato didn't recognize her but soon realized it was her friend from the ship and Immigration Building, Sachiko Jikemura. She seemed much smaller, as she was hunched over and scrawny. Her sad face smiled weakly as Chisato gazed at her. Still, Chisato's face beamed as she swiftly moved to the table.

"I go now," Sam said and moved to leave chuckling to himself in a self-satisfied way. "Ja-ne!"

Although shocked by his familiarity, she ignored Sam. "Sachiko-chan!" Chisato gushed as she sat down. "It really is you!"

Sachiko nodded.

"I never thought I'd see you again."

"Me neither." Her voice was weak, hoarse. She had changed so much, she had lost a lot of weight, her neck was so skinny and ribbed, it was a wonder it held up her boney head. Her hair was scraggly, matted, thinned out, and coarse. Her body exuded a faint odour of poverty and decay. Her clothes were frayed and ragged.

Only one coffee cup was on the table—Sam's, Chisato assumed, since it wasn't in front of her friend.

"How...how did you find me? What are you doing here? How do you know Sammu?" Her questions were many and rapid. She finally caught herself, stopped talking while taking in a breath. It was her friend's turn.

Sachiko began slowly. She seemed in pain and couldn't move easily or quickly. She shivered with the cold January air, even indoors.

"Akamatsu...I mean, Kimura-san, I asked Otagaki-san to help find you and arrange this meeting."

"Wait...how do you know Sammu?"

"Morii-san ordered Otagaki-san to help me."

That name again. *Who is this Morii?* She put that aside for the moment. "So, it was no accident that he met me in that Canadian restaurant."

Sachiko nodded. "I asked Morii-san for help, and he called in Sammu. I had to get a-hold of you..." Her voice trailed away.

"I am happy to see you again, but why so secretive about it all?" That was when she noticed the bruises shaded around her neck and on the exposed part of her forearms. Every time she moved, however slightly, her face grimaced. She also let out an almost imperceptible groan. Almost.

Chisato remembered Hideki's punishment wounds. He never thought she noticed the dark spots on his body. But she had. She didn't say anything to spare him and family members embarrassment. She knew Chiemi would deal with his problems.

"I...I...I need your help."

"Of course," Chisato said reassuringly. "How?"

"I heard you had married well. Your husband has a lot of influence in Powell Street and in BC. My husband is a monster. I think he's...not right in the—" she said, pointing to her head and lowering her voice to a conspiratorial whisper.

"Don't say that!" Chisato's voice rose unconsciously. She hoped that no one had heard or seen Sachiko.

"Look!" she said as she pushed up one sleeve of her blouse. Her entire arm was covered in the light and dark shadows of bruises, old and new. It was worse than Chisato had suspected.

Chisato was stunned. How could anyone do that, especially to his own wife?

"Most of my body is like that. I don't know why I'm still alive." She paused as Chisato let it sink in. "I need you...I ask you to help me get away. I live in Steveston... my husband is a fisherman. He'll be leaving soon to begin work. It's a good time to escape."

"But how can I help?"

"I'll need somewhere to go. Maybe your husband can find a place for me."

"I don't know—"

Sachiko reached out and grabbed Chisato's forearm.

"I'm desperate, Akamatsu-san. If our time coming over here together meant anything to you, you'll help me!"

Chisato noticed the customers around them had started to stare at them. She moved her arm to loosen the grip. She lowered her gaze.

"Why doesn't this Morii do something?"

"I'm too small to bother with," she said. Her lips curled into a sneer.

Chisato didn't know what that meant exactly, but she knew Morii was a deadend. "I'll do what I can...but you must realize—"

"That's all I ask. But I am depending on you. Convince your husband to help." Her voice anguished, she stood and made leaving noises.

"Wait," Chisato said loudly, "how will I get in touch with you?"

"Otagaki-san" was all she said and quickly shuffled out of the door.

Chisato was abruptly alone, and she felt all eyes on her. She too made her way out of the place.

❉ ❉ ❉

That evening, she stood at the dinner table serving dinner. Kiyoshi sat with legs crossed reading a newspaper while he waited for the food. She knew he would be leaving the house after he ate to go who knows where, so Chisato had to have the conversation.

"Kiyoshi, do you remember Sachiko Jikemura?"

"Hmm," he murmured, not looking at her.

"Sachiko Jikemura. Remember her from the Immigration Building when I first met you?"

Kiyoshi bent his paper down and looked at her with a questioning look. "Yes, yes, I remember her. You were concerned because her husband lied to her."

"Yes, well, I ran into her...at Ernie's today," she informed anticipating his next question.

"Oh?"

"Yes, she is being brutalized by her husband."

"And how is that any of our business?"

She was surprised by her husband's lack of compassion. Then again, he wasn't Buddhist.

"But we should help—"

"What happens between a man and wife is their business."

"Where is your Christian compassion for another Christian?"

"Is she Christian?"

She hesitated before answering. "Yes."

"Then she should go to her minister."

"In Steveston?"

"They have churches there."

"Too much local gossip. It would be easier if our church helped. No one knows her here. The farther away she can get, the better."

The argument seemed to convince Kiyoshi. "I'll talk to Reverend James, but she must get herself to Powell Street. We can't be accused of kidnapping her."

Chisato added, "Once fishing season begins and her husband leaves, she will come."

"How will we know?"

"Oh, I suppose, she'll send a letter." Again, she lied. She did not want to mention Otagaki's name, given his reaction to Sam's visit on *Oshogatsu*. But the problem remained. How was she going to get in touch? Otagaki?

❊ ❊ ❊

Her next appointment at the Gaiety Beauty Salon supplied the answer. The usual crowd of *Issei* women was there, touching up their dos, or getting a fresh permanent, and gossiping.

In an advantageous moment, she spoke to the owner, Mitzi Abe, who was on a break from her customers, in soft, conspiratorial tones.

"Abe-san, you remember Sammu Otagaki," she said and waited for a sign. "How do I get in touch with him?"

Michiko leaned towards her friend. "You don't want to do that."

"I do, actually. I need him to convey a message to a friend."

"You don't need a friend that is his friend."

"Please, stop telling me what I don't need or want. I just have to talk to him."

"I told you to stay away from him. He works for Morii."

"I thought he was working as a carpenter at—"

"He works for Morii."

"And who is this Morii that everyone wants to avoid talking about?" She thought of her husband.

"He is the boss of the Black Dragon Society."

"The what?"

"The Black Dragon Society. Yakuza. A gang of men who control gambling, alcohol, and other things I won't talk about. Morii is the boss, and he is dangerous. You don't want to get mixed up with him."

"But I have to talk to Otagaki-san."

A long pause as Mitzi seemed to be taking the measure of Chisato.

"I'm desperate," Chisato insisted. "It could be a matter of life and death." She didn't feel she was exaggerating if the bruises on Sachiko's body were any indication. Who knew how far Jikemura-*san* would go? She did not elaborate.

"Well, all right, it's your funeral. Otagaki is often seen at the Showa Club on Powell Street."

Strange expression, but Chisato ignored it. "Where on Powell?"

"Oh, I forget, somewhere in the 300 block."

"Don't you know where on the 300 block? It's a long block."

"Do you think I go to a place like that?" she said in an indignant tone. "Ask anyone there. Better yet, you'll see the watchman sitting out front...at the foot of the stairs. You can't miss him. He's always there. The place is upstairs."

"All right then. Thank you."

"But no women are allowed in there. At least, only 'working women' are allowed."

Chisato didn't understand what she meant by "working women" but she let it stand. So many mysterious Canadian sayings.

"Just speak to the watchman and he'll go fetch Otagaki, I reckon."

❊ ❊ ❊

A watchman indeed sat in the vestibule, hidden from a sideview from the street. He was a wizened old man with a sparse head of white hair, sunken cheeks, and a collapsed mouth, no teeth. His body sagged on both sides of the cheap metal chair, seemingly stolen from the Japanese Language School on Alexander Street—confirmed by the red lettering printed on the back of it.

Chisato approached the man gingerly. He looked like he was asleep.

"Please excuse me," she said quietly and politely.

Nevertheless, the man was startled awake. "Who are you?" he growled, inspecting her with one squinting eye.

"I am Kimura Chisato," she answered, reverting to the Japanese naming convention.

He pulled himself up to his feet with some difficulty. "Sorry, I was just resting my eyes."

"Yes, I'm sure," she said with a smile. "I'm looking for Otagaki Osamu. I understand he is likely upstairs at the..." She hesitated not wishing the watchman to know she knew about the place. "Can you help me?"

"Oh sure...sure. Wait here." He was friendly enough as he slowly got up, turned, and creaked before climbing the stairs.

About five minutes later, she heard the scurry of shoes coming down the stairs. At the door Otagaki-*san* stood with a wide grin on his face.

The old watchman walked up the street some distance to avoid the business between them.

"Kimura-san, so nice see you," Sam greeted.

Chisato would never get use to his Japanese. "Otagaki-san—"

"Sam," he corrected. He stood smiling and staring at her.

"Yes, Sammu, I understand you can get a message to Sachiko Jikemura."

"Who? Oh yes, at Ernie's," he said with confidence. "Yes, can. What message you have?"

"Tell her come see me in Vancouver...at my house...when... when the time is right."

"When the time is right?"

"Yes, she'll know what that means."

"All right. And what I get?"

"Get?"

"Yes, for service," he said with a lascivious leer. He then touched her shoulder with his index finger.

She shuddered at the implication. She quickly recovered and snapped back, "Maybe I should talk to Morii-san."

Otagaki's face drew back in horror. "No...no, you don't want to do that." He stepped back into the comfort of the vestibule.

"Maybe my husband—"

"I contact Sachiko. No worry. Don't talk to Morii...husband...no need worry them," he said.

Satisfied, Chisato turned and headed for home. *Morii is a magical name*, she thought to herself.

I grow sad at the loss.

14.   MARCH 1940

A BRIGHT SUNNY DAY—AN UNUSUAL occurrence in
Vancouver for mid-March. Chisato's outlook was lightened as
a result. She could not get used to the overcast days that seemingly went on endlessly. Hiroshima was sunny most days, hot,
burning hot at times. Just the other day, she looked for the sun,
but nothing but the heavy anvil of clouds. And so here it was,
finally.

Chisato enjoyed being outside in the backyard preparing the
vegetable and flower garden for the growth to come. *At least now,
there will be enough light for the plants and there will be colour and
wonderful fragrances*, she thought.

She turned her head when she heard a faint rapping in the
air. It didn't come from inside the house but from the front of it.
She walked along the side path until she was in front, near the
street.

Yet another phantom knock.

"Sachiko-chan," she called, more happy than surprised.
"Forgive me I was in the back. Come and we'll visit back there."

"Could we go inside?" she asked timidly, while turning every
which way.

"Of course." Chisato returned to the backyard, depositing digging implements, before entering the house and swiftly moving
to the front door. She opened it and welcomed her friend who
wore a cheap, worn beige coat and carried a small rough valise.

Sachiko Jikemura appeared the same as she did at Ernie's
a few months ago, perhaps not as skinny (might have been
Chisato's imagination), but certainly disheveled with a pronounced curve to her back. Her face was as thin as before with
more bruising here and there; her eyes tired with pronounced
dark bags underneath each.

Chisato noticed of course but didn't want to call attention to them.

Sachiko kept turning her head behind her to see through the front door.

"What are you looking for?" Chisato asked.

"My husband…" Her eyes bulged with fear.

"I thought he was away at sea."

"Maybe one of his spies. He has them everywhere." She meant one of her husband's friends, though Chisato couldn't imagine who would bother.

After Sachiko was safely in the house, Chisato scanned the street for anything suspicious. There were many more Canadian strangers, tall and in suits, overcoats, and fedoras in the neighbourhood of late. Some stood on a corner; some in cars parked on the street, while others walked as if patrolling the area.

At the kitchen table and after some green tea in charming China cups from Hiroshima and some colourful *manju* from Kawasaki Confectioner beside the nearby fruit market, Chisato explained what was going to happen with Sachiko.

"Only one suitcase?" she asked. "The rest of your belongings?"

"Left everything behind. The past is a curse and I want to forget it."

"I understand," Chisato said in sympathy. "I'm so happy to see you! And glad you made your escape."

Sachiko sat with lowered head, in a tomb of silence.

The room absorbed any noise Chisato made anyway. "I'll take you to the church where Reverend James will take care of you."

"No," Sachiko murmured and tensed up.

"Now, don't worry, he knows about your situation. He's a good man. You'll be in good hands. The fujinkai will provide you with new clothes, some money…anything you need."

Her shoulders relaxed somewhat.

"One thing bothers me though. My husband is at work, and I can't speak English."

"I speak a little," Sachiko said, suddenly raising her voice.

"Good. I bet there'll be someone there to help," she said. "Oh, are you Christian?"

"What? Me? No, I'm nothing."

"Well, don't say that to the Reverend."

✿ ✿ ✿

While walking along Powell Street towards the church, both women kept a sharp eye on their surroundings. When Sachiko thought she saw a "spy", they elected to go through the wide back lanes going east, lanes of garbage cans and animal leavings. The smell followed them like an insecure child.

They arrived at the front doors of the church, safe and sound. They entered through the back door at the top of a small wooden porch as a precaution. The yard was small and full of debris.

Chisato led the way up a short flight of inside stairs, which creaked with age. Despite the sun-lit day, the interior was dark and musty. Nevertheless, Chisato knew the way. Once they made it to the minister's office all was well.

It was an office full of books on shelves and filing cabinets. On the floor was what looked like decorations: crepe-paper flowers, small baskets with multicoloured eggs and white, green, and pink toy rabbits. Neither of the women had ever seen anything like it. Chisato examined the paraphernalia while Sachiko lifted a finger to touch the leather-bound books, but Chisato stopped her before she could.

✿ ✿ ✿

She later learned that Easter is the festival commemorating the death and resurrection of Christ, the Saviour. *The Jesus* in the living room came to mind. Chisato thought it odd that at this time of year Buddhists celebrate the birth of the Buddha with *Hanamatsuri*, a time of flowers, joy, and beauty, not toy rabbits. She would never understand these Christians.

"Chai-sato!" greeted Rev. James with his permanent smile and extended hand. "Please excuse the mess. Easter decorations.

The children love the candied eggs! You and Kiyo must come to that service. Lots of fun."

Michiko Fujino accompanied the minister to act as interpreter. Her smile reassured Chisato.

Despite her ignorance about the Easter celebrations and not understanding what he was saying (Michiko remained mum), she nodded while reaching out and took the hand. He predictably grasped, shook, and pulled; she pulled back, but he was too strong.

"*Sensei*, this my friend Sachiko Jikemura." That was the extent of her broken English. She stepped aside to reveal her friend.

"*Now, I don't need to know Japanese to know who this is.*" Again, he grabbed Sachiko's hand and pulled. Sachiko's eyes widened. "*Kiyo told me all about her.*" The minister then invited them to sit in his office while he left to go downstairs.

"*I Christian,*" she confessed in a timid English.

The reverend laughed. "*So am I!*"

Sachiko in Michiko's place quickly translated for Chisato. She was impressed by her friend's skill. Michiko confirmed that Sachiko's understanding of English was pretty good.

After some explanation by Michiko, Sachiko understood she was to accompany Rev. James and Michiko out of town to somewhere safe. "*You need to be as far away as possible from your husband and his friends.*"

Sachiko remained silent as Chisato advocated for her. She naturally wanted to know where. The reverend upon his return would not tell since knowledge would become a danger to her if the husband ever found out her role in all this. Chisato nodded.

"*Michiko,*" said the reverend, "*can we find some clothes for Sachi? The other ladies can help, I'm sure. Feed her as well. She looks like she could use a good meal!*" He was smiling the entire time. "*I'm sure we can do something about the bruises.*"

Chisato was taken aback as her face turned red. For Sachiko's part, she looked away and pulled down her sleeves and fingered her sweater as best as she could.

After a few moments, the Rev. James and Michiko took Sachiko down the stairs into unknown darkness. The last thing Sachiko said to Chisato was "Thank you. I will contact you, I promise."

Chisato sat in the office alone, thinking about what had just happened.

❊ ❊ ❊

A few weeks after Sachiko's rescue, in April in fact, Chisato received a letter. She first thought it might be from her friend but then she noticed it was from Japan—*Chiemi!* But no, it was from her father. *Strange*, she thought. She had written home infrequently because of all the adjustments she had to make and then only to her sister. But no, this time it was from her father. Only a single piece of paper and on it was written a *tanka*.

> *Death has no meaning for me,*
> *But when I give thought to the*
> *Moment of death,*
> *I grow sad at the loss of*
> *Warm family memories.*

What did it mean? And why did her father send it to her? There was no explanation, but the message made her tremble inexplicably. What was he trying to say? She immediately wrote to Chiemi. Principally, she wanted to know if her father was all right.

She did not receive an answer until September.

Chisato-chan,

Hello, I hope you are well. I am sad to say that, on August 6th, our beloved father died. I can't tell you why. The doctors don't even know. He didn't look ill; he didn't complain of any pain or even discomfort; he just passed away in his sleep.

I suppose the poem you received was a warning. He gave me a copy as well and he said he had sent one to Hideki, though I haven't heard from him to confirm that fact. Somehow, Ōtousan knew he was going to die.

Okaasan is grieving, of course, but she is generally doing well. The funeral was overseen by Sensei Kiyahara and well-attended. I told everyone that you are prospering in Canada.

Write soon.
Chiemi

Chisato wrote back immediately.

Chiemi Oneesan,

How can this be? Otousan was not sick, showed no signs of an illness, yet he died? Can't be true. Can it?

I don't know what to say. Please let me know if anything is found out.

Also let me know what Hideki has to say. I am destroyed.

Chisato

For most of the day and night, she wept off and on, to varying degrees. What was she to do without her father? Ridiculous since she lived so far away.

✿ ✿ ✿

When she told Kiyoshi that evening, his face filled with sympathy and quietly said to her, "He's in a better place. Let's talk to Reverend James."

Chisato wondered about the "better place". *He's dead, not on holiday*, she thought with anger in her heart, but she said nothing in return. But she did think, *This is a crazy religion.* She had no wish to listen to the minister, but Kiyoshi insisted.

In the same church office as before, she sat opposite Rev. James with Kiyoshi standing to translate. The reverend even looked tall sitting down. The place was heavy with dust causing Chisato to sniffle constantly, which both men surely mistook for grief. They said as much as they gazed at her with sympathetic eyes.

The reverend's chair creaked as he leaned forward. "*Chisato, I know how you're feeling, but he is with the Lord now. I'm sure he was a good man. Be comforted by the fact that your father will be saved come the Judgement Day. Can we pray together? Give me your hands.*"

Chisato sighed when he reached for her two hands and held them in front of her. She flinched with his touch, but he held firm and pulled her slightly towards him. She would never get used to the off-putting familiarity. He closed his eyes and uttered a few words, but she didn't hear his words. She shut her mind. And he and Kiyoshi did not see the disgust on her face as they prayed.

Whenever Kiyoshi left for the evening, not as frequently these days, she appreciated his absence. Even if he stayed home, she retreated to an empty, gloomy room in the house. Only one window allowed dull light from the street to enter. She missed her sister, her mother and even her brother. She wanted to see the Akamatsu compound again. To feel the cool of the surrounding woods, to warm in the bright sunlight coming from over the sea. To walk the Hiroshima streets to smell the familiar odours (sweet confections and fermented products like *miso*), to see the familiar landmarks, to take in the surrounding crowds of her fellow Japanese. She should've been there with her father.

Was coming to Canada a mistake? Was the Emperor wrong? The questions plagued her mind as she sat in the engulfing darkness.

The first chance she had, she went to the Buddhist church. She wanted to offer incense to her father's memory. She knew she was breaking with her vows to the Christian church, even though she was obligated to Rev. James for what he did for Sachiko, but this was her father she was thinking of. She would not tell her husband or the Reverend James.

The Vancouver Buddhist church was on two lots of Cordova Street near Princess Avenue. So, within walking distance. The wooden building with the familiar wisteria emblazoned above the entrance seemed new and indeed it had just opened in 1934. Chisato ventured up the curved stairs that acted like bookends to the entrance and walked into the musty congregation hall. It smelled so differently from the Christian church. It smelled familiar.

The incense and the faint sounds of a *sutra* being chanted comforted her. She was home as she sat at the back, with a good view of the altar. There were a few people gathered observing a memorial service, she guessed, since it was mid-week.

The *sensei* was at the front seated before the scroll of the *Nembutsu* and altar. His eyes were closed, his hands in supplication as he recited from the *Dharma*. One by one the parishioners approached the altar and offered incense, small fragrant crumbs, placing them in the burner. The smoke curled into the air above like a premonition.

Chisato waited her turn and then approached the large bronze *koro* to do the same. She thought of her father as she expressed gratitude to the Buddha. She bowed before returning to her seat.

Impermanence leads to desire which leads to suffering. Depend on the Buddha Dharma.

She had thought to talk to the *sensei*, but she just sat meditating for a while. She then quietly left and vowed to return when the *God Talk* got to be too much.

15.   FEBRUARY 1941

CHRISTMAS AND NEW YEAR'S 1940/41 were the same joyous occasions as the previous year with one significant difference. Kiyoshi bought Chisato a present: a gorgeous green dress
and a golden crucifix on a chain, which she was to wear around
her neck. She didn't receive anything as precious as this last year.
She didn't know what to say.

She wore the dress at New Year's as was the Japanese custom
of wearing something new. She of course wore the *Jesus Necklace*,
but never during her secret visits to the Buddhist temple. That
would've been absurd. Or even most times in public. When she
was with her husband and in church, that was about the only
time she did.

Every guest complimented her on her dress. People seemed
envious. She smiled to herself.

In February, she learned she was pregnant, making 1941 a
propitious year. She started making plans by asking for a carpenter to convert one of the rooms into a nursery (something
she learned at the church). It meant losing her hideaway, but a
new life lifted her spirits.

And Kiyoshi was supportive, not willing to do any of the
preparation work, but told her to consider a nurse maid to help
her through the difficult first months. Her mother and mother-
in-law were out of the question.

It was good news at the church as well. Michiko organized a
party, something called a "baby shower", to help plan for the new
addition to the congregation.

Chisato could not have been happier. She completely forgot
about her husband's late-night disappearances. She decided to

write her sister with the news. Unfortunately, she didn't have much of a chance to sit down and compose it.

✿ ✿ ✿

Starting in March, the government announced that all Japanese Canadians had to register with the Royal Canadian Mounted Police. She and Kiyoshi walked through Gastown and into the near downtown area to a non-descript building by the waterfront. He informed her it was the headquarters of the *Mountain Police*. She didn't like that the police had her on record. What would they want with her?

She soon found out: she began the registration process with an officious little man with a tiny mustache behind a desk. Two others stood guard near him. After loads of documents were signed and photographs taken, Kiyoshi and Chisato were labelled "Aliens". They were told to come back and pick up their identification cards. She didn't understand why.

"I suppose to keep tabs on us. There is a war in China."

"Yes, but—"

"Never mind. They don't trust us," he said with finality.

She bristled with indignation. *As if I was going to do anything subversive.*

✿ ✿ ✿

A few days later, she received a letter from Chiemi. Overjoyed, she read it with relish.

Chisato-chan,

This is your oneesan. I write to let you know Hideki is in ▮▮▮▮▮▮. He has fulfilled his dream. We are concerned for his safety. ▮▮▮▮▮▮▮▮▮▮

I made him a senninbari to protect him. The gods will deliver him back to us. I hope 1,000 stitches are enough. ▮▮▮

▮▮▮▮▮▮▮▮▮▮▮▮▮▮▮

Okaasan is growing lonely since her children are far away. Oh, I am married now. I married Ito-san back in November 1939. I am sorry I didn't tell you, but I did not know where you were.

I did miss your presence. That would have made the wedding tolerable. In any case, I will write again. Please write me sometime.

Chiemi Oneesan

Chisato was happy to hear from her sister, but the "tolerable" comment gave her pause. *What could she mean?*

She tried to write again, she had so much to tell her, but the times would not allow it.

❊ ❊ ❊

Kiyoshi Kimura soon fell into his old ways: frequently leaving the house shortly after or even before dinner and not returning until late at night. Chisato tried to ignore his drinking habit; she gave up waiting for him, but he made so much noise entering the house that she woke up with a start every time. She resisted the temptation to scold him, he had not after all beaten her like Sachiko's husband. Fortunately, he slept in another room.

However, whenever she cleaned his clothes, she noticed the perfume smell. It seemed to be getting stronger. She had no idea how to explain the mystery. It grew in such intensity that she decided to follow him one night.

One night, Chisato acted as soon as she heard Kiyoshi leave the house. As usual, he hadn't said a word; he just donned his overcoat and fedora, put on his shoes, and walked out the door. She immediately went to the living room window to see which direction he was heading. She thought about extinguishing the candles downstairs, left on for his return, but that would take too long; instead, she swiftly put on a sweater, a heavy coat, and wrapped herself in a cape with a hood. She had prepared well.

She slipped into outside shoes and opened the front door to a cold night, plagued by wind and darkness. Lucky for her it was not raining, and the moon was burning brightly.

Once outside, she pulled the cape tightly around her. She thought it was a good idea to wear a Western-styled dress that day instead of a *kimono* for easier movement. She was correct as she swept along the street.

Kiyoshi had walked the short distance to Powell Street knifing through the darkness with streetlights trailing his path and turned towards the community park. But Chisato laughed to herself: he wasn't going to see a baseball game. And in fact, he wasn't going to Powell Ground at all. He stopped short in front of an awfully familiar building.

Chisato recognized it as the entranceway to Morii's club. The watchman greeted her husband and scurried up the stairs as Kiyoshi waited in the street. He pulled out a cigarette and lit it. Chisato had no idea he smoked. The light exposed his face, a face of impatience, of anticipation. A few moments later, two men came out of the vestibule to make him feel welcomed. They bowed and apologized. She couldn't see their faces, but she knew one was the watchman.

When she heard the other man's voice, she recognized it immediately, it was Otagaki-*san*.

What's going on here? she asked herself.

With rather loud salutations, the two absconded up the stairs, leaving the watchman behind to sit on his chair and…well, watch.

There was nothing more to do, she couldn't follow her husband into the establishment. She decided to go home and return at the approximate time she thought he would be on the way home.

✿ ✿ ✿

While sitting in the dark front room surrounded by the still burning candles, she mulled over the situation. She was still in her cape. The light flickered gently, softening her mood. She was not so much angry as she was confused.

Why was Kiyoshi so angry with Otagaki if he knew him in a friendly manner? And Morii's establishment, the one Michiko warned against, what was Kiyoshi doing in there? Michiko said it was a drinking place. That explained the alcohol smell, but she couldn't imagine what else he did inside. She dismissed any further speculation. He was a devout Christian man, a leader in the church. It made no sense. She casually looked to *The Jesus* in the other room. Its mournful face looked upwards as the candlelight bathed his body in waves of light and dark shadows. The effect was mesmerizing, the splotches of light mottled the figure with what looked like splattered black raindrops.

Will I suffer as much as you have suffered?

After a while gazing at the figure, the light shimmied and fractured to distort *The Jesus* horribly. He wavered in the fire of night. A fright crackled through her.

At 11:30 p.m., Chisato woke with a start. The comfortable chair she was in had lulled her to a half-sleep. Most of the larger candles were still burning, even brighter to her mind. She suddenly remembered her purpose, she rose to her feet and gathered herself to leave. Her husband had not returned so her plan was clear. She hoped she was not too late and run into him in the street. She searched her mind for an excuse.

Once more in front of Morii's place, she gazed at the entranceway from across the street. The old guard was still there, his head nodding with sleep from time to time. No sign of Kiyoshi. She huddled in a cold corner of the vestibule of Soga's Department Store. There was no warmth to be had except in her coat and cape. She shivered but she maintained an eye on the place of her husband's sins.

About a half hour later, she heard a commotion. She spied Kiyoshi at the foot of the stairs with two others. She strained her eyes to see as a dull light switched on. It was two women in thin *yukata*. She could smell their cheap perfume in the air. They complained of the chilly weather and Kiyoshi pulled them both close to him in a laughing and drunk manner. He then kissed each in turn on the lips as he bid them a good night.

Acid pooled in Chisato's stomach. She took a step into the open and she lost her dinner. A foul smell masked her face. She cleaned her chin and cheeks with a handy handkerchief. Her head spun as she considered what to do as her husband staggered and stumbled in the distance. He was obviously going home.

It took some time to recover, but as soon as she had, she too walked towards home. Perhaps a little unsteady on her feet, but she had decided what to do—nothing. She just hoped his shenanigans were kept quiet and not get out on the *Nikkei* community grapevine.

As she quickened her pace homeward, she began to ponder the situation. *What kind of man was this Morii, who encourages married men to be with other women? And who are these women who throw themselves at men, married or not?* She imagined Morii-san to be a small, deformed man with hideous features: drooling mouth, close-set eyes, warped backbone, and withered hands ready to grasp at anything. He was like an *oni* in her father's domain.

When the house came into view, she could see that the candles were still lit, but she assumed Kiyoshi had gone to his bed in the spare room. That saved a face-to-face argument. She would hurry through the front hall and up the stairs to her bedroom. No one would ever know she had gone out.

But as soon as she stepped into the house and removed her shoes, she heard a strange sound. Crying. She moved to the dining room entrance where she saw a strange sight.

Kiyoshi was on his knees and with his hands interlocked in prayer before *The Jesus*, blubbering about something. She came closer without being noticed.

"Forgive...me, oh Lord. Please...I am a weak...weak man. Save me, oh Lord! Save me!"

All the time he was weeping out his words, *The Jesus* remained mute in His suffering. Flickering waves flowed over His body.

"Kiyoshi!" Chisato shouted. "What are you doing?"

"Leave me alone, woman! Go back to bed," he commanded not turning to look at her.

"Are you asking forgiveness? I followed you. I saw you. You should be asking forgiveness of me!"

That made him come to his feet, turning to confront her. His red eyes grew wide when seeing her. She could see his face wet with tears.

"You did follow me! The cape...how dare you!" he said with a voice full of anger and bile.

"Yes, and now I know what kind of man you are. How dare *you!*" she said in a voice rising in volume. Tears filmed her face, her nostrils filled with mucus.

Kiyoshi immediately grabbed a nearby vase and hurled it at her.

Chisato screamed but ducked in time. It crashed against the wall and fell to pieces on the front-room floor.

He then picked up a large, thick candle to threaten her. He quickly dropped it as the wax burned his hand.

Chisato laughed at him.

Enraged, he began kicking at all the candles in the room. They flew everywhere.

Chisato screamed, stepping back in fear, and headed for the front door. Outside, she realized she had no shoes, but luckily there was a pair of *zori* straw sandals on the veranda. She put them on and rushed down to the street in front. The screaming, crashing, and smashing continued inside the house. Neighbours came out to see the cause of the commotion.

She turned to look and just stared in anguish unable to say or do anything.

Flames throbbed and licked at the front window, the curtains ablaze. A shadow figure soon pressed against the front window. Its arms extended with the palms of his hands flattened against the surface. Its mouth opened and screamed silently. A radiance emanated around the silhouette, pulsating and glowing, seemingly kindling its body. Kiyoshi stood in agony.

The inferno inside grew in intensity as someone called for the Fire Department. Soon the brigade appeared but it was too late. The fire consumed the entire house.

HIDEKI

Kokumin Seishin
National Spiritual Mobilization Movement
October 1937–November 1938

16. LATE SUMMER 1938

AKAMATSU HIDEKI WAS A SICKLY child. Doctors suspected everything from diphtheria to cholera to consumption. But no one knew for sure; the doctors in town weren't particularly good. Then again, the doctor his father brought from Tokyo couldn't find an answer either.

Hideki survived though he became a thin and weak teenager. It didn't help that he was close to six-feet tall; made him look scrawny. His head seemed too big for his body and consequently he always stood with a stoop. His family worried of course. But no one would notice whenever he was with his sisters.

"It's mine!" shouted the obstinate Chisato.

"No, Otousan brought it back from Tokyo for me!" Chiemi responded.

"You don't want her. I found it in my room!"

"I must've left it there by mistake!"

"Hey you two!" Hideki interrupted. "Stop this noise. Don't you two know Otousan is napping?"

The sisters immediately stopped and looked sheepishly at their older brother.

"What are you two arguing about anyway?" he asked.

"Chi-chan stole my doll."

"I did not!" Chisato reacted.

"You did too!"

"Stop shouting!" Hideki commanded. "I told you, Otousan is sleeping."

Again, the two sisters muted their voices and hung their heads.

Hideki noticed for the first time Chisato clutching an *oningyo*, a thin fabric doll dressed in a red *kimono*. "Chiemi-chan, you're Oneesan. And you have dozens of dolls. Can't you be a little generous and let her have this one?"

"But Hanami is my favourite!" she explained.

"Favourite? You only got it a couple of weeks ago," Hideki said.

"She doesn't want it," Chisato insisted. "I only wanted to give it some love. I'll take better care of it than her."

Chiemi started to pout and remained silent. Hideki glanced at her and burst out laughing, which was choked off by his heavy cough. He bent over in convulsions.

She immediately started to cry, softly but emotionally. "I'm sorry...I'm...sorry," she stammered.

Hideki was alarmed, and he regained control. He instead apologized to his sister, bowed, and scurried away, hacking as he went.

Chiemi stopped crying and, seeing what had happened, addressed her younger sister, "Keep that old doll. I don't want it anymore."

❀ ❀ ❀

When Hideki entered high school, he discovered baseball, owing to his worship of the pitching wizard Sawamura Eiji. He was inspired and worked hard to become a passable ball player for his school team. He knew he could never be as good as Sawamura-*sensei*. But the sport was something he could commit himself to master. He loved the camaraderie, the quest for the championship. More importantly, he built his body up until he was physically healthy. His stoop disappeared, almost, and he stopped coughing.

Shortly after graduation, in the fall of 1938, he made a startling announcement to the family. Hideki walked into the house looking dapper but very unusually dressed.

"Who are you supposed to be?" Chiemi asked.

"You can't tell?" Hideki responded. He came to attention in front of his sister. The crisp, mostly brown uniform of jacket over white shirt, pants, cloth cap and boots was a bit baggy on him, given his height and slight build. "I've joined the army."

"You've what?" Chiemi's mouth fell open. "You can't do that."

"I can and I have. I am now part of the Emperor's army," he said proudly.

"Were you conscripted?" she asked with a skeptical eye.

"No, I just joined…voluntarily."

"Baka!" she cursed. "All you had to do was wait."

"Didn't want to. No matter when I was conscripted, I'd have to wait until the next January for induction. I won't take that chance. You see, since I've signed on now, I only have a few months to wait."

"Otousan won't allow it."

"Nothing he can do about it. I'm of age," he said, smirking.

"He won't allow it," she said. "Have you told him? And Okaasan?"

"That's why I'm here. Everyone is home, right?"

Chiemi nodded as he took off his boots and walked farther into the house.

* * *

What had made Hideki so patriotic? In hindsight, his family knew he was always looking for something to believe in, something to grab hold of, something to be part of. Less than a year ago, he read in the *Shuho*, a weekly government publication, that there was to be a rally at the Fudoin Temple, located a fair distance from the main part of the city, on November 3rd, the Meiji Emperor's birthday.

The grounds were filled with participants from all around the area. The children and mothers waved the *Hinomaru*, the Japanese flag with full rays spanning out from the central red orb, as speakers blared scratchy patriotic music. The flags fluttered in the unusually warm breeze. The men watched with rapt attention as officials prepared to address the crowd. Hideki's eyes were shining.

The place was normally peaceful. A rusty fence surrounded the property with woven *zori* sandals hanging from the entrance portion to indicate that the temple was a pilgrimage site. Just inside the gate was a statue of a wanderer welcoming all who came.

The *kata-kata-kata* sound of long strands of oversized prayer beads when pulled added to the serenity of the place. The abundant Japanese maple trees had turned to autumn colours, reminding Hideki that he had recently refused a trip to Arashiyama outside of Kyoto with his family to enjoy the autumn glory along the river.

The temple itself was a very ornate two-tiered structure, with two roofs with sharp, up-sweeping corners that pointed to the heavens. The huge main hall featured long and thick wooden beams and contained an almost-as-large *Yakushi* Buddha surrounded by paintings of twelve heavenly maidens—representing the twelve vows of the *Yakushi* Buddha, the *Healing Buddha*. A red-lacquered pagoda stood adjacent to one side. He knew of the cobbled path with a series of red gates leading the way and the shrine, painted a reddish orange to indicate a syncretic relationship between Buddhism and Shinto, in back and out-of-sight. But Hideki was not there to worship.

He listened to the speakers intently. They spoke of the programs: *The Boosting Production Service to the Nation* and the *Student Volunteers Corps Service to the Nation*. They encouraged the young to do what they could to aid in the war effort in China. The glory of the Emperor relied on what they did.

By the end of the presentations, Hideki was in tears, his chest and heart swollen with pride. He of course knew of the invasion of China back in July of 1937 and was excited by it. He fantasized the soldiers ripping through the enemy lines easily to win decisive battles. His older schoolmate, Honjo Tadanobu, had enlisted immediately to join the fight. Hideki was jealous that Tadanobu would find glory before him.

In his house's main hall with a gleaming floor made from maple trees, he encountered his father and mother. Chiemi soon joined them. Chisato, visiting home on a rare visit from Kure, wandered out of her bedroom and saw the gathering.

"Hideki-gun, what is going on?" Gunhei asked, pointing to the uniform.

Haruye, Hideki's mother, frowned. "Stop play-acting and take it off. Chiemi, get his yukata."

"No Okaa," he commanded. "I'm not play-acting. I have every right to wear this uniform."

"He's a soldier boy now," Chiemi chided.

Hideki frowned at her but did not act.

"Stop joking," Gunhei said, scolding his oldest daughter.

"She's right, Otousan, I've joined the army."

"But—," Haruye said, with gapping mouth and angry eyes mid-sentence.

"Because my Emperor needs me. You know what's happening in China. We have a duty to defend our country's honour after the Battle of Wanping."

"That's just propaganda," Chiemi replied.

"Damare!" Hideki shouted with a ferocity the family had not seen before.

"Hideki," Gunhei said calmly, "you can't be serious. Haven't you read that Shimura wasn't in any danger from the Chinese? He was lost but returned to his unit—"

"What of it?" Hideki interrupted with conviction.

"His absence was the reason Japanese forces surrounded Wanping. There is no good reason to escalate now."

"No, the Emperor's honour and therefore the country's honour have been defiled by these heathen Chinese!" Hideki insisted.

"Heathen?" Haruye scoffed and then demanded, "What business is it of yours?"

"Okaa, calm yourself," Gunhei said and paused a good long time before speaking again. "Okay...you understand what this means? The family needs you. I need you. You're the only son. Who will take over this house when I'm gone?"

Hideki lowered his gaze. "Otousan, we must sacrifice for the good of the country and the Emperor..."

"But what if you get killed in the war?" Haruye said nervously.

"Then I will find glory in my death," he answered.

She gave a little cry as Gunhei spoke, "Stop upsetting your mother! You do what you think is right."

"But Otousan—" Haruye started to say.

"The boy is of age and his own man."

"But..."

"Settle," he said as he placed a gentle hand on his wife's shoulder. "You know why he must do this, and you know it was expected."

She bent her head down, her eyes squeezed shut, nodded, and wiped away tears. "I suppose it was."

Both sisters looked confused.

"This is his fate," Gunhei declared. "We knew it the moment the boy was born."

Haruye nodded; Hideki, Chisato, and Chiemi remained in the dark.

✿ ✿ ✿

Akamatsu Hideki stood peering into the darkening paths throughout the garden while waiting. The truth was he wasn't officially in the army yet. As it happened, entrance didn't happen until Induction Day, January 10th, the anniversary of the Conscription Act becoming law. He knew that but argued with the recruitment officer vehemently to take him immediately. At least have him on record.

The officer instead said he could attend a "pre-military training camp" to get a "taste" of army life. It took place on the grounds of his local high school. That Hideki did, coming home to the compound every night until Induction Day. Near the end of his initial training, he asked Chiemi to meet after everyone else was in bed.

The lush, indistinct vegetation and trees of sturdy bamboo surrounded him, almost swallowing him. The night was settling, gently hugging the foliage. His uniform was chafing against his neck. Fortunately, the air was cool, and the full moon threw a cold light; still he scratched and fanned his face with his free hand. His other held a cloth bag.

Chiemi appeared out of nowhere, seemingly. She wore a light-coloured but thick *yukata*. The autumn cool wasn't going to bother her, he concluded.

"Why are you still in your outfit?" she asked in a kind of hostile way.

"I am a soldier of His Majesty's army—"

"Yes, yes, yes, enough," she said waving away his patriotism. "So, I'm here, as you asked...wait, what's that on your face?"

"What?" he said as he turned out of the moonlight and covered the left side of his face with a hand.

"That black mark," she said as she brushed away his hand. "Is it a bruise?"

"Nothing...it's nothing. Must be a shadow."

"What happened?" Chiemi pulled Hideki into the light and examined the black mark. "It *is* a bruise. There's more around your neck. How did you get those?" she demanded.

"My sergeant punished me, okay?"

"Punished you? What for?"

"I deserved it."

"Why?"

"I'm too tall. Tried to stoop...never mind, it's not important," he said in a near emotional state. "Listen, I have something important to ask you."

"Yes, yes. Don't tell me about your bruises then!"

"Promise you won't tell anyone, especially our parents."

"About the beating?"

"No, no, no, about what I'm about to tell you."

"Oh sure, sure."

"Do you promise?"

"Yes! Now tell me what you want," she said as she waved her hand in and out of the shadows. "It's getting cold out here!"

"I want you to hold on to this for me." He revealed the sack he was holding and made her take it.

"It's heavy. What is it?" She opened it and raised it to the moonlight. She reached in and pulled out a handful of coins. "It's money..."

"There're bills in there too. Hold on to it for me."

"Where'd you get this much?" she asked with an astonished face.

"Earned it and saved it over the years," he revealed. "I want you to keep it safe for me until I come back...and if I don't..."

"What do you mean?"

"If I don't come back, keep it for the family. Spend it on my funeral. Whatever."

"I will not!" she exclaimed as she tried to give the bag back. "There's...there's a curse on it already when you put it like that!"

"Chiemi-chan," Hideki said exasperated.

"No, you just keep the money for yourself. Spend it in China!"

Eventually, he convinced her to hold the money for safekeeping, but not unless he did something for her.

She glared at him. "Oh, why do you want to go in the first place?"

Hideki did not answer her. Instead, he remembered a similar question asked long ago.

"Why do you want to do that?" a very young Chiemi asked crossly.

Hideki, just a boy, crouched over the ground with a magnifying glass. Smoke curled into the air. Beneath him, ants writhed and crumpled under the focussed heat of the sun.

"I'm killing the enemies of the Emperor."

"Enemies? They're just ants."

"They're Chinese soldiers. Ant soldiers."

"Silly," she declared and promptly stepped on the remaining insects.

"Hey!"
Chiemi ran away with Hideki giving chase.

Chiemi produced her own cloth bag for him. "Take this. Take it and I'll accept your money."

"What's this?" he asked. "Don't give me any money."

"No, this is a soil bag."

He held it in his hands. "This is nonsense. Old superstitions."

"It's from this garden. You must take it as a reminder of home. As a connection to us."

"I'm a soldier in His Majesty's military! There's no room for sentimentality." He tried to give it back to his sister, but she resisted.

"Take it or I won't take your money."

He reluctantly gave in with the threat. Chiemi held his bag and said she would bury it until he came back. Uneasy at the thought of it, she claimed that he'd have to return because she won't tell him where. He agreed if she took care of it.

As he was about to leave, Chiemi called out, "Hideki!"

"What?" He turned to face her again.

"Take this as well." She held out a long piece of white cloth.

"Now, what's this?"

"A senninbari. Wear it around your belly. It'll keep you safe."

"More nonsense."

"There're one-thousand red stitches in it. It took me months to complete it."

"All right…all right, I'll take it just to keep you quiet."

✿ ✿ ✿

As they left the garden separately, Hideki noticed that the moonlight had shifted and caught the scowling face of the stone *samurai*. He dumped the bag's contents among the plants. The dirt fell in clumps. But he kept the belt of stitches.

Shosango Program for Victory
Seishin Kyoiku
Initiated during the Taisho era (1912–26)

17.   FALL 1938–WINTER 1939

AKAMATSU HIDEKI MAY HAVE HAD some doubts about his decision to join the military when he participated in the "pre-military camp". The army watched over the *Shosango Program for Victory*, which taught (as stated) students to defend the home islands to the last man. Both boys and girls joined initially in the physical education exercises held at a local high school.

Hideki was older than the others, so he could easily match and outdo their enthusiasm, stamina, and physical skills. Everyone knew of his determination, and he glowed seeing their eyes on him. He stood at attention in his army-issued uniform with his eyes glistening as brightly as his tunic's brass buttons in the sunlight.

The daily exercises consisted of marches, spearing maneuvers with wooden poles, and general stretching exercises. Sergeant Hayashi of the Imperial Army presided with a keen eye and a short wooden baton. Any lag in spirit was met with a stern rebuke; any weakness was commented on loudly; any incompetence was punished, severely in some cases—most times with corporal punishment.

Hideki was clumsy at first, despite his baseball prowess. He found the dexterity exercises particularly frustrating. One was the horizontal ladder climb. The sergeant placed a ladder on the ground before the students. Each then had to stand at one end and run forward, while twisting the upper body left and right alternatively and touching every space with the feet. The faster the better. Each effort was timed.

Hideki was not the most agile and so often tripped and fell to the ground. Sgt. Hayashi scolded him to no end, calling him *mushi* loudly to his face. *Bug!* It got worse when heavy backpacks and wooden rifles were required. Try as he might, Hideki just couldn't negotiate the course.

Hayashi showed no mercy and started to beat Hideki with his baton about the head and shoulders. Eventually, the young would-be recruit fell to his knees begging forgiveness in tears before the sergeant. Hayashi just snarled and nicknamed him *Nakimushi* (Crying Insect).

"Stand up!" the sergeant growled in the next moment. "Stand up straight!"

Hideki slouched out of habit.

"So you think you're so smart being tall, do you?" the sergeant shouted, and then struck Hideki's back so hard the young recruit fell to his knees again.

"Get up, you mushi!"

And so it went on.

✿ ✿ ✿

Induction Day in early January. The skies were grey and the temperatures cool, but the military building was buzzing with activity. Recruits stood in single file in front of a wooden desk where a sombre corporal wrote down each name before sending them on to the next station. The lineup was nearly out the door.

Hideki and his father came early that morning. No women allowed. The young man was eager to get on to the next phase of his life. He attended in a freshly cleaned and pressed uniform, polished boots, and smart cap.

He loved the snapping flags outside. The *Hinomaru*, the Japanese flag, a glorious symbol of the Emperor, made him proud the way it fluttered in the rising wind. Coloured streamers also decorated the building in celebration of the glorious youth about to commit themselves to the Emperor.

His father couldn't accompany him beyond the foyer, but he did have a final moment with him.

"Hideki-gun, last chance. You don't have to do this."

"Otousan," Hideki chided. "This is my time."

Gunhei smiled at him and appeared on the verge of tears, but none came. "I will be honest with you. I'm afraid for you, but I know you will make us proud, son. I know. Do your duty. Come back to us." He bowed as did his son.

Hideki snapped his heels, turned, and approached the wooden desk.

❀ ❀ ❀

The grandest day of Hideki's life was the formal celebration of Induction Day in late January 1939. The ceremony was at army headquarters in Hiroshima. Chiemi and parents attended, wearing their finest *kimono*, *Otousan* in his comical fedora and black *kimono*. With flags waving, banners flying and a full brass band, the Emperor's representative, Furusho Mikio, *Member of the Supreme War Council*, addressed the gathering.

"You will bring honour to Japan with your spirit and dedication..." he grandly pronounced, his full mustache slightly fluttering in the wind.

With a grin, Gunhei said that the impressive commander grew the preposterous long mustache to compensate for his bald head. Of course, the Emperor's representative had said nothing, keeping his reason for his affectation locked away forever.

❀ ❀ ❀

After that day, Hideki relished a long and rigorous training period. He was housed in the military centre with dormitories including showers, laundry, and lunchroom just outside Hiroshima, well-hidden from view, fenced-in with guards patrolling the surrounding area to ensure privacy and security.

The young recruit was surprised and perhaps a little shaken to see that Sgt. Hayashi, the same trainer at the high school, oversaw the new recruits. Hayashi was a hard man with a chiselled look to his face and a muscular body. His torso was particularly well-shaped, thick with developed muscles. He was loud with an order and quick with the baton if someone disobeyed. When he saw Hideki, he sneered at him.

"Still arrogant about your height!" he said and threatened a whipping.

Hideki cowered, causing Hayashi to bellow with laughter.

To say the young recruit was afraid of the man was an understatement, but he understood and accepted everything. The Japanese soldier was known for being fearless, ruthless, and merciless. Hideki had only three months to meet these expectations.

Indoctrination began right away. Every morning the troops stood in formation and recited the *Gunjin Chokuyu* or the *Imperial Rescript to Soldiers and Sailors*, a set of ethical rules written during the Meiji era to inspire the military. A ten-minute meditation on the message followed.

Each was expected to memorize it. Mistakes would not be tolerated, Sgt. Hayashi made sure of that. Hideki was struck several times for flubbing a word or two, especially when a solo recitation was ordered before supper.

For Hideki's part, he was not used to speaking under pressure, no matter how many were doing the same thing. By the end of the first week, he was so discouraged and sore, he wanted to quit, but knew he couldn't or wouldn't. An untenable situation. He was sure his family would be mocked if he left in disgrace and that could not happen.

Though Sgt. Hayashi started calling him *Nakimushi* again, Hideki got the point. Live frugally and devote yourself to the Emperor. And don't cry, don't whine, don't complain.

"Nakimushi!" the sergeant bellowed. "Where did you go to school?"

The question was odd, but he began to answer. The sergeant promptly cut him off. "Never mind, the past is nothing. You are nothing. There is only the Emperor. Remember that."

Turning to the assembled he continued, "You are all Ant Soldiers. Nothing but ants."

Hideki in his surprise unadvisedly spoke up, "But Sergeant, I thought the Chinese were the Ant Soldiers."

His perceived insolence was met with a vicious baton strike to the side of the head. Hideki fell to the ground.

"Ant Soldier!" growled Hayashi. "You are nothing but an insect, a little crying insect. Your life means as much as an ant's. Only the Emperor matters. You understand?"

Hideki nodded as he wept.

✾ ✾ ✾

Hideki's only solace was Takeuchi Shigeru, an old school-chum who had enlisted the same day he had. He called him Take-*san* for short. No matter how downtrodden either felt, for Shigeru was punished as much as Hideki, one would tell the other: "Faith equals strength".

Hideki often made note of his friend's baby-soft features; tears rimming his eyes; rosy, plump cheeks; and flawless skin. Though he was picked on by the sergeant precisely for his "girlish body", Shigeru experienced a gradual hardening of his body and spirit. His unshaven face, an uneven shadow forming under his chin. He looked considerably older. Hideki wondered if the same were happening to him.

Soon after the first week, Sgt. Hayashi stood before the troops and announced, "From today, you will be given rifles. Uppermost in your mind, you must remember that it is the personal property of the Emperor and any neglect of it will not be tolerated. The most precious part of the weapon is the bayonet. Once you affix the blade to the rifle, you are putting iron into your very souls. It is your samurai sword."

"Samurai?" asked some short, stocky, and naïve recruit.

The sergeant rushed to confront the idiot. "Tanaka, you think this is funny? There is no greater honour than to be a samurai, you understand. I doubt that you'll ever be one."

Tanaka Yusuke was a prep-school recruit wanting to prove his manhood to his father, so the story went. But his weight and awkward, rotund body worked against it. He was constantly victimized by just about everyone.

"No...no...I mean, yes..." he answered trailing off, half-expecting, Hideki thought, to be punished. And he was, the sergeant beat him, leaning into the blow with his shoulder and arm muscles. Shigeru fell to the ground shuddering and covering himself in a useless effort to protect himself.

Hideki then thought of his older high-school compatriot who recently died in battle, according to the newspapers.

Honjo Tadanobu charged the machinegun nest with a frightening determination. He raised his sword and shouted his kiai, his battle cry; he was ready to strike and draw blood. A glorious death as his body was torn to pieces. The glory of Bushido. The samurai spirit. For the Emperor!

Both Hideki and Shigeru took to heart that any neglect or misuse of the weapon was a corruption of the soul. Once at evening inspection, the idea was clearly demonstrated. All the recruits were lined up in front of their bunks as the sergeant walked down the line. Hideki was particularly nervous since he never knew if his weapon, uniform, or bunk would pass muster. He need not have worried...this time.

Shigeru was not so lucky. The private stood by his bunk next to Hideki's as the sergeant grabbed the rifle and inspected it closely.

"Takeuchi," Hayashi growled.

"Hai!"

"Your rifle is dirty! The oil is fouled with dirt."

"No, it isn't," he said disingenuously.

The sergeant suddenly and swiftly struck the hapless soldier across the face.

Shigeru fell heavily to the floor.

"Such insolence! When I say it's dirty, it's dirty."

Shigeru looked up in fear and cowered causing Hayashi to kick him viciously in the ribcage. Shigeru screamed in pain.

"You have fouled your soul! Do you understand? Do you?"

"Yes…Sergeant," he said with difficulty.

"Clean it and bring it to me for further inspection."

Sgt. Hayashi snapped to, turned, and walked away. Hideki thought he saw a smile on his face.

✿ ✿ ✿

The training continued with bayonet fighting. The ideal was a one-on-one battle. The superior Japanese soldier could never be defeated in a close fight. Hideki thought it strange that no target shooting was ever done.

Long marches were the second phase of the training. Without full packs at first but marching loaded down with equipment soon became a reality. They often started at the camp and ended some 50+ km away at the *Gokoku Shrine*, emblematic of Meiji architecture on expansive grounds. It was built for the dead of the 19th-Century *Boshin War*. The recruits soon talked among themselves and held the hope that their names would be added to the lists of dead *samurai* and soldiers in Tokyo's *Yasukuni Shrine* with its magnificent architecture of tall, peaked roof with criss-crossed masts towering above the building.

They came back to the camp after a few days exhausted, sweaty, and dirty.

✿ ✿ ✿

The final phase started when each recruit received dark glasses. During early evening, twice a week, when the sun was just above the horizon, Hideki and Shigeru, like everyone else, crawled outside and beyond the barracks area, their glasses rigidly attached. They soon discarded them as they performed man-euvers during the darkest nights, with or without the moon to light their way, in the roughest terrain. A few injured themselves while practicing stealth movements and had to be taken to the hospital with a broken bone or two. The obese Tanaka was one.

"That baka, too fat to crawl in the dark. There's not enough shadow to contain him!" the men joked.

When the hapless Tanaka returned, no one talked to him. Perhaps he heard the stifled laughter behind his back. Hideki observed from afar and began to question himself.

Kokumin Choyo Rei
National Service Draft Ordinance
March 1938

18.   SPRING 1939

THOUGH INTROSPECTIVE, HIDEKI DID NOT think of his
family and home during his training save one time—when his
sister Chisato was about to leave Japan. He resolved to write her
in the morning, more in an effort to strengthen his resolve than
out of any concern for her.

"What a stupid, stupid little girl," he growled in bed the night
before the wedding. The Japanese government had recently proclaimed that all citizens must fight to the last. No one was to
surrender, no one was to run away. Better to die by suicide if
necessary. *Glory to the Emperor; glory to Japan in the coming fight.*

Hideki got out of bed, the darkness holding him in place
before he could see the moonlight flowing in through a window.
He gingerly felt his way towards the light. With arms and hands
on the sill, he strained to see outside. His eyes soon adjusted to
the night, and he saw the exercise fields and other barracks. The
moon was high, bright as a shining disk.

He imagined the glow of the Emperor radiating His lustre
over all of Japan and beyond. His protective influence covered
all of Asia. And Hideki resolved, once again, to see to it that the
sphere of influence remained with Japan like a glorious beacon
for the world to see.

*Chikuso! Damn it! Live with the gaijin, be a keto, that's your
choice. A Canadian,* he snarled under his breath. In the end, he
sent no acknowledgement let alone a note of well-wishes to his
sister. He did harbour a fantasy about skewering the husband
with his bayonet in battle, the blood spewing out of the body
and splattering the ground.

On a fine early May morning, the soldiers rose as usual from their beds and made ready to assemble on the parade grounds. There was only a hint of summer humidity in the barracks.

"Hey, Take-san, wake up," Hideki shouted at his friend. "Didn't you hear reveille?"

"Huh…uh…no…I…," he muttered groggily. "Didn't sleep well last night."

"Well, get a-moving. You don't want to be late for line-up outside. There'll be hell to pay if you're not there!"

The sun was intense, eyes squinted in its glare. The cool wind reminded everyone of spring with new growth and the *sakura* blossoms of Arashiyama. Hideki ran out while Takeuchi Shigeru, half-dressed, stumbled along the way.

They soon joined the rest of the troops to fall smartly into the line awaiting the rituals of the day. No one was sharply dressed; the jackets and pants were spotted with mud from last night's maneuvers and generally disheveled; the boots scuffed, shirts sweat-stained, the uniform creased, crusted, and wrinkled. Some sported a day or two growth of beard.

It was about two weeks before the end of training. Accordingly, each man had marked each day either physically or mentally. The end was soon, and they would be in the war at last.

The Lieutenant stood rigidly in front of the assembly. He turned to Sgt. Hayashi and softly ordered him to begin.

"Before we all recite the Gunjin Chokuyu to honour the Emperor," the sergeant barked, "let's hear from a recruit.

"Takeuchi, step forward!"

Shigeru suddenly paid attention surprised to hear his name being singled out. His face heated red; sweat beads began to appear from under the peak of his cap as he awkwardly stepped forward.

"Stand here," Hayashi commanded as he pointed to the middle in front of the troops.

Shigeru moved into position.

"Begin the recitation!"

Everyone could see that his mind raced to remember the words. He began slowly without much confidence.

"Huh...the soldier and sailor should consider...loyalty their duty...essential duty. A soldier or a sailor in whom this spirit is not strong is a mere puppet—

"Stop right there!" Hayashi barked. "You have forgotten the second lines and dropped some words from the next!"

Shigeru hung his head in shame.

"How long have you been here, Takeuchi?"

"About three months," he muttered.

"How long?" the sergeant shouted.

"Three months, Sergeant!" he snapped.

"Three months and every morning I hear you flub our most sacred code of ethics. You have nothing in your head. It is like a sieve. It cannot hold anything. You are a disgrace. I don't know why you wear that uniform. You are such an ass. A bakatare. A nakimushi.

"Get back in line, Insect. Everyone else recite the Imperial Rescript! I will be listening."

Some of the soldiers managed to snicker, but Hideki lowered his head and closed his eyes. When next he looked, he saw tears run down Shigeru's cheeks as everyone began to go through the *Gunjin Chokuyu* oath.

That evening, Shigeru was inconsolable. He managed to hold back the tears during dinner, but Hideki could see all the soldiers turn away from the two. When it was "Lights Out", Shigeru wept softly into his pillow. Hideki could do nothing except say, "Faith equals strength."—the old saying they had said to one another for encouragement back in the school training days. Those days seemed like a thousand years ago.

✳ ✳ ✳

Takeuchi Shigeru performed his duties perfunctorily and always in a gloomy mood, his face sullen and brooding. He lacked energy and struggled to keep up during the daily exercises. Because of his lethargy, he often stumbled over a task, or he misspoke. And every time his behaviour drew the ire of Sgt. Hayashi.

"Takeuchi, you little insect, get moving. Maybe you need a little encouragement." He then baton-whipped Shigeru until he laid on the ground as a quivering and bloody lump. Sgt. Hayashi grimaced with no sympathy.

Hideki was always there to help his friend stand up and escort him away from the glare of the sergeant and others. Despite the torment and scrutiny, Take-*san* did memorize the *Imperial Rescript*, reciting it in a bumbling manner but he did get through it; he always ended in tears, sometimes quietly, sometimes intensely.

Sgt. Hayashi in turn meted out inappropriate punishment until Shigeru grew apathetic to it all. Shigeru simply closed his eyes and took it before crumbling to the ground.

Hideki did not know what would happen to his friend, but he resolved to be at his side no matter what. Unfortunately, he could not have foreseen what soon followed.

✿ ✿ ✿

The day before the last day, Sgt. Hayashi informed the men that they would pass in review before dignitaries from army headquarters and the government. They were then to be allowed to return home to say goodbye to loved ones for two days.

Upon return, each battalion was assigned to a division to be sent to Manchukuo or China, the destination was not announced.

"You hear that Take-san?" Hideki said enthusiastically. "China! That's where the Emperor needs us. Glory is coming!"

Shigeru just grunted.

That night when the moon was in its half-phase, Hideki decided not to go home. He suspected his parents were apathetic. They didn't care what he did one way or the other. Only one sister remained, and he had already given her instructions about what to do in his absence. He did write a letter, even though the light was thin.

To the household,

I am about to embark on the glorious expedition of my life. I cannot tell you where, you understand, but rest assured, I am bound to do my duty to the Emperor no matter what happens to me.

I am sure my sisters are wasting their lives in not learning how to defend their homeland. In fact, Chisato-chan is now in enemy territory. Mark my words, there is a war coming with the forces of Europe and North America. You must be prepared to fight to the end, but do not be alarmed. I pledge that I and my fellow soldiers will fight to the death not to let harm come to Japan. We shall be victorious in the end for we are superior in every way to the foreign soldier.

I hope that we will all be reunited as a family one day when all is said and done.

Akamatsu Hideki

The last line seemed too sentimental for him, but let it stand since correcting it meant starting over again. It didn't matter anyway. They would have his photograph to venerate.

His sleep was shallow later that night. When he felt himself slowly descending into the murk of a dream, a rustling and noise startled him awake. He looked to his left and found that Shigeru had sat up on his cot.

He was in his undershirt and *dorosu*, (baggy underwear). The sheen of perspiration painted his face even in the dull light. He seemed to burn with humiliation. But his face was contorted with determination. It strained with the exertion.

Hideki said nothing as Shigeru tied a *hachimaki* around his head. Where he got it was unknown. The headband was blank and not with the usual red sun emblazoned. Hideki remained motionless as his friend stood and moved to his footlocker.

From inside it, he pulled out his bayonet. It glittered in the pale moonlight. He shuffled to the large room adjacent to the sleeping area.

Hideki got up after a while and followed his friend, with a feeling of apprehension in the pit of his stomach. As he walked into the dressing room, the sweet smell of incense clouded his nose. Yet he saw no smoke curling in the air. It was dark, so he ignored the fact. *The Buddha is near.*

A single light bulb blazed in the room. Shigeru sat on his knees in the pool of light. He placed the blade on a handkerchief on the floor before him. Closing his eyes, he started to recite the *Imperial Rescript.*

> *The soldier and sailor should consider loyalty their essential duty. Who that is born in this land can be wanting in the spirit of grateful service to it? No soldier or sailor, especially, can be considered efficient unless this spirit be strong within him. A soldier or a sailor in whom this spirit is not strong, however skilled in art or proficient in science, is a mere puppet; and a body of soldiers or sailors wanting in loyalty, however well ordered and disciplined it may be, is in an emergency no better than a rabble. Remember that, as the protection of the state and the maintenance of its power depend upon the strength of its arms, the growth or decline of this strength must affect the nation's destiny for good or for evil; therefore, neither be led astray by current opinions nor meddle in politics, but with single heart fulfill your essential duty of loyalty, and bear in mind that duty is weightier than a mountain, while death is lighter than a feather. Never by failing in moral principle fall into disgrace and bring dishonor upon your name.*

Hideki stood mesmerized and couldn't help but listen intently. Remarkably, Shigeru did not make a single mistake: no stumbling over a word, no dropping of a word or two, no forgetting of a passage or phrase for that matter. Take's eyes blazed with conviction and patriotism. His voice growled with purpose, concentrating on the result.

Hideki was impressed, but it did worry him when Shigeru reached down for the bayonet with one hand and lifting his undershirt with the other.

"Take-gun!" he yelled and rushed forward.

Shigeru was shaken by the interruption and pointed thes blade at his intruder.

"What're you doing?" Hideki said excitedly as he stopped in his tracks at the threat.

With feverish eyes, Shigeru glared at his friend with anger rising in the heat of the moment. "The sword is the soul of the Emperor! The heart of Japan!"

"It's a bayonet!" he yelled as the realization of what his friend was about to do entered his mind. "Not a sword!"

Others awoke and began to move to the locker room. A small crowd of men who had stayed behind gathered but remained silent.

"It is the steel of the samurai. Bushido!" *The samurai spirit.*

"Don't do it!" And Hideki moved forward to stop him.

But it was too late. Shigeru raised his bayonet and sliced into his neck and across his throat. A gush of blood came out and splattered upon the floor. He gasped for air with a sickening sound. His body toppled over as his eyes went blank.

Hideki screamed as he reached for his friend.

✿ ✿ ✿

He pressed his palms against his eyes in a useless attempt to stop the tears. His friend was dead. *Seppuku.* Where is the glory in that? All the blood, the soiled bayonet, the ugly gash in his throat. Hideki felt drained, like all his conviction flowed out of him and pooled around his body.

His superior officers ordered him to go home for a week before he was to ship out with his comrades. His visit did not go well.

He stood in front of his father sullen and unsteady.

"Is something wrong, Hideki-gun?"

The voice was soft, kind. It felt inviting, open, and sincere.

Hideki shuffled a bit, looked downcast, before speaking. "Otousan, my friend…he committed seppuku."

"Why?" Gunhei asked as he gazed at his son with surprised kindness.

"He dishonoured himself…with his inability to recite the *Rescript*. He never could recite it perfectly."

"Yes, difficult."

"But don't you see, Father, that such a thing doesn't matter? He was a good soldier, willing to do his duty. If it results in a meaningless death, what good is there in being a soldier in His Majesty's army?"

"What are you saying?"

"I…I…I want to get out."

"Nanja?" Gunhei slammed with anger. "Desert? You want to desert, because there's no way they'll let you go."

"Can't you do something? You have influence," he said in a pleading tone.

"Not that kind of influence."

"But…"

"Do you want to bring shame to this family? Think of what will happen to your mother, your sisters and especially me! We'll never be able to go anywhere, do anything. Or even show ourselves.

"Are you that selfish? You made the decision to join the army. I tried to convince you otherwise. But you went ahead…"

Hideki shook with sorrow. He could not stop the tears from streaming down his face.

Gunhei grabbed his son by the shoulders and angrily shouted, "Men do not cry!"

Hideki suddenly stopped and regained control of his emotions. He had no choice to report for camp and ready himself for transportation to China.

19.

THE OCEAN BREEZE RAN ACROSS the tops of white caps and current to gently nudge the troopship towards a distant invisible shore. Akamatsu Hideki stood on the deck hugging his rifle close to his body. He shook, but not from the unusually cold wind.

It was more than a few weeks later, but his mind was still on his friend. Mystifying. There was no rhyme or reason to what Shigeru had done. No inquiry was held; no questions asked of Sgt. Hayashi, any of the men, or even him. The incident was simply written up, filed away, and forgotten by the superior officers. Judgement was left to Shigeru's compatriots.

He was weak...incompetent...good that he committed seppuku...he did the right thing...he died honourably...bushido, the samurai spirit...he completed his duty to the Emperor...he died as a samurai.

Hideki kept to himself, talking to no one. He sought a dark corner to crouch by himself. The act was contrary to his Buddhist way of thinking. Then again, his being in the military was just as contrary. He was raised a Buddhist and was supposed to approach life with compassion, generosity, and understanding. He suddenly realized he couldn't reconcile his beliefs with worshipping the Emperor who was god, a profoundly Shinto belief.

Hideki spent days deep in contemplation. *What glory was there in Shigeru's suicide?* he considered constantly. It was just a dead body lying in puddles of blood.

Others milled about the deck, some with rifles, some without but with backpacks by their feet, all in uniform, if dishevelled. *No one is thinking about Shigeru,* Hideki thought. Only the future battles existed for them: glory, honour, and a fulfillment of duty to the Emperor and country.

A new mantra was gaining popularity among the troops. From time to time, random groups of men chanted it: *Kill All, Burn All, Loot All!* Followed by a loud and repeated *Banzai!* *The Three Alls* epitomized the bloodlust the men felt. They ached to fulfill their destiny.

❀ ❀ ❀

Hideki's eyes casually drifted and landed on a clump of soldiers who weren't chanting but smoking to pass the time, no doubt. Quite unexpectantly, Hideki thought about the smell of incense as he had entered the locker room. He had not seen any glowing in the darkness. Shigeru had not lit any. Curious. *Namu Amida Butsu,* he whispered to the wind. *I rely on the Buddha of Infinite Light and Life.* He wondered if he would get to the point of suicide. His hands shook slightly even if he gripped the wood of his rifle tighter.

20.   EARLY SUMMER 1940

SHANGHAI WAS TOUTED AS THE *Paris of the Orient*. The twisted glowing lights of night shone intensely along the endless streets, from the wide main roads to the narrow and countless backstreets. The shops with incomprehensible signs covered with Chinese ideograms beckoned customers to come inside. The colonial-era Cathay Hotel dripped with glamour and exclusivity. The Shanghai Club vibrated with the noise of swing music, the pop of champagne corks, and the honking and revving line of expensive automobiles with uniformed drivers in front. Men in tuxedos and women in shimmering gowns milled at the gilded entrances until they sashayed inside. Movie stars like Douglas Fairbanks and Mary Pickford, Charlie Chaplin, and Sesshu Hayakawa were always rumoured to be about. But that was the past.

Because there was so much talk about Shanghai among the soldiers, Hideki was excited about being there. When he landed some months before and after much training, it turned out to be a case of the pursuit over the apprehension. His body slumped in disappointment.

Some streets were crowded with the hustle of city life, but there was no glamour. Just men and women pushing or pulling carts, others walking their poverty-stricken children, and there were those in Western business attire looking to make money. Some wretched women carried their scrawny babies, with open mouths begging for food and tired eyes shaded with death, in a sling on their backs while calling out, "Buy my baby. Please, buy my baby. Who wants a baby?"

Hideki had no idea what they were saying or selling, so he ignored them. What fascinated him as he marched along were the old posters. They were torn and frayed, some half torn off walls, but he could make out the images. Advertising a product, a night club, or an event, he was taken with the garish colours, inviting and placid backgrounds, and the women, unreal but alluring as they posed with a come-hither look. All images were stylized but harkened back to a time of peace and possibility. To him, they were posters of imagination, of beauty, of fantasy. Posters of dreams fallen to graceful ruin. Shanghai itself was a city of faded glory with the Japanese Occupation.

Akamatsu Hideki was now part of the Japanese China Expeditionary Army under Field Marshall Hata Shunroku, assigned as he was along with most of his comrades to the Chinese section of town. The International Settlement with its mix of Chinese and European architecture was abandoned, ruined as it was ever since the Battle of Shanghai took place in November 1937.

Still, Hideki was mesmerized by the city. He couldn't read the signs, the *kanji*, the ideogram characters, were too confusing, but at least they looked familiar, and he could pick out the odd word. The roads of low-lying, wooden storefronts held many secrets. A very few women still strolled in tight *cheongsam* dresses with the intriguing slits up the legs exposing an expanse of thigh. They were a sight to behold for the young soldier. Each called to him as they passed by. He remembered going to a Shochiku theatre in the Shintenchi District in downtown Hiroshima not that long ago to see *Shanghai Express*, an early "talkie", for Japan at least. The film's atmosphere was mysterious and forbidding, and every character appeared to be evil. Though Marlene Dietrich was exotic and sexually stimulating, he loved Anna May Wong, the Chinese American actress in a *cheongsam*, which displayed an ample amount of thigh. She was the real star of the movie; her scintillating and smouldering looks stimulated him to no end. She was a poster come to life. He knew he could never marry anyone like that, but he sure wanted to meet someone like her. Maybe this was his chance. And then perhaps not.

Hideki had a keen interest in the Bund, a waterfront area in central Shanghai. The Zhongshan Road ran along side of it marking the outer border of the International Settlement. Just beyond was the Huang Pu River. He saw from a distance the grand architecture of the Sassoon House, the Hong Kong and Shanghai Bank Building, and the Broadway Mansions. He longed to go there to see and meet people from around the world. The Bund held that promise. Maybe he had some of that need for adventure his baby sister possessed.

His spirits uplifted, he conjured up the image of the Akamatsu Compound, his sisters, and his parents. His body ached. He would write home, he resolved, when time permitted.

His father's words weighed heavily upon him. He cannot disgrace the Akamatsu name. In the training camp before Shanghai, he once again embraced the military life and decided to dedicate his service to his family.

The International Settlement itself had been drained of foreigners, everyone fearing for their own lives. And for good reason too: ever since the Japanese Expedition had moved up the Yangtse River to Nanking, the force carried out a six-week campaign of fighting and slaughter, eventually conquering and occupying the city.

Despite Hideki's ambiguity about the military, he knew the anti-rebel action had to be done, since there was so much resistance to their presence. They were in the Chinese Sector primarily to ferret out the resistors and stop any armed uprising from taking place.

Soon word finally came down that a detail of men, including Hideki, was to go into the International Settlement to search for and "clean up" the dissidents. His patrol was one of many that went on a daily basis. Hideki grimaced at the "sanitation" job, but orders were orders. He thought he would be staging a police action: taking into custody all dissidents in the section of town and depositing them in a holding centre to be dealt with by the justice system.

Sgt. Hayashi surveyed the men with a scrutinizing eye: Akamatsu, Inokuchi, Honda, Saito, Tamaki, Tsuchiyama, Hirabayashi, Inefuku, Iguchi. The Sergeant did not know most of them; Honda, Hirabayashi, Inokuchi, and Akamatsu came with him to China. The rest, more than half, had been here since the Battle of Shanghai in 1937.

They were a ragtag group of soldiers. Not having bathed, shaved, or washed clothes in quite a while, they appeared well-worn, but fierce. Most were what Hideki considered to be fanatics, duty to the Emperor above all else. He could see it in their eyes, bloodshot yet intense. The Chinese were ant *mushi*. But it wasn't long before Sgt. Hayashi called him a *"mushi"* again. His life meant nothing. Shigeru was proof of that.

"We overwhelmed them," Saito stated, a man confident in his purpose. "We hit them with naval and air power. Then we attacked with tanks and mobile cannons."

China reinforces Shanghai defense.
32 Tokyo warships mass at Shanghai.

❊ ❊ ❊

Hideki remembered the headlines in the *Shuho* magazine and other newspapers at the time.

"But the Chinese resisted," interrupted Tsuchiyama, a soldier with a hint of sadness about him. "Even with small calibre weapons, they fought like dogs."

"And they died like dogs in the streets!" Saito added. *"Kill All!"*

Hideki did further question their presence.

Tsuchiyama quickly responded, "We have to protect our people in Little Tokyo. Do you want to see them slaughtered?"

Hideki's face must've given away his ignorance.

"In the Bund. You know."

Hideki nodded, not really knowing for sure.

Saito insisted, "We're here for revenge. Those small calibre weapons killed hundreds of our troops back in '37!" Saito grew emotional. *"Burn All! Loot All!"*

Such was the talk in the barracks.

A Chinese man soon joined the patrol. Wang Jingwei was a politician smartly dressed in a suit and tie. The tall man with a full face was considered a "quisling" by the military but a useful one. He was on his way to Nanking to rule Japanese-occupied China. This was his last act in Shanghai.

The men went into the mostly deserted International Settlement in the morning. Each man, except. Sgt. Hayashi who held a pistol and sword by his side, carried his rifle with bayonet affixed. Rubble from cannon-fire lay in piles inside and outside every hollowed-out building they passed.

Hideki was not expecting such devastation. *Were there bodies underneath?* he wondered. He thought he heard muffled cries for help but, since the sergeant ignored any sounds, he moved on and tried to ignore them. The Sergeant did stop every so often and gave the order to set fire to the wooden debris.

Eventually, Wang stopped in front of a mostly intact building of about four stories. There were cannon holes in the walls, but the structure stood. He turned to Sgt. Hayashi and whispered something to him.

"Yoshi," he said conclusively. "Inokuchi, Honda, go in there and report what you find."

The two snapped to and moved to inspect the premises with rifles at the ready, but before they could enter, a group of about ten men emerged. They were clothed in anything but uniforms: torn and ragged everyday shirts and pants. They held clubs and what appeared to be bags of stones. Their weary faces of despair were menacing as if ready to fight.

The detail raised their rifles in self-defence. Sgt. Hayashi raised his arm.

"Who is Chiang? Step forward, make yourself known," Wang ordered.

A particularly defiant man stepped in front of the others. His eyes were intense, angry. Not saying a word, he threatened with his crudely fashioned wooden club.

The Sergeant rushed forward and in one swift movement drew his sword and swung it at the man. The *Sukesada katana*, a sword specially made for him by Master Sukesada, caught the front of the man's neck and the head flew off behind in one stroke. Blood spurted like an open faucet for a short time. The body collapsed into a heap immediately.

Hideki stood shocked, horrified, and couldn't move even when he saw the other Chinese men turn to flee. Sgt. Hayashi wounded one with his pistol. The man fell to his knees in obvious pain. Most of the others froze in their tracks. At least two disappeared into the building.

"Akamatsu, the rest of you, secure those prisoners."

Suddenly another voice thundered. "Hayashi! What are you doing?"

It was Captain Fujimoto with another patrol of about ten men. His face was hard with anger.

"Sir," he said coming to attention. "I was ordered to find Chiang and his men. I'm just dealing with them now."

"Well, stop wasting bullets. You let two escape!"

"Sorry, sir. We'll find them."

"Never mind," he scoffed. "Sergeant. Tsujiuchi!"

"Hai!" A muscular sergeant rushed to present himself to the captain.

"Take these prisoners for the burial detail."

"Hai." He motioned for the men behind him to take charge of the prisoners. They herded them away.

Hideki turned to Inefuku, the soldier standing beside him, and whispered, "What's the burial detail?"

"Sergeant Hayashi, this sector still needs securing. Carry on," Capt. Fujimoto ordered.

"Hai. Okay men, let's move on."

Before they lined up in formation to march out, Inefuku turned to Hideki and said, "The prisoners will be buried."

"But they're still alive. Are they going to be executed?"

"No."

Gunjin Chokuyu
Duty is heavier than a mountain;
Death is lighter than a feather.

21.   AUGUST 1940

THE INTERNATIONAL SETTLEMENT INCIDENT STAYED
with Hideki a long time. The head lopped off and fell like it
was a sack of water. It bounced and rolled, spraying blood as it
tumbled, before nestling among the rocks and boulders on the
ground, the expression on its face was one of…shock and dis-
belief. Shigeru was bad enough with his throat cut open. His
face had the same look to it. *Is death meaningless?*

Hideki would never forget the sound of Chiang's execution:
the spurting of escaping blood, the flop of the head to the ground,
and the gurgling afterward. The image came back to him time
and time again in his dreams. One made him laugh out loud: the
head dropped, rolled, and ended face up, eyes open and staring
at him. Then it started talking to him. "I am Chiang, and I am
a human being," it said clear as a bell. And then it blubbered
incomprehensibly. Hideki burst out laughing in his dreamscape.
He woke up in a cold sweat.

The night surrounded him, and the snores of his fellow soldiers reverberated in the darkness. He uncovered and shifted his
legs over the side of the bunk to be flat-footed on the floor. He
then slumped in contemplation. He knew the sergeant could be
cruel, but he never imagined he could be so brutal. His acts to
discipline them had some purpose at least, but this…this execution meant nothing. No conscience, no compassion, and certainly no hesitation. The Sergeant's body odour from exertion
rose in the still air.

Surely the Emperor didn't want this, Hideki considered to himself. *The generals must've come up with the Three Alls.* He knew his

duty to Him, but he ruminated on the Buddha's call for benevolence, for gratitude, for grace.

The Chinese were the enemy, and those in Shanghai were bent on resistance, killing as many Japanese as possible in the hope of demoralizing the invading force. But surely, they knew that was impossible. *We are here to stay*, he thought. *Yet all our lives are meaningless.*

The horror of the moment, however, made him sweat and tremble like he had the plague.

✻ ✻ ✻

It was fortunate for Hideki that he was never called on to perform a beheading or any other atrocity while in Shanghai. He did witness some.

On another occasion, the patrol discovered the unofficial mayor of the Settlement, a Fat Chow Yang. He was a short, rotund man. His rosy cheeks attested to his jolly reputation. Hideki thought him pleasant, but it was clear the "mayor" was scared as the sergeant dragged him out of the old and ruined bank building where he was found. He then ordered him tied to a chair in the middle of the street.

Sgt. Hayashi turned away as Iguchi approached the hapless victim.

"Where is the gang known as the 'Axe men'?" Hayashi asked loudly, his voice pinging off the surrounding walls.

Iguchi translated.

"I…I don't know," he answered to which Iguchi flexed his arm muscles and struck the man across the face.

"I ask again—"

"I said…I don't know…"

To which Iguchi struck him again and again. Hideki watched and wanted the beating to stop but could do nothing. *How could this cherub of a man know anything?* he wondered.

The beating became torture as it went on to for another half hour. Chow Yang was unconscious, his face pulpy and bloody.

"Revive him," Sgt. Hayashi ordered.

Hideki took out his water canteen and tilted Chow Yung's face upwards. He gently poured a trickle into the mouth.

"Baka!" the sergeant screamed and grabbed the canteen away from Hideki. He glared at him with murder in his eyes.

"Don't coddle him," he said as he poured the contents over the man's head, instantly bringing him around.

The man screamed awake as Iguchi brought a knife to his neck. The sergeant stood in front. "You'll tell me what I want to know, or this good man will cut your throat."

"All right, all right," he gasped. "The Axe Men meet at the Suzhou Creek every other night. I don't know if all of them show up but a good number."

"The Double Snake River?" said the sergeant. "Where? It's a long river."

Hideki stood astonished.

"Near the Waibaidu Bridge...at the Huangpu River."

"I know where that is," informed Iguchi.

"Good. Untie him."

Hideki seized the moment. "Sir, I'll escort the mayor back inside."

Sgt. Hayashi glared at him again and then laughed, a good loud laugh.

Hideki looked at him in shock.

"Tamaki, Tsujiyama, take him away. Iguchi, you know what to do."

"And what is that?" Hideki asked defiantly, surprising himself.

"Well, since you ask. Iguchi will cut him, not so he's dead but incapacitated, and the men will bury him."

"Alive? Why?" he said with a shudder, spit hanging on his lower lip and tears welling in his eyes.

"Because of his unwillingness to co-operate."

"But he told you...even if he had co-operated, you would've executed him."

"But more mercifully." Sgt. Hayashi guffawed in Hideki's face. "Tamaki, you stay and Akamatsu will take your place.

"Be a soldier, you nakimushi ass."

They marched, dragging the mayor along, about five kilometres away until they came to a riverbank. The wind was up and cooled their faces and bodies. A small mercy. Hideki was certain Chow Yang didn't know what was happening since they hardly spoke and, when they did, it was in Japanese.

No one knew the name of the river, but they could see a large cruiser making its way downstream.

"That's the *Izumi*," said Tsujiyama, a young, tall, and skinny man. "I'd know that ship anywhere." He had made a study of all the fleet as a way of passing the time. He also wanted to join the navy, but they didn't accept him. Something about seasickness.

In a remote part away from the water. Hideki noted the nearby thick stand of trees, the view of the water, and distant landscape of soft rolling hills, a pleasant spot if not for the gruesome duty about to take place. Iguchi took a small shovel from his backpack and gave it to Chow Yang. He ordered him to dig.

The mayor suddenly understood what was happening and started to cry, loudly and uncontrollably. He fell to his knees in front of them and begged for his life, Hideki guessed.

It was gibberish to Iguchi who pulled out his knife and sliced the backs of his two legs.

The mayor screamed and rolled to the ground, grasping at his wounds.

"Akamatsu, Tsujiyama, dig!"

"You don't have to do this," Hideki complained. "We could just let him go and he'll disappear into the city."

"Yeah, and what if he's discovered sometime? It's our heads that'll be coming off." Iguchi grinned sardonically. He saw the sergeant in his face. "Now dig."

Hideki dug a swallow grave before Iguchi said that was enough.

"Now, put the fat man in it."

Tsujiyama and Hideki tried to pick the mayor up, but he suddenly started twisting his body, his face contorted with terror and anger.

Iguchi sprang into action, grabbing hold of one of the shovels and began striking the victim about the head. Several blows later and the man lay still and groaning; he was conscious but unable to move.

"Now bury him," he said without emotion.

"But...but..." stammered Hideki.

Iguchi sighed and said, "Oh all right." He then proceeded to take out his knife and slit the man's wrists. Surprising to Hideki, the mayor only let out a quiet groan. "Okay? He'll bleed to death now."

The two wanted to wait but Iguchi couldn't so he shovelled dirt on the body until he was covered. The detail of three only heard muffled choking from underneath.

Hideki kneeled on the ground sick to his stomach. He vomited.

Iguchi laughed like the devil again. "Don't tell anyone of our mercy," he warned with a smile.

Wiping away the debris from his face, Hideki scowled at Iguchi in disgust.

✾ ✾ ✾

The "Double Snake River Battle" came soon enough. Two days after the mayor's execution, Hideki found himself part of a force of about thirty men. Sgt. Hayashi had been told by Capt. Fujimoto that other informants said the Axe Men would be amongst trees near the Waibaidu Bridge, well away from the numerous warehouses of the area, about 10 o'clock in the evening. They would be ready in full battle dress, bayonets fixed on their rifles.

The Axe Men were not an organized group, not a gang, or military unit. They were a hostile force, to be sure, ready to slaughter any Japanese patrol they happen to come across. And they did. Fifty men so far in the back alleys of the Settlement. There was no obvious leader, but a Chai Yee Fung was the most prominent name. They carried hammers and not axes. The Axe Men was a nickname coined by Capt. Fujimoto's superiors. Some suspected the name came from the prewar triads in China, famous for the axe as a preferred choice of weapon. But no one knew for sure.

The heat, despite the night, was heavy, as Hideki and his comrades took up positions near the meeting site. The full moon was almost at its height. At least they could see the supposed battleground from a distance. Nearly invisible insects tormented them, but most men crouched absolutely still, out of fear of punishment or discovery by the enemy.

As Hideki squatted in the darkness, he felt the sweat on the palms of his hands as he gripped his rifle in anticipation.

"Akamatsu, rub your blade with dirt," growled Sgt. Hayashi. "The moonlight's making it shine. It'll give us away."

Hideki obeyed right away, though he wondered why he was to soil the Emperor's soul, his *samurai* sword. As he dirtied his bayonet, he thought he heard some movement. He then saw figures rustling and moving in the distance.

From that point, events accelerated and progressed in a flash. Sgt. Hayashi stood and drew his dreaded sword. He said nothing but motioned everyone to move forward. Like insects swarming on their prey, everyone began amassing and then rushing toward what Hideki presumed were the Axe Men. The night exercises during training came in handy.

The sound of gunfire soon erupted as the forward men announced their presence. Hideki could hear the mantra rising like locust in the night. More shots rang out the closer they got. Not so distant bodies fell. Return fire came soon enough. *The Axe Men have rifles? I thought they only had hammers.* Hideki saw some of his comrades fall, but he and everyone else kept going, until they arrived at the battle site. The smell of cordite and urine rose into the air. More gun fire and then hand-to-hand combat broke out. More bodies collapsed.

Hideki himself engaged in close battle with one of the Axe Men, shorter than he but with strong legs. He led with his rifle and caught the enemy's chest with his bayonet. An audible cry and the man dropped to his knees and just sat there with eyes open and blood oozing through his shirt. The ambient light caught the face and Hideki could see he was just a boy, maybe fourteen-years-old, not older. He didn't even have a weapon, no rifle, no hammer. Hideki recoiled. He dropped his rifle with the shock. Just then someone hit him in the middle of his back, not a blow meant to hurt but to bring him back to the business at hand.

"Pick up your rifle, Akamatsu," ordered Sgt. Hayashi with a shout. "Come on, move!"

"But...but...I killed a boy!"

"Good. We've got more to go! *Kill All!*"

The battle continued until all the Axe Men were dead or captured. One was identified as Chai Yee Fung, the *de facto* leader of the bunch. Fung was wiry with a face contorted by a cause and maybe madness.

No one noticed that Hideki had stayed back of the fray and did not engage in any more hand-to-hand combat. He would not be the cause of anyone else's death, especially a boy. He did stand near his comrades when the leadership approached.

Capt. Fujimoto, the battalion commander, was pleased as he surveyed the captives. Sgt. Hayashi, in turn, was ecstatic and ordered the prisoners to be taken away. Hideki knew what fate awaited the enemy survivors.

Death has no meaning for me.

22.   LATE SEPTEMBER 1940

HIDEKI COULDN'T SLEEP. HE EITHER paced the floor or lay
in bed awake, bleary-eyed, and sobbing quietly. His pillow was
damp. It had been a month since the battle, and he had been
on a few more patrols, but nothing happened to the extent of
the events leading up to and including the Double Snake River
Incident, as it was called.

As he later gazed out of the barracks' window, he found
some comfort in the open sky above. The distant stars were cold
and remote, if only he could rise into the air and travel to them.
His friends and enemies celestial beings. He would bow to them
and ask forgiveness.

When he joined the military so long ago now it seemed,
he knew he would be in battles and killing would happen, but
he thought he would find glory. His own death would be sun-
lit, immaculate, and encapsulated in the glow of the Emperor.
He thought of Shigeru, his body lying on the floor, the mess of
blood from his gaping throat underneath and beside him.

Desertion means disgrace for the family.

And in Shanghai, he constantly saw the faces of Chai Yee
Fung, the mayor, and Chiang. He shook in the pale light. Then
there was the Snake River Incident; the boy combatant's face
was exceptionally clear. It floated before him.

Sgt. Hayashi was evil, as cold as the heavens above, capable of
such a callousness that stunned Hideki. His stomach crunched
into knots, aching with an indistinct pain.

He soon learned that Honda and Tsujiyama had died in the
ambush. Both were as inexperienced as he. Honda was young,

younger than Hideki, and had been nervous about the coming fight. His face bled innocence in the face of battle. Hideki could see his eyes trembling, even in the darkness within the trees. His small hands also shivered as he gripped his rifle tightly. Tsujiyama, a soldier of fierce, unwavering patriotism, was clear about his duty and encouraged Honda as best as he could. He was anxious to get into the fray and said so, his face taut with violent intention. He embraced the *Three Alls* as his reason for being and so was one of the first to engage the enemy. Almost immediately, he was shot through the heart. Hideki mourned both though he hardly knew them.

Hideki's lack of sleep dizzied him, made him unsteady on his feet. He dragged through his duties, sometimes losing balance and flopping to the ground. He was indifferent to the insults and yelling of his superior officers and his fellow soldiers. He just didn't care, no matter how many beatings he endured. Once sent to the hospital after a particularly savage thrashing by the sergeant, Hideki groggily saw the army doctor who gave him sedatives and confined him to his barracks. He slept, but he never really felt rested.

During his convalescence in late September, he received two letters from home. One came from his father, mailed last June. The second from his sister, Chiemi, dated at the beginning of August. Yet both arrived together on the same day.

His father sent him a *tanka* with no explanation. *Curious.*

Death has no meaning for me,
But when I give thought to the
Moment of death,
I grow sad at the loss of
Warm family memories.

He didn't understand its purpose, not until he read his sister's letter. *Otousan* was dead. No one knew why, the cause was never discovered. He just died in his sleep.

It seemed ridiculous to Hideki or at least anti-climatic given all the slaughter around him. *Death is meaningless.* He harrumphed and tossed the letters.

Hideki and his fellow troopers learned in early fall 1940 that they were ordered on the road to Nanking. He knew the old capital was the site of a major battle back in 1937 where some 4,000 Chinese soldiers had been eliminated, but the braggart Inefuku said otherwise.

"4,000? More like 400,000! They offered up much resistance, but we as the superior Emperor's Army easily defeated them."

400,000? Hideki was stunned by the number. *How can you kill 400,000?* ran through his mind constantly. *Is it even possible?* It stayed with him as they marched along the road to Nanking. Burned out houses and buildings, scorched fields and the ruined lives of people greeted them as they passed. Peasants staggered out to plead for water, food, anything. Half dead, hollow, with bloodshot eyes and emaciated bodies. But they were met with indifference, some with derision. Hideki, himself haggard, his body wasted, held a glimmer of understanding, which soon vanished as he passed-by.

Their mission was to deal with any force who would confront them. Some of the poor begged in front of Sgt. Hayashi but were simply knocked to the ground. He said, "Akamatsu, drop to the rear and throw out some provisions."

Hideki did as he was ordered, falling to the back of the line to toss some of dried grub from his backpack along the road. No one said anything even as a mob of peasants swarmed the road behind the line of troops. He was perplexed at the sergeant's sudden change of heart, change of character.

He later understood it was a lesson from him: he ate very little for about four days after having given away most of his provisions. The Sergeant ordered no one was to share food with him. Hideki felt the sergeant's grin every time he walked by him.

Hideki and company were marching to Nanking (about 300 kilometres); from there, they were to move across the Yangtze

River and then north towards Peking to relieve the 9th Division. All along the journey, Hideki mumbled to himself. Anger and hunger forced him to gather whatever green plants he could find and gnaw on the branches and leaves. His eyes widened, taking on a crazed look.

Death is meaningless.

23.   OCTOBER 1940

NANKING WAS ALL BOMB SITES, soot, and ruins. Half-
buildings were torn apart and burnt out, a wall or two still
standing without a roof, or window glass resting amongst piles
of rubble. The telltale odour of rotting flesh told Hideki of what
was hidden beneath. He could also smell the familiar cordite
and urine emanating from somewhere. He clenched his teeth
and muscles as he marched past various wasted parts of the city.
Even after nearly three years since the take-over and occupation,
about a third of Nanking was still in ruin.

The 10th Division had arrived through the Taiping Gate,
basically an arched hole, a ruined architectural feature with bits
of blue ceramic tiles as the only testament to a glorious past, in
the city wall that surrounded the place. He had heard that the
16th Division, a much larger contingent of soldiers, had entered
the city through the same entrance and the Zongshan Gate a
few weeks before. Simultaneously, the 9th Division had entered
through the Guanghua Gate. That must've been a magnificent
sight, with fully dressed troops marching smartly and with the
towering Zijin Mountain in the background. The summit was
partially hidden by its famous purple clouds that day.

Hideki's division went straight to what was once known
as the International Safety Zone in the western end of town.
The commanders had not recognized it as a neutral area and so
ordered it to be "cleaned out". Perhaps the first heinous order.
Headquarters and barracks were now located there.

The sleeping quarters were like any other Hideki had known,
except most of the walls and floors of the commandeered bank
building were covered in burnt umber stains. The discoloura-
tion soaked into the surfaces and could not be removed by work
crews. He could feel tears coming on.

He had heard that mobs of Chinese citizens fled to the Safety Zone for protection with the Japanese advance from the countryside, but they were fired upon without thought and without mercy. Scores of enemy soldiers and young Chinese men were bound and shot by the Yangtze River. As was customary, the bodies were bayoneted and tossed into the water. By the Taiping Gate through which he had arrived, 1300 soldiers and citizens were blown up by artillery fire, doused with gasoline, and burned, alive or dead. Survivors were bayoneted.

Bodies were piled up in six-foot high mounds outside the Yijiang Gate in the north end of town. The young soldier gritted his teeth and walked with his head bent, not wishing to look or imagine. He was no longer self-conscious of his height.

✿ ✿ ✿

How many? How many dead went through his head with no answer coming. He had heard 4,000, but he suspected the alleged 400,000 was more accurate. He knew each victim had a name, an identity, a family, yet they were all unknown to him. Names, identities, families…all erased. A huge number makes the dead anonymous.

Rumours and gossip floated about Hideki's ears. In the barracks, a small gang of compatriots talked in a circle of camaraderie. They were smoking and drinking *sake* casually on their beds. Hideki didn't know their names, but he had seen them in the street from a distance. They had surrounded a poor peasant woman.

"Did you see how scared she was?" one said with a laugh.

"Yeah, especially when we tore her clothes off!"

"Oh, she was a honey."

"Quit it, she was a Chinese mushi."

"Good body, you gotta admit it."

"Ach. Average."

They guffawed.

"Hey, why didn't you partake? You know, have at her?" one asked an older soldier.

"I like virgins," he said with a grin. "She had a daughter."

"She was a child. Must've been six or seven."

His grin grew wider. "I liked her."

Hideki turned away as the image of the woman, with legs splayed wide, a stomach sliced open, blood everywhere, and a face full of horror, materialized before him. And the daughter raped, bayoneted, and raised high in the air.

He ran to the latrine to vomit.

✿ ✿ ✿

Surely, none of these acts could be done to honour the Emperor. In his dreams, he swam within the overwhelming numbers of dead. Bodies piled on bodies. He tried in desperation to save even one…but could not.

He dragged about with head hung down, his shoulders hunched and arms limp. He was constantly in a nervous sweat. His eyes always at half-mast. He kept to himself, though he continued to follow orders; he would not, however, engage with others. Except Tsujiyama, the soldier who stood beside him when they buried the mayor before the Double Snake Incident.

Tsujiyama Hideo's thin body was always perspiring, like Hideki, or so it seemed. The smell of dried sweat was palpable, but no one cared.

One night, Tsujiyama sat up talking to Hideki in their side-by-side cots. His face was animated, his voice filled with earnest anxiety. Hideki just saw another soldier serving the Emperor, but there was something more in this one.

"Akamatsu, we got a two-day pass coming. You wanna do something?" Tsujiyama asked.

"No, not really. I thought I'd stay here and clean my bayonet and rifle."

"Clean…? Are you…? Listen, we may not get another chance to see the city. Not get to see China in our lifetimes. We should get out there—"

"What's there to see? Everything is in ruins. Only officers live in comfort and luxury."

"Wanna go visit the Ian-jo?"

"The what?"

"You know, get one of them Jugun Ianfu. I know where to find them."

There was a Comfort Station or brothel in the Japanese Concession of Shanghai. Hideki had never gone, but many of his fellow recruits did. The idea made him shake and sweat more. He imagined alluring women flashing their thighs and covered with a putrid perfume. In Hideki's mind, his comrades were fools to open themselves up for disease, theft, and possible murder for a few moments of pleasure. He was teased mercilessly, but no real harm came to him. He was just considered too young, inexperienced, and ignorant of the ways of the world.

He did wonder, again and only for a moment, how Japanese soldiers could treat Chinese women the way they did. The casual conversation by the soldiers in the barracks then came to mind.

✿ ✿ ✿

After much persuasive argument and haranguing by Tsujiyama, Hideki finally agreed. He gave in, but he did consider "knowing" a woman to be of vital importance. Hideki slept nervously with the prospect of the next day.

The Comfort Station was in a hidden and squalid corner of the Security Zone. The single, stand-alone building was one floor high, with a cracked and caved-in roof and scarred wooden walls. All the windows had been boarded. Cracks in the concrete foundation left debris everywhere. The whole place looked ravaged by war. Similar anonymous buildings lined the street, more like a back alley.

There was no one to greet the two soldiers outside, but Tsujiyama confidently opened the front door. Inside, a short and slight man greeted them. He called himself "Kawasaki", but it was obvious he was Chinese.

"Gentlemen, come in. Welcome to the Comfort Battalion. What is your pleasure?" At least his Japanese, though accented, was clear.

Tsujiyama consulted with him quietly for a bit. Kawasaki with a wide grin pointed the way to the back rooms.

As Hideki walked down the long corridor, he was aware of every footstep he took, aware of the cracks and the peeling paint of the walls, aware of the too few lights trying to pierce the dull darkness. Every wooden door, and there were many, was anonymous. All he felt was Tsujiyama's hand on his back guiding him to the very back of the hallway. They came to stop before the crude door facing forward.

"Go on in," Tsujiyama encouraged. He smiled and walked to an adjacent door.

Hideki noticed his breathing quickened as he opened the door. He first thought to knock but decided that would be silly.

The door swung open with a great yawn. What greeted him inside surprised him. A woman, older with creped throat and crow's feet about the eyes, stood as if waiting for him. Her hair was painted black, ink trails down the back of her neck. Even standing on a soiled mattress, she was slightly shorter than he; she wore a loose-fitting *yukata* of faded cherry blossoms. She was indifferent to the fact that it gapped open, exposing her naked body.

Her breasts were plump but drooping, like twin hanging pears. Her rib cage thinned out, the bones showing. Her face had no makeup, lined instead with age and abuse, her eyes hollow. The face hung like sad, withered fruit. Her legs were dirty, maybe bruised, definitely spotted and had none of the vigour of a healthy body.

She approached him and, without a word, proceeded to disrobe him.

Hideki remained silent and began feeling dizzy. Once naked, he was pushed to the floor. She soon straddled him and proceeded to perform mechanical intercourse. He breathed even more heavily than he had until he could hold no longer. And just like that it was over.

The experience was all new to him. Guilt came over him; he felt dirty. He wondered if this absurd and awkward exercise was necessary. Yet he knew all his companion soldiers sought women for this precise reason. He then gazed at her as she stood and walked to a corner of the room.

"What's your name?" he asked. He felt like he should say something. Seemed appropriate given what had just happened.

She said nothing; instead, she took a piece of soiled fabric and cleaned herself. She appeared uncomfortable, but not embarrassed at all. Still, Hideki decided it was necessary to connect somehow.

Before she could answer, if she were going to, a scream came from somewhere down the hall. It sounded like a woman being murdered. Hideki came to his feet immediately and clumsily put on some of his clothes. As he made for the door, the Comfort Woman grabbed him with her hands and said something incomprehensible. He pushed her aside and entered the hallway.

The screaming continued along with convulsive crying. Once he got to the door, he didn't hesitate, he opened it and witnessed a naked muscular man grinding against a young girl beneath him, her thin legs splayed apart. She was pushing and striking against him but to no avail. She screeched in his face. Tears filmed her contorted face.

Hideki could instantly see she was young, undernourished, and weak. The tormentor suddenly grabbed her by the throat to quell the screams, no doubt. She started gasping, clawing for air. Her eyes looked ready to burst.

Hideki yelled, "Stop! You're going to kill her." His face was flushed, his hands outstretched and shaking.

The man stopped momentarily and looked around him. Hideki gulped in surprise. "Sergeant Hayashi..." was all he could say.

Hayashi stood and faced Hideki. He was nude but not self-conscious.

"Mind your own business," he hissed.

The girl had curled into a ball and tried to recover and hide her nakedness. She wriggled to a corner.

"But she's a little girl! Leave her alone."

The Sergeant burst out laughing. "What do you care? I paid for her."

Hideki would not be deterred. "There must be a hundred Comfort Women here. Why her?"

"She's a virgin, a Korean virgin," he said as if to say she was worthless in every other sense. "I paid extra." With those words, he turned his back to reclaim his prize.

The girl shrieked again and cowered in the corner as the sergeant approached her. "Come here, you little mushi."

Hideki reached out and grabbed his Sergeant to put a stop to it. Hayashi was momentarily stopped but twisted around and struck Hideki across the face, his cheek instantly red. Hideki fell backwards and to the ground.

In the next split-second, Hideki grabbed a nearby weapon, Hayashi's sword, resting against the wall next to him, and, in one swift motion, unsheathed it and blindly swung the raw blade and caught the sergeant in the abdomen. *Sukesada*, a *samurai's* sword.

Hideki gasped at Hayashi as he realized what he had done. Hayashi stood for a moment as if stunned by what was happening. Blood gushed forward and Hayashi fell to his knees. With contorted face, he looked up at Hideki. He then toppled over in a dead fall, still gripping his wound, the blood oozing between his fingers.

Hideki took two steps back, dropping the sword at the same time. The girl leapt to her feet and ran out of the room, screaming with her hands in the air. He was vaguely aware he had sullied the blade, the Emperor's sword. He dropped it with a rattle and clang. And in the next moment, someone held Hideki by the shoulders and pulled him out. It was Tsujiyama.

Neither said anything. His friend made sure Hideki was soon out of the building and out of the district quickly. No one yelled at them, no one gave chase.

❋ ❋ ❋

Back in the barracks, Hideki sat on his cot, shaking in the darkness. Tsujiyama brought him a cup of water and told him to drink, which he did quickly.

"What am I going to do?" Hideki fretted. "I should give myself up. Confess everything."

"That would be signing your death warrant. No, don't say a thing. They won't come for you. No one knows your name there…No one'll say anything at the Comfort Station."

"But most of my stuff is there. I left it behind."

"Yeah, a generic uniform? And army equipment? In a place full of military personnel? No one'll trace it back to you."

"But—"

"Trust me," he said with a confidence that inspired acceptance. "The Chinese'll sell all your stuff."

❀ ❀ ❀

Tsujiyama was correct. No one came to accuse and arrest him. A captain announced that Sgt. Hayashi was killed by a young Comfort Girl, who was apprehended and quietly put to death. No trial, just put against a wall and shot. *Or worse*, Hideki imagined.

Sgt. Hayashi was given full military honours; his body cremated and sent to his family in Japan for commemoration. The sword had disappeared.

Hideki was left quietly crying, remorse hanging over him like a cloud of sadness.

24.

RUMOURS ABOUT SGT. HAYASHI'S MURDER abounded. One
of the most compelling involved five men, including a Kawasaki.
They were part of a Resistance Movement in Nanking, con-
spiring to kill as many Japanese as possible. They, it was said,
ambushed Sgt. Hayashi, who fought bravely and wounded one
or two of them, killed at least one, but their number was too
much. He died a glorious, noble death.

The murderers were apprehended and beheaded; their bodies thrown into the Yangtze River. Kawasaki was said to have
begged for mercy in Japanese. The Execution Squad laughed.

Odd that the story of the Comfort Woman was no longer
mentioned. It was as if she and her alleged action had never
taken place. There were no tears for the woman and daughter in
the street, Hideki thought.

Hideki and Tsujiyama knew the truth of course and made
no comment about the claim. Privately, Hideki wondered how
such a story could be propagated. The Sergeant was found in an
Ian-jo. Kawasaki, he knew, but who were the other four men?
Wouldn't they be women, if they existed at all? His *Jugun Ianfu*,
the young Chinese girl, was put to death anonymously suppos-
edly on a fresh, quiet early morning outside the Nanking city
wall. Or so he had guessed.

He knew he could not do anything for her. Her life had been
a misery from the moment the troops arrived in China, maybe
before. He sat up in the night trying to remember her face, as
terrified as it was. It was soon replaced by an image of a girl in a
Shanghai poster: cherry lips, rosy cheeks, bright eyes, and hair
tied together and black as a streak of night down her back. The
darkness was his comfort, his shame his companion.

One night, he found himself talking to Tsujiyama, softly but earnestly.

"How can there be glory in death? How can you die well?" Hideki asked. "Did the executed Chinese soldiers die gloriously? And the civilians? It was a mass slaughter."

Tsujiyama stared at him with a confused look before saying anything. "Think I know? You better shut up about things like that. You want trouble? You want to die as *gloriously?* Look, the higher-ups can't say Sgt. Hayashi died in a Comfort Battalion. He wasn't in a fight with prostitutes; he was killed by some Chinese girl. That would not sit well with Hayashi-san's family or the public for that matter. He had to die in a battle of some kind. It had to be an ambush because it happened in a city we control. Don't you see?"

"I know…I know," Hideki repeated until he bent his head, covered his eyes with his hands, and started sobbing.

"Quiet down, now. Get some sleep. It'll all be better in the morning," Tsujiyama advised.

At a later hour, Hideki sat up; his forehead was damp, his eyes red. Anger contorted his face. He came to his feet.

"Tomorrow won't be better," he said. His voice started to rise in volume. Words came out in a torrent. "Sergeant Hayashi was killed in a brothel. He doesn't deserve anything for bravery. He didn't die an honourable death. He was a horrible man. A sadist, a brute…a monster… murderer. And why did that girl have to die?"

"Bakatare!" "Damare!" "Go back to sleep!" Voices of disturbed sleep called out in the dark.

Tsujiyama in his drowsy sleep stood and faced him to try and calm him down. "Akamatsu! Akamatsu, lower your voice. You can't say things like that. It'll only bring trouble. This is war, remember? Japan needs men like Sergeant Hayashi. Now be quiet," he ordered. He scanned the room before continuing, "I don't think anyone paid attention to what you were saying."

Hideki softened his voice and sat down on his cot, his face wetter. "She didn't have to die…she didn't—"

"You mean the Jugun Ianfu?"

"Don't call her that," he said with a flash. "She was just a young girl...a country girl."

"Don't you understand, it's better this way" Tsujiyama insisted. "She no longer suffers, and you're not suspected of anything."

"Bakatare! Couldn't they just punish her and be done with it? I mean if they had to blame somebody...had to do something."

"Punish her how?"

"Well..." he groped for the words. "They could've had a bunch of men have her and then let her go."

"You mean, gang rape her?"

"At least she'd be alive," he reasoned in his innocence.

"I don't think so. You know what happens to those girls."

"No, I don't." His lower lip trembled as he lied.

"Never mind. You don't know what you're saying," Tsujiyama said to comfort Hideki. "Look, you should be grateful she's dead. Quick and easy. No blame can come to you now." He kept harping on that same point, perhaps trying to convince himself rather than his friend.

Hideki thought about what his friend had said and immediately felt pity and sorrow. He couldn't believe his suggestion. *Death is meaningless.* His father's words began to haunt him.

He sought sleep but none was to be had. He tossed and turned, he shivered, he perspired profusely until his bedclothes were wet. In his semi-conscious and incoherent state, Hideki's eyes opened wide, and the night poured into them. Yet he could make out shapes—one in particular. Various parts of the dark air broke off in jigsaw pieces and coalesced into a distinctive form. It was human yet had no face, no distinguishing features. It was a shadow. It moved forward to stand next to his bed. It pulsated with energy. Hideki looked up and his lips formed a word: "Otousan."

In the morning, Hideki was found to have a high fever. He continued to perspire copiously, shaking with the chills. He was dizzy and disoriented.

"I didn't mean it...it just happened," he kept mumbling over and over.

Tsujiyama feared Hideki would incriminate himself and so he and a few others helped him to the Infirmary where he received treatment for pneumonia. Hideki was in bed for a month.

25.

A CRISP DAY GREETED HIDEKI when he left the army hospital. The leaves on the ground crackled as he stepped on them; the branches rustled with the wind; the choreography of the leaves sliced through the air as they fell to the ground. He breathed in the cold air and shivered with the weather as he trundled towards his barracks. His lungs expanded with wellbeing. The hospital was clean, the staff friendly and compassionate. He had finally found some peace there.

While in his hospital bed, he dreamed of her: the young girl of the Comfort Station. He recalled a Shanghai advertising poster along the city streets. She was the most beautiful girl in the world.

Back in his barracks' cot, he dreamed the girl was beneath the naked man clawing and punching to get free. She screamed and spit at the same time. Hideki quickly approached them and grabbed the man's shoulder.

The man twisted to face him, and it was not the sergeant; it was Hideki glaring back at him. It was like looking in a mirror. Hideki returned to the girl, who no longer struggled. Instead, she groaned and placed her hands over his ears. Her face expressed ecstasy as her eyes closed. Her mouth opened sucking in air, while her lips, ringed by a bright red lipstick, exhaled his name.

Hideki squirmed under the cot covers as he felt his groin solidify.

❊ ❊ ❊

The next morning, he decided to go back to the *Ian-jo*. He dressed making sure he donned the *senninbari*, the protective cloth belt his sister had given him, mixed in with his clothes. He hadn't worn it or even thought about it until this very moment.

He needed to talk to his friend Tsujiyama, who was in the barracks playing *gaji* with others. There was money on the table;

his boney head bobbed up and down to the action before him. Hideki apologized when he interrupted and pulled his friend's arm to get him up from the game.

"Akamatsu, what are you doing?" complained Tsujiyama, holding his cards up to his friend's face. "I'm gonna win. I already have two yaku sets! I've got big money coming to me."

"I need your help."

Tsujiyama stopped struggling when he saw the look on Akamatsu's face. He got up from his crouch and pulled his friend aside. "Okay, what's the problem?"

"You have to take me back."

"To where?"

"To the Ian-jo."

"What? Why do you want to go back there?"

"To find that young girl's name. I've got to find out. Don't you see? Don't you?" His voice rose to desperation.

"She's dead!" he said resoundingly and then surveyed the room. No one had paid any attention. Tsujiyama's game was lost and a new one had started.

"I know, but maybe I can help her family—"

"But—"

"But nothing. I have to go, and you've got to help."

"All right, all right. Just stop it."

Things calmed down and Hideki bowed and smiled.

"Look," Tsujiyama said, "the place is probably no longer there—"

"Why, what do you mean?"

"The brass isn't gonna let that place stand. One of their own was killed in there." He was careful not to say any more.

Both remained silent but they each knew they were going back to that *Ian-jo*.

❊ ❊ ❊

Night closed in on the two aimlessly wandering the streets. The darkness slowly swallowed and disguised everything, yet Tsujiyama seemed to know where he was going. There was little light, some streetlights, but nothing substantial, not even room lights coming from windows. Still, Hideki could see the buildings, mostly shuttered and anonymous.

Clouds streamed out of their mouths into the cold air the more they exerted themselves. To Hideki, their breath looked like ghosts straining to escape.

He didn't remember it being so far with all the twists and switchbacks along the way. Eventually Tsujiyama came to a stop in front of a dilapidated building, the wooden walls scarred with cracks and gouges. No windows. No identification at all. Hideki told himself it looked familiar.

"So here it is," Tsujiyama announced. He banged on the door, which rattled with the intrusion. No one answered.

"Just as I thought, no one inside," he said after an appropriate amount of time. "I told you."

"Try again." He did and still no answer. Hideki then pounded on the door harder. Then kicked at it. It cracked, dented in, comically.

"Hey! Don't attract attention!"

Hideki stepped back, disappointed and wondered what to do next.

A voice came out of the darkness. "Gentlemen, are you looking for something?"

The two confronted a rather fat man with balding head, dressed preposterously in an old tuxedo, ragged and dishevelled. He spoke perfect Japanese.

"My name is Kawasaki and I believe I can help you. Are you looking for the Ian-jo that was here?" he said in an oily voice.

"Yes," Hideki offered, even though Tsujiyama tried to hold him back. *Are they all named Kawasaki?*

"Excellent. Follow me." The little rotund man turned on his feet and began walking into the better yet inadequately lit end of the street.

Tsujiyama looked skeptical, fearful perhaps, and tried to warn Hideki wordlessly, but Hideki was determined and followed the man.

As he walked, their guide spoke, "Gentlemen, I will lead you to the paradise you seek. All your dreams will be fulfilled."

The two stayed quiet even as they walked down an ominous laneway or two. As they turned one last corner, Hideki saw a doorway with a single lightbulb burning pathetically in the shadows.

The trio stopped in front of another cracked wooden door.

✿ ✿ ✿

Inside, it was as the first *Ian-jo* Hideki visited the other night. A small reception room in front with a wizened old lady sitting, waiting for customers, Hideki presumed. He addressed her.

"I'm looking for the name of the girl that was arrested and executed a little while ago. You must remember her. Her customer was killed in the room."

The old lady looked at him with a confused expression.

"She can't speak Japanese," Kawasaki informed.

"Can you translate?" he asked.

"I know that girl of whom you speak."

Hideki's eyes lit up. "What was her name?"

"I don't know, but I can take you to someone who might know. And she speaks Japanese. You like this idea?"

"Yes, please."

"You have money?"

"Money?"

"You think information is free? Maybe American dollars?"

The haggling continued until Hideki gritted his teeth and pulled out all the money he had in his pockets. Tsujiyama did the same. He had less than Hideki. The *gaji* game had depleted his stash. Kawasaki looked disappointed, but he snatched the money from their hands and motioned for them to follow.

A short trip down the hall to yet another door. Kawasaki opened it with a wide grin and motioned them inside. A middle-aged woman squatted on a rickety chair in the corner. She sighed and stood. She was dressed in a loose and soiled *yukata*.

Besides the rolls of weight, her legs were bloated and ugly with blue veins.

"Two?" she exclaimed. "I get more than double!"

Kawasaki acted as translator as the conversation continued.

"No, no," stammered Hideki. She looked familiar. Was she the one he paid for that night? He did not pursue that idea. "We're not here for that! We're looking for information."

She looked at them with a suspicious eye. "What kind of information?" she said as she tightened her *yukata* around her abdomen.

"Kawasaki-san says you know the girl who was arrested for killing a soldier."

"You look familiar somehow. Do I know you?"

"No…no," Hideki said as he stepped back into shadows. "Do you know her name?"

"Maybe…" she said coyly.

"Please, I want to help her family. Maybe give them money."

"Maybe…first, you give me money."

Tsujiyama erupted. "Stop playing games! Do you know the name or not?"

Her eyes grew wide at the abrupt emotion. "Information is not cheap!"

"We paid—"

Kawasaki then stepped between the two and the woman. "I think the interview is over." He pushed the two out the door.

"Thank you for your time," he said to the woman with the fading beauty.

❊ ❊ ❊

Once outside the establishment, Kawasaki confronted the two. His eyes narrowed in the dull ambient light as he spoke.

"I know that wasn't satisfying. I will continue to ask around for you. But first you must pay the bill."

"What bill?" Hideki asked, his face twisted with confusion.

"For my time, her time…for the service."

"But we paid you."

"That was for information. You pay for time now."

"We have no more," Hideki insisted and began breathing harder.

"You lie. Soldier boys always hide money." Kawasaki flashed a sardonic grin. "You asked for help, and I gave it. I can't help it if you didn't find answer. Now pay!"

"Ketsuno-ana!" Tsujiyama swore, his voice becoming hoarse. *Asshole!* "He told you we have no more."

"Pay up!" he said offering his palm in front of them.

Tsujiyama slapped it away.

"Ach," Kawasaki said with finality and raised his hand as if to signal.

In the next few moments, the two were surrounded by five thugs. Each held a pointed weapon or a hammer in his hand. Knives.

"The Axe Men!" Hideki uttered in a rasp.

"Akamatsu, why didn't you let me finish the game back in the barracks?" Tsujiyama said, his voice quivering.

Before either could react, one stepped in to Tsujiyama and swung his knife. It caught him in the stomach, and he screamed in pain. He fell to the ground, holding his gut to prevent it from spilling.

Hideki began to run; the remaining men gave chase. He felt their hands on him, their stinking breath on his face. For some reason, he did not feel the sting of knives to his body, though he anticipated them. Instead, body blows, some hammer blows, came furiously. Once he dropped to the street, kicks to his rib cage caused him to curl into a defensive position. He felt something crack inside him and he begged them to stop. But they wouldn't.

Soon, foreign hands pawed him and took his money pouch; it left like some internal organ.

Eventually, they did stop when they found nothing. He lay on the wet and cold road as he heard the men run away. Steam rose from his body, the steam of after-violence.

Gunjin Chokuyu
Duty is heavier than a mountain;
Death is lighter than a feather.

26.   DECEMBER 1940

WHEN HIDEKI WAS RELEASED YET again from medical care,
he was not fully recovered. He walked slowly and with a slight
stoop. Four broken ribs nagged at him; fractures and contusions
stayed unhealed. Again, the staff were very friendly, compassionate, even funny.

"We'll have to provide your own room," a nurse quipped. "Or
put in a revolving door!"

He couldn't laugh as pain would stab at him.

The day before he left, an army captain appeared bedside.
Captain Inouye Shinobu was a career officer; he was a tall man,
with such distinctive features as shining eyes and strong jawline.
His body was well-sculpted and strong. Hideki thought women
would think him handsome.

"Private Akamatsu. I hope you are feeling well, or at least,
better."

"Y...y...yes," he stuttered. "Sir."

"I want to assure you, the men who assaulted you are being
pursued and will be captured and punished."

"Thank...you."

"I have a few questions, however. Feel up to answering?"

"Hai."

"What were you doing there?"

He thought for a moment and then let the truth out. What
was the point hiding anything? "I was looking for a girl...actually,
her name."

"A girl in that neighbourhood?"

"Not for what you're thinking," he said quickly.

The captain stood up straight, insulted perhaps.

"No, I was there with my friend for a girl who was arrested and executed—"

"Stop right there," ordered the captain. "I'm sorry, such information shall remain unsaid. Do you understand?"

Hideki nodded.

"I see then, nothing more needs to be said."

"What happened to my friend, Private Tsujiyama?"

"I'm afraid he was killed," he said and paused. "That's why it is imperative that we find the perpetrators."

Another friend dead? Hideki squeezed his eyes shut before asking, "Why didn't they kill me?"

"Nearly did. I think it was a matter of killing one and punishing the other…as a kind of warning. Can you tell me who they were?"

"The Axe Men," Hideki said.

"No, that's impossible. They were eliminated shortly after the Snake River Incident. And that was in Shanghai. Quite a distance from here."

Double Snake River, Hideki corrected to himself. So, these men were not the Axe Gang. Who were they then?

Capt. Inouye turned on his heels to leave, but he stopped when Hideki called to him. "Sir, can you tell me what happened to my senninbari? I wore it that night."

"I don't know, it's probably with your belongings. Ask the nurse."

✿ ✿ ✿

After Hideki left to resume his duties, his face drooped with fatigue and depression; his pained back curved with some indistinct burden. Not embarrassment over his height.

It was not a happy reunion. No one really talked to him or even acknowledged his absence. His friends or those he chummed around with were no more. Hideki kept to himself and shied away from any conversation that may have come up. He couldn't sleep.

One night, he bolted from his bed and started yelling to no one in particular.

"It's my responsibility. I'm to blame…"

He flailed about, ignoring his own body pain, and pulling up blankets, throwing them to the floor. Whatever possessions he came across, he grabbed them too and smashed them against the wall. His face contorted and strained against the anger. He continued his frenzied rant.

"Shigeru! Shigeru! I could've done more! The girl! The girl! I should've left well enough alone. Now she's dead. If I had done nothing…"

Desertion means disgrace for the family.

❀ ❀ ❀

By the time his raving descended into incoherence and blubbering, men in their underclothing grabbed him by the arms to try and calm him down. Or at least, control him. Hideki twisted and struggled to get free, swinging his arms wildly. He struck one or two men, but they were too many and too strong. The soldiers finally pinned him to the ground.

Sergeant Akiyoshi, Hayashi's replacement, rushed forward and saw what had happened. "Take him to the infirmary," he ordered.

After a few days of treatment and isolation, Hideki returned to the barracks. Some mercy was shown the young soldier; he was assigned light duty. But he soon found out that his division had been ordered to cross the Yangtze River and move towards Peking. Again, they were charged with "cleaning out" any resistance.

"Can't have an able man wasting the hours away doing nothing," said the new Sergeant, pointing to Hideki and grinning in a friendly manner. He delivered the fresh orders to the assembled men.

Sergeant Akiyoshi continued, "Men, we are boarding a troopship just outside the city. It'll take us up and across the Yangtze where we'll disembark and begin our task. You'll be in full battle dress."

His face was filled with something unfamiliar to Hideki: kindness and humour. He was taller than Hayashi and probably heavier. He wore a mustache, which was highly unusual for a non-commissioned officer. Gave him a distinguished air, designed to impress the men, no doubt.

Hideki heard that the sergeant was a teacher in civilian life. Could be why he was compassionate.

"Maybe he came from the Samurai class or he's the son of a Baron or something," someone offered. "Otherwise, they would've ordered him to shave it off!"

The speculation meant nothing to Hideki. Instead, he prepared for the voyage and march. While packing his equipment and clothes, he searched for his *senninbari*. The captain's words were true: the amulet was among Hideki's possessions, soiled and a little blood stained, but the red stitches were intact. He wrapped and tied it around his abdomen; it gave him the comfort of a rare sister's hug.

❀ ❀ ❀

The short voyage across the river was pleasant enough for Hideki. Reminded him of the trip from Japan. It was a substantial operation since there was a significant number of men and equipment. The five troop carriers on hand had to make several trips back and forth. The time gave Hideki a chance to think, ideal in his weakened state.

His mind drifted to the spectre that had stood beside his cot on that night seemingly so long ago. He decided it was an hallucination, brought on by his lunacy, something no one ever mentioned about him. But there was something so familiar about it. Maybe it was his father.

He wondered if his sisters and mother had the same experience. Writing home would've been out of the question. A letter from him out of the blue? He hadn't sent one since he couldn't remember when. And with such a ridiculous message! They would just worry. He decided against it while listening to the lapping grey-green water and watching birds gently flying near the ship as if accompanying them. The cold wind made him shiver but he didn't mind. It was refreshing somehow.

He didn't think the censors would allow it anyway.

Once upon solid ground, Hideki's body nearly gave out. He stumbled and, if not for a nearby compatriot's quick reaction, he would've been on the ground. What was surprising was Sgt. Akiyoshi's reaction.

As the sergeant rushed over, Hideki expected a scolding, maybe even a beating. Instead, he heard a note of concern.

"Is Akamatsu all right?"

"He's fine, sir. Just slipped on the wet dock," Sato explained, a long-time soldier with a young face but a lot of experience. He was new to the unit.

"Okay, but I know he's been injured," Akiyoshi smiled as if he cared. "Akamatsu, if you need medical attention, just ask. Sato, keep an eye on him."

Lifted by his comments, Hideki couldn't believe what he just heard. The ghost of a grinning Sgt. Hayashi materialized and faded in his mind.

✾ ✾ ✾

The countryside was either barren, scorched by the military, or filled with bombed-out buildings and homes. Skeletal trees, scrawny bushes, and other vegetation dotted the landscape. They acted like sentinels along the dirt road. Mysterious smoke curled into the air, some of it was dust but some, he was sure, came from hidden fires. At least, he could see no bodies strewn about. He tasted bile at the back of his mouth.

Hideki did note how peaceful war seemed at that time. His fellow soldiers were mute, heads hung low as if exhausted. He thought they were on the verge of tears. Oh, there were those still caught in the patriotism and Emperor worship, but most looked...well, defeated.

That night, something happened that played in his mind. The battalion pitched tents by the side of the road. It was unseasonably warm, especially for December. Sleep was not easy to come by, but Hideki did close his eyes and felt himself drift.

But then something woke him; he didn't know what, a cold, stray wind, noise outside. He opened the tent flap, and he encountered a strange world. Fog rolled along the ground to invade the campsite. A cold gauze wrapped itself around the rocks, trees, bushes, ruins and tent canvas. It was so thick Hideki couldn't see the guards standing nearby.

But something emerged from the fog. Before his eyes, ghost soldiers, their faces pale and gaunt, moved forward in formation toward him. His mouth fell open, but he didn't recognize anyone. They were the nameless dead marching out of the clouds of the world beyond. The spirits started to spin, slow at first but then faster and faster until blurring their bodies in a mess of sad and distorted faces.

An invisible *shime* rapped just once. The sound of wood, the manifestation of the Buddha. And music rose in the air, surrounding the translucent figures before him. A harmonious choir chanted the *Heart Sutra* with a peaceful beauty.

...in emptiness no form, no feelings,
perceptions, impulses, consciousness.
No eyes, no ears, no nose, no tongue, no body, no mind;
no color, no sound, no smell, no taste, no touch,
no object of mind; no realm of eyes
and so forth until no realm of consciousness.

Hideki fell back into the tent and shook into merciful unconsciousness.

✿ ✿ ✿

Just south of Chuzhou, an ancient city near Hefei, the capital of Anhui Province, rifle shots rang out. They came from nearby ruined buildings, perfect for snipers. Hideki's unit scattered, taking cover wherever they could. A couple of men died instantly.

Hideki was behind some protruding rocks. He strained his eyes looking for the enemy riflemen. Nothing. He then looked to the road. There were a few bodies, still and bleeding, he guessed. He glanced around him and found that Sato was missing.

"Oh no," he said. He stood and attempted to move out from behind his cover.

Sgt. Akiyoshi grabbed his shoulder and pulled him back.

"Akamatsu, stay here," he commanded.

"But Sato is out there. He needs my help!"

"Your help will mean your death. Stay!"

"But Sergeant…"

"I said, Stay!" His voice was stern, almost callous. He threatened with his baton.

Hideki's lower lip trembled; his eyes closed with the realization that this new man and potential friend was probably dead.

More shots were heard. Dirt and rock fragments flew into the air while pings of bullets could be heard. Hideki lowered his head, but he saw men had started to maneuver to get to an advantageous spot. Return fire finally came. A familiar chant rose in the air mixing with screams and then groans somewhere in the distance. An incantation to flush out the enemy combatants.

The battle went on for what seemed like an eternity. In truth, it was maybe half an hour before everything came to a standstill. Time had lengthened.

After several men worked their way across the open road and fields to the buildings, chaos and confusion reigned: gunfire, smoke, the acrid smell of cordite, and more screams rose in the air. When it was declared safe, Hideki and his fellow soldiers stood and walked into the open.

He looked and realized the extent of the destruction around him. The land had been scorched, vegetation smouldering, bare tree trunks with bark singed off swayed in the wind. Bomb craters gaped open at the smoky air above. The devastation was endless.

We have destroyed everything. Where is the glory?

He rushed to Sato's side, hoping against hope. His suspicion was right. Sato was on the ground with a bullet wound in the middle of his forehead, the cap flung away. A minimal amount of blood stained his face, the eyes were open, surprised to be killed. Death must've been instantaneous.

Something made Hideki look up. Before him and in the distance, ghosts, shadows of the past, rose from the ground. Their faces grey, their bodies translucent, no legs. They were a scattered army of unknown dead, raggedly clothed, slumping towards him. They slowly evaporated into the air, clouds like breath in the cold formed and dissipated.

Hideki lowered his bayoneted rifle. He thought of the spirits that had visited him the other night. The dead. Added to them were the 400,000 of Nanking combatants and civilians, all equal now, all without thought or emotion, all nameless and without a story, all extinguished from the earth. *Form is emptiness, emptiness is form.* He imagined Japan laughing at him and at all the war dead: soldiers and civilians, Japanese and Chinese.

There was no honour in death, except only for the Emperor. He unconsciously bowed to the sun. He reached for the *senninbari* underneath his shirt, but it was not there. Nirvana awaited.

He could feel the white eyes of the Buddha on the back of his neck. He felt his own eyes liquefy.

❀ ❀ ❀

His ears pricked up to a soft, indistinct sound. He twisted around to see a tiny figure with hands in the air running towards him. But not in capitulation, not to surrender. Hideki's body froze, and then swayed, hardening and cracking like ice during a late winter thaw.

As the figure drew closer, Hideki could make out a boy, dressed in well-worn peasant clothing. He was barefooted and bore a determined look. He was not an illusion.

We are all ant soldiers.

❖ ❖ ❖

Even closer, Hideki noticed something gripped in both of his hands. Couldn't tell what they were holding. He thought he heard his comrades' voices saying something. But their voices were muffled by his thoughts. He stood alone in the battlefield with the boy charging toward him.

It was the *Double Snake River Incident* again. Hideki raised his rifle to defend himself, ready to shoot, but the memory of his young victim's face became stronger and stronger. It was replaced by the young girl, Shigeru, Tsujiyama in a sullen Nanking street, Sato, freshly dead, and then Sgt. Hayashi in his moment of shock and death. The images grew stronger before him as the hordes of ghosts in the fog came to mind. He shivered on the spot as he lowered his rifle until the long bayonet touched the ground.

Tears began to flow down his cheeks. *Chiemi. Chisato. Okaasan.* His sisters and mother materialized before him. He wanted to embrace them, tell them how much he missed them, how much he loved them. The childhood arguments. The laughter. The comfort of a mother's wisdom. His free hand sought the feel of the *senninbari* again, but it was still not there. Had he forgotten to wear it? He ignored the mystery as the Hiroshima bag of soil his sister had given him in the garden floated into his consciousness. He yearned to stand in the pile of soil in bare feet, to feel its softness, its familiarity of...of home.

His father's shadow then appeared in front of him, emerging as it did out of thin air. The edges reached out for him, and a smile appeared.

> *But when I give thought to the*
> *Moment of death,*
> *I grow sad at the loss of*
> *Warm family memories.*

He understood the poem. Just then the boy leapt onto his body in a tight hug. Hideki heard two metallic clicks and realized the boy held two hand grenades. They detonated, obliterating their bodies.

All are dead.

CHISATO

It is God's will.
God says, "My purpose will stand,
and I will do all that I please."
Isaiah 46:10

27.   INTO EXILE :: FEBRUARY 1941

THE FLAMES CONSUMED THE VANCOUVER house in minutes. When all was said and done, Chisato's home was an empty
black shell, though the two floors remained intact, skeletal but
intact. The contents lay strewn on the floor, charred beyond
recognition. *The Jesus* still stood, though barely, one arm having
disappeared. Its countenance was black and unrecognisable save
the eyes—as mournful as ever, maybe more so.

No one knew Kiyoshi's fate since no body was found.
Someone said she thought she had seen him or someone like
him run out the backdoor and into the night. Chisato saw her
husband withdraw from the front window and heard a maniacal
laugh accompanied by shouting, something in English within
the flames. In any case, she made no comment.

She herself was lucky Michiko took her into her care.
Michiko's house, a small, simple one-storey place with stucco
walls and garden in front, was two blocks away on the other side
of East Hastings Street. The roar of Chinatown was faint but
ever present. Chisato found herself lying in the bed of an extra
room while Michiko prepared a comforting cup of barley tea.

The two soon sat together in the room, Chisato warming her
hands as she palmed the cup.

"I don't know what happened," confided Chisato to a worried
Michiko. "He came home late as he usually does and prayed in

the living room. He suddenly got up and started yelling about something! That's when he started throwing and breaking things."

"I suppose that's how the fire started," Michiko opined. "Where were you?"

"Upstairs."

"But you were fully clothed outside...and with a coat on." She lowered her eyes, having realized she may have caused embarrassment.

Chisato paused before saying, "I was just about to get ready for bed when Kiyoshi came home. I came downstairs once he started breaking things. I grabbed a cape when I saw him and ran away."

Michiko sat with a smirk. Chisato knew her words hadn't explained her street clothes, but her friend let it go.

"I think I heard him inside the house; he kept screaming about something...and laughing...laughing. I don't know what he was saying. I couldn't understand..."

"I heard it too," Michiko informed, "It was so loud. He said, 'My God, my God, why hast thou forsaken me?'"

"What does that mean?"

Michiko lowered her gaze and explained, "...Jesus said it on the cross."

❁ ❁ ❁

The late hours put Chisato into a confessional mood. She was too tired to sleep, and fatigue played on her. Her body slumped, her eyes drooped, but she wanted to say something as she looked at Michiko's own hangdog face.

"Michiko-san. I followed Kiyoshi...to the Showa Club. I saw what he was up to."

"You went inside?" Michiko said somewhat alarmed.

"No...no. I waited outside," she said and then paused. "What would make him go there?"

"He's been going a long time, long before he married you."

"Why?"

"Because he could. He has the money...he has the desire."

"But he's married."

"I'm sure you know nothinig about Morii-san and his place of business. He controls all the vices that attract men. He and his Black Dragon Society convince wealthy men that they deserve what he offers. Meanwhile, he pulls in all the money."

"So, Kiyoshi had to be convinced…"

"No, he was tempted."

"But he's a devout Christian!"

"He's human. Even the Lord was tempted. Kiyoshi just gave in, even though he knew it was wrong. The women and alcohol were just too much for him to resist."

"Then why did he marry? Marry me? He could've just gone on indulging himself without bringing shame to his wife. His family," she said rubbing her belly.

"Doesn't look good if the president of the church is single. Makes people suspicious."

❊ ❊ ❊

She felt good having confessed, but what to do now? Fortunately, the next day, after a breakfast of *miso* soup, fried fish, and rice, Michiko insisted they go see the Reverend James for help. The day was sunny, breezy, and cold, but Michiko offered a heavier coat that was a good match for the weather.

While on the way, Chisato asked to see her house. Michiko complied of course. The charred remains were heartbreaking. A skeleton stood where walls once were. The roof had partially collapsed during the night. The ground was black.

The contents were mostly gone, though she could make out the outlines of furniture. *The Jesus* stood as it had late last night. Its face charred and forlorn, its body and cross slightly bent and disfigured. The icon was in ruins.

Is this my fate? Chisato questioned silently. She resisted the urge to cry.

Her mind flashed to the moment outside the Immigration Building when the truth about Sachiko's husband was revealed. Chisato saw her friend shake perhaps out of anger, perhaps out of fear. She had been duped; he had lied to her. Like Jikemura-san, Kiyoshi had kept his truth hidden from her. In that moment, something changed for her. Chisato's eyes watered.

Because the sun shone brightly, she spied the odd glint amongst the debris. The metal crosses had survived. She resisted the urge to pick one out of the ashes—they seemed to be mocking her. She also saw the cross necklace. It seemed untouched. She left it.

Michiko patiently waited for Chisato.

"We had better go," she insisted at length.

Chisato nodded and they continued to walk to the church.

❀ ❀ ❀

The reverend's office was as musty as before, but it represented a pocket of peace for Chisato. The good reverend smiled as he usually did and welcomed her with open arms. But as he reached for her, Chisato stepped back, resisting him.

Rev. James let the moment pass as he informed that he had heard about the tragic events. Chisato supposed everyone had by that point.

"*Chai-sato-san,*" Rev. James opened, "*any word about Kiyo?*"

As Michiko translated, she looked at the floor and shook her head.

"*Well, I'm sure the police will find him.*" Rev. James turned to Michiko and said, "*Will you be able to take care of Chai-sato?*"

"*Yes, Sensei.*"

"*Good, you're in good hands,*" he said to Chisato.

He then escorted them downstairs to a *fujinkai* meeting. He entreated the gathered to open their collective heart.

She could stay with Michiko for the time being until a more permanent solution could be found. Her husband, Tamio, had no objection but avoided talking to her. Suited Chisato. The *fujinkai* provided all the clothing Chisato would need. The reverend went to the bank with Chisato since she had no money and no way of accessing the accounts. Michiko acted as interpreter. Although the bank officials were sympathetic, they balked since

Kiyoshi was not officially dead. The police were charged with finding him and a lawyer would have to be hired.

Chisato marvelled at what good people the Christians were. *Was this a trick?*

About a week later, Rev. James summoned Chisato and Michiko to his office again.

"*Chai-sato-san,*" he addressed, foregoing the niceties. "*There has been no word about Kiyo. He seems to have simply disappeared without a trace.*"

Michiko translated until Chisato understood.

"*I know you must be worried, but we have to be patient. Let the police do their job.*"

Chisato turned to Michiko to ask, "Is he dead?"

"*We don't know,*" Rev James said as an answer and then paused before continuing. "*Whatever his fate, it is God's will.*"

Chisato grimaced, unsatisfied with the pronouncement. *Empty words. They don't mean anything,* she thought. *Why would God will such a thing?*

She did ponder what *Sensei* Fujita would say. *Desire leads to suffering.* Probably, but again, the words would be meaningless, given her situation.

The Reverend James hemmed and let out a little cough before continuing. "*I know what he's been doing all this time. He sought advice from me. I of course could not and did not condone his behaviour, but I could see it was something he…something he greatly regretted…struggled with. I assume he was asking forgiveness of our Lord.*"

"You knew what he was doing?" Chisato said, somewhat astonished. And yet he never let on. He had said nothing to her. "So, he was asking forgiveness?"

"*I'm sure he was.*"

"I cannot forgive."

The reverend looked away and shuffled some papers.

"*We have to get you settled,*" he finally said. "*Would you like to stay in Vancouver?*"

"Where else would I go?"

"*Difficult to find you a place where you would be safe and can afford. Say, I have it!*" he suddenly said. "*Do you remember your friend? Sachiko...um...Sachiko Jai-gee-mura?*"

He had an unfortunate way of pronouncing Japanese names, but she understood and nodded. *What is it with these gaijin? These foreigners? Can't they speak properly?*

"*Well, you could join her, away from...um... 'misbehaving' husbands,*" he said with a smile, almost laughing. "*Would you like that?*"

Chisato didn't see the humour, but it did seem like a good idea. Michiko agreed. Who knew when and if Kiyoshi would reappear and in what kind of state of mind. She guessed she was in some danger and quickly warmed to the idea.

"When can I come back?"

"*Honestly, I don't know, but I'll keep in touch. The place I'm thinking of is part of my rounds where I minister to the needs of Christians. I'll see you from time to time.*"

"And where is that?" she asked tentatively, afraid to betray a confidence.

"*A place called Britannia Beach.*"

THE STEAMER OUT OF VANCOUVER was smaller than the *Heian Maru* and certainly not as luxurious, but it wasn't going across the Pacific. Chisato grumbled but remained silent to those around her as she boarded, her swollen stomach making it difficult to climb the gangplank. The *Marigold* slowly chugged up the coast towards an unknown destination. At least the landscape was beautiful, the sky cloudy, but the day pleasant enough despite the rain and the cold. The sea was calm.

Before they landed, Rev. James gave Chisato a pair of black rubber boots. Ugly things.

"*You'll need these. Wear them always,*" he told her as Michiko nodded.

She had seen her father and brother wear such things when working the fields, but she and her sister never had to. What kind of place was she headed? She linked arms with Michiko.

Britannia Beach, only reached by boat, was a small, rough settlement located about thirty-five miles north of Vancouver. It sat on the shores of Howe Sound. The surrounding mountains, frosted with snow, held up the cloud-heavy sky effectively. Chisato was somewhat comforted by what she encountered when the trio arrived in the early fall of 1941. The place reminded her of Hiroshima with its verdant and rugged terrain.

The town itself featured a line of ramshackle wooden structures along both sides of a muddy road with wooden planks as walkways to avoid caking good shoes with muck while climbing up the mountainside. She saw the wisdom of wearing boots even if she avoided the lumps of mud with every step.

The main industry was copper, located in Britannia Mine, a going business that produced enough ore to warrant a smelter in town. The smell was intense, inducing tears in Chisato and Michiko; oddly, Rev. James seemed to be immune.

"You can get used to anything," he explained.

The settlement itself was not her final destination. Instead, they climbed a winding pathway surrounded by lush forest high up above Britannia Beach to a settlement called Mount Sheer. The buildings there were the same as below, perhaps more dilapidated with cracked single-panelled walls and rough hewn roofs. Alarming most of all, they were perched on the side of the steep valley, the land just seemed to fall away. What she found in a corner of the tiny community of mining families was a community of Japanese.

She started to warm to the idea of living there, but then she stopped in her tracks.

"What is that?" she exclaimed as she plugged her nose.

"Oh, that's the abattoir," Rev. James explained. *"Like I said, you'll get used to it."*

Used to it? It's worse than the copper mines and smelter.

Turns out, the Japanese were the sole workers in the abattoir. *Maybe Buraku were the only ones willing to do the job.*

A fear grew within her. *Eta, buraku, the untouchables.* She placed a hand on her expanding belly to protect her baby.

The mud she slogged through added to her suspicion. The lumps she tried to avoid, as the minister revealed (as tactfully as he could), were piles of pig excrement. *Eta* was right.

❀ ❀ ❀

A harried woman soon came down the road to greet the trio. She was scrawny, frail with a drawn face. Her neck skin looked like crepe. Chisato didn't recognize her at first, but then it dawned on her.

"Sachiko-san!" she said eagerly, bowing before her friend. "It's you!"

She didn't look well, but at least, the bruises had well faded from her face, neck, and arms. Skinny with arms like wooden sticks, but she seemed fed well enough.

"I'm happy to see you, Chisato-san." Her voice was weak, but she looked her straight in the eye. "Come, let's go to your new home. Sensei explained everything to me. When is your baby due? Must be soon by the looks of you!"

On the way, Chisato introduced Michiko and marvelled how well Sachiko looked. A bit of a lie, but there was no need to bring up her past.

About ten cabins away, they came to a stop in front of a makeshift structure with hanging laundry in front and piles of wooden debris from carts, barrels, and the like lying all around as far as she could tell. There were mud splatters on some of the sheets; Sachiko stood in front of them. Chisato didn't care; she would help her friend with the laundry, perhaps asking *Sensei* to move the clothesline. But then, from inside, she heard a sound Chisato had not expected, a crying child.

Sachiko scurried inside soon to return with a baby in her arms. She introduced her child as Mary Jikemura, the name said in a flat Canadian accented tone.

"So cute, so precious!" Chisato enthused. "Mariko-chan, you're so beautiful."

"*Mary*, her name is *Mary*," Sachiko insisted.

Mary was born in the winter of 1940. Sachiko must've been early in the pregnancy when she was rescued. Chisato did shiver at the thought of Sachiko's husband forcing himself upon her. The pregnancy, however, was a blessing in her friend's mind. By the way Sachiko held and coddled the baby, it was obvious the mother treasured her child. It was lucky Sachiko hadn't lost it because of the beatings. Chisato did feel relieved that Sachiko had had her baby despite such dire circumstances.

The entrance to the one-room shack glowed, illuminated by an unknown source. Chisato again was stopped in her tracks. From the doorway, she could see candles burning everywhere. She could also make-out a crucifix or two displayed on the rough-hewn furniture. There were various pictures of *The Jesus* on the walls. *No statue, thank God*, she quipped to herself.

Sachiko had become a Christian. The obligation to Rev. James fulfilled for his help. But she seemed to have gone too far in her devotion.

"*God is great*," she declared in English as they stood amongst the adorations.

Rev. James uttered "*Amen*". Michiko bowed her head and mouthed some prayer. The two then left.

Chisato and Sachiko sat in the flickering lights of the candles as they communed over a simple meal of rice, tea, and *denbatsuke (pickled radish)—ochasuke*. She spied more than a few crucifixes around the room, more than the one or two she had seen initially from the doorway. *Do all Christians live like this?*

"God is looking over me," Sachiko started. "I am blessed to be taken care of by Him. He delivered me from my husband and for that I am grateful."

Who delivered her? she questioned silently. *Wasn't it me, Sensei, and Michiko?* Chisato was confused but she knew better not to speak. She turned her mind instead to her circumstances. How had she come to this: living in a broken-down shack in the middle of the wilderness with a baby on the way? She longed for the open space of the Akamatsu Compound in Hiroshima. She thought of her Hiroshima cloth bag in one of her suitcases. Her sister, her brother, her parents, only happy memories of them. She remembered her "isolation room" in Vancouver. Now only the constant foul odour was her companion. The air stung her eyes, and she surreptitiously dabbed them with a handy handkerchief, hoping that Sachiko wouldn't notice. Good thing her companion was lost in Jesus.

Chisato resided in a corner of the shack, uncomfortable with the cramped space and her pregnancy. But she felt safe, she reasoned, sharing the security with her friend and child. Kiyoshi and Sachiko's husband would never find them. At least, she learned what child rearing entailed. She even took her turn to bathe "Mary", wash her handmade cloth diapers, and even change them. *Sensei* had kindly moved the clothesline out of the way of mud-splatters.

And when the time came to deliver her child, Sachiko was a great help. There wasn't a doctor, of course, not even in the Britannia Beach settlement (an itinerant served the townsfolk's needs), but Sachiko acted like an efficient midwife. Some women in Mount Sheer also tended to her needs. They may have been *eta*, Chisato thought, but she drew close to them.

In late October 1941, with winter winds flowing down the mountainside to chill the bones and the occasional snowfall decorating the trees, baby Hideko Kimura greeted the world. Chisato held her child and her eyes beamed. Hideko seemed small but the air in her lungs blew out a deafening noise for the entire village to hear. The sound of happy laughter greeted the newborn.

Chisato snuggled her baby with great joy.

✿ ✿ ✿

Life settled into a routine. Both women did not worry about finances since the church sponsored them. The babies were well cared for; the villagers pitched in. The Reverend James was right, she could get used to anything. The only thing Chisato hated was her aromatic clothes. No amount of washing in lye soap could ever get rid of the smell.

The situation created an obligation, however, and Chisato could not let that stand.

The slaughterhouse town was filled with men rough-hewn and hard tempered to the work. They bathed once a week, but the choking, cloying smell always lingered. The women were hardy, the kind you might expect in the backwoods of a wild country. They may not have liked the unpleasant life, with all the trials, but they never complained.

There was no socializing during the week, but Saturdays, after the men bathed themselves in a jerry-rigged bathhouse yet again, and spruced up in their best clothes, stained and smelly as they were, everyone gathered in the Cookhouse, situated just far enough away from the slaughterhouse to make things tolerable, for a pie, coffee, and conversation party.

The ingredients were plentiful in the Cookhouse kitchen. Chisato volunteered to help Sachiko bake the pies, especially raisin, lemon, and apple, as many as were needed. The raisin was not too sweet, the lemon not too tart, the apple just right. Sachiko as it turned out was an excellent baker.

Chisato dreamed of opening a bakery on Powell Street after all of this was settled. Just like Furuya Store in Hiroshima's *Hondori*, a half-kilometre shopping mall. She would be Sachiko's partner. She liked the idea of being the "public face".

The first Saturday, the room bustled with workers and their wives. Chisato was nervous, until she saw everyone dig into the desserts with relish. She won many accolades that night even if Sachiko had done most of the work, still, Sachiko retreated to the cooking area.

But then Chisato committed a cardinal sin: she hadn't saved anyone a piece of pie to take home. Whatever was left she put away for meals during the coming week. This was not done; Sachiko was not there to tell her. Chisato subsequently suffered vicious gossip.

"I bet she sells them on the side... She has a rich husband, you know. Probably used to the fineries in life. No, look how fat she is...she keeps 'em for herself... she's so tight a coin squeaks in her hand."

Though Sachiko helped Chisato to correct the practice in the weeks to come, the villagers never let her forget it. So intense was the gossip that she couldn't even eat pie. In her mind, it always tasted bitter.

"I hate it here," she confessed to Sachiko. "I can't stand the looks from everyone, the loud whispers from those...those...dirty mouths. And you know they make sure I can hear them."

She needn't have fretted for long. On December 7th, life changed irrevocably.

29.   JANUARY – FEBRUARY 1942

THE GOVERNMENT UNEXPECTEDLY ANNOUNCED, AT least
to the inhabitants of Mount Sheer and Britannia Beach, something called an "Order-in-Council". It proclaimed a 100-mile
protected area along the coast. Both Chisato and Sachiko did
not know what to make of the order, and if it had any implications for them.

At the beginning of February, they were awakened by the
noise of men marching into camp. The cabin was solidly dark,
but the noise was as plain as day. Chisato looked outside and saw
numerous soldiers (army she guessed since they bore rifles) with
two grey plain-clothes men leading the way against the back-
drop of moonlight and glistening snow; they rousted out the
men, no matter how they were dressed, of each cabin ordering
them to the middle of the road.

Two came to their place with portable lights and searched
the inside to find nothing they wanted. The grim look on their
faces frightened Chisato as Sachiko ran to sit beside the two
sleeping babies. It was a wonder that they were not disturbed.
The soldiers left, the door gaping open. The wind streamed in
carried by the darkness.

Once the detachment was satisfied that they had what they
wanted in camp, one of the grey leaders left a piece of paper with a
woman, one of the wives, Sachiko identified. The man, an RCMP
officer as it turned out, then signalled the "prisoners" to be taken
away. And just like that, the procession of shivering Japanese men
(some only in muddied stocking feet) departed in single file with
soldiers pointing their rifles menacingly around them.

"What's going on?" Chisato asked.

The remaining gathered in the shining moonlight around
one of the wives who had the piece of paper. Sadayo Takehara,

an older and bilingual *Nisei*, translated as she read the paper. Holding it with both of her thin and shaking hands, she strained her eyes holding the document in front of her.

> BY ORDER OF THE GOVERNMENT OF CANADA IN ACCORD-
> ANCE WITH ORDER-IN-COUNCIL 365, ALL MALE JAPANESE
> BETWEEN THE AGES OF 18 AND 45 AND LIVING WITHIN
> THE 100-MILE PROTECTED ZONE OF BRITISH COLUMBIA ARE
> ORDERED TO BE REMOVED.

"But why?" screamed another wife within the darkness.

"I don't know," said Sadayo as she waved the paper. "That's all that's written here."

"He's done nothing. None of them have. Nothing illegal..."

A wave of worry rippled through the crowd. "What do we do now?"

"Canada is at war with Japan," Chisato whispered to Sachiko. But what she thought to herself was *I am not at war with Canada*.

❀ ❀ ❀

Last December, Chisato had read in a stray copy of the *Tariku Nippo*, brought by Michiko, that Canada quickly and perhaps rashly declared war on Japan. Japan had bombed someplace called Pearl Harbor. She thought it silly. *Why should Canada care? Was the country going to fight Japan on her own?* Of course, the United States soon declared. But the question remained: *What did this have to do with the Japanese in Canada?* She had not heard that German and Italian citizens were imprisoned. She soon learned that these *Enemy Aliens* or *Fascists* were in camps in Alberta, New Brunswick, Ontario, and Quebec. The *Nippo* emphasized that less than a 1,000. No way to tell the accuracy of the number.

The first Order-in-Council announced that all Japanese nationals must register with the Registrar of Enemy Aliens. Another required all persons of Japanese origin, regardless of citizenship, to register.

Chisato didn't know what to make of all this. She and her husband had already registered with the RCMP and not that long ago. Was this different? She was already declared an *Alien*. Now she was an *Enemy Alien*? She wasn't a naturalized citizen and had no plans to be, but she wanted to live in Canada. Was she suspected of planning to commit violent acts against the country? *Ridiculous*.

Then came the next Order-in-Council: P.C. 365.

At first, Chisato didn't believe any of it. She had been fooled too many times—Sachiko's husband and Kiyoshi's identity as a "man of God". Both she and Sachiko had to run away. Whom was she to believe? Yes, her brother was in China fighting a war, but that was China. How could Japan go to war with the world? She was never sure of the truth.

She longed to write her sister, but Canada cut off all mail to her home country. She wrote anyway.

Chiemi Oneesan,

Tell me it isn't true. Japan is not at war with Canada. I have no idea what will happen to me and all the other Japanese here. Many say they are Canadian, especially the Nisei, but I have no confidence the government will recognize the citizenship even if some of us were born here.

Have you heard from Hideki? Perhaps he knows something. How is Mother taking all this? I wish Otousan was still with us so he could bring reason and wisdom into our lives. How has the war in China affected you and Japan? I can't imagine how conflict in such a faraway land can mean anything to the Japanese people. Such a stupid war brought to our country by anonymous military leaders. What does the Emperor say?

I know you won't get this letter, but I feel better just having written. I hope I am in your thoughts. You are in mine.

Chisato

Her chief source of information was *The New Canadian,* the only community newspaper allowed to keep publishing. The women gathered in the Saturday Cookhouse to listen to a translation of the paper by Sadayo-*san.* The gathered rustled and grumbled after each meeting.

By February 1942, Order-in-Council P.C. 365 saw to it that all Japanese males, except the aged or in infirm health, were removed. No one knew to where. Some women broke down holding themselves to stop shaking. Chisato wondered about Kiyoshi. *Was he even found?*

Within that month, all women, children, and older males were ordered into the city of Vancouver to a place called Hastings Park or *The Pool.* At the beginning of March, a contingent of white men in heavy overcoats and with fedoras pulled down to hide their faces came to Sheer Mountain. Chisato and Sachiko observed two of them heading towards their cabin.

They stepped back from the doorway when the men came to stand in the opening. One said something that Chisato didn't understand, but he handed the two a sheet of paper. They then turned on their heels and walked away.

"What does it say?" Chisato asked.

Sachiko shook her head and said, "Let's find Takehara-san."

By the time they searched for their interpreter, many if not all the townsfolk had gathered once again in the Saturday night hall. A constant murmur rippled through the crowd. Many concerned faces greeted the two.

Eventually, Sadayo stood at the head of the gathering to address everyone. She cleared her throat before speaking.

"I'm sorry I took awhile to come here. It took some time to translate the difficult English." She cleared her throat again nervously. "We with our children have been ordered to report to Hastings Park in Vancouver with as much of our possessions as possible. 150 pounds, maximum."

She said lowering the page, "Hastings Park is in the Pacific National Exhibition Grounds."

A chorus of complaints reverberated. *The fairgrounds?* *There's no place there for us to stay! Are we staying with the horses?*

Ignoring the questions she couldn't answer, she continued, "We have forty-eight hours to appear at the docks of Britannia Beach where the BC Security Commission men will give further instructions."

"Commands, you mean!" a voice called out, greeted by other voices, loud and hostile.

"150 pounds is how much?" another yelled,

"If any of you have any property, like land or fishing boats, you are ordered to surrender it to Custodian of Enemy Alien Property. This is a 'protective measure' only."

The murmur turned into a loud grumble.

"According to Order-in-Council 1665," she finished.

"That's a laugh!" someone shouted. "Who has a fishing boat here? Or even land?"

Sachiko must've thought of her neighbours and friends in Steveston, Chisato guessed.

"If we owned land, wouldn't we be on it?" The grumble turned into a bitter laugh mixed with groans and complaints.

About forty-eight hours later, Chisato with Hideko in her arms, Sachiko and Mary stood on the Britannia Beach dock. Mary in a heavy green coat with a small crucifix around her neck stood among their boxes, suitcases, and trunk, brought along by volunteer white men from town. She had no idea how much her possessions weighed. They sat on the wooden planks of the dock waiting to be loaded onto the *Marigold*, the same steamer that had brought them so many months before.

Volunteer *gaijin* men from Britannia Beach and Mount Sheer had helped them haul the belongings down to the dock. Once women had deposited the luggage on the pier, they too retraced their steps to lend a hand.

Other men, Sachiko pointed out, had appeared and started ransacking the empty cabins, taking whatever they found that was useful. They heard shouting and crying at one point and saw Takehara-*san* wrestling with someone over an axe.

"*It's my husband's,*" she screamed in Japanese. "*He'll need it when he comes back!*"

She lost of course. The man slapped her face in the end, and she let go. She stood shaking and crying. Other women moved to comfort her.

Sachiko and Chisato walked away. Nothing could be done.

"Such a pig. He should be in the abattoir," Sachiko growled. "*Bokenasu.*" *Ass.*

It was a cold day, though it wasn't raining, which was a blessing. The sun however was well-hidden behind a press of clouds. The two women pulled their winter coats tighter. They looked odd in their Japanese farm garments, boots, and overcoats. They didn't care; the cold and mud weren't going to chill and soil them.

An officious *gaijin* approached them and inspected their belongings. He bent his long body over the luggage.

"*No radios, record players, cameras, or other restricted items?*" he growled.

They had no idea what he was saying.

The *gaijin* did a cursory inspection and grunted. He then spied Mary and the crucifix. "*What do we have here?*" he said and ripped the metal cross away.

Mary screamed and Sachiko confronted the man. "*Give that back!*"

"*Can't be no Christian! She probably stole it,*" he accused and walked away.

"*Stinking lousy Japs. Take a bath once in a while,*" he said as a parting shot.

Sachiko bent to her knees and hugged her daughter to console her. She rubbed the red mark around the neck away.

A familiar voice said, "Pay him no mind. He knows not what he does."

"Michiko-*san!*" Chisato squealed in surprise.

"Chai-sato!" called out Rev. James. "*So good to see you again.*"

He rushed forward and jerked and shook Chisato's hand, something she would never get used to. She growled under her breath.

The two had made the trip to greet the church's charges. Both women were glad to see them. Rev. James' wide smile gave them a measure of comfort. Michiko nodded in sympathy as she translated.

"Why are they doing this to us?" Sachiko pleaded.

Rev. James took a breath before speaking. "*We're at war,*" was all he said as an explanation.

"But we're not the enemy," Chisato insisted.

"*I know that,*" the minister said reassuringly. "*But they think you are.*"

"Where are they taking us?"

Michiko leaned in and whispered something in the reverend's ear. He nodded. "*To Vancouver.*"

That sounded good. They were going back to Powell Street. A warm feeling came over Chisato and she smiled to herself.

"Where's my husband?" Sachiko asked with trepidation. A cold sweat appeared on her brow.

"*Don't know exactly, but I heard the Mounties did a 'clean sweep' of Steveston.*"

She looked to Chisato as if to question the term. No answer was to be had. Not even Michiko said anything to clear the mystery.

✿ ✿ ✿

Vancouver was a welcome sight. The majestic mountains, the blue sea, the smells of the logging industry, the brown, anonymous buildings, the varying widths of streets, the lights, and appetizing aromas of Chinatown, and the Buddhist church, Ernie's, Fuji Chop Suey all meant home to the two women. She hoped Powell Street was intact, but in her heart of hearts, she knew it was no more, even if Michiko and a few others still lived there. It was disintegrating, its component parts breaking off and disappearing.

Chisato settled into the serenity of the voyage back to civility. She loved the smooth sailing of the boat, the tranquil shoreline, and the gentle lapping of the water. Even the cold air felt good on her face and in her lungs.

She had only one concern. Chisato had no idea where she would stay since her house, she assumed, was destroyed beyond repair; she couldn't live there amongst the rubble. Sachiko too had no desire to go back to Steveston. The haunt of old violence.

"Sensei, are we going to live in the church? In Powell Street?" Sachiko asked through Michiko.

"I'm afraid not," Rev. James said glumly. *"You're going to Hastings Park."*

They looked at one another. *"What is Ha...ing Park?"* Sachiko asked as best as she could in English. They had clearly ignored or forgotten that part of the order to leave Britannia Beach. It made no sense to them anyway. Not even the complaints raised by some in the crowd.

"It's a 'distribution centre' set up by the Security Commission. For everyone from out-of-town. You'll be there until they can send you to a camp outside the 'protected area'."

"Where?"

"I don't know. I'm sorry."

They held their daughters close to their bodies. There was obviously something he wasn't telling them, and he wasn't about to.

Another thing Sachiko wondered about was the fate of her husband. She confessed to her friends on the boat that she didn't know what the *Sensei* meant by "clean sweep". Michiko finally explained to her that her husband was probably arrested and taken away to the interior road gangs that were formed earlier in February.

Sachiko hissed, "Good."

Michiko confessed her own husband, Tamio, suffered that fate. She held faith in the Lord that he would return to her.

30.   MARCH 1942

HASTINGS PARK BROODED ON EAST Hastings Street in
the far east side of Vancouver. The grounds housed a racetrack,
where confiscated cars were stored temporarily, and the Pacific
National Exhibition, an annual provincial fair held in the summer and enjoyed by all. The racetrack's facilities, a collection of
buildings, became a holding centre for Japanese Canadians from
outside Vancouver until they could be sent to ghost town internment camps...eventually.

The Pool was the horse pavilions. The cavernous mostly
concrete buildings segregated men and women. The Livestock
Building's horse stalls were quickly converted, but not removed,
for mothers and their children. There was no privacy, so blankets
were hung between stalls. Otherwise, cots in the Horse Show
Building were lined up for people to sleep side by side. Open
toilets, more like troughs, were set for the "convenience" of the
prisoners. The food was meagre at best in the makeshift mess
halls, separated by gender. No consideration to the Japanese diet
was given. No rice, no *shoyu*. The place was dusty, crowded, and
smelly—the horses left their calling-card, and nothing could be
done to get rid of it. The odour was tear-inducing. Various diseases festered and hunted.

Chisato and Sachiko with their babies were summarily
dropped into these conditions. Rev. James said his goodbyes
as he and Michiko were asked to leave. "*Godspeed*," he invoked.
Michiko promised to come visit.

"Tell us about your husband," Chisato said.

Michiko nodded and left.

Inside, Sachiko observed it was like the Immigration
Building. Chisato said it was worse as she held her nose and

wiped her eyes. It was more concentrated than Sheer Mountain with its abattoir, though it was hard to compare the two. At least, her fetid clothes wouldn't be noticed. They were assigned adjacent stalls. Small comfort.

Besides the smell, the two were greeted by a chorus of crying. Here and there, Chisato spied mothers convulsing in tears on their cots, some into their straw pillows, others in a seated position, or heard behind hanging blankets. She wondered what was wrong but then decided it was *The Pool* itself. She felt like crying herself as she held Hideko close to her. She entertained the thought of returning to Hiroshima. Was there anything really keeping her in Canada? She had warm and sad thoughts of the Akamatsu compound, with all its rooms. Even the *Whispering Oni Room*. She longed for the peace and solitude, the fresh air. Perhaps the authorities would let her leave. They don't want her, she reasoned. They didn't want Terumi. Maybe she could get consumption. *Can't be that bad.*

One nearby woman was weeping inconsolably, incessantly. Finally, the two women approached her in her stall.

Yaeko Ebisuzaki was a young woman with the palms of her hands over her face. Her hair was tied into a bun, and she wore a plain *kimono* and *zori* on her feet. Though she was seated, she appeared small in stature, her feet did not touch the ground.

"What's wrong?" Chisato asked as gently as she could.

Sachiko grimaced and said, "Are you afraid?"

Yaeko looked up, her soft features contorted with grief, it seemed. Smooth skin distorted by pain.

A neighbour watched from the edge of the stall. "They took her baby away."

"They did what?"

"They took her baby away," she repeated.

"But why?"

"She was sick and had to be *quarantined*."

"What is *quar…*?"

"Separated and isolated" was the answer.

Seemed simple enough and Sachiko said so. "Nothing could be done."

"Don't be cruel," Chisato rebuked as she sat next to Yaeko.

"Nonsense, God will provide and protect her baby."

"How can you say that? Look around you! Why did God put us here? Was He really looking out for us?" Chisato obviously had had enough of the *God Talk*.

"The Lord delivered me from my husband, and He will deliver me from this place!"

Chisato looked at her incredulously.

"I don't know God's plan," Sachiko continued. "None of us do, but we must maintain our faith. He will deliver us unto the Promised Land. He always has and He always will."

"Well until He does, we are going to have to take care of ourselves," Chisato said with finality.

* * *

Chisato was tired of arguing about God and "His mysterious ways". She fell silent whenever Sachiko talked to her. Sachiko didn't seem to mind or even notice. She went about decorating their stall with the one crucifix she had hidden from the authorities and brought from Sheer Mountain. She had scrounged a candle from around the mess hall. Where she found the matches was anyone's guess.

She placed both on a wooden box she had found, and twice a day, Sachiko kneeled before the makeshift altar, lit the candle, and prayed. She had asked Rev. James for a Bible, but none was forthcoming. Chisato tolerated it all, the candle helped with the smell of the place.

Chisato decided she would hold on to her faith in the Buddha. He taught that we must be grateful for all we have. She was alive, her child was a joy, her future was unknown and somewhat bleak, but she never believed that the Canadian government would do them irreparable harm. Despite the obligation she had to Rev. James and the Christian church, she moved away from the idea that an external and invisible being of enormous power would rescue them. Even if all she had to do was pray.

Besides, there was a present danger that posed a threat in Hastings Park: the spread of disease. Measles, mumps, chicken pox, dysentery, scarlet fever, and other communicable diseases ripped through the dormitories like an *Oni Wind*.

Sachiko of course believed God would protect her if she prayed for "deliverance from evil". Chisato was more circumspect. She did everything she could to protect Hideko. She laundered her child's clothes and diapers everyday. She cleaned and washed the stall as well. She stayed away from anyone she suspected of coming down with something.

She found out that Yaeko's baby had been taken away because the child was sick with scarlet fever. Chisato assumed she knew where but was not saying; instead, Yaeko's face had grown pale, and her eyes trembled in fear. The authorities would not let her visit.

Chisato began feeling a weight on her shoulders.

To avoid embarrassment, both women and most others avoided Yaeko, who simply sat on her cot in her stall whimpering most of the time. She could not be consoled anyway.

✿ ✿ ✿

About a month later, Chisato received a notice, in Japanese of all things, that made her laugh. It was another Order-in-Council. The government in its wisdom informed her that all of her and her husband's property must be surrendered to the Custodian for Enemy Alien Property. It would be well taken care of as a "protective measure".

"They can have my house for all I care!"

She then thought of her husband's businesses, though she never knew exactly what he owned. Maybe she could claim them or, at least, the money in the bank once the war was over. She chuckled and tore up the letter.

She later pondered the implications of the order as she made her way from the mess hall. With Hideko in her arms, she

suddenly heard a wailing commotion. It was Sachiko screaming and pleading with two uniformed nurses in her stall. As she
drew closer, Chisato saw one had grabbed Mary, while the other
kept Sachiko at bay. Sachiko struggled against the nurse, desperate to secure her child. She howled at the top of her lungs.
Mary's legs grew red in the nurse's grip.

Chisato tried to interfere, but with Hideko, she could do
little to help. A tall, white doctor in a white coat stood in her way.
He said something in the cursed English language. She called
out to Sachiko, asking what was happening.

"They're taking Mary away. Put her into *quarantine!*" Her
voice was ragged, but understandable.

"Why? She's not sick!"

"They say she is. I told them...I told them God and I can
take care of her...but they won't listen. They won't let me go
with Mary..."

The burly nurse pulled at Mary with must've seemed like
unfamiliar, large, and rough hands. She kept Sachiko at bay as
she strained against the strength of the tormentor, while Mary
continued to scream, wail, and squirm to get away. Her face was
flushed. She reached pathetically for her mother.

With one final push, the nurse knocked Sachiko to the cot.
She let out a groan and gave up as she quivered silently in her
sorrow.

Chisato quickly moved to her side and tried to offer comfort. The doctor and nurses stole away with Mary. The child continued to scream for her mother, the sound fading away.

Sachiko immediately fell to her knees beside the bed, clasped
her hands in front of her and began praying intensely. Shaking
her clasped hands.

Chisato didn't know what to do. Fortunately, Hideko started
crying and so had to be soothed.

Once her baby was settled, Chisato immediately went next
door to find Yaeko. She would know where the children were.

Yaeko was asleep in her cot, but that didn't stop Chisato. She
grabbed her by the front of her chemise and shook her awake.

"Yaeko-san! Yaeko! Wake up!"

She groaned and cracked open her eyes.

"Yaeko, you've got to tell me where they put your baby! Wake up, wake up!"

When she fully came to and understood what was being asked of her, she shook her head and then buried her face in her pillow.

Frustrated, Chisato let her go and told her to watch her child. Yaeko agreed and came to a seated position. Chisato then began wandering the crowded aisles of *The Pool* asking any if they knew where the sick babies and children were taken. No one knew, so she decided to walk to the hospital area of the building. Seemed like the logical place to find a patient.

It took awhile, but a Japanese orderly finally pointed towards a distant corner of Building A. A former poultry barn was set up as a makeshift hospital with 180 beds. Stray lumps of straw supported about sixty beds. Adjacent to the area was an isolation ward for TB patients.

Were these people to be deported?

Chisato, as luck would have it, met a tall Japanese doctor with a toothy smile. Dr. Uchida kindly directed her to another area of the building,

"You want the *quarantine* area," he said in a soothing voice. "For general disease." He pointed in a direction diagonally opposite the crude facilities. He looked concerned with furrowed brow but wouldn't say why.

She soon found out. She wasn't sure what to expect but, once she got to the other side, she found a hole in the floor. Upon closer inspection, she discovered a staircase that led down to a dark basement.

In all good conscience, who would separate mothers and their children, sick or not?

An exhaust of stale and fetid air rushed up from below as if to coat her in slime. Chisato covered her mouth and nose with her hand, before stepping back. Her eyes watered. She wiped them with the sleeve of her other arm. The smell was evil. She hesitated to step on the first step, but she did and then stopped. It was like the blackness licked at her feet, pulling her down into the depths.

She heard a chorus of babies and children calling, weeping, and wailing. Many asking for their mamas. She shook and retreated carefully, stepping back onto the main floor as the sound of steps came rushing up. A woman in a nurse's uniform materialized as if appearing from behind a curtain. She spoke sharply to her and motioned for her to move away.

Chisato didn't understand her words, of course, but she obeyed. A nearby inmate told her the doctors keep the very sick children down in the *Dungeon*, a cramped, pitch-black room with no ventilation, coal dust, and little light. It was normally an underground coal and animal feed storage area. A true *Oni Room*.

"How long?" she asked.

"Until they're better or dead," the woman said ominously. "Usually ten days but some for weeks."

※ ※ ※

The next night, Sachiko was sick with worry, her strength sapped by it. All she could do was pray since no one listened to her pleas.

After Hideko was sleeping soundly in their shared cot, Chisato sat up and saw that Sachiko was also asleep. The weight on her shoulders had grown noticeably heavier. Sachiko could do nothing to relieve the pressure. She sought peace in dreamless sleep.

Chisato looked at Hideko and wondered what she would do if they came for her. She decided to look for Mary again. She stood up and moved out of the stall. The light was dull but there was enough to be able to find her way.

She soon enough came to the hole in the floor, a gaping grave. She took a deep breath and stepped down the steps. They creaked. She bent down and felt for the running board of the staircase. Her other hand touched the wooden wall beside the staircase; there was no handrail.

As she made her way down in a crouch, the darkness poured into her eyes, blinding her. She slowly sank into the blackness like wading into an inhospitable ocean.

At the bottom of the stairs, she noticed there was a dull light source coming from somewhere. A small opening for an ancient coal chute; there were no windows. Some light came down the staircase offering hope for escape, but no patient moved.

Chisato sensed the small size of the room. She could barely make out the large number of beds all crammed together. She felt the enormity of the situation. The place was hardly silent with soothing sleep. Coughing, crying, and desperation reigned.

No nurse was on duty; in fact, no one was, not even guards. She perceived older girls moving about taking care of or comforting the younger children; they coughed steadily and loudly as they did so. Everyone wallowed in their illness; no medical staff was present.

Chisato started to whisper in a soft but hoarse voice, "Mari-chan. Mariko." Then she remembered. She said as best as she could, "Mary." She repeated the name as she felt her way among the beds.

Some children asked, "Okaachan?"

"No, dear child."

"Please take me to her. Please. Take me out of here."

An older girl lying with a baby asked, "Have you come to take us out?"

"I'm sorry, no."

"I can't take care of all of these babies by myself. They need their mothers."

"Why are you caring for them?"

"Who else is there?" The girl began sobbing.

Chisato lifted her hand to caress the teenager's hair.

At that moment, a phalanx of light beams pierced the darkness from upstairs. Several footsteps rushed down the steps.

Voices called out as the children sat up, some startled, and began to cry.

Chisato froze as hands grabbed her and began dragging her out of the *Dungeon*. She protested in vain. "Stop! Stop! I'm looking for Mary, Mary Jikemura. You must let me find her!" Her words were in Japanese of course and the anonymous staff couldn't understand a word.

The next thing Chisato knew, she was sitting in some office with a Canadian man in a suit and tie sitting behind a desk in front of her. Two others were there, a nurse and a *Nisei*, a kind looking woman with a round face and sympathetic eyes, the interpreter no doubt.

The *gaijin* looked tired, but he stared at her intensely. "What were you doing down in the quarantine room? Don't you know that you're not allowed in there in case you catch something and take it back to the general population. You could infect everyone!"

"I was looking for Mary Jikemura," she said through Sachi Tokunaga, the *Nisei* interpreter. "To see if she was all right."

"*Are you her mother?*"

"No...I'm a friend. My name is Chisato Kimura."

"*Why didn't the mother come with you?*"

"She's in no condition to do so. She may be sick herself. Sick with worry, for sure."

"Well," he said conclusively, "*I have some bad news for you and the mother.*"

Chisato didn't like the sound of that.

"*Mary Jik...Jik... your friend's daughter died earlier today. She was taken out to be 'dealt with.'*"

The news hit Chisato hard. She gasped and held her throat. The weight crushed her body as she thought about Hideko and felt the guilt of fate.

"How...how?" was all she could muster.

"*Doctor's report says she died of...*" He shuffled some papers in front of him until he found the page he was looking for. "*...pain.*"

✳ ✳ ✳

Chisato with Sachi accompanying her walked back to her stall. They found Sachiko on her knees again in front of her altar, the candle unlit, praying and whispering, "Oh Lord, how could you forsake me? How could you?" Someone had obviously told her, and she reacted with prayer.

"Jesus will save her. He will save me."

You bokenasu. You damn fool. What did your lord do to save your child? To deliver you from evil? You damn fool. Her thoughts kindled with anger inside her.

A neighbour said the authorities wouldn't allow Sachiko to see her daughter. There was no funeral, no last rites. The Reverend James had not come to comfort her. She was Christ on the cross.

Sachi Tokunaga turned and left without saying a word.

Chisato ignored her stall-mate, brought Hideko closer to her and fell asleep. Her lingering thoughts drifted to the Buddha. A few hours later, something woke her. She looked over to Sachiko and saw that she was slumped with her head on the cot, her arms and hands fallen to the floor, her legs collapsed underneath her body. Her face was awash in the salted remnants of tears. She was mercifully asleep.

Chisato gazed into the dull night. Thoughts raced around her brain when disparate parts of the darkness started to gather. She watched in awe as the shadows formed into a figure—no distinct features, just a mass of black air. It soon expanded and drifted to float over her.

She was immobile. She gazed at it in wonderment lying on her back. And in the next moment, she whispered, "Otousan."

31.   MAY 1942

AFTER HER DAUGHTER HAD DIED, Sachiko left *The Pool*. Two
suited men, a doctor, two nurses, and a guard came to escort her.
Chisato watched closely. Sachiko looked terrible as she gathered
her belongings. Her back was curved as she struggled until one
of the nurses helped to pack everything. Sachiko's eyes were hollow, her face thin and weary, all strength seemed to have abandoned her. More worn down than when she was being abused
by her husband. There was no telling where her friend was going,
but Chisato hoped it was to see Mary for the last time.

It wasn't long after that Chisato received word that she and
Hideko were to be transported to someplace called Sandon. She
had no idea where it was; she had a hard time pronouncing the
word. But a weight lifted off her.

A warmth spread over her abdomen. Someone had told her
Sandon was a camp for the Buddhists in the community. The
government had resolved to segregate the Japanese community by religion. She had no idea who had told the authorities
Buddhism was her religion, but her burden felt lighter.

But then Rev. James and Michiko came to visit her. The minister stood before her with a worried look. Michiko was ready to
translate.

"Michiko-san, how is your husband? Did he return?"

Before she could answer Rev. James spoke up, *"Chaisato, I've
been told you're going to Sandon,"* he began. *"That's got to be a mistake. You should be going to Tashme or New Denver...Christian
camps."*

She of course had no idea what he was saying. Places like
Tashme and New Denver meant nothing. It soon became apparent that he didn't want her in Sandon.

"N...n...no," she said nervously and quietly in English.

"*Now, you leave it to me...*" the reverend reassured.

"*No,*" she repeated louder.

"*I'll have this all cleared up in no-time.*"

"*No!*" she insisted.

Rev. James' words caught in his throat. It made him stand up straight.

"*No? What do you mean no?*" he asked, his forehead furrowed with confusion and worry.

Michiko translated. "*It means I am not going to those places. I want to go to Sandon.*"

"*But it means—*"

"It means, I want to be with my own. Your Jesus did nothing to help my husband. Your Jesus did not prevent *The Pool.* Your Jesus did not protect us from being exiled. Your Jesus did not save *Mary.* Your Jesus...did nothing for me...you—"

She stopped in mid-rant. "I'm sorry, Sensei. I misspoke. I...I..."

"*No,*" Rev James said as he recovered. "*You meant every word. I don't understand, but I forgive...*" He stopped mid-sentence. In a moment or two, he said, "*We'll leave you now. Despite how you feel, I will say, God bless and God speed.*

"*I forgive you,*" he repeated.

As she watched the two leave, Chisato felt a scream catch in her throat. *Nothing to forgive*, she thought.

Michiko turned and glared at her. She sneered, "You never had the true faith." Chisato felt for Michiko, but she had decided to discard her obligation to Rev James and the Christian church.

✿ ✿ ✿

So, it was in early May, when the sun was bright and warm on the horizon, that Chisato, her luggage at her feet, while holding an exhausted and slumbering Hideko in her arms, waited to board the train that would take them to Sandon. The platform was crowded with other Japanese. She thought she recognized some from her secret visits to the temple. A young, new priest had taken charge. Rev. Tsuji was the first *Nisei* Buddhist priest and the last to leave Japan for Canada just after he was ordained, as it happened. He beamed with compassion as he saw to everyone's needs.

In a moment of contemplation, Chisato thought of Sachiko and Kiyoshi. She hadn't seen either since they left her life. Neither Rev. James nor Michiko had been seen since their visit. Chisato hoped she would be forgiven some day. She would probably never know.

What she did know was that the next chapter in her life was about to begin for her and Hideko. She just didn't know what that meant. Sachi Tokunaga had told her that Sandon was a "land of perpetual night".

"The devil's breath runs through the valley where the ghost town is. Don't breathe or the air will turn to ice in your lungs!"

Sachi was a silly girl dependent on rumour to get through life. Chisato harrumphed and thought, *I'm used to oni and cold rooms.*

How she missed her sister, Chiemi, and even her brother, Hideki, a pest but a loving pest. Her mother must be worried for the three of them. Regret visited her for insisting on leaving for adventure in this damnable country. Would she have been happier in Japan?

The shadow that had visited her in her stall drifted across her imagination. She hadn't thought of it until now. She felt a comfort rise in her body as she suddenly knew all would be well despite the uncertainty and adversity. *Otousan will watch over us.* She held on to that feeling as she kissed her sleeping daughter.

The devil's breath.

CHIEMI

The Buddha Dharma: the Eightfold Path
The 4th Noble Truth
Right View

32.   LATE SUMMER 1939

IMPERMANENCE. FUJITA *SENSEI* SPOKE OF impermanence,
back when Chiemi's mother took her daughters, she and Chisato,
to the Daisho-in, an expansive temple complex on Miyajima
Island. The tall red gateway standing in front welcomes worshippers into the island's sacred embrace. Chiemi's favourite
had to be the Itsukushima Shrine, which juts out into the water.
Though considered a Shinto shrine, its distinctive orange colour
reflected the amalgamation of gods and the Buddha. A syncretic
place of worship.

For the girls, the lit lanterns along the shore were particularly pretty at night. Their mother, Haruye, too found peace in
walking along the path.

Fujita *Sensei* was a handsome man, with intense eyes but
with a face of soft features. Chiemi didn't understand what he
meant by the word until much later.

When the girls became women, Chiemi made a point of
going twice a year, *Hanamatsuri* and *Obon*, birth and death,
rebirth, the circle of life, to sit in meditation and contemplate the
Buddha. Chisato usually accompanied her, but the younger sister had married last year, and her immigration papers had finally
been approved by the Canadian government far sooner than the
usual two-year waiting period. She left to join her husband earlier in the summer. With all the activity surrounding her sister's
departure, Chiemi delayed going to Miyajima until the end of

the *Obon* season. In the first letter to her sister, she quipped that the Buddha wouldn't mind if she were a little late.

The small-craft ferry ride from Ujina Port was fun, always was; the lapping blue-green waves put her mind at ease. She once spotted jellyfish floating along side. Their diaphanous bodies seemingly the suspension of body and soul in the eternal sea. She always brought a colourful bib for the stone statue, the Shinto protectors of young women and children, that lined the stairs of the temple.

She let out a slow sigh. Impermanence leads to change and change leads to suffering, *dukkha*. All three link together in the flow of life. She placed her faith in the *Three Jewels of Buddhism: the Buddha, the Dharma, the Sangha; the Buddha, the Buddha's Teachings, the Buddhist Community.*

❁ ❁ ❁

In the cool *Oni Room*, Chiemi sat on her legs sitting *seiza*. Her father had relaxed his prohibition of the use of the room since there were only the three of them left at home. The acrid smell of incense that filled her nostrils and lungs came back to her in a reminiscence of her childhood visit to Miyajima. A large statue of the Buddha down a corridor of Itsukushima sat in peaceful repose. His hands poised in a *mudra* of compassion and generosity—the palm of the right hand faced outwards, and the index finger touched the thumb in the perfect circle of the *Dharma*. The Buddha was always near as memories abounded.

She contemplated her recent life. Chisato had married Kimura Kiyoshi, a son of a naval shipbuilding family in Kure, in the spring of 1938 and emigrated a year or so later. Their parents worried, not knowing what hardships she would have to endure in a foreign country. But that was what she wanted.

Akamatsu Hideki was ambitious to get-on with his army career. He had kept ranting about the campaign in Manchukuo. All could tell he was frustrated that he wasn't yet into the fray.

"Did you read about Honjo-san?" he shouted to the family one day before he entered the army. Honjo Tadanobu was

Hideki's classmate, a preposterously skinny boy who worked his way into the army through physical work. "He charged a machine gun with raised sword. Cut down, being torn to pieces in the effort. Such an honourable death!"

Chiemi objected. "But he died horribly! So many are dying in Manchukuo. I hear about 10,000 so far."

"That's not true! Stop reading the paper!" he chided. "Don't read what you don't understand! He shines with glory!"

She walked away, the odour of burnt ants enveloped her.

❀ ❀ ❀

When Hideki was finally and officially inducted into the army, Chiemi and family attended the marvelous ceremony. She loved the pomp and ritual. Though she didn't approve of her brother's zeal for military service, she was taken in by the events of the day and grew excited at the sight of her brother in full uniform, so handsome and resplendent. It was a day to remember.

Once in the army, Hideki came home intermittently, though he had every Sunday off and twenty military and patriotic holidays during the year. It seemed he didn't want to see his family. Whenever he did, however, he received a hero's welcome, especially the first time about two months after induction.

Chisato made a point of being there for that auspicious occasion. Chiemi could see the glee on Chisato's and *Okaasan's* faces in seeing him, *Okaa* especially. She was so proud of her son that she arranged a lavish dinner, including his favourite dishes: *maze gohan* (rice mixed with vegetables), steamed fish Chinese style, and steamed *tofu*. The white rice must've cost a small fortune on the Black Market.

He had changed in appearance: his hair was cut close to his scalp, with some scabs where the razor's blade had cut him, he had a three-day growth of beard (which he shaved off immediately after returning and before his sisters could tease him), his eyes had darkened with bags under them, and he appeared sullen, rarely speaking. He was still skinny, perhaps skinnier, but no one commented on it. For most of the meal, he sat hunched over, mute about his experiences in the military even as his father praised him.

"We received a letter from your Commanding Officer, a Colonel Hashimoto," Otousan said at dinner. "Very reassuring. He said we should consider him your father of the army. I like that. He'll take care of you. You should have a sword," he observed. "Let me buy you one. Maybe get a better fitting uniform—"

"No, Otousan, no!" he replied adamantly coming alive.

"But why? We can afford it."

Silence was his answer.

✾ ✾ ✾

Chiemi was the only one who had any insight into Hideki. After that night in the garden the summer before when Chiemi gave her brother the pouch of home soil and saw the bruises on his face and neck, she constantly worried about him. More so after a night bath.

> The nightly hot water ofuro took place in a separate extension of the large concrete kitchen. Otousan had built a comfortable but small room just off and attached to the cooking area. It featured an oversized, steep-sided wooden tub with comfortable wooden benches and stools surrounding. There was a crude drainage system for family members to wash before relaxing in the tub. The kitchen stove was fired up to boil the water from the pump. It was the girls who filled the tub with buckets of hot water.
>
> Chisato thought the tub was made from a shoyu casket, but Hideki said they were too small to accommodate their bodies. When the three were babies, Haruye dutifully washed the children before handing each off to Gunhei who was in the tub. But that was years ago. In any case, members of the household enjoyed the ritual: Otousan first, followed by Hideki, Okaasan, Chiemi, and last Chisato.
>
> Chiemi became visibly distressed when she saw her brother's naked body covered with bruises during his first visit home,

much more than just his face and shoulders. She never com-
mented on them, too embarrassing to call attention to them.
After all, Hideki said nothing.

The shadows of brutality inspired her to take a long piece of
white cloth and stitch it with red thread, 1,000 knots, for a *senninbari*, a belt to protect him. *He will suffer but will survive China.*

She gave it to him and the Hiroshima bag of soil in the
garden the night he left for the army, for war, for glory. Chiemi
sighed with relief afterwards, even if the arguments continued.

"We are invincible," Hideki proclaimed. "It's because of the
Emperor's divine spirit. It's in all of us. The Nankin are weak…
nothing. We can't be defeated."

Ever since the destruction of Nanking, *Nankin*, a slang word
for the Chinese, came into popular use.

"But everything is impermanent. Everything changes,"
Chisato argued. "Yes, our military is everywhere, but that will
change."

"Don't talk blasphemy!" he yelled. "We defeated Russia. We
defeated China and we conquered Manchuria. We are again at
war with China, and we'll defeat them again. Look at how easily
we invaded and subjugated Nanking. We are working towards
invading the Philippines and Indochina. There is no end to our
ambition and power."

"What will happen when Europe and America get involved?"

That gave him pause.

"They're…already involved. But just with words. Nothing
but…complaints. They're weak, afraid of Japan's might!" he said
with some trepidation. "They are!" His voice had faltered.

She looked at him with a skeptical eye. He spoke patriotic-
ally but more to convince himself, she thought.

A few months later, Hideki came home unexpectedly. He
appeared haggard, like he hadn't slept in days. He was sullen,
weak, and noncommunicative. Though he did say he wanted to
talk to Father.

Chiemi, horrified at her brother's condition, followed the two at a distance to the *Oni Room*. She stood just outside and listened as best as she could.

"What's wrong, son?" Gunhei asked as he sat in his favourite position.

Hideki did not sit; instead, he positioned himself in front of his father and bent over slightly as if a weight was pushing him down.

"Otousan, I will come straight to the point, I wish to leave the military."

Gunhei didn't say a word. Instead, he let his son continue.

"I am but an insect among insects. If I am killed, there will be no glory."

"Have you seen men get killed?"

"Yes," he said and paused before speaking again. "I don't see the point of it all."

"I understand, but you were the one who chose to be in the army." Gunhei stood and placed his hand on his son's shoulder.

"And now I am the one who chooses to leave," Hideki said emphatically.

Chiemi turned away. Still, she heard her father talking about bringing shame to the family. Hideki had committed himself to the military life and *Otousan* impressed upon him the imperative of seeing it through. There wasn't anything Father or anyone could do.

Chiemi walked away in order to avoid being discovered by her brother or father.

That night, Hideki left in the darkness.

33.

ABOUT MID-AUTUMN 1939, AFTER SENDING off Chisato and trying not to worry about Hideki, Chiemi's parents came to her after she returned from work at the city hospital. She wasn't a nurse or any other kind of medical professional; instead, she helped make comfortable the elderly and/or some of the convalescing soldiers. She did as her betters bid her to do.

Because of the government's policy of drafting civilians to man various positions connected to the war effort, she couldn't quit even if she wanted to. She received the notice of conscription from General Araki Sadao, head of the *Spiritual Mobilization Movement*, himself. Chiemi was surprised that she should warrant such attention. She reasoned it was due to her father's status in Hiroshima.

The wind was up that day. The maple trees surrounding the compound bristled perhaps foretelling rainy weather. Chiemi appreciated the breeze since it took away the heat. Her aversion to hot weather made her seek coolness wherever she was.

"Chiemi-chan," her father opened, "I'm glad we can talk."

"Of course, Otousan."

"Your mother and I feel...that is, it's time you..."

Growing impatient, Haruye stepped forward. "You should be married," she said bluntly. Chiemi's mother was a no-nonsense kind of woman; she always seemed to have a scowl on her face. Like her husband, she was completely devoted to the children, but she had no patience for indecision and delay. She knew what she wanted and when to expect it. She told her husband from the beginning she was to have three children and three only: first a daughter, then a son and then another daughter. Gunhei was solicitous and tried to prepare his wife for disappointment. He needn't have bothered.

Chiemi was taken aback. It was clear, she had not expected such a thing.

"You are twenty-three now, the perfect time to get married," Haruye reasoned, her face crunching with concern.

"Chiemi-chan," her father interrupted while glaring at his wife. "You are a young woman who needs to become a wife."

Chiemi did not disagree but needed a moment to accept the idea. "Who would marry me?" was all she could ask.

"Stop that!" Haruye said. "No need for that now. Your father has a friend in town who has a son of marrying age."

Chiemi gave a small smile, thinking her father has many, many friends with eligible sons.

"He's chonan so he stands to inherit his father's business," her mother informed. "A profitable kimono store, near the centre of town."

Taisho-ya Kimono was indeed a popular shop, due to its location in the middle of the Hondori shopping arcade.

"What's his name?"

"Ito Haruo."

"Such a plain name," she said with a frown.

"What's that got to do with anything?" Haruye chided.

"All right, I'll meet this plain Ito Haruo," she said with a grimace.

✿ ✿ ✿

On an unusually warm October night, when the cicadas sang loudly, the Ito family met the Akamatsu family at the compound. Haruye served cold tea and multi-coloured rice cakes, much to the delight of Ito *Okaasan*, a slight and frivolous woman who wore, some would say, a too garish *kimono* of red-and-white blossoms. Her thoughts centred on possessions and money; the Akamatsu house with its many hallways leading to dark and mysterious enclaves deep in the building made her blink in wonderment. She owned the face of a simpleton, overly concerned with what people thought of her.

Ito Ginaburo, the patriarch, looked impressive in his plain, grey *kimono*, an overly formal garment for the weather, but appropriate for the occasion. He suffered the heat in silence with a small amount of perspiration on his high forehead.

"The tea is quite good," Ito *Okaasan* commented. "So refreshing, ne? And expensive, I'm sure."

Everyone nodded.

The two young people sat behind their respective parents, each stealing a glance at the other. Each catching a smile of the other. Chiemi was beginning to warm to the idea of marriage.

Haruo was a tall man, a good thing since Chiemi didn't want to tower over her husband. One thing that bothered her was his crooked front teeth. They made him look like a country bumpkin; his thick, black-rimmed glasses emphasized them. She resisted showing her displeasure, though her mother did notice her daughter's slight consternation.

In the privacy of the late evening, Haruye sat unraveling and combing her daughter's long hair. Chiemi's *ofuton* was rolled out and ready to be used, but there was still time for conversation.

"He's not a handsome man," Chiemi said honestly. "Looks like an idiot, actually. Takes after his mother."

"Chiemi! Don't you say anything to the Itos," she scolded. "Such talk."

"I won't. It's just that…well…I have to live with the man."

Haruye said nothing and continued to comb the long lustrous hair.

"And what about that Ito Okaasan?"

"What about her?"

"Did you see her kimono? So gaudy."

"Well, some people are like that."

"But how am I to deal with that? So embarrassing…in public, I mean."

"Yes, but you'll live in your own house, away from your in-laws."

"I suppose."

"The kimono business is doing quite well. Everyone I know goes to their store."

"You know, he can't see...with those glasses."

"Don't be silly," Haruye said and paused. "Good thing he won't be able to see you then." She laughed as Chiemi frowned. The wedding date was set.

✿ ✿ ✿

Mid-November, when the skies darkened and hung heavy with rain, Chiemi married the lanky Ito Haruo. She enjoyed the journey across town. Walking as a diversion with her parents along the Nakajima Hondori with decorative paper lanterns suspended above, the lily-of-the-valley shaped streetlights, and the *Hinomaru* draped everywhere, she wondered if she would ever be able to visit her favourite shops again. Maybe she could visit Yoshioka's fabric shop one last time or the Watanabe Toen to buy her china. The *Ebisu-ko* festival would start soon. Great bargains then; so many shops offering discounts. So many customers, so much colour.

She wondered what Chisato was doing at that moment. How she wished her sister were there to celebrate her marriage. She desperately tried to put the thought out of her mind, but it persisted.

The wedding ceremony was not as elaborate as Chisato's, but it was surprisingly dignified, given Ito *Okaasan's* proclivities. It gave Chiemi some sense of hope. A few words of wisdom by Fujita *Sensei*, whom Gunhei sponsored to come officiate, and the blessed couple in traditional wedding *kimono* entered their names in the family register. And that was that, though Ito *Okaasan*, who now insisted on being called *Giri-no ha-ha*, Mother-in-Law (*Giri* being the operative word: obligation), hosted an elaborate dinner in their house, a simple two-storey wooden building on the banks of the Ota River.

In the central *tatami* room, a long, light-coloured dining table held a feast of seafood, fragrant rice, and assorted dishes for all to partake. It was prepared by the Ryoji Hachigo, a chef of some renown in Hiroshima. All sorts of guests were invited to the dinner: distant and close relatives, local businessmen, associates and rivals in the retail *kimono* trade, and old friends.

"I know this place isn't as grand as yours, but we do what we can," she gushed to Akamatsu Haruye, who smiled politely.

Gunhei and Ginaburo drank *sake* to the couple and deepened their friendship. Gunhei especially liked the *chawan mushi*, an egg custard with bits of fish and shrimp embedded. So tasty with its fragrance of the sea and plump morsels of shrimp and octopus. He was impressed and repeated many times, "So amazing!"

❀ ❀ ❀

The wedding night was nothing special to Chiemi's mind. She knew it had to be done, part of the ritual of life. Her mother did talk to her a week before the wedding. *You would think she was getting married!* she told her sister in a letter. Chiemi was surprised how nervous *Okaasan* was.

A cool breeze wafted in from the garden and throughout the house. It tasted of rain. While Okaa combed her hair, Chiemi remarked how familiar this was.

"Yes, well…yes, are you…um…prepared for the…wedding night," Haruye asked stumbling over her words.

Chiemi said nothing, keeping mum to spare any embarrassment. She must've had this same discussion with Chisato-chan, she thought. Not used to it yet.

"Just do what your husband says…and you'll be all right…you…understand?"

Chiemi nodded and that was that.

It was silly of her mother to be so worried. Chiemi had seen a naked male body before—her brother and her father for instance. And she had seen the boys swimming nude in the sea at a nearby beach. She did worry about the actual act of coupling; it was something her friends had giggled about. The talk was nonsense, she decided; they were foolish and stupid girls after all. But she listened intently, never commenting.

Haruo disrobed behind a screen and came out for her inspection. He was too skinny, and those teeth! His rib bones were showing, his skin was pale and sallow like an office clerk's. Thank you to the Buddha he took off his glasses. She suddenly felt a bout of embarrassment. *He won't see my body clearly,* she thought drawing some consolation from the idea. Still, she could see he was excited and slowly took her clothes off as well, blushing as she did so. Would he comment on the budges around her stomach, her thick thighs, and large calves? On the other hand, she was happy to get out of her formal attire.

She then crunched down to the *ofuton* and dutifully waited for him. It was then she noticed her breathing was faster, deeper. Her heart began to race. She was surprised at her reaction. He lay down beside her as she lay back. The warmth of his body comforted her, thin and boney though it was. Skin touching skin was luxurious.

The act was uncomfortable, a bit painful and messy, but mercifully, over quickly. He rolled off her and soon fell asleep with his back to her.

"Is that all there is to it?" she whispered to herself. She turned on her side and wondered if she was pregnant.

That same cool breeze tasting of rain entered the room through a window and gently nudged her towards sleep.

From that night onward, she addressed her husband as "Ito-san", a term that made her smirk.

34.   SUMMER 1940

THE *KIMONO* SHOP THRIVED AFTER the wedding. Chiemi
surprised herself by how much she enjoyed being a shopkeeper.
Taisho-ya Kimono was such a popular shop for women to buy
fabric material that Ito-*san* decided to open a second location
within sight of the Ota River in the prosperous Hondori shopping street. Chiemi thought it unwise to invest so much money,
given the war. But despite the deprivations, people still came
in and bought. Who was she to argue? She didn't know about
business.

She really liked the lily-of-the-valley lanterns just outside
and along the main street, lighting the way until closing at night.
She was there late most times to greet and help customers.

She avoided reading the newspapers. She turned away from
radio reports. Despite her efforts, the war intruded at every
turn. It was everyone's favourite topic of conversation. Japan
had joined Germany and Italy in a pact to come to the defence
of the others if a conflict were to erupt with an adversary. As a
result, the United States moved its Pacific Fleet to some place
called Pearl Harbor, Hawaii. She had never heard of the place
but thought it a "nice" enough name.

In the meantime, Japan moved into Vichy-controlled
Indochina, and the United States, as a countermeasure, closed
the Panama Canal to Japanese ships and placed an embargo on
scrap metal to Japan. *Maybe Hideki was right*, she thought. *The
two sides are just arguing with little or no consequence.* She concluded that there would be no war; the United States feared the
might of Japan.

These actions had little effect on Chiemi and family though
the military needed the scrap metal. Purchasing rice, however,
was beginning to become a problem in 1940. Businesses like the

Fukuya Department Store kept their basement bins full, but the cost was going up. And the rice stocks were from foreign countries, like Taiwan. Most agreed, not as good as Japanese. The small neighbourhood shops found it difficult to replenish. They certainly couldn't afford to stock the imported kind. Neighbours like the Mizuyabu family resorted to eating millet or barley mixed with a few grains of precious rice, whatever they could get.

There was no need to patronize the Black Market yet, given the Itos' prosperity, but Chiemi wondered when she would have to go there. She didn't worry about her parents.

The government, *in its wisdom*, scoffed Chiemi, soon began to appropriate land for the war effort. In Hiroshima, work to improve port facilities was done as well as construction of industrial zones within the city.

Military barracks sprouted in Ujina for soldiers from all over Japan. That made sense to Chiemi since the port was the departure point for them to destinations in China and the South Pacific, she assumed. But there would be no more visits to Miyajima at *Obon*.

She felt sorry for Mizuyabu-*san* whose candy shop was appropriated for an officers' club. The business had been in the family for three generations. About a month ago, Chiemi treated her neighbour, Mizuyabu Aiko, to tea and cakes in the Shintenchi district, with its many lights and fashionable shops and cafés, to commiserate.

"I don't understand," Chiemi opened as they sat at a small table in the window of Toranomon Café, away from the crowded counter that faced the coffee roaster and pastries. It was a new place, cleanly white and almost monastic in appearance. But it was popular with crowds on weekends.

"Why pick on such a small shop like yours for their own pleasure?" she wondered.

"It's the solid concrete and sturdy building, not the store," Aiko answered. "Bomb proof. They took it because they can."

"They think Hiroshima will be bombed?"

"I don't know, but they said, 'In case.'"

Chiemi paused as she remembered General Tojo's declaration that Japan would never be touched by the enemy. He sounded so sure of it.

"Have they no compassion?" Chiemi said as she turned back to the issue at hand. "Have they no shame?"

"Ito-san," Aiko fell into a confessional mood. "I don't mind telling you, we're heading into desperate times." She quietly lowered her gaze, and her voice became almost a whisper. "I opened the rice can the other day...the last of our rice...and...and I found ants all over it..." She gulped her emotion down.

Chiemi was disturbed by the revelation. "What did you do?"

"I picked the bugs out. Threw them in a can of water..."

After a long pause, Chiemi asked, "Is there anything I can do?"

"No...no." She bowed her head.

Who has caused all this misery? Chiemi asked herself. *And why? I know what the newspapers say, but I don't believe them.*

Later that day, Chiemi placed a small bag of rice inside Mizuyabu-*san's* house through one of the open doors.

❀ ❀ ❀

One night, after Ito-*san* had fallen asleep, Chiemi found herself thinking about Hideki, for some reason. It had been some time. Maybe because Mizuyabu-*san* had said during the tea she heard disturbing facts coming to light about a mass slaughter of Chinese civilians in someplace called Nanking. Chiemi recalled Hideki had mentioned the place, and she did read about the original campaign as a major victory for the Japanese military back in early 1938. Hence the disparaging nickname for the Chinese: *Nankin-san.* One newspaper proclaimed Nanking was revenge for the Marco Polo Bridge Incident. *4,000 for one missing Japanese soldier? Was he dead?* she questioned. *Seemed to be overkill,* she thought with a slight grin.

She then recalled Hideki tormenting the "Ant Soldiers" on that hot summer's day so long ago. He saw himself as the Emperor's *samurai* destroying the hated Chinese. But no one in the family had ever met a Chinese person to hate them. Maybe *Otousan* during his business trips, but he never said. Curious. In any case, her brother couldn't have taken part in Nanking since he was still in Japan at the time.

Maybe he had changed his mind. He had wanted to get out, after all.

She dismissed the rumours in the end, calling it *Nankin* propaganda.

✿ ✿ ✿

Remembering her brother did put into her mind the bag of money he had left her in the garden of the Akamatsu family compound. She had brought it with her when she married and placed it in her bedroom clothing chest. Ito-*san's* house was a modest two-storey building close to the *kimono* shop. Built out of stucco, the walls were grey and stippled. The green shingled roof was in the Chinese style with sloped and pointed corners. The two front windows were in the Western style and the front door was wooden and heavy. The upstairs bedrooms were functional and featured Western beds. People called her filthy rich in their whisperings. She dismissed such a notion.

She had never counted Hideki's money or ever looked at it. But the next day, she decided to take it and bury it in the back lot (small as it was). She found a spade and began digging in a likely spot among the bushes that hid the house from the street.

Ito-*san* caught sight of her from a back window. "What are you doing?"

She growled and snapped, "Nothing for you to worry about." She strained against the weight of the dirt and the size of her stomach as she hunched over the spot. She dug about a foot deep.

"You shouldn't be doing that."

She didn't answer; she just grunted.

"What's in the bag?" he asked as she finished digging and lifted the bag into the hole.

"Something my brother gave me to take care of." She began to back-fill the hole.

"Like what?"

"Never mind," she said crossly. "Just forget about what you saw."

"All right, but you should stop and let me do that."

She ignored him.

After a moment's pause, he spoke again. "Chiemi-chan, there's something I want to talk to you about." He sat on a convenient rock.

She put down the spade after packing down the dirt and glared at her husband. "What is it?"

Nervously he continued speaking, "I…I…I…had to…"

"Well?" she said impatiently.

"I joined the military…the navy in fact."

"You did what?" she said as she picked up the spade again and gripped it tightly while glaring at her husband.

"I joined the navy." His voice was filled with newly found conviction.

"Nonsense, you're too old."

"Not anymore. They're starting to recruit older."

"Why do you want to join the navy? You can't swim."

"I was conscripted."

"Well, you could fight it. Tell them of our circumstances," she said standing straight up and rubbing her stomach. "Are you too stupid to have forgotten?"

He turned away. "No, I won't do that," he replied. "I want to be patriotic."

"Patriotic?" she scoffed. "Why get involved in a stupid war against a people we have no business with?"

"It's not so much the Nankin we worry about—"

"What? Then who?"

"Europe and America. There's a war coming with them."

"Who told you that?" She kept mum about her brother's foreshadowing.

"I listen."

"Nonsense, you don't listen to me," she dismissed. "Okay, you go off and play sailor…but remember you'll have a family soon."

"The store will take care of you. No need to worry."

"What about the babies?"

"Babies?"

"The doctor said I was big enough for twins," she revealed and continued anticipating his next question. "Yesterday, he told me yesterday. I'll need help!"

Haruo was stunned for a moment as his thin head shook slightly. "I'll ask my okaa to help."

"No, you will not! If anything, I'll ask my mother," she harrumphed.

✤ ✤ ✤

Ito-san is so stupid. He could've argued against conscription because of her condition and his age. But he complied. She wondered if he just wanted to get away from her. From the children. His mother.

As it came about, he became assigned as a clerk at naval operations in Hong Kong, far from the fighting. *At least, he wasn't on a ship that could sink and drown him,* she thought. She was surprised to learn she felt relieved.

She had the twins, named Kuniya and Takeshi, and decided to live with her parents on the outskirts of Hiroshima. They were beautiful babies, Kuniya constantly fussing while Takeshi remaining still and quiet. Chiemi and her mother-in-law kept an eye on Kuniya, suspecting that he was going to be a rambunctious and perhaps difficult child. Chiemi then announced her move home.

"What is your last name?" asked *Giri-no ha ha.*

"What's that supposed to mean?"

Ito *Okaasan* bristled. "It's a simple question. What is your last name?" she asked with emphasis.

"Ito."

"Then you should stay with the Ito family. You and the babies will come to our place, and you'll work at the store."

"I choose not to," she said and turned away. She knew her *giri-no ha ha* wanted a daughter-in-law under her thumb. A slave in other words.

"You belong to us."

"I don't belong to anyone!" Chiemi exploded. "I'll work at the store, but I'll live with *my* family!"

And so, it was decided. Chiemi would move to the Akamatsu compound. Her mind was made up. The city house would remain empty until her husband returned. All was well until impermanence took hold.

On a late-spring day of 1941, when the sun rose high in the sky and glowed with a warmth that was welcome, Chiemi sat in the *Whispering Oni Room* waiting. It was characteristically cold within the confines. The room was open to the inviting garden where the vegetation was moist, lush, and inviting. A comforting wind rustled the bushes and trees. She loved standing in the breeze, feeling invisible arms around her.

But she played the obedient daughter, though she shivered in her seated position. There seemed to be a transparent barrier between the garden and the *Oni Room*. The stone *samurai* scowled at her. Nothing unusual about it except to her the statue seemed somewhat menacing that day.

Akamatsu Gunhei swept into the room, his long black *kimono* fluttering in the air. Chiemi looked up and grimaced. She was tired of this game. Still, she was happy to see her father; he had been away for a few days. Probably in Tokyo. Probably since he had said nothing.

His face was ashen and haggard, his full head of hair a tad greyer. What had happened? Thin and tired, he sat in front of her.

"Are you all right, Otousan?"

"I'm fine...fine," he replied, turning to evade her inspection. "I have something to say to you."

Chiemi quelled her concern to listen.

"Come August 6 at 9:15 in the morning..." His voice faded.

She remained quiet, not wishing to offend him with her impatience.

"On August 6th at 9:15 a.m. ....I..."

"Yes, on August 6th at 9:15 a.m., what?" Her patience was at an end.

"I will be no more. I will die."

She quivered slightly as she continued to sit. How was this possible? True, he appeared a little sick, more fatigued than anything, but that could be from the travel and business. There was nothing catastrophic going on with his body. He was hale and hearty before he left for Tokyo.

"What do you mean? What are you saying?" she said quickly. "That's just nonsense."

He sighed and continued, "On that day and time I will be no more."

"Don't be ridiculous. How do you know anyway? Are you joking with me?"

"I just know. And no, I'm not joking. I am serious."

"Did you see a doctor while you were away. Did he say something?"

"I didn't see a doctor."

"Then this is all a joke, I know it. How can you be so cruel?"

"No, it's true. Chiemi-chan, I have something for you." He reached underneath his *kimono* and pulled out a piece of paper. He gave it to her.

Death has no meaning for me,
But when I give thought to the
Moment of death,
I grow sad at the loss of
Warm family memories.

"What is this?"

"A tanka. I sent it to your brother and sister as well. They should know."

"What does Okaasan think about all this?"

"She doesn't believe it, like you. You are your mother's daughter."

"Ach," she said dismissively. "There's nothing wrong with you that a good night's sleep wouldn't cure. How can you be so cruel to send Hideki and Chisato this…this tanka?" she said waving the paper in the air. "I'm sure they have bigger problems."

Gunhei closed his eyes, not disclosing his thoughts. Instead, he said, "I regret not seeing my grandchildren grow up, but I'm sure they'll become fine young men. I love holding them in my arms. They are a great and sincere comfort."

"Then, don't die," she said under her breath.

* * *

As fate would have it, on August 6th, 1941, at precisely 9:15 a.m., Akamatsu Gunhei died in his sleep. His wife kneeled by his side and recited the *Nembutsu. Sensei* Kiyahara lit the incense in the family altar, rang the chime, and chanted the *Heart Sutra*.

Chiemi was in shock. She couldn't understand how this could happen. *Otousan* was in perfect health as far as she was concerned. He showed little signs of ill-health. He just took to his bed the night before and died—as predicted. He was only fifty-eight.

In late September, Chiemi was again sitting in the cold *Oni Room*. The funeral was simple with only her mother and her with the priest presiding. Haruye was rather stoic in her reaction to Gunhei's passing. She took care of the details efficiently and quickly, showing little emotion. *This is what he wanted. He just wanted to go* was all she said about it.

Chiemi said nothing to her. But she did wonder how her siblings reacted to the *tanka* and pronouncement. Chisato did write to clarify; Hideki never responded.

It was late at night when Chiemi heard a Buddhist chime. She went to the altar and found the small bell in position and still and the cloth-covered hammer undisturbed. But after she returned to her *ofuton*, the sound started again, softly and, this time, coming from the *Oni Room*, she swore. As she moved to the room, the chime stopped.

Chiemi shook her head. *Must be my imagination,* she thought, even though she knew she had heard the sound clearly. She went back to bed and quivered to sleep.

* * *

In the depths of night, she awoke with a start. No bell, no noise, not even the sound of cicadas singing in the air disturbed her. She sat up and felt a distinct presence in her room.

She scanned with her eyes, straining to see, but it was too dark. But then she heard a rustling as if someone were moving. The night fractured right before her like a cracked mirror; she thought she was looking at the inside of a dream. The blacker-than-night pieces slowly dislodged and floated before coming together into a mass. She couldn't make out what it was. She called out, "Who's there?" But no answer.

Eventually she recognized that the fragments formed into a figure, a human being, a featureless person. No face but certainly a body, like an inert shadow. She watched as it silently moved across the foot of her *ofuton*. It moved some distance before blending into the darkness and disappearing. Though she pulled up her legs under the covers, she couldn't move from the bed.

Chiemi was shaken, an eerie sensation tingled through her body as she stared into the darkness. She rubbed her eyes and tried to dismiss it as a dream, but she knew she was fully awake. *What could it possibly be?*

A thought then flashed through her consciousness: *Otousan.*

35.   DECEMBER 1941

SHE HAD NOT THOUGHT ABOUT the shadow or her father since his funeral last October. She shook at the thought, but she soon dismissed the apparition as part of her stress, a figment of her imagination. A product of her grief.

Her immediate worry however was her move back to the family compound. Her mother-in-law refused to speak to her afterwards, not even wanting to see her grandchildren. Whenever Chiemi was in the store, she imagined what her customers were thinking. Whether they knew or not.

"You were always a willful girl," Haruye *Okaasan* commented.

"Willful? What does that mean?" Chiemi said with more than a little anger in her voice.

"I mean, you always did whatever you wanted, never mind how it looks."

"How was I supposed to take care of the twins, the business, and my giri-no onibaba?" The commute was much longer, but it was worth it to get away from the constant mother-in-law nagging.

Haruye turned away from the obvious insult, grimacing at the same time. "Don't call her that."

"Well? But tell me, tell me!" Chiemi nagged. "Am I right?"

Her mother remained silent as she sat to pick up her mending. She refused to make eye-contact with her daughter.

"Okaa, Takeshi is a sickly child and needs extra care. Do you think that the onibaba can help? Do you? Do you?"

"Stop calling her that! She is not a devil woman."

❊ ❊ ❊

The newspapers indicated that the times were getting dangerous. On December 7th, the *Asahi Shimbun* reported the "victorious and glorious" attack on the United States at Pearl Harbor. The American Pacific fleet had been moved there, she recalled reading some time ago. Back then, Chiemi thought the Americans foolish for such a provocative move. She read of the estimated number of dead, but it meant nothing to her. It was just a number. *Death is meaningless*, whispered a shadow in the dark.

Leading up to the attack, the newspapers had reported an oil embargo by the US and a demand for the total and unconditional withdrawal from China. She sniffed at the idea and thought the demands and actions unreasonable. *How will we survive without China? We need China's rice, soy...oil.* The US then froze Japan's assets.

In rapid succession, Japan attacked and occupied the Philippines, Singapore, Hong Kong, and other South Pacific islands. The news flooded the minds of the population; everyone swelled with pride and patriotic fervour. No one could stop the Japanese Imperial Forces, invulnerable and unstoppable. It was a matter of self-preservation, according to the editorials. Japan was truly an empire now. Chiemi saw a wall forming around her country, fortified by the Divine Emperor, General Tojo, Admiral Yamamoto, and the combined might of the military forces. The Empire of Japan presented a formidable wedge against the US and European forces who wanted to harm Chiemi and the Japanese.

But others claimed that it would be disastrous for Japan to enter a war with the United States. Admiral Yamamoto, it was rumoured, said as much in high-level meetings. Pundits speculated that any conflict would last six months before Japan lost. Chiemi wondered why they weren't arrested for treason.

Despite the embargoes, Japan nevertheless dictated terms with the Americans. They wanted the guarantee of the Greater East Asia Co-Prosperity Sphere: the linking of all of East Asia culturally and economically, led by Japan. The Roof Over Asia.

❊ ❊ ❊

But Chiemi remained indifferent to what was happening among politicians and with the military campaigns, even as the war crept steadily into the Spring of 1942. She was appalled by the rationing which was still enforced and in fact intensified with time and situation. Rice became scarce, even to the wealthy, as everyone mixed in millet (mostly barley) to stretch the supply (encouraged by government propaganda). The same blend went to the soldiers. Japanese vegetables were still easily had, the domestic production had not waned...yet. But seafood was getting hard to come by. American submarine patrols curtailed deep-sea fishing. Fishermen were only able to harvest squid and sardines. She was worried how to keep her children nourished, especially Takeshi. Her breast milk wasn't enough for both, but she reserved most of it for Takeshi. Whole milk was expensive, but she bought what she could for Kuniya. As for her and her mother, thank the Buddha for *tofu* and *shoyu*. Add a little dried baby sardines and everything tasted Japanese. Didn't feel as deprived then.

Besides the food issues, Chiemi was concerned about the two men in her life: Hideki and Ito-*san*. But she had no say in what the two did. Neither listened to her. She scanned the lists of the dead posted on neighbourhood announcement boards or printed in the newspapers. She still harboured the notion that they were idiots for having run off to join the military. She didn't want to see them dead, especially with Hideki's change of heart. *Stay safe, Hideki. Stay safe.*

Concerns at home soon took over.

Even so, her father's death after a while returned to play on her mind. It was such a mystery. And had he visited her in the night? The moving shadow had had to have been him. What did it mean? Perhaps he was telling her he was all right. There was no way to know.

He became another ancestor to venerate at *Obon*; a photograph accompanied by the *tanka* was placed in the *butsudan* (the family altar). From time to time, she sat *seiza*, meditating, in front of the altar in the *Whispering Oni Room* and offered incense to remember him. She came to appreciate the ritual and the sanctity of that part of the house.

So, every morning, she kissed her babies, bid her mother farewell, and walked off along the dirt road towards town. The road rose slightly before descending to the trolley station. A thick forest of trees stood on either side, keeping the area cool and shady. The smells of spring greeted her every day and lightened her mood.

Once on the trolley, it was a simple ride to the covered shopping street of Hiroshima where the store, Taisho-ya Kimono, stood inside the Hondori. Her mother-in-law took care of the second shop within sight of the Ota River so that was a blessing. Chiemi would not have to deal with the *onibaba* (the devil woman).

Above all else, she worried about her mother. Since *Otousan's* death, *Okaasan* had grown old. Her hair sprouted much more grey than her age called for, she walked with a stoop and chores became harder and harder. It didn't help that the twin grandchildren were so mischievous, even at one-year-old. Kuniya, the one with the rascal smile, especially would get into things, fearlessly climbing on furniture and the like, while Takeshi, who had gained weight and was seemingly out of danger, observed and then followed. Invariably, they knocked things over, upset things, broke things. *Okaasan* and Chiemi chased after them trying to contain them at the same time. They both looked so beautiful, yet they possessed the hearts of *oni*.

Chiemi spent the day in the shop in relative peace. Though from time to time, something would happen to upset things. Like the time, she caught a woman shoplifting some material. Chiemi grabbed her by the shoulders, a simple task since she was so much taller than the thief.

The woman had a small bolt of patterned cloth under her arm as she made for the door.

"Stop, what do you think you're doing?" Chiemi shrieked.

"Let me go! I don't mean anything—" she insisted. "I can pay! I can pay!"

The voice was familiar for some reason and Chiemi turned her around. It was Mizuyabu Aiko, the candy store owner whose property was confiscated. Chiemi immediately let go.

"Mizuyabu-san? What are you doing?"

"I'm sorry…I'm sorry," she said nearly in tears. Aiko bowed deeply in front of her. "I didn't mean anything. If I had known you were…I never would've—"

"You didn't have to steal anything."

"I'm…we're so poor," she confessed in a humble voice. "I can't pay…"

It was then that Chiemi noticed how thin her friend had become, her arms especially, like sticks. Her face was haggard, pulled down by worry, poverty, and perhaps shame. She pushed Aiko towards the back of the store, past the displays of *kimono* and stacks of colourful cloth to a small table with two chairs against the wall.

"You sit here," she commanded quietly. "I'll make some green tea."

Aiko smiled weakly and obeyed, sitting on the edge of the metal chair, holding on as if her life depended on not falling to the floor. Her face drooped with fatigue.

Chiemi tipped the teapot gently, her left hand supporting the bottom to control the pour. The set, decorated with bamboo fronds and enameled in a deep dark green, was delicate and pleasing to the eye. The cup elegantly received the pale green liquid until nearly full. The steam rose into the cool air.

Aiko at least looked relaxed as she picked up her cup, holding it gently with two fingers at the cool area at the top of the cup while her left palm cradled it. The moist, warm steam felt good against the skin as she closed her eyes and smiled approval.

"Now, tell me what's happened to you since I last saw you," Chiemi said.

"I thought I could make a decent kimono, so I'd look presentable for a job some—"

"No, you're not listening. Since I last saw you…"

"My husband was drafted into the navy shortly after our place was taken."

That was not unexpected, but she did have a question. "Isn't he too old?" An odd question since her husband was not immune because of age.

"His time in the navy during WWI got him in."

"Where is he?"

She fell silent.

"Mizuyabu-san?"

"He's dead."

"What…how?" Her face betrayed her surprise.

"His ship, the *Izumi*, was bombed and sank somewhere in the South Pacific…they wouldn't tell me…last year," she revealed with her head down. "We've been struggling ever since, my two daughters and me."

"I'm so sorry."

"Two men in uniform came to our door…they gave me a kotsutsubo." *A white funeral box.*

"His remains—"

"No…no…not really. They couldn't recover his body…so they placed a rock inside to represent his body."

Chiemi fell silent, not really knowing what to say.

"At least, his navy pay was something…but now we have nothing. And you know how hard it is finding work," she said almost out of desperation.

"Yoshi," Chiemi said, "you come work here."

Her face suddenly grew animated. "Really? Is this true?"

"I'm serious. I could use the help."

"Thank you, thank you, thank you." She bent over to bow. "You don't have to—"

"Nonsense. As I said, I need the help. You go home and prepare for a full day's work tomorrow. And take the cloth with you. You've got to look presentable…" she said with a smile.

Chiemi breathed out thinking of her mother. Had her father not provided for Haruye in case of his passing, she would just as badly off as Mizuyabu-*san*.

36.   AUTUMN 1942

MIZUYABU AIKO WORKED OUT RATHER well. She was at
the store bright and early every morning with a smile on her
face and ready for the job. She swept and mopped the floor first
thing; got down on her hands and knees with a rag for difficult
areas. She made sure the bolts of fabric were aligned just so and
put on display the material that needed to be sold. Signs were
adjusted and placed in advantageous spots, if necessary. Later,
she would wash the windows and wipe and dust the counters.
Thus, the store was ready every day.

Then and only then would she open the front doors and
greet any customer who happened to be waiting outside.

Chiemi was pleased to have made the right decision to hire
her. Aiko was a real benefit despite her mother-in-law.

"You can't trust that woman," Fumiko warned. Her sour
expression angered Chiemi but she said nothing. "You watch her.
She'll rob us blind if given a chance."

"You should go back to the Ota store," Chiemi suggested. "I'll
watch her."

"Well, you'd better. I don't want to impoverish my grandsons!"
At least, she was thinking of her grandchildren.

What worried her then and into 1943 was not thievery but
the war. As far as she could tell, the Axis powers were beginning to lose their grip on Europe and in the South Pacific. The
Tripartite Pact was not working well. Still, she could not tell if
the newspapers and radio reports were reporting the truth. She
knew better than to take things at face value. The lists of War
Dead, however, were getting longer and more persistent.

Other signs the war was going badly cropped up on a con-
sistent basis.

✿ ✿ ✿

By April 1943, Tokyo and other city-targets were bombed continuously despite assurances from the military that the skies over Japan would be "clean" forever. Everyone talked about a Jimmy Doolittle who led the first of the raids in 1942. An impossible name to pronounce and so was mocked later. Although there wasn't much damage, people initially were shocked by the attack on an "invulnerable" Japan.

"Chiemi-chan," *Okaasan* said, her voice trembling, "they're bombing Tokyo more and more...the enemy. We'll be next, I know it."

"Calm down Okaa!" Chiemi turned away and busied herself getting ready to go to work.

"But...but...the Americans are coming for us."

"Look how far away we are from Tokyo," Chiemi pointed out. "General Tojo will protect us."

"What does he care?" she said. Good thing the military police didn't hear her outburst.

"Calm down, I said. We'll be fine. Tokyo is far away from here!"

Until then the war had not touched Japan in daily life, except for the abstract lists of the dead. Even so it was names and numbers on paper that meant nothing to Chiemi. Then there was the scarcity of food items. Above all else, Japan was attacked unopposed; that was unsettling.

All she advised was to hold faith in the Emperor. "He will protect us, not the generals." Her mother's face continued to be smeared with worry.

What bothered Chiemi most was the fact that American aircraft carriers were close enough to stage the raids. Is Japan on the verge of defeat? Worry painted her face as well. *Will they slaughter us in our sleep? Who is responsible? Who started all of this?* The questions nagged at her constantly.

This was less than a year after the battle of Midway. The defeat of the Japanese navy was bad enough but then there came the portentous death of Admiral Yamamoto, commander-in-chief of the Combined Japanese Fleet, in the spring of 1943.

The newspapers never gave a full accounting of battles; instead, there were glowing reports of Japanese victories in the South Pacific campaign. Everyone knew it was all disinformation. Even Admiral Yamamoto's death was said to have been "glorious and heroic" during the Solomon Islands campaign. *A resounding success for Japanese forces!* But rumours told of American ingenuity in ferreting out Yamamoto's schedule and route. His plane was brought down by enemy fighter aircraft.

None of this seemed to affect Aiko, who happily went about her job at the *kimono* store. It was as if nothing were happening. Sometimes, it bothered Chiemi so much that she lashed out at her employee for no apparent reason.

"Mizuyabu-san! Do a better job mopping the floor. It's filthy."

Aiko said nothing. She bowed as an apology and proceeded to clean as best as she could. Chiemi barked even louder.

When Chiemi received a letter from her husband through military post, she suddenly realized she hadn't thought of him much all this time. Letters were a rarity since the service was disrupted because of the war, so she hadn't expected any from her sister and husband. Her brother never wrote anyway. *Was he still in China?* Still, it would've been nice to hear from Chisato and Hideki. Her indifference to her husband surprised her.

Chiemi-chan,

I hope you are doing well. Life in Hong Kong is good. I live in the barracks; I cannot tell you the location. I'm sure you understand.

I have made many friends as I go about my daily work. Again, I cannot tell you what I do. But it is important.

Don't worry about me. I am very safe. I don't know of any military action planned where I am involved.

How are the children? And my parents? I have not heard from anyone in a long time. I know mail is suppressed and is

slow, but please write and encourage others to write. I do miss you all.
*   I heard Tokyo...* ███████████████████████

Please write soon.
Ito

What an idiot, she thought aloud. How could he call me Chiemi-chan? - chan! She sat in the *Oni Room* brooding and simmering with anger.

DISTANT MORNING THUNDER ALWAYS GAVE Chiemi pause. Yet there was no rain or lightning one late fall morning. It had to be an air-raid bombing. From her family compound, she looked to the skies over Hiroshima and saw nothing except the clear cold steel blue that she had expected. Farther to the southeast, she saw the horizon wounded by rising black smoke. She guessed it was the Kure Naval District, the shipbuilding yard, that had to have been bombed by the Americans. But there were no reports of a raid, no sirens, no street announcements by the local civil defense men. She let it pass, thinking she would learn soon enough.

She then wondered about Chisato-*chan's* in-laws. The father (*what was his name?*) worked at designing and building warships. Kimura Hideo, she eventually remembered, was quite prominent in the industry. His wife Fumiko was severe but kept the household together. What would happen to them if there had been a bombing?

By evening, Chiemi learned it had been an explosion in a factory just outside Hiroshima. Five men were killed, but no explanation was given. One paper speculated that it was sabotage.

"Why would anyone do that? Blow up a building, I mean," Chiemi said.

"I don't know," *Okaasan* replied, as she served bowls of rice to accompany the plates of *tofu*, sweet potatoes, and sardines for dinner. "Where did you get such lovely rice? It looks so delicious."

"Black market. It's from Korea. Can't get Japanese rice anymore."

"Expensive then," *Okaasan* concluded with a worried look on her face and the delight gone from her voice.

The *kimono* business had slowed of late. Not that many customers came to buy. In fact, some days, no one at all. At some point, Aiko had to be let go, but Chiemi brought her on as a domestic at the compound for a small stipend and room and board. With her two daughters and the two boys, the place became quite raucous though there was plenty of room. Aiko's children, Mitsue, the older one by a year or so, and Keiko, were older than the boys by about seven plus years, but they were inspired by Kuniya's mischievous nature. All four were constantly chasing each other around the house. And Kuniya was the leader. Aiko constantly scolded her daughters, but the girls never blamed Kuniya. *Okaasan* scolded her grandchildren. Chiemi enjoyed the chaos and simply sat watching everyone. They were a family again.

By the middle of 1943, her *giri-no ha ha* had closed the shop by the Ota River and Chiemi closed the other before the beginning of winter. All the material was stored at the Ito's house. Chiemi continued to live at the Akamatsu Compound. Her mother-in-law disappeared from her thoughts.

Money was tight and food rations were getting slim. Milk was a problem. Chiemi turned to soymilk. When she ran out of that, she resorted to using the milky water obtained from washing the rice and barley. The children complained of the chalky taste, but she ignored them.

All four children grew thinner and thinner. No one, thank the Buddha, was hospitalized or bedridden at home. Chiemi noticed that clumps of her hair came out with a gentle pull.

✿ ✿ ✿

When the weather turned cold and grey skies dominated, Akamatsu Haruye received notice to come to the Military headquarters near the Prefectural Industrial Promotion Hall downtown. The official invited her to bring along older family members.

"What do they want with us?" *Okaasan* wondered. "We must go. Have you caused any trouble?"

"No!" Chiemi complained. "Why would you even think that?"

Okaasan remained silent.

The two donned heavy dark *haori* or *kimono* jackets and scarves to ward off the cold outside and walked along the familiar path to the trolley stop. The trip was the usual for Chiemi, but her mother enjoyed the change of scenery. Being away from the children was good, though Aiko's daughters were in school while Aiko looked after the twins.

Once they arrived at the wide and tall administration building, Chiemi led them to the headquarters nearby according to the letter. Inside they were met by a solemn young man in a lieutenant's uniform. He knew who they were right away.

They were brought down a long corridor of linoleum and bare walls to a clean, well-organized office. Inside was an older, higher-ranked officer decorated with many garish ribbons and insignia. The young officer left them.

Lieutenant Colonel Tasaka introduced himself in a pleasant but mannered way and invited them to sit.

"Akamatsu Haruye and ..."

"Ito Chiemi, desu. I am her daughter—"

"Ah yes, in any case, I asked you here to extend my condolences."

Chiemi immediately thought her husband was dead, a victim of the war. But then she thought about it, and a sudden realization came to her. Her stomach clenched and her arms weakened.

"Your son has given his life for the greater glory of the Emperor and Empire. His was an honourable death."

The words hit Chiemi like a punch of wind. It took her breath away. Hideki never wrote so she could never tell how much danger he was in. She looked to her mother.

Haruye remained calm and showed no emotion, but she lowered her gaze.

"How..." Chiemi began.

"He was lost in action. I can't tell you many details, but while participating in a military operation, he lost his life in a courageous charge at the enemy. He killed more than a few of the enemy. His was a glorious death."

"When?"

"Yes, that is a matter of contention," the lieutenant colonel said. "We think early 1941 or late 1940."

"1941? Why did it take so long to inform us?" Chiemi said with a hint of irritation in her voice.

"Forgive us. Communication lines have become frayed. Reports from the front have become few and far between. His battle was in an obscure location."

It was a poor excuse, but Chiemi said nothing. She felt her face turn red.

The Lt. Col. paused to let the facts sink in and then gestured for the young lieutenant to re-enter the room. He carried with him a box wrapped in a plain, unadorned white cloth. He handed it carefully to Haruye.

"We respectfully bestow Private First Class Akamatsu Hideki's remains to you. Inside you will find a kotsutsubo."

Haruye gripped it tightly and began to cry, silently. Chiemi, the Lt. Col., and the young officer bowed before her and said nothing.

"You will shortly receive the China Incident War Medal," the Lt. Col. informed. "Please forgive the delay. There are shortages everywhere."

He looked up and added, "You should know that inside the urn is a stone, representing your son's body..."

"Why?" Haruye asked in the pause.

"Quite simply, the body could not be recovered. That's another reason it took us so long. We spent a great deal of time looking for any remains. What little was found was unidentifiable for the longest time. The stone gives the kotsutsobo some weight while, at the same time, representing your son. His spirit will always be with you."

Aiko came to mind, but again Chiemi said nothing. How odd that the fate that befell their loved ones was the same.

Haruye shut her eyes tightly, bowed and stood to leave with Chiemi.

❀ ❀ ❀

Both remained silent all the way home. Haruye tightly and carefully held onto the box, her face grim and sullen, while Chiemi looked exhausted and slumped in her trolley seat.

Home was quiet. Aiko must've taken the twins out for exercise and play. Good thing, too, Grandmother and mother could not have handled their mischief at that moment. They moved directly to the *Whispering Oni Room* where the family altar rested. It was colder than usual since it was winter, even with the screen doors closed. Chiemi still felt the stone *samurai's* stare just beyond the screen. Haruye placed the box before the altar and sat on her legs. She silently wept and muttered the *Nembutsu.* Chiemi did the same.

At an opportune moment, Chiemi spoke, not so much to her mother but out loud for herself. "Why did Hideki have to join the army?" she said almost in anguish.

Her mother stirred and looked at her daughter.

"It's in his blood," she said.

"What do you mean?"

Her face settled into a serious conversation. "We are a samurai family."

"I know that."

"Yes, but we are warriors first."

"What's the difference?"

"Loyalty is one thing, but the Akamatsu ancestors were first warriors, then samurai. You know the statue in the garden?"

"Yes, of course."

"You probably believe your father bought it as some kind of decoration."

"We all did. He bought it in Tokyo."

"Yes, but that's not the reason he bought it."

"Never thought about it."

"Well, it was purchased to remind us we are warriors and not samurai."

"Again, what's the difference?"

"A warrior does battle to win the peace; a samurai battles to serve his master."

"So, you think Hideki was a warrior?" asked Chiemi.

"Yes, and if he had lived, he probably would've become a Buddhist priest. So many of our ancestors did after they won the peace. It is the logical progression from a life of violence and duty to a life of spirituality, serenity, and peace."

"Hideki may have become a priest then," Chiemi surmised. "To find peace."

Haruye closed her eyes. "Perhaps...his spirit is with the Buddha."

Chiemi resolved to write Chisato. Her sister must be told, but the mail was not getting through. Chiemi would write the letter and then wait.

38.   LATE 1943–EARLY 1944

HARUYE PLACED HIDEKI'S *KOTSUTSUBO* BESIDE the family
altar in the *Oni Room*. She draped the cloth wrapping over and
down the sides of the white box. She sat and looked at her husband's photo inside. He seemed to be smiling. Chiemi scoffed at
such a notion. No one smiled in pictures.

Chiemi once knocked the box accidentally. The inside rattled. *The government couldn't even wrap the rock in cloth to secure it,*
she grumbled to herself. She thought she heard Hideki laughing.

She felt the presence of the stone *samurai* just outside in the
garden. She knew it was scowling at her as usual. She turned to
face the screen to the outside. Sliding the door open, she saw the
figure of the *samurai* emerging from within the shadows.

"And who do you serve? Or are you a warrior?"

At night, the haunting began. Late in the darkness, Chiemi
awoke to the sound of a Buddhist bell chime, just as before with
her father. Not loud, but soft, a gentle ting. Not just once or
twice but continuously. She rose from the futon and followed
the sound to the *Oni Room*. She trembled. The chill of the room
turned into the chill of the supernatural. The altar stood as
expected, open and without anyone hitting the bell bowl in front,
Hideki's *kotsutsubo* also remained in its place, yet the chiming
continued. It seemed to be coming from all directions.

What is going on? she said to herself. Her spine tingled. She
searched everywhere but found nothing. *It's not Joya-no kane.*
She sensed that the bell would keep going for one hundred
and eight times, like the New Year's bell ringing. Not that she
counted, but it continued insistently.

Sensei Fujita might call this "mindfulness", but there's no reason for it.

Chiemi sat in front of the family altar, closed her eyes, and placed her hands together in *gassho* (supplication). She decided she must be rid of the one hundred and eight desires within her and all who are living. *Desire leads to suffering. Eight-fold Path to Enlightenment.* So, she patiently waited until the ringing ended. And then it did, silence prevailing in a space of reverberating peace. She opened her eyes.

And the shadows in front of her came together and coalesced into a mass. This had not happened since the night of her father's death.

"Otousan?" she whispered.

No answer came back. Instead, the shadow spread before her as if reaching out, enveloping her, the altar, and the *kotsutsubo*. She closed her eyes. An unidentifiable sensation came over her, then a loving sensation.

She no longer shivered.

✿ ✿ ✿

Two weeks later, Haruye received the *Sina Jihen Jūgun Kishō*, the *China Incident War Medal*, from a smartly uniformed officer. He didn't say much, presented the medal and said something perfunctorily and walked away. The plain brass medal came with a red stripped ribbon.

Haruye placed it on top of Hideki's *kotsutsubo* and faded into the house...

✿ ✿ ✿

Changes came rapidly and copiously in 1944. Evacuation plans began in earnest. Children were to be removed from industrial cities to the countryside to protect them from the anticipated bombing. The government planned to do it by school. The students were to be moved; the parents left behind.

Civil defense forces became the *Peoples Volunteer Combat Corps*. Men up to the age of sixty and women up to forty were conscripted. Rumours of a rigorous training program were circulated. It would be put into play soon. Invasion was imminent.

Chiemi did not feel the panic yet, but neighbours and citizens like Aiko started echoing the government's initial refrain of the *Grand Suicide of the One Hundred Million* during the final decisive battle with the Americans. But all they had for weapons were bamboo spears.

"You can't stop the invading army with that," Chiemi reasoned.

"You have no faith!" Aiko said in a raised voice as she practised stabbing the air in the Compound courtyard. "With our magnificent army in front of us, we will push them back into the sea."

Chiemi stared but remained silent. She ruminated on the Emperor. He's the embodiment of Japan's national identity, but the country is losing the war, defeats everyday, the neighbourhood death lists are not kept up to date, too many. She turned to the Buddha. Compassion and Gratitude. Respect life.

Damn the war. Damn those who started it. Life is dukkha. War propaganda. Life had become a series of slogans.

* * *

She herself was assigned to the annex of the Shima Hospital. The main building was a modern two-storey, concrete and stucco building used to treat the wounded from the battlefront in China and then from the South Pacific. It was located just across the way from the Hiroshima Prefectural Industrial Promotion Hall. Her building stood a few blocks away.

Chiemi enjoyed dressing in a white nurse's uniform with a red cross emblazoned on her cap and traveling downtown to the hospital. She had to stop when the Head Nurse told her she wasn't allowed since she was not a true nurse. She surrendered the uniform where she had found it in a basement closet. On the other hand, she began wearing a "uniform" of tunic, skirt, nylons, and shoes, all white. She felt like a nurse, at least. Other than that confrontation, the staff were friendly enough and the wounded were so appreciative. She did not see the worst off.

Dr. Shima himself came to visit the building and to look in on the patients. His kind, bespectacled face gave off a compassion that was welcomed by everyone. He in turn talked to any and all who talked to him. He made sure the patients were comfortable and reassured them they would recover soon. Chiemi didn't know if that were true, but she understood.

She often closed her eyes tight to the first ritual of the day. A government official, a lackey as Chiemi liked to think, came to lead the recitation of the Morning pledge. His fat index finger always stabbed the air when he talked.

Today, all day, we shall be loyal.
We shall worship the gods and revere our ancestors.
We shall not forget our filial duties.
We shall not be selfish.
We shall be kind and modest.
We shall endure hardship.
We are subjects of the empire.
Today, we will do our best to help destroy America and
    England.
We shall pass these ideals on to our descendants.
This we swear.

Everyone in the hospital gathered on the first floor to recite the words, even the injured and bedridden. The helpless were wheeled into the large central hall by orderlies. And even if the patients couldn't speak, they mouthed the words; even if they couldn't see, they were prompted into the recitation; and even if they couldn't rise, they were propped up with pillows. And so the day began. With patriotic catchphrases and propaganda.

The rest of her time was taken up with comforting the patients in the wards on the first two floors of the building. Each floor featured a cavernous space with light streaming in from the row of windows that lined the walls. Rows of beds sat against those walls as doctors, nurses, and volunteers administered to the patients' needs. Chiemi often helped those who could rise to their feet to hobble about the place.

✿ ✿ ✿

Every night, Chiemi came home to the four children running around, though the girls not so much anymore since they had schoolwork and chores. Her mother, Haruye, simply went about her business, helping to clean and prepare whatever ingredients she could find for dinner. She tended to the supply of rice especially. She even measured the level in the tin cans daily. She soon started adding millet to the cooking, more millet than rice, it seemed.

Chiemi never discussed the war with her or Aiko; she also never mentioned the haunting. But every evening, she sat in the *Oni Room* and waited for the chiming to begin again. The anticipation settled in the pit of her stomach.

But no bell chime ever came. No ghost. Just dark silence and an indistinct fear.

39.   OPERATION STARVATION 1944

LUXURY IS OUR ENEMY! YET another slogan emblazoned in red on the street banner was everywhere in Hiroshima and probably Japan, Chiemi guessed. It was generated and distributed by the *National Spiritual Mobilization Movement*, which the government established in 1937 but only in the 1940s was coming into prominence. They propagated the idea that Western decadence, baseball, movies, and especially jazz, made the Japanese forget their true nature. War was necessary to restore the pure spirit of sacrifice within the people. The Emperor was Japan and everyone must be loyal to Him to bring glory to the country.

Other mantras appeared on posters. *Follow the Example of the War Dead; Increase Production; Our Homeland is a Battlefield too; Success is Determined by Character and Strength of Mind.*

Some repeated the phrases in daily conversation; others recited them loudly in the streets. Chiemi turned away from them.

❊ ❊ ❊

Chiemi sat in front of the *butsudan* trying to meditate, but she instead gazed at the black-and-white photographs contained within the home altar. Her father's forlorn face, Hideki's picture with so much optimism in his eyes, and grandparents and unknown elder uncles and aunts, maybe cousins. No photos or paintings of the warrior ancestors. She thought about Chisato and felt the tears drip down her cheeks.

She didn't know her husband's fate, sniffing at the thought. She always held her children close to her, their warm bodies comforting her.

The papers were full of military victories all over the South Pacific; that too she sneered at. Instead, she depended on rumour and private publications, distributed by anonymous people in the streets, to know the truth. She never knew where the information came from; she always looked side to side and behind for fear of arrest.

The walls of Japan were buckling.

Food was becoming scarce. The enemy navy sank so many supply ships surrounding Japan. They patrolled like sharks. Rice was abandoned for millet altogether. Enough could not be grown for the population and importation was now impossible. There was also the possibility of the bombing of the rice fields. Fishing boats no longer went out for fear of submarine attack. Vegetables were scrounged, dandelions and other weeds took their place. Spent fish, spoiled meat, and once discarded vegetable stalks and leaves were reused for soup stock. Fortunately, she and her mother had pickled cucumbers and cabbage in the last few years. And their supply of dried fish was still plentiful.

She constantly worried for the children in the compound. How would they grow without adequate nutrition? It was all part of the Americans' *Operation Starvation*, primarily aimed at the military, but affecting the civilian population as well.

❊ ❊ ❊

The oil and scrap metal embargoes, the frozen assets overseas, and the shipping blockade all served to strangle the economy. Despite these strictures, the success of the air and sea operations, and the steady takeover of Japanese bases in the Pacific, the military leaders refused to surrender. They could see everyone, men, women, and children, fighting in the street to beat back an Allied invasion.

The numbers of dead were becoming all too real for Chiemi. Death was no longer meaningless. She held onto the words of a sermon by Sensei Fujita, delivered the last time she went to the temple to seek comfort, if not advice.

The autumn moon of the Buddha over Nirvana is hidden behind the clouds full of...trouble. Nobody remains to jolt us awake from this long, dark dream of birth, death, and rebirth. In the not-too-distant past, there was an emperor who embraced the Three Jewels of the Dharma and showed benevolence towards His subjects. He happened to have an inspired dream, and for the sake of peace in the realm, He built a magnificent temple. The temple was destroyed in a fit of vanity by local peasants. Our reigning Emperor deeply regretted its destruction and wishes to erect a temple of temples. It will be a lotus among sacred lotus flowers. And peace will reign.

Though he didn't mention the war, some considered such talk treasonous, but Chiemi saw the wisdom in the words. She brought her hands together before the ancestors, bowed her head, closed her eyes, and clapped her hands before saying,

I take refuge in the Buddha; I take refuge in the Dharma; I take refuge in the Sangha.
The Three Jewels

But there were few left to form a *Sangha*. She lit the incense in front of the *butsudan*, the family altar, and recited the phrase again and again.

✿ ✿ ✿

At the beginning of 1945, the Americans staged an invasion of the Ogasawara Archipelago and Iwo Jima, specifically.

40.   1945

IWO JIMA WAS A SMALL, volcanic island south of Japan. It was remote even if it was part of the Ogasawara Archipelago, mere dots in the Pacific south of Tokyo. Chiemi had never heard of it until it appeared in the papers as a "Glorious battle for the soul of Japan". The three airfields situated there made it of paramount importance. She understood why the Americans wanted it. Attacks on the Japanese main islands would soon follow. The "arch" of the archipelago, like a sword, pointed straight at the heart of Japan.

After the American victory, the US military began a systematic bombing campaign across the country. Walls closed in on Japan. The misinformation machine could not deny the attacks, even though the national newspapers tried.

Victory over Nagoya as our glorious military shot down enemy bombers.

Chiemi gnashed her teeth at the lies.

The air raid sirens blared day and night. To Chiemi, it seemed like Hiroshima screamed in fear and pain. Kure became the primary target in her area since it was a ship-building town. She wondered about the Kimuras, her in-laws.

Some were false alarms, others not. There was always a pause between the sirens and the explosions. Chiemi insisted that the children wear helmets. The boys loved playing Soldier, while the girls thought they looked ugly. In any case, they followed Chiemi's wishes.

✿ ✿ ✿

Chiemi found solace in two sanctuaries, two places of refuge, two *Sangha*. The Akamatsu Compound was one. Her twin sons were nearly five and naughty as could be expected. They ran everywhere and upset things, much to the distress of their grandmother. But Chiemi didn't mind. She would grab one or two in mid-flight and hug them tightly even as they struggled to get free.

Kuniya seemed to be becoming the more handsome of the two. Both were lovable, as most children were, but Kuniya possessed a solid body with well-defined leg muscles, kind eyes, and wide, friendly smile. It was probably Chiemi's imagination, but Takeshi always seemed sullen, eyes always downcast, even if he was revelling in play.

She quite often said to one or both, "Do not be a soldier. Never." She never explained why. She talked about neither their uncle nor their warrior ancestors.

The Mizuyabu girls were becoming beautiful teenagers. Mitsue wore her hair long, which showed off her soft feminine features. She was kind and demure. Keiko was more tomboy than her sister, but her constant running, jumping, and exercising bestowed upon her a fine figure. In front of their elders, they were always demure, which served to charm anyone who met them.

Chiemi's other sanctuary was the hospital. She enjoyed the work and the people there. The place and staff were her true *Sangha*. She knew she confronted the effects of war daily but nursing the wounded made her work harder.

Dr. Shima was more and more present, probably because more and more injured soldiers came as patients. His constant smile was replaced with a permanent scowl. With so many more questions about every patient's condition, a heightened sense of urgency emerged in the man's voice.

Every morning, he addressed the usual gathering of personnel and patients. His speech came right after the Morning Pledge.

The enemy's counter-offenses are becoming more massive and widespread. Now, in a battle of might, the more valiant soldiers there are the stronger. But it's our spiritual power that

*produces that warrior might. Every single one of you must
become an outstanding human being. Only strict discipline,
a vigilant attitude, an unwavering sense of responsibility,
and a respectful silent hospital will yield good health and
solid bodies. Always bear that in mind during this emer-
gency. I want all of you to help the soldiers to recover fully,
to get them on their feet so that they may return to the fight.
And you patients, endeavour to make your bodies whole,
gain strength, and restore your fighting spirit. Above all else,
improve your character. Follow the example of the* WAR
DEAD!

His words were always met with a cheer: *Banzai!* Chiemi
only half-heartedly joined in the enthusiasm. She thought of
her brother and his "example." What were the benefits of his
death? Hideki was wrapped in words, patriotic, heroic words,
yet he was no more, obliterated from the world.

Still, she enjoyed working with the staff. Isomura Fumiko,
Abe Eiko, and Fujiwara Ikue were her closest colleagues. The
four tightened their bonds with each passing day.

Fumiko was short, a little heavy but full of good cheer and
optimism. "When we win the war, everything will go back to
where we were," she would say just about every day. Eiko, by
contrast, would worry a great deal. "The Americans wouldn't
bomb a hospital, would they? There's a huge red cross painted
on the roof. The bombers couldn't miss that...could they?" And
Ikuei, known to all as Iku-*chan*, saw the world in pastel hues,
pink especially. Naïve perhaps, but she more than the others
brought cheer to any patient she attended. The four made
quite a team. They laughed a great deal in the lunchroom. They
encouraged and supported one another even when they heard
bombs exploding near the hospital.

"I'm scared," Eiko whispered as they cowered in a corner
of the hospital ward during an air raid. She was shaking. The
explosions grew in intensity as if they were coming closer and
closer to the building.

"Don't worry, Eiko-chan," Fumiko assured. "Our air force will defeat the American devils."

Chiemi knew the "devils" now dominated the skies. The newspapers said over fifty enemy ships were destroyed during the invasion of Okinawa. That meant, to Chiemi's calculations, that over fifty *kamikaze* pilots died and fifty planes were destroyed. Multiply that by three, since one plane couldn't sink a ship, and that is probably the actual number of losses. *Such a waste*, Chiemi thought. Most pilots were boys, she reasoned, younger than Hideki.

"Kamikaze," she sighed.

Fumiko picked up on the word. "Yes! Let's sing the *Kamikaze Song!* You all remember it. The Mongol Invasions... We all learned it as kids. Come on, sing!" Her smile broadened with her spirit. She stood in defiance of the bombs bursting in the distance outside and gave forth full-throated:

Rising from all over China
A 100,000 Mongol riders advance.
Our nation in crisis
In the summer of 1281.
We have nothing to fear,
Our Kamakura warriors stand ready.
With our righteous military spirit,
We proclaim to the world
With a thunderous roar...
We vow to fight like demons,
To die defending our country...
Heaven is enraged.
The sea surges with massive waves.
The enemy approaches, Mongol hordes, 100,000 strong,
They disappear to the bottom of the sea...
The moon is clear above the Genkai Sea.

The ward reverberated with what sounded like a thousand voices. Besides her three friends, every patient who could was singing at the top of his lungs. Some had tears in their eyes. Other sat up as best as they could, bandages and plaster casts and all. Nothing could stop these men in their patriotic fervour.

After the singing stopped, Fumiko stood with raised arms and wet cheeks and led the crowd in shouting *Banzai!* The bombing coincidentally stopped. Iku-*chan* gushed, "It's true, the gods are with us!" It was a glorious moment.

✿ ✿ ✿

Chiemi watched the patients with a caring eye. She knew most of them by name. Her favourites were Hashimoto-*san*, Tabata-*san*, and Miki-*san*.

Hashimoto-*san* was young, too young to be in a war. He should've been working on his family's rice farm in Fukui. His legs were shattered, probably cannon fire or an aerial bomb, though the doctors managed to save his limbs. How he survived was anyone's guess. Yet he put much stronger men to shame. He displayed a determination to get healthy every day, to be whole again. His smooth youthful features strained with the effort to pull himself up to look around the room, to see the activity carried out by the attendants and medical staff. His arms were consequently muscular even if his upper body was frail. He was ambitious for the future, even wanting to rejoin his unit. Chiemi didn't have the heart to tell him that he would probably never walk again.

Tabata-*san* was blind. Bandages wrapped around his head were applied in a vain attempt to heal him. They most likely gave him some hope, but he instinctively knew he would never again work in an optical factory near Atami. He possessed a gentle manner; he never wanted anyone to bother with him, even if they offered. His body too was frail, most others too. Not surprising.

Miki-*san* was the worst off. He was in a seemingly permanent coma. He just lay in his bed, still and silent. Chiemi found out he was the parent of two boys, like her, and was a business-man in Osaka. She saw in his face compassion, kindness…and optimism. At least, Chiemi imagined it was so.

Such were the ravages of war.

She always welled up with emotion every time she saw them. She couldn't help herself, though she knew she must remain positive. The broken bodies and ruined lives, overall, made her emotional.

Things became considerably worse when the previous January the government began an intensive training program for the entire civilian population of Japan. The "last decisive battle" with the American invading forces was coming. Though the hospital staff was exempted from the training with spears and sticks, Chiemi watched a co-ordinated exercise in a nearby city square. Old men, old women, housewives, young teenagers, boys, and girls, in a formation of straight lines stabbed the air with their spears. Pathetic, but each wore a white bandana with the full red sun printed on the front. They all yelled a *kiai*, a battle cry. She supposed the drills uplifted their spirits. Really though, wooden spears could never stop a soldier with a flamethrower (as the Japanese soldiers on Iwo Jima found out).

The government and military leaders envisioned the entire population would be killed in the invasion; thus, the program was announced as the *Grand Suicide of the One Hundred Million*. A hundred million lives sacrificed for the Emperor.

Mizuyabu Aiko would die for the Emperor, willingly. She took in all the propaganda and threw it back in Chiemi's face. She attended every patriotic rally, exercised with her spear religiously, and recited every pledge she heard. Chiemi couldn't believe her three hospital friends, Fumiko, Eiko, and Iku-*chan*, would do the same. Being loyal to the Emperor was one thing but worshipping Him was another. She just couldn't see the sense in getting killed for Him. She didn't believe Hideki had.

Her children came to mind, and the two Mizuyabu girls. They had everything to live for. The girls would be women soon enough. She argued with Aiko, but she wouldn't listen to reason. Her girls practiced with spears just as hard as their mother.

And her two sons—so *kawaii* (cute) playing with so much energy. Kuniya's impish ways always touched her heart. She was always quick to forgive. She worried about Takeshi and his weak constitution, but she held firm in her belief that all would be well with him. She would not let them join the training squads. As much as Kuniya begged, she did not relent; she saw his great desire to play soldier, but that was anathema to her. She did admit his spirit made sense, given Hideki's nature.

Aiko begged her; she would look after the boys, but Chiemi wouldn't relent. She may be treasonous, but she couldn't see sacrificing their lives for Japan. If she survived and they didn't, what would she do?

Her mother stayed out of it.

The sea will not "surge with massive waves" and destroy the enemy. The *kamikaze* gods had forsaken them.

41.   CAPTAIN INOUYE SHINOBU

A LIGHTNESS SOON ENTERED CHIEMI'S life. Shortly after the defeat at Iwo Jima, a new patient was wheeled into the convalescence hospital. He could walk, albeit with some difficulty, but, according to Dr. Shima's instructions, all patients must be assisted inside by wheelchair. Probably in case of a mishap, Chiemi surmised.

She was drawn to him and found he was a friendly man. She was happy to adjust his bedding, to bring his food, and to read to him. She soon conversed with him, tentatively at first and then more at ease with time.

Captain Inouye Shinobu was a handsome man, with strong facial features, a muscular body, and tall height. His skin was smooth, odd for a man who came from various battle zones. He was from Sendai in the north, a business family. Married with children, he had not seen them since the war started. He had been stationed in China when he fell victim to a sniper's bullet in one of his legs.

The Japanese doctors in a hospital outside Nanking performed surgery, and he recuperated there for about four months. He was then transferred to Hong Kong before moving to the Shima Hospital in Hiroshima. Here he was to finish his recovery.

Chiemi insinuated her way into taking care of him, exclusively, even though she wasn't a nurse. No one minded since there were so many patients.

Iku-*chan* was the first to tease her.

"How is Capt. Inouye coming along?" she asked in her innocent voice.

"How would I know?" Chiemi said incredulously.

"Oh, I don't know. Maybe it's the way you're constantly fussing over him. Always around his bed. Always first to help him with...with everything!"

"Nonsense. I take care of Shinobu-san just as much as any other patient."

"Shinobu-san? You're on a first name basis?"

Caught in a trap, Chiemi tried to extricate herself. "That's his name, isn't it?"

"Yes, I suppose it is," she said with a coy smile.

"Oh, stop it!"

She continued in the lunchroom with Eiko and Fumiko joining the fray.

"You know, he's married?" Eiko informed.

"Yes, I know," Chiemi confirmed, more than a bit irritated at Iku-*chan*. "How do you know?"

"I checked the hospital records."

"Eiko-chan! How could you?"

"Just looking after you."

"And he has two children," Fumiko added.

"You too?"

"That's what friends do," Fumiko said with a smile.

"Honestly, you three!" Was she in high school again?

✿ ✿ ✿

The captain's soft tone of voice and the mellifluous quality of it told Chiemi he was a man of compassion, a kind man. Her spine tingled with the nearness of him.

"Excuse me. May I have a drink of water?"

She stood frozen to the spot. She stared at him for what seemed like an eternity.

"Hello?" he said again.

She suddenly awoke, aware of the situation. Awkwardly and with a stumble, she moved to fulfill the request. She returned with a broad smile as she handed the glass to him.

The captain smiled in return but made no comment.

The long hours of conversation between the two continued throughout the days ahead.

Capt. Inouye had first been stationed in China, near Nanking as it was. He was charged with investigating incidents in the city that involved Japanese soldiers. In most cases, he found that Chinese dissidents were at fault in assaulting or killing infantry men or committing terrorist acts upon military facilities. He was often involved with the arresting of the perpetrators. He said no more about their fates.

He himself fell victim to an ambush. Late one night in December 1940, he was on his way to an *Ian-jo* (a brothel) to probe the circumstances of a murder of an infantry man. He didn't mind confessing that his orders were to keep the whole incident under wraps.

As he turned onto a dark street that led to the establishment, a shot rang out. He felt the sting of something hitting his leg and he collapsed. The winter air made it hurt even more as he related later. His subordinate took care of him while the other men of the patrol tried to ferret out the sniper.

"My time in hospital was painful yet boring," he offered. "Then again, if this hadn't happened, I wouldn't have met you."

Chiemi blushed. Saying nothing, she adjusted his pillow and generally fussed with the bedsheets. She hoped the moment would pass.

She called him "Captain" ever since she misspoke to her friends. "Shinobu" was just too intimate to say in public. Despite Chiemi's discretion, her friends continued to take notice.

"Chiemi-chan, do you know what you're doing?" asked Fumiko.

"No, what?"

Eiko jumped in. "Don't be so coy. You shouldn't spend so much time with Inouye-san."

"What are you talking about? You mean with the captain?"

"The way you hover around his bed. It is getting noticed. Aren't you embarrassed?"

"I don't know what you're talking about." She turned away only to be confronted by Iku-*chan*, her innocent eyes bent with concern.

"I heard the Head Nurse talking to some doctors about you."

"Look," Chiemi said in an angry tone to all three, "mind your own business. There's nothing going on. So what if I pay attention to one patient more than another. As for the Head Nurse, she can fire me if she wants."

"I think it'll be more than that!" Fumiko said. "You'll be disciplined. Transferred somewhere else."

"What if this comes back on Dr. Shima?" Eiko added. "The shame he'll have to endure. Could be the ruin of him."

That gave Chiemi pause. Such an honourable man. She also thought of her family. Her poor mother. Everywhere she went, *Okaasan* would hear whispers.

✿ ✿ ✿

The following late afternoon, Chiemi stood beside the captain. The sun streamed in through the windows and bathed his body with a brilliant and expansive embrace. He was asleep but soon awoke to look up at her.

"Oh, you-ka?" he said smoothly.

"Inouye-san, I must talk to you," she began. "I can no longer take care of you."

"Why not?" he asked.

"Because…because …," she said hesitantly. "Because people are starting to talk."

He pondered as he weighed the significance of what she was saying. "Oh," he said finally.

"I can't let my 'diligence' harm Dr. Shima's reputation." She didn't mention her family.

"I understand."

"So you see, I can't—"

"I said, I understand." He was firm in his conviction.

Chiemi fell silent and turned to go. Just then she heard the captain's voice.

"Perhaps...perhaps we could meet for an afternoon tea? Somewhere. I'm due to be discharged sometime this week. I'll leave a note for you. Discreetly, of course."

Chiemi did not face him but closed her eyes and nodded as she moved away.

42.

CHIEMI CONTEMPLATED THE CAPTAIN'S LAST words to her. Should she see him outside the hospital? What would people say? Would the gossip intensify? She would have to do it, as he put it, discreetly. But to what end? He was married; she was married.

Then Fumiko said something in the hushed environment of a hospital corridor that gave her pause.

"It's a good thing you stopped fussing over the 'Captain.'"

"Why?"

"I've heard things." Her face turned into the shadows. "He's been with other women. Lots. Using them and then leaving them. You've done well being rid of him."

She breathed relief. His easy ways, his charming presence, she grinned secretly. She thought of her husband with the too skinny body, the buckteeth, and weak chin. By contrast, he was the plain-looking and dull office clerk, whereas Capt. Inouye was dashing and so attractive. A true hero.

At home, she looked at the note he had handed her surreptitiously. It proposed that they meet in Chinatown for tea and *dim sum* in about a week. At 11:00 a.m., at a place called Club China House near the Hatsukaichi train station.

She thought it strange that a Chinese restaurant was still in operation during the war. She didn't think about it too long; instead, she began to fantasize while in her bed.

When the darkness closed in on her, she felt safe and alone. In her half dream, she imagined what it would be like—a cool and quiet room of light green and flowers with an *ofuton* and *tatami*. A slight wind wrapped around her naked body. Nearby was the captain, just as naked and glowing in the dark. He approached her, kissed her, and led her down to the *ofuton*. She felt his hands explore her, diving into intimate places. She groaned and submitted to her revelry.

She opened her eyes and found that her hand had descended to her nether region. It was wet with the manipulation. She smiled as she rolled back her eyes. Ecstasy. A state of joy came over her.

❀ ❀ ❀

It was early April, and the skies were overcast. The train ride west of the city to Hatsukaichi was long but tolerable, the cars rumbled and lurched their way across town and out from there into the countryside.

Omachi train station was clean, noisy but tolerably attractive. A cherry tree grew in the middle of one of the platforms. It was not in blossom even though it was spring. She guessed it didn't have enough sunlight. Beyond the station, though, the street was wide and open, and the sun shone brightly.

The Club China House Restaurant, a short block away, was decorated with Chinese flourishes. Golden dragons guarded the front door. The primary colours were red and gold, of course, and ribbons and garlands festooned the walls outside and in. Many tables and chairs dotted the dining room. Waiters flew around the large room serving an endless number of customers. They held mysterious but sumptuous platters of food. The smells were heavenly, if not exotic. She had not seen anything like it. The establishment was inexplicably bustling like a grand train station.

Capt. Inouye greeted her and, with a wave of the hand, invited her to sit at one of the tables in the back.

"So nice to see you again," the captain said. "I'm glad you came."

"Didn't think I would," she said with a worried look.

"Why not? This is an innocent tea between nurse and patient."

"I'm not a nurse."

"Friends then."

Chiemi blushed. She soon learned why the place had survived the war. The owners were Japanese. Endo-*san*, the patriarch with a large belly and jovial nature enclosed by a tight-fitting and old-fashioned tuxedo, had been born in Tokyo but raised in Shanghai. With the approach of war, his father decided to move the family back to Japan. The family then opened a Chinese restaurant since that was what they knew best.

The captain and Chiemi spent the next hour dining on dumplings of what she thought was shrimp (most likely chopped up bamboo) and conversing. She did wonder where the restaurant got the ingredients, the flour especially, for the *har gow*. Only for a second or two since she spent most of the time gazing at the captain's face.

At some point, Inouye reached to touch Chiemi's hand. "You are quite lovely."

She blushed again, but his touch was electrifying.

❀ ❀ ❀

At the end of the meal, the two sat in companionable silence in their seats. The restaurant too was quiet. Sunlight shone through the windows and bathed the room in a bright radiance. It seemed an understanding, like the light, had settled between the couple.

The captain looked to a nearby waiter, dressed in a shabby tuxedo. He as it happened was Endo-*san*'s maître d.' The suit fabric, stained and wrinkled, hung loose over his slight build but stayed in place. The captain nodded as did the waiter, who motioned for them to follow him.

They walked upstairs to the second floor. Chiemi walked past several rooms. She thought she heard fragmented and hushed conversations behind several. Finally, she came to a stop at the end of the hall. The headwaiter graciously opened the door and invited her inside. The captain followed, slipping a few bills into an outstretched hand.

The room was small and dingy. A torn curtain offered a semblance of privacy over the double dirty window. There was no furniture, but there was an *ofuton*, thin and ragged. There was an odour that floated about the room, the smell of uncleanliness and age. The wooden floor was well scratched but sturdy.

Chiemi, disappointed, said nothing as the captain approached her. He kissed her; his lips were as soft as she had imagined. She reacted by embracing him, feeling his muscles grasping her in return. He then moved away slightly and wordlessly began undressing her. Her *kimono* loosened and then dropped to the floor. Her undergarments too. Her hair unravelled and draped over her bare shoulders and breasts. She trembled with the cold and anticipation, her breathing intensified. He led her to the *ofuton*, and she lay down. It was stained and coloured brown with misuse. She noticed but was quickly distracted. The captain disrobed in front of her, his glorious body coming into full view before her. The scar on his left leg was quite prominent, quite ugly, but somehow it excited her even more. She reached for him, and he collapsed into her arms, his mouth enveloping her mouth; probing tongue exploring her mouth and then her body.

Waves of pleasure came over her. And a smile traced across her face. She began to sweat with the manoeuvring and the friction. She moaned as she never moaned for her husband. Her legs rose in the air almost independently. She wanted to take him into herself and never let him go. And at the peak of emotion, she felt release. Soon thereafter, the captain rolled off her and lay beside her breathing deeply trying to recover.

Chiemi looked to the window and could see nothing through the grime. It didn't help that the sun had disappeared.

✽ ✽ ✽

She returned to the Club China House Restaurant a few more times with the good Captain, whenever she and he could get away from their responsibilities. She soon found out that Chinese food was not the main source of income for the establishment; Endo-*san* made his money from renting the rooms upstairs to military officers. The place was in the business of clandestine adultery.

She didn't care. The temptation was too great. Too much suffering in the world anyway. The walls around Japan strengthened but threatened to collapse. She never knew where he slept at night, military headquarters she assumed, but simply did not know. Again, she didn't care; she didn't want to live with him. She glowed from within whenever she returned to the hospital. Her friends noticed but she never said a word.

Eiko especially had become the hospital gossip and was the first to notice Chiemi's inner change.

"Why are you so happy?"

"I'm always happy," Chiemi said.

"No, you're not. Have you been seeing Captain Inouye?"

"What a ridiculous thing to say. How can you say such a thing?" Chiemi's face contorted with anger. "I don't even know where he is these days."

Iku-*chan* stepped forward. "Do you love him?"

Chiemi barked, "Enough! I am not seeing the captain and I don't love him!"

The conversation abruptly ended.

43.

SPRING 1945 AND THE CHERRY blossoms, the *sakura*, painted
the landscape in pink beauty. Chiemi, Aiko, her mother, and the
children celebrated *hanami*, the festival of cherry blossom view-
ing, with a picnic at near the end of the season in early May. They
sat among the nearby trees planted by her father so many years
ago. It became a tradition to appreciate the transient nature of
the flowers. *Impermanence.*

The boys chased each other around the tree trunks. Naturally,
Kuniya climbed onto one or two branches. Takeshi did not; he
was starting to exhibit signs of caution, another side to his character was emerging. Kuniya soon tired himself out and lay by his
mother in a contemplative mood. The girls sat with the parents,
demurely sipping their tea and biting into their *mochi*. Haruye
made the sweet morsels with the last of the white rice, red beans,
and sugar.

It was the kind of activity and day that took their minds
away from the war, except for Chiemi. She thought of her last
day with the captain.

As usual, they sat in silence at the end of lunch in the Club
China House. This time, however, Inouye broke the quiet.

"Chiemi-chan," he opened, "I have to tell you something."

It was the first time he had called her by the term of affec-
tion. It felt like a betrayal of some kind. She said nothing and
the moment passed.

As she fell into her thoughts, he continued. "I've been
assigned to Tokyo."

She suddenly became aware of the revelation. "What do
you mean?"

"I have to go to Tokyo. I've been reassigned."

"For how long?" Her eyes began to quiver; her hands clenched into fists.

"Permanently."

Chiemi cast her eyes downwards towards the table.

"You know this couldn't've lasted forever. I will rejoin my family…"

Her face flared with anger. Her cheeks turned red. She abruptly stood disrupting her plate and hashi, chopsticks. Her hands covered her face as she ran out of the restaurant. She even pushed Endo-san aside as he tried to block her.

It was the last time Chiemi saw Capt. Inouye. Reason soon descended afterwards. She knew their liaisons could not last forever, she should've expected it. In fact, she surprised herself with her reaction. She yearned for more time together. Their affair was too brief, not enough really to know him, to take in his spirit to become a part of her. Her body ached for him in the quiet darkness of her home.

In late April, when the hospital was exceptionally busy with new patients needing attention, Eiko ran up to Chiemi and tried to talk to her quietly.

"What is it Eiko-chan? Can't you see I'm busy?" She continued to make one of the beds for a freshly wounded soldier in from the Philippines.

But Eiko insisted. She tugged on Chiemi's sleeve until she paid attention. "Chiemi-san, I've got something to tell you!"

Chiemi stopped and stood to confront her bothersome friend. "Oh, all right, what do you want?"

"I was reading the list…you know, the War Dead List… and…," she gasped.

"And what?"

"I saw Capt. Inouye's name on it."

"What? You must be mistaken."

"No, I'm not. I checked it several times, just in case."

***

Chiemi dropped everything, grabbed her light jacket, and ran out into the street, not really caring how it looked. She headed straight for the Hiroshima Prefectural Industrial Promotion Hall. The War-Dead List in front was the closest one.

The sun blinded her temporarily, but she soon regained her sight. The city streets were quiet for some odd reason; birds twittered from the trees; a few cicadas sang to the slight breeze. The nearby Ota River flowed with whitecaps through the delta into the Seto Inland Sea.

Out of breath, she saw the bulletin board outside the administration building. A small but insistent crowd had formed, but she pushed her way to the front. Her eyes trembled as they scanned the lists in front of her. The names were not in alphabetical order; instead, they were arranged chronologically. And since she didn't know the relevant date, she had to finger-trace to find the name and to steady herself. Name after name after name, hundreds of them, flew by as she sought the familiar. Her breathing became more pronounced.

Finally, on page three, she came across Captain Inouye Shinobu. She read and reread the ideograms to see if it was a mistake. But no, it was her captain, the spelling familiar from the hospital records. He had been killed in the early March incendiary air raids of Tokyo, Japan. No mention of the captain's whereabouts other than Tokyo, his circumstances; no mention of his family. She later learned that the bombing was part of *Operation Meetinghouse* when 500,000 died in total. Another prosaic number, so simple, so matter of fact in black-and-white.

She stood transfixed, concentrating on the name despite the jostling of others reading the list. She could not move on her own. She wanted to scream; she wanted to cry like the others around her. But could not. She was there forever, it seemed, until the crowd pressed on her to leave.

A dull pain formed in her stomach as she went back to the hospital. It stayed with her, but it subsided to a tolerable irritation. She said nothing to her friends, and they didn't ask. In fact, they avoided eye contact. She resumed her duties.

At home, she sat in the *Oni Room* before the *butsudan*. She considered placing a photograph of the captain inside the altar to join her ancestors, but soon dismissed the idea. How could she explain the missing photograph from the hospital records? How was she to explain his inclusion? She did light an incense stick for him.

As she meditated in *gassho*, that stomach-ache came back. It was not from hunger or something she ate, neither indigestion nor gastric discomfort. Yet it was there and made her skin crawl as it expanded. Emotion rose in her, colouring her face red and causing mucus to run out of her nose. A moment later, she burst into tears.

✿ ✿ ✿

Haruye's voice brought her back to the present. "Chiemi-chan, are you all right? Where were you?"

"Oh, just thinking of an old friend."

"Who?"

"No one special. Let's enjoy our day of peace while we can." The boys squealed with delight.

44.   MONDAY AUGUST 6, 1945

CAPT. INOUYE WAS DEAD. THE walls around Japan had cracked and collapsed, turned to rubble. Chiemi had thought about him over the months since she had learned of his death. Less so when summer finally arrived. But, in quiet moments, she did savour the memories of their times together: the sumptuous lunches, the grotty upstairs room, the nefarious Endo-*san*, and the secret satisfaction she derived. She continued to sob in the *Oni Room*—discreetly and always alone. The cold settled around her like a grieving companion.

From old newspapers, Chiemi saw the destruction of Tokyo. She gasped at the photographs. She shivered as she imagined the victims caught in the attack, buried in the debris. Then there was the captain's last moments. His body must've flared like a match ignited.

She sat before the *butsudan* much more often. She gazed at the photographs of Hideki and her father. An absent Capt. Inouye came to mind, and she thought of Chisato until her hands grew pale as the blood drained. She raised her fists and shook them. The lines of her face deepened. Her eyes moistened; her breath quickened. Perspiration appeared on her forehead. She envisioned the *Hinomaru* flag waving in the wind, snapping and flapping, and she growled, "Chikuso." *Damnation.*

❊ ❊ ❊

The skies were always clear in August, noticeably clear, a bright, bright blue, wide-open over the city. Nary a cloud. Certainly, before that day; certainly after, but not on that day.

The sun was just starting to make its climb to the top of the day, the heat and humidity were building as they always did.

Chiemi as usual wore her uniform to go to work. Her clothes were smart, and she was proud of her look but a bit too hot for the weather. A light *yukata* would've been better, but appearances must be kept. The *yukata* she wore at home was light with a bright pattern of maple leaves from Canada decorating it, the fabric a wedding present from her sister a few years ago. It comforted her in these days of strife and war. She smiled as she recalled calling her *gaijin* as a tease.

Chi-chan, I haven't seen her in, what?...ten, no, fifteen years, maybe longer. I suppose not, it just feels like it. Probably more like five. I miss her, of course. Then again, I miss the three of us being together with our father watching over us. What happened? We got lost somehow.

The trolley, green and yellow with a blunt front, clanked and jostled its usual self as it made its way to the centre of Hiroshima. The surrounding tall, three or four-storey buildings dreaming or in silent contemplation were not yet busy with the comings and goings of scroungers, shoppers, and businesspeople. All was quiet except for banners that festooned most walls, each with some patriotic slogan seemingly blaring out its message. She noticed a new one just the other day: "FORGET SELF! ALL OUT FOR YOUR COUNTRY!" And then there were the loudspeakers squawking from every corner and lamppost about the war even at this time of day—loud and painful to the ears. *Slogans, slogans, slogans, loud, misleading, and insidious slogans rule our lives.*

Mysterious music magically arises and carries me away. Temple bells and gongs, Sensei chanting the Heart Sutra calms the noise of the cityscape. I slowly spread my arms and fly across the skies. Music is invisible, like a benign spirit that lifts and soothes.

War must not intrude.

❋ ❋ ❋

She always liked it when the city opened to the wide mountainous horizon as the trolley rattled across the Yokogawa-*bashi*, a small tied-arch bridge over the Yokogawa River, a waterway with cement shores. The iron arches were elegant in shape. The noise faded away behind her. She imagined herself embraced and enveloped by nature: the forest, the water, the mountains, the very landscape itself. Unfortunately, the trolley crossed too quickly.

It was hot. Humid more than anything else. She shouldn't have worn so many undergarments. It was summer. What was she thinking?

I wish I could run down the street in my all-together! Don't be stupid. Imagine that. My shame would be my family's shame.

❋ ❋ ❋

At least, the breeze, a hot, moist breeze, coming in through the trolley window offered some relief.

Just after 7:30 a.m. The reliable clock tower was always true. She'd be early, but she could get an early start on finishing those bandages she started rolling yesterday.

She walked into the Shima Hospital and went downstairs to the locker room. She quickly shuffled past the beds carefully so as not to disturb the still sleeping patients. In the locker room, she stored away her possessions before heading back into the patient area.

A new ward had to be added for the too many wounded soldiers admitted. At least it was filled with light from the several windows lining the top half of the walls. Her thoughts turned to the heat.

The hospital is stifling even in the basement. Poor soldiers.
They suffer so much. Why am I here? It's not like I'm earning
any money; I was conscripted into doing this. Not like Hideki.

He volunteered. He should be here. What time is it? Almost 8:00.

The day would start soon, and her friends will be arriving. She wondered what new bit of gossip Eiko-*chan* will be armed with. Oh well, she'd hear it at lunch.

As it happened, Eiko along with Iku-*chan* were the first to arrive. "Chiemi-chan, good morning!" they greeted with a cheery smile. They both looked as fresh as a spring day.

Others soon came into the room. Their initial banter was warm and friendly. Some patients stirred. Chiemi knew their spirits lifted with the activity.

The *Morning Pledge* and Dr. Shima's address would take part at 8:30, so they began to prepare the men for transport to another hall nearby since it was too difficult to take them upstairs to the main hall. The basement room was equipped with speakers.

For some reason, Chiemi decided to go upstairs, possibly to help Dr. Shima with whatever. When she first mounted the steps, she heard the air raid siren warning of imminent attack.

So early, she thought. *Why can't the Americans just stop? Why can't General Tojo negotiate peace?*

A pause at 8:15 a.m., and then Chiemi heard a deafening explosion, she turned to see the windows smash open with a blinding flash, shards of glass flew everywhere, and a wave of fire hit her, blowing her up the stairs. She folded into the stairs and lost consciousness.

45.

WHERE AM I? SHE ASKED herself when she regained full consciousness. She was in front of the Aioi bridge. It had been destroyed but remained intact. She vaguely recalled walking to that point. Her memory faded in and out. She turned her head and then the pain enveloped her. She nearly collapsed.

She saw that most of her clothes were gone, burned off. What little was left was nearly ash and crumbling, sticking to her skin. Her joints ached. Her body ached. Her head too. Her skin was blotched with oozing blisters: pus seeped out of them, all yellow or clear. Her breasts were fully uncovered except that they were burned black with slashes of red exposed. She was in her altogether, but her nakedness meant nothing to her.

Every step felt like she was lifting a concrete block. She came to a stop to mitigate the pain. It didn't work. She twisted around with much difficulty to look at the nearby Shima Hospital. Most of it was destroyed but three of the walls remained standing, half standing. The thick concrete must've prevented total annihilation.

But what of her friends in the hospital? Iku-*chan*, Fumiko, Eiko... She tried calling out, but no sound came out of her mouth. Her throat was sore. She did taste the bitterness of charred remains. What about the patients? Hashimoto, Tabata, Miki... Dr. Shima? What happened to him? What could do all this? How many bombs fell? The Americans were so cruel. *Karma* in its purest form.

The *samurai* outside the *Oni Room* was laughing at her. No, there was something different about him. His countenance had changed. Not a smile...but a look of compassion. Or so she imagined.

Aiko-*san*, the girls, her children, were they all right? *Kuniya, Takeshi? Okaasan?* Was the Akamatsu Compound destroyed? She must get home. She knew that now; she remembered her resolve.

❀ ❀ ❀

She turned and began walking eastward across the Aioi-*bashi*, with its t-shape, it was the most distinctive bridge in Hiroshima. She passed a trolley burning on it. The metal twisted in the flames. The seats warped. She turned her head to the river below and noticed that there was very little water in it. A harder look revealed skeletal black bodies stuck in the mud standing in grotesque poses of agony. In fact, all around her were piles of burnt corpses, hardly human, certainly dead. *This must've been the captain's fate...the Shimo Hospital staff...her friends.*

She saw in the distance most buildings were razed, a few still stood but the bones of the buildings laid bare and smouldering in the muted sun. Prominent among them was the Hiroshima Prefectural Industrial Promotion Hall, the grand building where her father had brought her when she was a little girl. The dome's structure, though shattered, remained suspended as a hollow shell, intricate lace like a spider's web. A few walls supported it but most of the Promotion Hall had lost its integrity and had collapsed to the ground as rubble. Its shiny floor smooth enough to slide along, the various halls leading to secret parts, the overhead lights that illuminated like the brightest day were gone, all gone.

What had happened? An incendiary bomb attack? Like Tokyo?

She fell to the red-and-white linoleum covered stairs and squeezed herself into the crease of wall and steps. A fierce wind roared up the staircase. A Fire-Wind. Her clothes, her body were set ablaze; her skin scalded, she twisted in pain, in agony, she screamed before crumpling into unconsciousness. She thought she heard her friends, patients screaming from below. But no, only silence as her mind darkened.

She stepped off the bridge with difficulty and stepped northward, towards home. It began to rain. The water was cool and a touch of relief for her. But then she realized, the rain was black. *Black rain.* Fragments pasted onto her skin, sealing the blisters, stopping the pus from oozing. For that she was grateful. But what is this *black rain?*

The riverbed underneath the bridge was turning wet with it. The rain turned into a torrent replenishing the evaporated river. Bodies in the mud floated to the surface and bobbed in place. Were they alive? Barely recognizable arms and legs reached for the skies from underneath the black water. An *oni's* blood flowed towards the delta.

Bodies sank into mud, ash, and dust. All part of the scattered army of the dead.

✿ ✿ ✿

From the other side of the bridge, she moved in the direction she thought was home. The trolley tracks were a good guide marker. *Follow the river upstream.* That was her plan. She struggled to get her legs to obey. They rebelled. Her left leg dragged behind as the right pulled her ahead. Her arms were numb and useless, her head heavy and dull. It was a wonder she remained upright.

The landscape around her was grey, from the sky to the ground…grey. Rubble in piles everywhere. Half-walls stood but looked like they were about to disintegrate and collapse. Black skeletons swaying in the hot wind.

No relief anywhere.

Occasionally along the way, she saw shadows against low walls or on the sidewalks. They were shaped like bodies. *Otousan?* Could it be? Had he returned to help her? She needed him now. But no, there were too many of them and they didn't move with her.

They were the shadows of human beings incinerated against the wall and where they stood. She tried to close her eyes to the evaporated horror, but she could not. Her eyes were seared open, it seemed.

She could only move onwards towards home.

Where are the posters…the slogans? The comfort of the people. What good are slogans now?

Her mind wandered. Chisato was always bothering her growing up together. *Make a kimono for me; teach me the latest odori; feed me. What a bother!* The worse times came when she fought with *Oniisan.*

> "Here, I'll be the samurai," Hideki said as he wielded his toy katana. "You be the Chankoro!"
>
> "Why am I the Chinese?" Chisato complained. "I want to be the samurai."
>
> "Baka! I'm the boy."
>
> "What's that got to do with anything?"
>
> "The Chankoro are like little girls. Weak and stupid. I am a man doing his duty for the glory of the Emperor!"
>
> "Aho! I can do my duty for the Emperor too!"
>
> "Don't be ridiculous—"
>
> "Will you commit hara kiri after you've done your duty?"
>
> "What?"
>
> "You know, cut your stomach open once you're done."
>
> "That's ridiculous."
>
> "I would! That's what true samurai do," Chisato insisted. "I bet it hurts."
>
> "Damare! What do you know?"
>
> The shouting brought Chiemi to intercede. Always.

Hideki was the patriotic one with a vivid imagination. He constantly saw himself in battle, fighting whatever enemy of Japan he saw at the time: the Chinese, the Mongols, the Russians, the Koreans, the British, the Americans. Did he know the family was of the Warrior Class? *Fight for peace.* Did *Okaa* tell him? Chiemi had only heard about it the one time. And she never heard Hideki bragging about it. That was something he surely would've done.

Chiemi smiled, or thought she had, at the memories. She missed her siblings terribly and mother especially.

❊ ❊ ❊

She remembered the day her mother called her to the kitchen.

"Ah, Chiemi-chan. Come learn how to make rice," she said.

Chiemi must've been six or seven-years-old at the time. Okaasan thought it was time for her daughter to make the basic ingredient of a meal. Chiemi was tall for her age so she could reach all the supplies and lift the cooking implements.

From a large tin can, Okaa scooped four or five cups of rice into an iron pot. She filled it with water and swished it about with her hand three times, until the water was clear. She then measured the water up to the first knuckle on her right hand, adjusted the level, covered the pot, and placed it over the fire.

The rice boiled until it overflowed. Okaasan took it off the high heat and let it stand over a low fire. In approximately half an hour, the rice was ready, perfectly cooked.

"You see how easy that is, Chiemi-chan."

Chiemi took it all in and marveled at how the grains of rice had become fluffy steamed rice. The steam from the open kama, rice pot, warmed her young, plump skin. It felt like…home.

She tried it herself the next time and, though it was a bit burnt, brown and too crisp on the bottom, she was forgiven and told she would get better as time progressed. Her mother was filled with love while she watched.

That Chiemi remembered.

Her father was a reserved, quiet man. He hardly ever expressed emotion. But she knew he loved her and the family. He made a good life for them in growing rice, in lumbering, and in fishing, with a fleet of boats. He built a beautiful compound with a distinctive bushy fence surrounding the estate. They never wanted for food, clothing, or anything really. Well, after he was gone, in the time of war, they experienced hard times just like everyone else. Maybe the various measures enacted by the government were necessary. She didn't know; she ached for rice most of all, since it was in short supply, even in the Black Market.

When *Otousan* "left" them, Chiemi feared for the future.

Hideki should've taken over, ensuring our well-being. He is Oniisan. He just did that stupid thing he did and left. Selfish.

She suddenly realized her father had not known his grandsons particularly long. He would've loved them for their spirit and for their *kawaii* looks as they grew. But they were so precious when they were born. He would've spoiled them, that she knew. Even in the short time he was with them, he gave them candy indiscriminately.

And when she complained, "Why do you give them so much? You never gave me so much. You'll rot out their teeth!"
"I am Ojiichan. Their teeth aren't my responsibility," he explained with a wry smile.
Kuniya, Takeshi. My babies, so precious…so precious.

She liked the hospital work most of all because it was a chance to get out of her parents' house, away from her rambunctious sons. She loved them, but they were a handful at the best of times. More irritating than her younger sister had ever been. She never understood how her mother and Aiko could manage them. The hospital was a nice break. Had been.

Tears flowed down her cheeks…or at least, she thought she could feel the wet.

Maybe the Black Rain is my sorrow.

The Perversion of the Buddha's 8-fold Path
for the Emperor's War
Enlightenment

46.

HOW LONG HAVE I BEEN *walking?* There was no way of telling what time it was. Or how much time had passed. She did know the coming of night. In the gathering darkness, she saw creatures wandering; the apparitions with hollow but shining eyes, elongated arms of loose skin dragging behind them, and faltering legs, looking for...what...salvation? Maybe praying for an end... for death. She saw the petrified bodies standing in place, some impaled by shards of wood or glass. Other bodies burnt to a crisp but still standing, like dead trees after a forest fire. One was comical in posture; like the *dokekata* comic character in *kabuki.* Two pieces of lumber had spiked the body of a young woman and anchored it in position in the ground before her. Her half-facial expression was one of total surprise. Comical if not for the horrifying implication. The surrounding landscape dark and shadowed mounds of rubble, a landscape of horror. Hiroshima had become an eternal Hell.

She fell asleep as she lay on the ground. No mean feat to lie down, but she managed with some effort. She vowed out loud, "I will not die, not now...not here."

A bowl of rice, hot, fluffy white rice, appeared in her dreamscape. Stomach pains woke her. She touched her abdomen and the aching disappeared. Water gurgled somewhere nearby. Was she thirsty? She couldn't tell, but she noticed a broken lead pipe jutting out the ground. A spigot with an arch of water flowing out of it. She realized she had seen many pipes along the way. She pulled herself along the ground; fortunately, it wasn't far away. She felt the liquid against her lips, her mouth, down her throat, but it offered no relief. It wasn't even cold. Then again, she really couldn't tell.

When she finished her fill, she fell asleep on the spot and dreamed of a shining bowl of rice.

✿ ✿ ✿

Morning. Morning was not morning with the sun shining and flowers dancing in the breeze. It was grey, hot, and foul smelling, like unseen corpses rotting. Chiemi stirred and remembered what had happened. The pain came back as she rose in the still, smoky air. She continued her journey gingerly.

Her left leg, her curse, still dragged; it was useless. But she pressed on, keeping in mind her children.

The hours slid into hours as she moved along the trolley tracks. A ghostly monster saw her and followed for a pace. The elastic skin of his arms dragged behind, leaving a trail in the black ground. He soon fell by the wayside, exhausted by the exertion, mercifully dying or dead.

Chiemi could not stop to help. Her mind would not allow her to feel compassion. Her own skin had opened even more, the wounds gapped like hungry birds waiting for nourishment, but none came, no relief from pain. And no blood oozed out. Blisters all over her body (those she could see) grew larger and new ones formed; the blood and yellow-green pus seemed to coagulate in contact with the air. Was she turning into a wandering ghost?

Sometime during the day, she came face to face with a nearly blank wall. Nearly because a huge red circular splotch adorned it. *It must be blood*, she thought. There was no sign of a body, anywhere, but she knew what had happened.

She grimaced and grinned a sardonic smirk. The splotch was in the shape of a rough circle. *The Hinomaru, the Japanese flag*. She lurched away from the telling symbol.

✿ ✿ ✿

Night fell again and again she found a spot to sleep. But this time something was different: she discovered she was lying on grass! Green and cool soft grass. It was a small patch of vegetation, but the aroma, even if tinged by smoke, was intoxicating. Her spirits were raised as if some gigantic burden was lifted. *Hope...hope.* She slept soundly.

Her babies squirmed on their *futon*, always busy, always restless. Her Takeshi, cute and endearing, smiled up at her. Kuniya can take care of himself, she thought, but what about Takeshi?

She awoke in the moist aftermath of happiness. But she was not lying on grass. It was morning with a sun weakly shining behind the eternally overcast sky. The ground was grey and black around her and in the distance. All ash and sharp-edged cinders had cut into the bottoms of her feet. Numb to the pain. Fatigue slowly overcame her consciousness.

No grass, it was the memory of grass. Words poured onto her dreamscape.

The Americans are a cruel people. They bomb indiscriminately. They kill blindly, without conscience or compassion: babies, young girls, young boys, the elderly. Captain... How could they do that?

Her thoughts once more faded into a dark sleep.

✿ ✿ ✿

Once she recovered somewhat, she climbed to her feet and continued walking for a good long time. She struggled along until she saw trees surrounding her, slowly but surely. The ground gradually changed from scarred and scattered ash to green. She approached a familiar hill, a grass-covered hill. She looked to the top and saw it was the rise to the Akamatsu Compound. Sure enough, as she reached the modest summit, she saw the thick stands of trees and bushy fence around the estate. *Could it be?* She reached out to grasp the vegetation in the distance.

Suspecting it was real, she quickened her pace as best as she could. *Only a few steps more.*

In excruciating agony, she lifted her right arm until her hand caressed the bushes. The morning dew was cool. She brought her hand to her mouth and tasted it. She beamed.

She struggled along the fence until she found an opening. She stepped inside only to hear a scream. It was Mitsue, Aiko's eldest daughter.

"Obasan!" she said startled, shocked, and concerned. "Is that really you? Look what they've done... Oh my... Where've you been? It's been over two weeks since..." Her voice trailed away.

Chiemi's body was stiff from her injuries but was able to move. Mitsue helped her into the house, though she hesitated to touch her aunt.

Once inside, Chiemi collapsed to the *tatami* and wood as Mitsue called for others to come help. The floor was cool to the touch. In the rush of household members coming to her, she heard familiar voices.

"Chiemi-chan, it is you! I can't believe you're here."

"Okaa...okaa," she rasped.

"Okaasan! Okaasan!" Her babies shrieked. "What happened? Are you—"

"Mitsue, take the boys away!" Haruye ordered.

Relief came over Chiemi. Her babies were safe. She felt her mother's arms propping her up. "Okaa...Aiko...?"

"We don't know... She went to the high school to practice as she always does. Then... We haven't heard from her. How in the world did you survive? Look at you! We'll get you Dr. Kubota. He's nearby," she said assuredly. "Go get him, Mitsue."

"Okaa...okaa," Chiemi said as she reached up and touched the sleeve of her *kimono*. Her mother's perfume enveloped her.

Okaasan reached and embraced her daughter, something she hadn't done since she was a baby. She held Chiemi in the crook of her arm.

Chiemi widened her eyes as best as she could. The blurred image of her mother came into focus, but then faded. But her words came back to her. A deeply black shadow quickly enveloped Haruye's outline. It expanded and embraced Chiemi's body. And she immediately understood. Chiemi tried to sit up and, in a hoarse, rasping voice yelled, with the last of her strength,

"Otousan, we are warriors. Otou…sa…a search for peace, peace…"

CHISATO

The Three Jewels of Buddhism: the Buddha,
the Dharma, and the Sangha.

47.   1940S

SANDON, THE CANADIAN BUDDHIST INTERNMENT camp
during WWII, proved to be a curse and a blessing. It was as
everyone had said: plagued by the devil's cold breath. The high
mountain ranges of the Kootenays on either side of the thin
strip of cabins running up and down the valley gave the place
only limited sunlight on a good day. A freezing wind screamed
up the chasm.

The settlement itself sat beside Carpenter Creek right near
its junction with Sandon Creek. A three-storey wooden building,
the old City Hall, dominated the area. There were other buildings: an abandoned dry goods store, hotel, and bars, but they
were all in disrepair. A Methodist church stood empty, mute in
its spreading of the Word of God.

Sato-*san*, a fireplug of a man with a determined look, of
Vancouver led a crew of a dozen carpenters to fix up the existing
buildings and build new cabins for about 1,000 internees. The
place became busy with noise and activity for awhile. In time,
the places were all ready for the new inhabitants.

The church was quickly selected and converted into the
Buddhist church since everyone in camp was Buddhist. Reverend
Tsuji, fresh from his education and training in Japan (on the last
boat back to Canada), arrived to preside. His duties included all
the internment camp churches in British Columbia though he
was centred in Slocan. He was a *Nisei*, young but considered to
be a good man, mature beyond his years.

The large congregation celebrated with a special service and meal when *Sensei* brought a gold-painted statue of the Buddha. Where he got it was anyone's guess. Reminded Chisato of *The Jesus*.

Chisato, weathered by experience and with a daughter to raise on her own, often wondered what became of her husband Kiyoshi. He disappeared after he set their house on fire. It was gutted as a result. He was last seen, someone said, running down the back alley behind the house.

Kiyoshi Kimura seemingly had everything. A beautiful wife, she immodestly thought. A grand house, well-respected in the community and in the Christian church, successful businessman, and a wonderful child. Yet, he wallowed in sin. She supposed he was a typical Japanese man: outwardly an upstanding citizen while hiding a seedy side. She would never understand. She secretly hoped he was dead, having met a grisly end. Would she ever know?

Life in Sandon wasn't all that bad, even if she was an *Enemy Alien*. The injustice, the injustice. She wondered who to blame for all the misfortune and suffering. *Life is dukkha*. But she had survived and in her own community. There was no need to be a "pretend Christian". In camp, she got to know and befriend several Buddhist *Nikkei*: the Yoneyama family; the Yonekura family (the "Yo-Yos" she called them to herself with a smile); the Kuroda family.

Hide Hyodo, the only BC accredited teacher in the *Nikkei* community, was a Christian but full of compassion. Hideko, Chisato's daughter, would continue her education once Hyodo-*san* set up a school system among the internment camps. Hideko started calling herself "Hi-de" in admiration of the principal.

The high school was the top floor of the old CPR train station. Hideko and her fellow elementary school students were somewhere else in the lower portions of the building. The Catholic nuns of the Sisters of Christ the King convent acted as teachers along with some of the older high-school girls. Hyodo-*san* organized them well. Chisato paid no mind to the Christian influence; Hideko was continuing her education.

A hospital, with twenty beds and run by Dr. Shimotakahara, an itinerant physician, provided care for anyone who needed medical attention. It had a clinic, surgery, and isolation ward. No coal storage bin for the dead and dying. The staff stayed upstairs from the converted BC Security offices. Dr. Tanaka, a dentist, came once a week.

The landscape was beautiful with the tall mountains, rocky terrain, and rushing waters. The air was clean, free of the lumber industry, the abattoir, and Hastings Park, but Chisato gazed at the Colossuses surrounding her and the settlement. She was struck by the natural wall of rock in front of her; she felt small, a mere speck in a vast wilderness. If she stepped into the surrounding forests, the depths would swallow her, and she would be lost forever.

The best part of the place was the fact that there was only one *keto-jin*: a provincial police officer named James Kennedy. He really had nothing to do; of course, the *Nikkei* were law-abiding people.

He used to joke with the older *Nisei* men. "It's such a quiet life here! If they'd locked up a thousand Irishmen up here, they'd be at least two-thousand cops to ride herd on them!"

His laugh was hearty and Chisato didn't understand until someone translated. She felt a sense of pride in that. She decided he wasn't such a bad man, even friendly.

Internees took up gardening when the weather permitted, and they sold their crop to the Doukhobors who lived nearby.

If it wasn't for the fact that they were forced to live there, she might've enjoyed the place. On the other hand, the winters were severe. People worried about avalanches preventing government supplies from getting through.

Kondo-*san* opined one snowy day, "It cost the government a lot more money to keep this place going than other camps!"

He has such a big face, Chisato chuckled to herself. It matched the rest of his corpulent body. Fortunately, no avalanches occurred until after they left.

The days were short in the winter; the mountains had something to do with that. They blocked out the sunlight, limiting it sometimes to two hours a day.

Late 1942, just before *Oshogatsu*, a truck rolled up the road into camp. It came to a stop in front of the Buddhist church where a large crowd of internees gathered. Everyone rustled in anticipation as a short man in a suit and overcoat stepped out of the vehicle. His nub of a mustache sat underneath his nostrils and his hair was cut short, nearly bald even in the dead of winter.

"Who is that?" Chisato asked from her vantage point.

"Morii Etsuji."

So that's Morii. Short. He didn't look so dangerous.

Morii arrived bearing a gift: a couple hundred pounds of rice. People gasped at the precious and rare gift. The kids salivated at the prospect of hot, steamed rice.

Morii puffed himself up as he spoke, "You cannot celebrate the New Year properly without rice! Please enjoy this as a gift from your leader and protector. I want nothing in return, except maybe your gratitude." The breath escaping his mouth made him look spectral.

Who is this man? Chisato questioned. *He gives a magnificent gift so generously, yet he does terrible things to women.*

No one complained, of course. They accepted the rice with the appropriate amount of grovelling.

The New Year's feast was a communal meal: the rare treat of cooked rice with dried mushrooms, harvested from the surrounding area and revived in water, fashioned into *sushi* rolls wrapped in sheets of seaweed brought to Sandon by Mizuno-san, a Powell Street grocery store owner. Others brought what they could to the church, where Rev. Tsuji gave a *Dharma Talk* about gratitude even in these mean and miserable times.

The celebration brought back memories of New Year's in Vancouver. A tear came to Chisato's eyes as she noticed just about everyone felt the loss. It seemed like an age ago.

❊ ❊ ❊

On a crisp January morning in 1943 with rare sunlight reflecting off the snow, Tohana-*san* scrambled out of his cabin, screaming to the high heavens. Clouds of his breath pillowed into the mountain air as he waved a piece of paper in front of anyone who would listen. A crowd soon gathered.

He screamed at the letter he had received from the government. His small hands clenched the paper tightly as he explained it was from the Custodian of Enemy Alien Property.

"He sold my farm, ten acres in the Okanagan! I received pennies on the dollar. The amount is nothing to what it's worth."

"Who did they sell it to?" someone asked in the crowd.

"The bastard Custodian lied to us" was the consensus as others confessed to receiving the same notice.

"Some soldier. I don't know," he said as he pulled at his thinning hair. His face distorted with rage as he continued. "And they sent me a bill for room and board—"

"Room and board?"

"Yeah, for this goddamn place!"

"Chikuso!" *Damn!*

There was nothing to be done. Another cursed "Order-in-Council" gave the anonymous Custodian the power. Chisato wanted to laugh out loud, but she stifled herself. She had no property to be sold. Whatever she had was gone in a fire. Kiyoshi had probably lost everything to the Custodian, though she did not know what that was. She frowned at the prospect and squeezed her hands tightly.

✿ ✿ ✿

In early 1944, everyone was told they had to choose between staying in Canada, just not on the coast, or move back to Japan, giving up any claim to Canada. That meant, the *Nisei* had to give up their citizenship, their birthright.

Chisato was tempted. It would be nice to see Hiroshima and her family again. She smiled at the memory of her siblings. But no, she would not accept, fearing what it was like in Japan. She also thought of Hideko. She was speaking more and more English with her friends. But she should meet her *Baachan* (Grandmother) and venerate the graves of her aunt and uncle —just not now but one day.

Sandon would soon close, the first of the camps as it turned out, most likely because of the costs as Kondo-*san* had surmised.

Chisato and Hideko moved to New Denver, a larger camp by a placid lake. Religion was no longer a factor. They were assigned to a crude cabin in what was known as the Orchard, a vast settlement of cabins. At least, she was close to many more people than Sandon. Winters were still snow-heavy and cold; pots with water in them froze by morning, fingers of frost slipped through cracks in the walls. But the many men of the camp cleared the roads quickly and efficiently; they also provided firewood for free.

In 1945, the pressure to choose whether to stay in Canada or go to Japan mounted. The news in *The New Canadian* was not looking good for the homeland. And on August 6th, a terrible new weapon was unleashed on Hiroshima. One bomb, one single bomb was exploded over the city and killed approximately 70,000 citizens. Two days later another was dropped on Nagasaki, a city filled with Christians.

Chisato dreamed about her sister and mother. Their bodies caught fire and flared into the night sky until they blackened and crumbled with the flames. She often screamed herself awake. While sitting up in the dark, she found it odd that she did not dream about her in-laws in Kure. But then that thought disappeared. She was more upset that she could not be sure of her family at the Akamatsu Compound; all communication had been cut off since the war began. And what of Hideki? In China? So, she waited for word from somebody, anybody. The dreams of fire and incineration continued.

Chisato decided to stay in New Denver for the duration, a relatively short time as it turned out, and then move east of the Rockies.

They came to Hamilton, Ontario, by train in late 1945. Chisato heard Toronto was a much larger and cosmopolitan city with more Japanese, but it instituted a ban on Japanese Canadians coming there in 1944—yet another insult to add to the pile. You had to be a University of Toronto student to be allowed to live there. Hamilton was considered a reasonable if not perfect compromise. She could see Hideko going to university. That was when they would move.

It was ironic that the Methodist Church helped Chisato settle in the small city. She stayed in a church-sponsored rooming house right next to the Balmoral Tavern, something called a "Public House" or "Hotel" as Chisato learned. When she found out it was a bar, she bristled at the thought. She watched Hideko like a hawk. The house at 50 Balmoral Street was a three-storey building with many small rooms and a communal kitchen and laundry room in the basement. With its Victorian flourishes, it reminded Chisato of Vancouver houses.

She was encouraged by the landlord to come to service on Sundays where many Japanese congregated. She would feel so at home there. As friendly as the invitation was, she declined, considering it a trap.

The church officials were nice enough, however. Mr. Anderson, a church deacon, even found her a job as a laundry person. Working for a Chinese owner didn't bother her. The long hours and the stifling conditions did. But it brought in money. She saved most of it, unless it was to buy a necessity for Hideko, like a new dress or school supplies.

Toronto lifted its restrictions in 1949 and so Chisato and her daughter moved to the big city. Before they left, Chisato received two letters from Japan. Trepidation entered her mind as she fingered the envelopes. She took them away so she could read them in private.

Hideko could not help but notice a change in her mother. Chisato's face was dark, and a gloominess came over her like a shroud. Hideko asked what was wrong, but Chisato turned away and said, "Nothing, child. Nothing is wrong."

It was quickly forgotten since they had leaving on their minds.

Again, the Methodist Church helped by meeting her at Union Station and taking her to their rooming house on McCaul Street. The station was the grandest she had ever seen. A ceiling so high she thought it next to the Shinto gods. Hideko liked the stone floor, sliding on it as much as she could. The place reminded Chisato of the Hiroshima Prefectural Industrial Promotion Hall, a fond memory of a visit there with Chiemi and her father. Like Hideko, she loved running and gliding along the floor.

Chisato had enough money saved from Hamilton to find a better place to live. She met much hostility. If a house had a sign that said *Room to Let*, she inquired with Hideko's help. The owner simply said she was too late—they just rented it out. Chisato knew he or she was lying but said nothing. She finally found a place on Huron Street near Spadina and Dundas. It was a backroom next to the kitchen. Mr. Levy was kind and willing to rent to her and her daughter. She liked his broad smile.

She also found a job as a factory worker nearby, a dress-making business called Nu Mode. Though the owners were Jewish, the manager was an older *Nisei* with kind eyes and short thin body. Mr. Shintani, a distinguished man with slightly grey hair, welcomed her with open arms. Inside, the place was filled with *Issei* and *Nisei* workers. Chisato was finally home, though she had to learn on the job. Good thing, Nobi Kihara, the floor manager, was a patient man and assigned Fuzzy Ohashi to teach and guide her.

Hideko went to Orde School, an elementary school, and then to Jarvis Collegiate, many Japanese Canadians at both schools. She was making her way to university when she met and fell for Hidematsu Hide Nakamura, a student enrolled in the University of Toronto's dental program. He was only a few years older.

They met at the Oddfellow's Hall when the *Bussei*, a club for Buddhist youth, threw a Hallowe'en Dance. Chisato approved of the occasion since it was run by the newly founded Buddhist Church *Nisei* Club. The place, according to Hideko, was decked out in all the Hallowe'en decorations: haystacks, jack-o'-lanterns, scarecrows, bedsheets for ghosts, and other things. They played bobbing for apples and pin-the-tail. And the music—swing music by a *Nisei* band, the Swing Kings of Harbord Collegiate. Hideko, telling her mother, couldn't believe how much fun it all was. She and her girlfriends from school had the best time. Even better when Hidematsu approached her and asked for a dance or three.

"Care to trip the light fantastic?" he asked, his hand extended and smiling face beaming. They danced all evening. His strong arms carried her away. By the end, she was smitten with the tall, handsome man with bushy hair, strong chin, and slight body. She was also tickled by the fact that his *Nisei* name was the same as hers.

They married once he finished his education and established his practice.

I take refuge in the Buddha.
The Three Jewels

48. OBON SEASON :: SUMMER 2000

CHISATO STARED AT THE TOPS of her hands positioned on her lap as she sat in her comfortable lounge chair. The skin was withered and pockmarked with age. *Almost 80,* she thought. *Amazing I lived to be so old. And yet here I am.*

Agincourt is filled with strip malls on the banks of wide thoroughfares; within numerous neighbourhoods, there are real estate developments largely consisting of bungalows; with the recent 1980s influx of numerous Chinese immigrant businesses and multitudes of residents with monster homes, the long-time Canadian inhabitants grew angry enough to stage protest marches and picket lines to boycott the "ethnic invasion" of businesses.

Such racism didn't bother Hidematsu or Herb (he had adopted a new name to avoid confusion) and Hideko or Helen as they were accustomed to it. They bought into a new neighbourhood development once it was promulgated in the late 1970s. The developer was only interested in the colour of their money. The Nakamura house was a four-bedroom affair with a side kitchen, dining and living room, and a basement with a walkout to the backyard. There was no second floor. Hideko thought the downstairs would be perfect, once finished, for her mother.

After about a month of construction and a lot of convincing, Chisato moved out of her Huron Street rental and into her daughter's place to enjoy her "golden years". She settled in with a double bed, Sears living room furniture, and a Sony television set, all bought by her accommodating dentist son-in-law. Chisato enjoyed what was called a "middle class life". She hadn't enjoyed such comfort since her childhood.

She ate with her children and twin grandchildren upstairs. She enjoyed her two girl grandchildren and watched them grow steadily into adolescence. Chiemi or Emi and Diane were full of energy, always into things. They seldom talked to her, since they knew no Japanese and Chisato only had a rough command of English, broken at best. But it seemed they liked her company. Chisato was tickled that one was named after her long-lost sister.

Chisato once suggested to Hideko that they be sent to the once-a-week Japanese Language School, but her daughter said no. They were to be raised "Canadian". Besides, the school was either downtown, Orde Public School in Chisato's old neighbourhood, or at the Don Mills Japanese Canadian Cultural Centre (which Chisato had heard wasn't particularly good—spoke more English than Japanese). The classes weren't "real school" to the students and so just became unruly. So, the girls spent their Saturday mornings watching Bugs Bunny cartoons.

It was an easy life. Her son-in-law was afraid she would object to the large Chinese population in the area. But she simply said, "I lived near Chinatown in Toronto and Vancouver for that matter. Why should this be any different?"

She liked that the area was nicknamed *Asiancourt* once she understood it. She was comfortable and loved to walk to a nearby market filled with Asians of all sorts. She shopped for fresh vegetables, the Chinese greens especially, though she had to get used to the barking store clerks with the rude manners.

"They aren't so bad," she remarked. "Not as bad as them in Vancouver."

* * *

What she did miss were her Buddhist friends from Sandon. She knew many of them attended the Toronto Buddhist church at Bathurst near Bloor, a downtown modern building, designed and constructed by *Nisei*, dominated by white maple wood, and featured many levels, like a split-leveled house. The congregation hall was beautiful with high arches, incense-soaked interior, and glorious altar. She couldn't convince her daughter and son-in-law to go on a regular basis.

"But it's good for the children!" she insisted. "The Sunday School will teach them Japanese traditions and customs."

"I like my Sundays off," Hidematsu quipped.

But they were willing to join bowling and curling leagues, even if they were *Nisei* leagues. Diane played hockey in the *Sansei Girls League* in the winter, while Emi was shortstop for the Urabe Blue Jays softball team in the summer. Their parents helped as volunteers for both activities. Hidematsu drove the girls to Christie Pits, a large park in the heart of the city, and George Bell Arena in the west end, so they could attend their respective practices. Whenever the family went to a Chinese restaurant (again downtown and not in *Asiancourt*), for a birthday or some other significant celebration, Hidematsu always ordered *soba, wonton* noodle soup really; the *Nisei* thought it a reasonable substitute for the traditional Japanese noodle soup. And they patronized Japanese food stores for supplies. Dundas Union on Dundas near University Avenue provided all they would ever need. There was even fresh *tofu*! Chisato liked the place because it reminded her of the old Union Fish on Powell St., Vancouver. It no longer existed out west, but the Ryoji family carried on their ownership of the business in Toronto. And they delivered, once a week, if desired. A beat-up van brought an assortment of food items (including *tofu*) to be chosen by the customer. The driver, a tall young Japanese man was very accommodating. The family went to the Japanese Canadian Cultural Centre in the near suburbs for the annual bazaar, the *Harumatsuri, Spring Festival*, and others. But the parents wouldn't let either of the daughters join any of the youth groups there.

Herb bragged to his colleagues that he was a "meat and potatoes kind of guy", whenever he was asked where to get good Japanese food.

Chisato just harrumphed and didn't say anything.

* * *

They were not Christians. Chisato guessed that's where they drew the line. They were "holiday Buddhists." But they hardly ever went, even if Chisato was happiest there. The annual bazaar in November was one of those times they did go.

Chisato walked into the building, the noise of activity rising through the air like familiar conversations and the aroma of the *tempura* gilding in the basement kitchen welcomed her back into the fold. The upstairs bustled with people looking for that bargain of clothes and accessories, baked goods, and packages of *sushi*. The White Elephant table groaned with bric-a-brac and other useful products at low-low prices. The Youth Groups set up a raffle table while the "adults" sold their own raffle tickets with Japanese dinners, money, and a trip to Japan provided by a *Nisei* travel agent as prizes. Everywhere friendly faces greeted old friends, interested Buddhist novices, and bargain hunters.

Chisato noted that the *Nisei* had taken over the leadership roles, despite Kondo-*san's* presence as the President. *It's good. Buddhism will last at least another generation.* If not for the *Nisei*, there wouldn't be a church on Bathurst. The *Issei*, her generation, didn't want to be saddled with a mortgage for twenty years or so. At least, that was the argument of the pioneer generation. But the *Nisei* won out since they understood "Canadian ways".

Chisato laughed and relaxed as she caught up with the "Yo-yos," the Yoneyamas and the Yonekuras. Hedy Yoneyama, a woman wrinkled but youthful in her joy, came alive at the sight of her.

"Kimura-san! It's been forever since I last saw you!" she enthused. "How are you?"

"So-so ne? You know, old age."

"So-ne."

She looked for Kondo-*san*, the church president, remarkable given his age. But he was nowhere to be found. *Must be downstairs helping with the food,* she guessed.

She was right. There he was with his *fat face* putting together the set lunch of rice, Japanese *chow mein*, and shrimp *tempura*. Despite his girth, he seemed comfortable in the kitchen among the dancing *Fujinkai* and *Dana* women. She wished she could join them but how would she travel to the church? Public transit was impossibly complicated, and she would have to walk great distances just to get to the bus and church. What would she do about her mobility problems?

Rev. Tsuji was gone to be Bishop of the Buddhist churches of America somewhere south of the border. Chisato and everyone else was so proud of him but missed him at the same time.

Fusae "Fuzzy" Yoneyama joined her and her family at a rare open table just outside the kitchen. Fuzzy was a tall thin woman with a sagging face of tiny cheeks and still sharp eyes that belied her friendly disposition. She would talk to anyone, even in English, though she was in conversation with Hideko in Japanese at the moment.

"Haven't seen you at church," she opened.

"We're not members," Hideko replied.

"Oh well, you're always welcome. Your daughters might like the youth groups for teens here. They go to Camp Lumbini every summer…up at Wasaga Beach. Trips to Chicago and Washington for conferences…maybe Japan in a few years."

Hideko smiled. The church bought the camp property back in the 1960s as a retreat for members. Harry Yoneyama, a professional carpenter, led a team to build a few cabins to be rented for members or for church use (conferences, workshops, campouts for the kids, and the like). It was ironic to Chisato, but she made no comment.

"You know, you speak Japanese well," Fuzzy observed.

"Her children don't," Chisato inserted.

Hideko ignored the dig and began to complain about her daughters, who by that point had scurried upstairs to find a choice dress or two or costume jewelry. They were spared the embarrassment of adults talking about them.

"Emi and Diane can't speak Japanese and they know nothing about the past. They don't respect the traditions or customs. They eat the food but don't know the significance of the dishes…"

Fusae nodded in sympathy. Chisato just grimaced.

Her favourite Buddhist event of the year was *Obon*, the summer festival when the ancestors came back to be commemorated. As she did in Japan, Chisato spent many days leading up to the day in August hanging paper lanterns outside the house as she and her siblings had done so many lifetimes ago. She lit the candles and incense in front of the open family altar while she sat in *gassho*. Unfortunately, she had no photos of her family, so she expressed her gratitude blind.

Every year, Emi was curious and approached her grandma to ask what she was doing. Chisato knew what she was about to ask but couldn't answer. Instead, Hideko scurried her away ordering her to *Stop bothering Baachan*. Chisato was happy that one of her grandchildren was at least curious. Perhaps one day she would satisfy that curiosity.

But she did not participate in the *Obon* ceremonies and traditions with other Japanese Canadians. Her daughter and son-in-law wouldn't have it. "Too much trouble. No parking," Hideko explained. "We're Canadians," Hidematsu grumbled.

A shroud of sadness descended as Chisato dabbed her eyes while in her bedroom.

❀ ❀ ❀

Chisato soon decided to take a different approach. She bothered her daughter to take the family to the *Bon Dance*, the community gathering filled with joyous music, sumptuous food, and demure *kimono*. The public event was an acceptable compromise.

The *Bon Dance* was held at various locations over the years. First, at High Park where dancers came from all around the region. Then, the church moved it to City Hall, before settling in Mel Lastman Square, North York's City Hall, on Yonge Street north of Sheppard Avenue. There was talk of relocating it to the JCCC. But that was just talk.

The crowds were good; it was the one festival that attracted most of the *Nikkei* community. And playing host was the congenial Kunio Suyama, a *Nisei* with an animated face and voice. His loud accented English made everyone feel welcome, even the Canadians in the audience. Chisato guessed he was a *Kika Nisei*, a *Nisei* educated in Japan before the war. His signature piece was his narration during the *Tanko Bushi*, the *Coalminer's Dance*.

"Clap three times and you dig and you dig and you carry and you carry the coal over your shoulders...and you push and you push the coal cart...you end by clapping again."

The High Park *Obon* came closest to her childhood *Bon Dance* in Hiroshima. The surrounding trees reminded her of the woods near the Akamatsu Compound. The impromptu picnic afterwards was reminiscent of the food kiosks back then. All the participants in their colourful *yukata* in a circle swaying to the small wooden flutes and vocal music and *taiko* beat.

All the Japanese Canadian families had gathered and sat on the grassy hills surrounding the dancers. It was so wonderful. The cool wind was in her face as she reminisced. She could see her sister Chiemi dancing with her. Not the *Tanko Bushi* of course but something she couldn't remember. Emotion swelled her chest. Her eyes dampened at the memory.

Her mother died in the Akamatsu Compound in the 1980s. She was informed by Ito-*san*, Chiemi's husband. Such a surprise; she had never met him, after all. Seemed like a good man.

She then recalled the old two letters from Japan. She had received them while living in Hamilton. The post office had found her from her address in Vancouver. The news, though new to her, had taken so many years to reach her.

They were water-stained and crumpled but they were intact. Chisato treasured them, smoothed them as best as she could before opening.

The first was from Chiemi.

Chi-chan,

I am writing to tell you our brother, Hideki, died in a military campaign in China. They say he died bravely...

She stopped reading, shaking and silently shedding a tear. *I suppose it is what he wanted.*

The second was from her mother. She sighed and felt an ominous feeling come over her body. She gingerly opened it and read slowly.

September 1945

Chi-chan,

I am sorry to have to tell you that your Oneesan died in the Hiroshima bomb. The Akamatsu compound was spared so the children and I are fine. The city does not look so good... everything...

And Ito-san's message. Her stomach churned with acid; her body ached with grief. It occurred to her, she was the last. Chisato felt so lonely with the news of her mother. Maybe she should've stayed in Hiroshima. *I would've survived.* The boys, Chiemi's boys, need their aunt. How happy her grandchildren would be with cousins. Her absent loved ones descended into her silent grief, her quiet sorrow. Their faces had started to fade, Hiroshima was becoming a pale memory, the final tragedy.

"Kimura-san?" a voice interrupted her musings.

Chisato looked up to see a tall and old thin woman. Maybe her age.

"Are you Kimura Chisato-san?" she asked.

"Yes."

"Forgive me but I am Yasui Sumiko. You don't know me, but I think I know your husband."

My husband? Kiyoshi? She didn't know what to say or look for that matter. Chisato hadn't thought of him since that day he had disappeared into the darkness.

"Or rather, I knew your husband." Sumiko sat beside Chisato on the grass. Her eyes lay half closed. It's a wonder she could see. Her cheeks were flat, and her mouth possessed thin lips. Her body too was slender, her legs neatly folded under her.

"How do you know me?" Chisato asked.

"Yoneyama-san pointed you out for me," she revealed. "I've been looking for you a while now. Normally, I don't come to Buddhist things, but I wanted to keep a promise."

"Oh?"

"Yes, let me explain."

Quite a chatty woman, she began.

"I am a friend of Fujino Michiko. You know her?"

Before Chisato could answer, Sumiko continued.

"She was in Castleview-Wychwood up on Christie Street, you know, in the west end, the retirement home. She was on the Extended Care floor. She suffered a stroke and was there. Anyway, I was visiting her because I'm a volunteer of the Women's Auxiliary at the Japanese United Church on Dovercourt. We visit the sick around the city.

"We were at Lemon Creek together. You know, one of the Christian internment camps." She stopped as if to let that sink in.

"Anyway, she told me about Kimura Kiyoshi, your husband, I believe. I knew he had wandered into the camp looking a mess about six months after the war started. No one knew where he came from, and it took a long time to get him to say anything, and even then, most of us couldn't understand him. But Michiko-san said she knew him.

"Last time anyone had seen him was in Vancouver when he burned down his house. I couldn't believe it myself. Why would anyone burn down his own house? Then again, he seemed awfully guilty about something, maybe the fire. He just walked around the camp with a vacant look on his face and muttered scripture."

"How is Michiko-san?" Chisato managed to ask.

"Oh, she's dead." Succinct and to the point.

Chisato did not betray emotion. She turned her attention to the dancers. But that didn't deter Sumiko from finishing her story.

"Your husband one day walked out of the camp. He muttered something about Jesus Christ our Lord and just walked into the woods. Without a by-your-leave.

"Search parties found nothing. He just disappeared like he had in Vancouver. He was presumed dead."

Chisato sat silently as she listened, but a visible tremor went through her body as she saw a ghost walking into and out of the camp. She hoped Yasui-*san* had not noticed. She needn't have worried.

"Before she died…naturally, before, Michiko asked me to find you and tell you about your husband's fate. And to tell you she forgives you."

More God talk. Sachiko continued but Chisato had stopped listening.

✿ ✿ ✿

An integral part of *Obon* was the memorial service at the church and the commemoration at the loved ones' grave sites. Once Chisato had convinced her daughter to take in the *Bon Dance*, she persuaded her to visit the cemetery for Hidematsu's sake. His parents were the only relatives in Toronto to venerate.

The children fussed at their grandparents' graves and wanted to leave quickly. Their parents scolded them, and Chisato heard her daughter whisper, *Know-nothing Sansei.*

And whose fault is that?

The lay minister, Kondo-*san* himself, stood with the family and offered his greetings before leading everyone in the *Nembutsu*. He was dressed in casual clothes as befitted the warm weather and beating sun. He wore a short purple sash worn around his neck that gave him an air of spiritual authority. His meaty hands came together in *gassho* and he bowed his head and recited *Namu Amida Butsu* three times.

Everyone followed, even the granddaughters, though Chisato suspected they didn't know what they were saying. Perhaps they would learn once they did it for her.

Chisato was soon able to attend the *Obon* service by herself, her son-in-law having dropped her off, picking her up afterwards. She didn't know where he went. The church service soothed her brow as she smiled in her seat. Even if it was mid-August and only ceiling fans above offered any coolness to the main hall during the Japanese language service, she sat in her *kimono*, quietly listening to the Rev. Kawabata deliver his Dharma Talk.

Kiyoshi and Michiko. She had not thought about either of them, Kiyoshi especially, for decades. She needed to survive, not live in the past. But now that she knew Kiyoshi's fate, she dredged up her feelings about her husband. She understood that most Japanese men did what he did back then.

Maybe they all wanted to visit Morii-san's club, but most lacked the money. The temptation was too great for Kiyoshi. We could've had a good life together. He chose otherwise. Too long ago to care. I can't complain. My life is good now. Maybe I can forgive him. And Michiko, too. A good person at heart. She didn't deserve such a fate. What a Christian thing to do!

Sensei was resplendent in his flowing black robe and golden sash around his neck, which represented his vows. The looped hanging cloth necklace, which featured a white wisteria, glowed in the sunlight. With handsome young facial features and expressive hands, Rev. Kawabata quoted the Heart Sutra as his central message.

"Form is emptiness, emptiness is form... All things are empty of intrinsic existence and nature. We own nothing; we are nothing. Therefore, our empty selves are our form."

Sensei spoke in riddles for Chisato; nonetheless, she was reminded of her loved ones in Japan and realized they abided as empty forms now, devoid of ego, hatred, delusion. They felt no pain, no desire. Thus, the lesson became clear.

Desire leads to suffering which can lead to the Dharma. Life may be suffering but we can all escape the cycle of suffering.

That day, she offered incense for Kiyoshi and then Michiko.

49.

A S I A N C O U R T
LATE SEPTEMBER 2000

CHISATO SAT IN HER GREEN fabric easy chair one morning, enjoying the sunlight bathing the room with its brilliance. She was unaccountably weak. Strange since she slept a full ten hours, disturbed maybe once for the bathroom. Her arms fell limply by the side of the chair. After a time, her head bent down, and she closed her eyes. She drifted away wondering if it was her time to die.

"*Baachan,*" interrupted a sweet voice.

She quickly awoke and raised her head out of its torpor. It was Emi-*chan* holding a package in her hands and offering it to her. Her bright eyes shone, and her long hair shimmered in the morning sun. She was such a demure girl, so unlike her namesake.

"Arigato," Chisato said and accepted the mail. "*Hai, you-wa good girl, ne,*" she said in broken English.

Emi smiled as if pleased with herself and skipped away.

The box was from Ito-*san* in Hiroshima. Her brother-in-law, that much she remembered. Chisato wondered what was in it, shaking it just to see. Something rattled inside. Not a *kotsutsubo,* she feared. Who was in this one? And why did it rattle? *Not Ito-san,* she whispered in dread.

She struggled to open it, not wishing to rip the brown wrapping but had no choice. It made a mess on the floor since it was so well-taped. Such were the Japanese with the over-packaging. Inside was a letter and a grey rock. A rock? What was this all about?

Upon closer examination after she donned her cursed glasses, she saw it was no ordinary rock. The mass was two, maybe three, rows of what looked like coins, Japanese coins. They were uniformly grey, having lost their shine, and they seemed to be melted solidly together with bubbles of non-descript material surrounding them. She could distinctly see the *kanji* ideograms around a square hole on some of the coins. *Meiji* era. Each row, each coin was bent and warped against the next. A black and grey coating cemented all of them together in one contorted and twisted mass. No sharp edges.

"What is this?" she asked herself.

She unfolded the letter and found two pages. She began reading. Perhaps an explanation could be had.

Hello Chisato-san,

Ito Haruo desu. It has been a long time since I last wrote. Your poor okaasan. She did not suffer.

Inside the box you will have found a rock, more accurately, a mass of coins fused together. Let me explain.

One day during the war with China, the Fifteen-Year-War, while I was still home in Hiroshima, I found Chiemi-chan digging in our backyard. I was concerned since she was pregnant with the boys. I asked what she was doing, and she scolded me for asking. Such was her character, as you know. I could see she was burying a pouch, a heavy pouch, but I let it go.

I later confronted her and insisted on knowing what she was burying. Turns out, it was a bag of money your brother had given her. For his return as I understood it. She didn't know how much, too many coins and paper money, and she never counted it.

In any case, I forgot about it until long after the war.

I was stationed in Hong Kong for the duration. I worked as a clerk for the Adjutant General of the Army in China. It was a safe job as I saw no combat.

When I came home...well, you know what happened to Hiroshima. Nothing was left of Chiemi and my home, burned to the ground like so much kindling. Chiemi was working at the Shima Hospital as she usually did when the bomb hit. Perhaps Okaasan told you? She was lost to us that day.

Takeishi curiously said his okaasan died at home. He swore to it. But must be imagined out of grief. You know how children are. I asked your okaasan but she said nothing.

My family was gone as well. Your mother was kind enough to allow me to stay at the Akamatsu Compound since it was unscathed in the bomb. The distance and the encircling mountains must've protected it. I was well taken care of.

My sons, Takeishi and Kuniya, were such rascals. They got into everything. Eventually, they grew up to be fine men. Takeshi has a family of his own now: three children, one boy, two girls. Good children. He's a policeman, of all things, in the city. Kuniya studied at the University of Tokyo and graduated as an architect. He is still single but is happy in his chosen career.

You will have found the rock in the box. It is what we call "bomb money". As I said, I completely forgot about Chiemi digging a hole in the backyard. Shortly after Okaasan passed, I remembered the incident.

I recently went back to the site of the house. Though a completely different structure was in its place, I recognized the space. I went into the back and guessed where the hole might be. I found a shovel and began to dig. Not sure what I would find, if anything.

Eventually, I dug up the remains of the pouch. As you can imagine, the bomb really devastated everything. It even affected something that was buried maybe two feet below the surface. Inside the charred remains was a grey mass of coins. The paper money was crumpled black ash.

The bomb blast was so intense it reached down and burned up and melted all your brother's money. I know it's hard to believe, but I swear it's true.

I met with my sons and daughter-in-law to show them the artifact and to discuss what to do with it.

Shizue, Takeishi's wife, suggested we donate it to the Peace Museum near the Genbaku Dome, perhaps you've heard of it? I thought it was a good idea, but Kuniya disagreed. "We should keep it in the family as a reminder of what they did to us." I liked the idea of keeping it as a family heirloom.

I then decided we should break it into three separate but equal pieces: one for each of my sons and one for you. I don't need one since I can see it anytime at my sons' houses. But we all agreed, you should have one so you may pass it on to your children and grandchildren.

You will agree, it is a profound gift from your siblings. As Kuniya said, "Show them what they did to us."

With all sincerity, I wish you well.
Ito Haruo

I take refuge in the Sangha.
The Three Jewels

50. THE END OF OBON SEASON

CHISATO PUT DOWN THE PAGES after having read them three times. She took off her glasses and placed them on a table beside the easy chair. She pinched the bridge of her nose as if to lessen the impact of the letter. *Okaasan* had told of Chiemi's death in a previous letter, but no details were given; her sister was killed by the bomb. Her child's story was puzzling.

She knew nothing of Hideki's money left behind. Perhaps he was foretelling his own death. Like *Otousan*. Who knows? She was not privy to the exchange. That hurt a little, but she put faith in Chiemi's judgement in not telling her. She was either going to or in Canada by that point.

What bothered her most was Takeishi's claim that Chiemi died at home. The Akamatsu Compound was not touched after all. How could she have been home when she died downtown? Ito-*san* was right: the child was probably speaking out of a yearning to see his mother. But what if it were true? *Okaasan* would surely have told her. Maybe not. *A ghost?*

If she had died at home, where was the grave? She let it go.

* * *

That evening after the sun had set and the shadows of the day melded with the darkness, she sat on her bed still thinking about the letter and the *Bomb Money*. She gripped the artifact in her right hand while the left rubbed her forehead. A headache tormented her.

Despite the pain, her thoughts turned to her family. She could not see their faces, Chiemi, Hideki, *Okaasan*. She knew *Otousan* was a shadow that she had not seen in years. She couldn't quite remember what he looked like.

Life is the progression from love to separation and finally to disappearance.

She wondered how she could see them again. She could ask Ito-*san* to mail her some of the old photographs. Her children and grandchildren could use a computer, of course, but she didn't trust an electronic device to send photographs, despite having been told that such a thing was possible. *But such a distance!* Besides, she wanted something tangible to hold in her hands, something she could gaze at for a good long time without having to ask a family member to turn on a device and then conjure it up for her. An image of light and magic was not satisfying.

There must be another way. Going to Japan was out of the question at her age. She also. didn't have the money to afford such a trip. The Redress Money, won in 1988, was saved for the grandchildren. She assumed she would stay at the Compound if it were still there. Ito-*san* seemed to imply it.

When the campaign was going on in the late 1980s, Chisato had no interest. She read in *The New Canadian* that they were asking for an apology and $20,000 in compensation. Such an outrageous amount! *They'll never get it*, she thought.

Her daughter and son-in-law too refused to participate. Even going to information sessions, never mind rallies, was out of the question. They thought the National Association of Japanese Canadians (the NAJC) full of radicals and troublemakers. Better to stay in the shadows and quietly disappear.

Haruo summed it up by saying of the campaign organizers, "The Sansei have a good life, better than we did. They weren't even there!"

Of course, they accepted the money when the apology was said in the House of Commons, and the money granted. They renovated the kitchen with it.

✿ ✿ ✿

She looked at the bedroom mirror near the foot of the bed. She saw an old woman with a slumped face crisscrossed with wrinkles and pockmarks. The ravages of age had stolen her youth. It has been a long, long journey from Hiroshima, when she was so full of energy and optimism, to Vancouver, where happiness was promised and then taken away in a devastating fire, to the rough beauty of the BC coast, and the primeval Mount Sheer. Then there was Hastings Park, the separation of babies from their mothers, and the horrifying fact that barely older children took care of the younger. Sandon with its devil's breath still frightened her even though she made lifelong friends there. And now Asiancourt. Manicured lawns, convenient shopping, and the racism of white residents.

Fatigue combined with the darkness bobbed her head up and down as she fought the urge to sleep. She laid down on the bed, upside down. No pillow except on her feet but she was comfortable. She closed her eyes as the dark sealed her eyes and pulled her to dreamland. Her last thoughts were of her sister. She heard the laughter, *taiko*, and *odori* music of *Obon* back in Hiroshima, and she smiled though no dream conjured before her.

✿ ✿ ✿

Chisato awoke refreshed to the morning sun. *Strange*, she thought, since she was so tired yesterday after a ten-hour sleep. She was still holding the *Bomb Money* in her right hand though her grip had loosened. It rolled to the top sheet as she swivelled to a stand. She laughed to herself when she realized she had slept upside down all night.

A thought floated into her mind. She moved to her bureau and searched through the bottom drawer. There she found something odd. She was looking for the small, grey sack, the one Chiemi had given her when she left Japan. But instead, she discovered a carefully folded light blue dress with flowers all over it, soiled, torn, a rag really. She pulled it out and a musty smell rose in the air. It was her dress she had worn when she first arrived in Vancouver. Memories of the vile immigration process flooded her mind. It had been ripped away by the officials and destroyed by the delousing. But she had thrown it out, she remembered.

No, Kiyoshi had deposited the rags in the garbage on the first day, had he not? Maybe not. Questions splashed in her mind.

She felt around the lump of cloth and uncovered the cloth bag.

How on earth…? she asked herself. She had no recollection of wrapping it in the dress. She shivered with the mystery.

She examined the pouch closely. She had not looked inside it since the day her sister gave it to her though she had carried it everywhere she went in Canada. It was soft, she squeezed the cloth and then opened the top. It was the expected soil, a reddish-brown soil.

It was part of an old tradition: emigrants often hand-scooped dirt from their homes to take away. Her sister had said, "Remember the poem; remember your home; remember us."

But what was she to do with it now? She contemplated and soon decided. *It is still Obon. I'm not too late.* She quickly changed clothes and hobbled to the back door. She carried with her the bag and the *Bomb Money*. She put on outside shoes, discarding her slippers.

Once outside and finding a suitable spot, she crouched down and emptied the dirt onto the green lawn. Also partially covering the *Bomb Money*. She slipped out of her footwear and stood on the patch of dirt in her bare feet with the artifact between her feet. The Hiroshima soil was soft and warm. The acrid aroma of home rose in the air and touched her nostrils. She tried to remember the accompanying chant, but nothing came immediately to mind. She concentrated hard with only fragments entering her mind.

The soil brought to this foreign land,
The blood of forefathers,
The soil on which I was born.
The scent of it brings back memories:
Walking barefoot through it…my mother's skin;
My father's voice.
I am where my spirit is…at home.

A sense of something surged within her. A sense of something familiar. She looked up, effectively blinding herself in the glare of the sun. Suddenly, she began chanting the *Heart Sutra*, specifically a certain passage.

Form is emptiness, emptiness is form.

And she repeated it over and over until she smelled the sweet perfume of her mother, felt the tight embrace of her sister, and the strength of her brother. The three were fine in their young and strong selves. She saw the outline of the Akamatsu Compound…home. The trees around her swayed and rustled like the woods of Hiroshima. The darkness and secrets comforted her. A deeper shadow then descended. *Otousan.* He enveloped everyone and the house; a sense of contentment came over Chisato, and she knew their emptiness was her *Nirvana.* Family. *Sangha,* the third jewel.

EPILOGUE

Hideko-chan,

Since you are reading this letter, I must be in the Pure Land, passed into Nirvana. Form is emptiness, emptiness is form. Remember and you will not grieve. I no longer desire; I feel no pain, no sorrow.

I ask little of you, except to observe Obon. Remember me during that time. Take your children to my gravesite and wash my headstone, light incense, and say gasshou. Listen to the priest and heed his words.

The Bon Odori was among the happiest times for me. All the colourful dancers circling the yagura tower. The music was loud and festive. It was all so wonderful. My sister and I danced to our hearts' content, and we enjoyed the savoury food: teriyaki chicken, shrimp, and beef; the scented rice; the noodles. Seeing all the friends was such a joy. It is my wish that my grandchildren have the same experience.

I have left you three things. The first is the Hiroshima Bomb Money. Do not throw this away. Read Ito-san's explanatory letter. Tell your children the story, impress upon them the importance of the artifact. Tell them what they did to us. I hope the Bomb Money passes from generation to generation.

The second is my money. I expressed my gratitude to the NAJC everyday for the redress. I know you have inherited it anyway, but it is for a specific purpose. Use it to take the family to Hiroshima. Let them see the Akamatsu Compound and meet the relatives, the cousins especially and Ito-san, their uncle. Also take half my ashes and place them in the family plot. I want to be reunited with my sister, your Aunt Chiemi, Hideki, your uncle, and your grandparents. Then I'll be happy. To close, I leave you the final poem your grandfather composed. It is for the family. Cherish the memories as much as I cherished you.

Death has no meaning for me,
But when I give thought to the
Moment of death,
I grow sad at the loss of
Warm family memories.

Do not grieve for me. I survived and raised a family, and I am at peace with my duty done.

Okaachan

AUTHOR'S NOTE

HIROSHIMA BOMB MONEY IS A work of fiction but rooted in the reality of family stories. My wife's family live in Hawaii but came to the US from Japan in the 19th Century. They did experience the attack on Pearl Harbor. Her father, who lived in Waikiki at the time, was woken by the bombing. He complained angrily, "Who's making all that racket on a Sunday morning?"

At the end of the war, the family heard about the atomic bomb attacks on Hiroshima and Nagasaki—of great significant since the extended family lived in Hiroshima. Many were lost including Chiemi Tanigawa, maiden name of my wife's Great Aunt. She did survive for a few weeks as she made her way back to the Akamatsu Compound just outside the city limits to make sure her two babies were alive. When she finally made it home and found her babies, she died. In the aftermath, her husband, Ito-*san*, dug up a bag of money buried in the garden before he left for China in the early days of the Fifteen Year War (the Japanese term for the war period from 1930 to 1945).

He found a grey mass of coins melted together because of the intense heat. The paper money and the bag itself were burned. That was surprising since the cache had been buried at least two feet underground.

The family decided to break the mass of melted coins into five pieces and give a share to family members—to three sisters and both of Chiemi's sons. One of the sisters was my wife's grandmother.

Years later, during a visit home from her job in Rochester, New York, my wife announced she was going to participate in an anti-war rally in New York City. Her grandmother gave her granddaughter her "bomb money". She simply said, "Show them what they did to us."

The bomb money became a family heirloom when we married.

GLOSSARY

8-Fold Path: Right View, Right Resolve, Right Speech, Right
    Action, Right Livelihood, Right Effort, Right Mindfulness,
    and Right Concentration. These are the practices the
    Buddha observed to attain enlightenment and nirvana.
Ahotare: stupid
Baka, bakatare: idiot
- bashi: bridge
Bon dance: community dance at the Obon festival
Butsudan: family altar
- chan: honorific for young girl
Chankoro: Chinese (pejorative)
Char shiu: BBQ pork (Chinese)
Cheongsam: Chinese dress
Chichi-ue: Formal term for Father
Chonan: Eldest son
Dana: Buddhist Women's Club (Canada)
Denbatsuke: pickled radish, invented in New Denver
    (Canadian)
- desu: copula: It is
Dharma: Teaching of the Buddha
Dorosu: Underwear (archaic)
Dukkha: Buddhist term for suffering (first Noble Truth)
Ebisu-ko: Fireworks festival
Fujinkai: Buddhist women's club
Gaijin: Foreigner (pejorative)
Gaji: Japanese card game
Gasshou: the act of expressing gratitude to the Buddha
Giri: Obligation
Gohan: Steamed rice
- gun: honorific for young boy
Hai: Yes
Haikara: "High collar", snobbish
Hanamatsuri: Buddhist festival, celebrating the birth of the
    Buddha

Happi: Short, light jacket
Har gow: Shrimp dumplings (Chinese)
Harumatsuri: Spring festival (Canadian)
Hibachi: Portable grill
Hinomaru: Japanese flag, refers to the emblazoned sun
Hondori: Main street, usually a shopping area
Ian-jo: Comfort station during WWII, house of prostitution
i-in deso yo: It is good.
Issei: first generation Japanese Canadian (immigrant generation)
Ja-ne: See ya.
-jin: Person
Jugun ianfu: comfort women (sex slaves)
Kadomatsu: a New Year's decoration made of bamboo and pine
    branches
Kama: metal pot or kettle
Kamikaze: a god of wind
Kanji: Japanese ideograms
Kata–kata–kata: sound effect
Katana: sword
Kawaii: cute, lovable
Keto: : (pejorative) Caucasian
Ketsuno-ana: (vulgarism) asshole
Koro: incense burner
Koseki: family register
Kotsutsubo: funerary urn
Kusotare: (insult) shithead
Maze gohan: mixed vegetables and rice
Meiji: era of the Emperor Meiji (1867–1912)
Mizu: water
Mochitsuki: rice pounding to make mochi (rice cake)
Momiji: maple tree
Mountain Police: Japanese Canadian term for Mounted Police
    or RCMP.
Mudra: hand positions with religious meaning
Mushi: insect
Nakimushi: crybaby

Namu Amida Butsu a Buddhist expression: "I rely on the Buddha of Infinite Light and Life."

Nankin: (pejorative) Chinese

Neesan: waitress

Nembutsu: an expression of gratitude to the Buddha (recitation of Namu

Amida Butsu

Nikkei: A Japanese emigrant

Nisei: second generation Japanese (born in Canada)

- ne: particle used for confirmation, "Right?"

- no: particle indicating possession

Noppera: faceless demon, ghost

Obaachan, Baachan grandmother

Obasan: Old woman, aunt

Obi: Cloth belt

Obon: Buddhist festival of the dead, celebrated from July to September

Ochasuke: rice soup with green tea

Odori: Folk dance

Ofuro: soaking bathtub

Ofuton: mattress

Ojiichan: grandpa

Okaasan, Okaa Mother: mom

Okaachan

Oneesan: Eldest sister

Oni: Devil, demon

Onibaba: devil woman

Oniisan: Eldest brother

Osechi ryori: New Year's food

Osenko: Incense

Oshogatsu: New Year's Day

Oshoko: Offering of incense

Otousan: Father

Sakura: cherry blossom

-san: Mr., Mrs.

Sangha: community

Sansei: third generation of Japanese Canadians
Sashimi: raw fish or meat
Seiza: Meditation
Senninbari: a cloth belt with red thread stitches woven into it worn around the
waist to keep the bearer safe during war
Sensei: teacher or master, commonly used to refer to a minister
Seppuku: suicide
Shamisen: Three-stringed Japanese instrument
Shoji: Rice paper walls
Showa: era of the Emperor Showa (1926–1989)
Shoyu: soy sauce
Sukesada katana: sword made and signed by Bizen Osafune Sukesada
Sutra: Buddhist scripture
Tai: Sea bream
Taiko: Japanese drum
Tairiku nippo: Continental Daily News
Taisho: era of the Emperor Taisho (1912–1925)
Takoyaki, tako: Grilled octopus
Tamago: egg
Tanka: five-line poem
Tatami: Straw floor mats
Torii: Gate
Toro-nagashi: Ceremony of boats (performed at end of Obon)
Toshikoshi soba: buckwheat noodle soup to "cross over" into the new year
Umeboshi: Pickled plum
Yagura: Musicians' tower at Obon
Yakitori: Grilled chicken
Yaku: card set in a game like Bridge
Yakushi Buddha Buddha of medicine
Yoshi: expression: All right, Okay
Yukata: casual kimono
Zori: straw sandal

Note: the Japanese refer to WWII as part of the
"Fifteen Year War", 1931–1945.

In memory of my maternal grandfather.

Death Has No Meaning
by Iwakichi Takehara
February 1944

Thanks and love to:
Tane Akamatsu
Ruby Hirano (nee Akamatsu), Aunty Ruby
Francis Wu (nee Akamatsu), Aunty Fran

A special thank you to the Toronto Arts Council for the sizable writers' grant in support of this project.

Gratitude to Jim Wong Chu for his unwavering belief in my work.

TERRY WATADA is a well-published author living in Toronto, Ontario. He has three novels, six poetry books, and a short story collection in print. *Hiroshima Bomb Money*, his fourth novel, is the culmination of his exploration of the Japanese and Japanese Canadian experience. *Hiroshima Bomb Money* comes from the heart, more so than any other, since at its core, the novel encompasses the Japanese experience during World War II. The book illuminates the events, incidents and atrocities of the Hiroshima bomb, the invasion of China and the Canadian Internment.